VAPORS

Also by Wes DeMott

Short Stories

The Fortune Teller

17 Days on a Raft

The Island of Tatanaroo

Novels

WALKING K

"If you're patriotic enough to get goose bumps when "The Star Spangled Banner" plays, you'll love Wes DeMott's debut novel, *Walking K*" –**Naples Daily News**

"DeMott, a former FBI Agent, writes movingly about ex-POWs struggle with wartime horrors"–**Publishers Weekly**

"An exciting climax and conclusion"–**The Virginian-Pilot**

"An intriguing plot with all the twists and turns to keep you riveted"–**United News Service**

"Absolutely, a must read"–**Ken Lindbloom, KCMX radio**

"*Walking K* is a novel stamped with intelligence, humanity and courage"–**Sterling Watson,** *Deadly Sweet*

"I thoroughly enjoyed Mr. DeMott's book and look forward to the next"–**Senator Larry E. Craig**

"A fantastic book"–**KVEN Radio**

"*Walking K* held me spellbound and in suspense through to the final page"–**Admiral Harry D. Train II** (ret)

"*Walking K* generates a lot of goose bumps"– **Orlando Star-Advocate**

VAPORS

WES

DeMott

ADMIRAL HOUSE PUBLISHING

ADMIRAL HOUSE PUBLISHING, Box 8176, Naples, FL 34101
AdmHouse@aol.com

The Library of Congress has catalogued this hardcover edition as:

DeMott, Wes
    Vapors / Wes DeMott.— 1st edition

    p. cm.
    ISBN 0-9659602-7-7 (hardcover)

                                                98-074460

ADMIRAL HOUSE first hardcover printing April 14, 1999

10 9 8 7 6 5 4 3 2 1

Printed in the U.S.A.

DEDICATION

To the beauty and spirit of those women who give
men a reason to give a damn about anything

ACKNOWLEDGMENTS

As a former special agent of the Federal Bureau of Investigation, I want to thank the F.B.I. for the experiences that allowed me to write this book from an insider's perspective. The many fine men and women—and the occasional son of a bitch—in that elite organization are well represented in the pages of *Vapors*. Many will recognize themselves and smile or rage at the way they are portrayed. I call 'em as I see 'em.

I also want to thank the readers of *Walking K*, my first novel, for their incredible support. The enthusiasm we all shared over that book, and the fanaticism with which they sent their friends into bookstores to buy it, helped make *Vapors* a reality.

As always, thanks to my girls, Stacy and Kelsey, for thinking that I'm the best dad on earth, and my own parents for showing me the way.

Captain Richard Perkins (USN), a heroic aviator and respected skipper, has been a faithful friend since high school, and unknowingly served as an inspiration for pieces of many characters in my writing.

My love to the real Melissa Corley—an incredible woman.

"In the councils of government we must guard against the acquisition of unwarranted influence, whether sought or unsought, by the military-industrial complex. The potential for the disastrous rise of misplaced power exists and will persist."

President Dwight D. Eisenhower
Farewell Address
January 17, 1961

1

Peter Jamison hadn't heard a sound since seven P.M. His last three hours in the sprawling research center had been darker than normal, and cemetery-quiet. Only emergency lights were burning, starry spots at each end of the hall casting eerie shadows along the corridor and through the glass beside his door. The F.B.I. agents had gone, reeking of the power a puny badge and photo ID gave them. But they were sure to return tomorrow, and the next day, as long as it took to catch the person leaking information.

Jamison was rushing to finish his work and get down to Jonah's Bar. As the chief engineer on the Wombat's weapons modification, he always worked late and missed much of what happened in the world of happy hours, movies, and restaurants. He'd wanted tonight to be different. But Dillon Aerospace's board of directors was making its final decision tomorrow and he had to make sure it was an easy one. So he worked late, checking and rechecking every statistic, refiguring the costs and confirming the allowances for manufacturing delays and conversion complications. He had it all on his desk, black-and-white documents and full-color charts—clear, concise answers to any questions that might be asked.

He raked his fingers through his thick blond hair, which much to the aggravation of Dillon management he wore in a shorter version of the surfer's cut he had in high school, back when good waves meant cutting school and weekends were spent surfing the hollow barrels of Cape Hatteras. He rubbed the back of his neck then stacked his presentation. He felt confident, fully prepared, ready for tomorrow's assault by the board.

At forty-seven years old, Jamison was the youngest division head at Dillon. He loved his work, even with the threats and fears that had erupted after the leaks began eleven months ago. He'd made good time at Dillon after two years in the army and his late start on college. His hard work and confident leadership had shot him ahead of the normal promotional curve. He was a blue-flamer, and he knew people said so when he wasn't around.

It hadn't hurt his career that Dillon's management liked him, in spite of the strain he put on some restrictive company policies. The aerospace industry was competitive, and infighting for government contracts was fierce. Jamison had proven that he was tough and would fight like hell for his projects. His quick movements, youthful face, and wild blue eyes always looked ready for a challenge, and Dillon had given him plenty over the years. He had made good on every one of them.

He liked to believe that those battles were the reason he stayed in such excellent shape, corporate motivation to keep his lean, six-foot frame powerful. But it was a lie. Although Dillon provided a gym and encouraged its employees to use it, that wasn't the reason Jamison stayed strong and fast.

The unsettling truth was that he stayed fit, absolutely battle-ready, because the crazy man demanded it.

Jamison pushed back from his desk, locked the data in the credenza behind him, and tried to ignore the little worries about tomorrow. "Okay," he said, "everything's ready. The target ident parameters, the accuracy data and the cost projections. All my stuff's organized, so I guess I'm out of here. Time to knock back a few with—"

From out in the hall's gloom, a sound slipped under his door and burrowed into his ears—the scrape of a shoe. Then a click followed, light as breath but mechanical as the antipersonnel mines that had laced the foot trails and paddies of Vietnam. He snapped off his desk lamp and turned the room to black.

The click came again. The doorknob was turning. Slowly, the shadowy glow of the emergency lights leaked into the room as the door cracked open. He watched with the quiet stealth of a predator, half-thinking that he didn't have to worry because he was protected by Dillon's security force, but on some basic level doubting it. Then the alarm bell rang in his head and demanded that he trust himself for his own defense. He jumped to his feet and rushed for the door.

Like everyone who'd ever walked patrol in Indian Country, he would always respect the value of speed. Regardless of how badly he wanted to flush the war's damage from his soul, a combatant still lived inside him, holding on to the skills that had kept him alive. He knew that speed was his friend. Stillness too, at times. But speed was best when suddenly put on the defensive.

Jamison despised the way these old instincts controlled him, even as they propelled him across his office. He would often fantasize—it was his greatest fantasy—about how wonderful it would feel to be normal, expecting nothing dangerous, able to turn slowly to the door and trust that its opening wouldn't bring a threat. More than anything he wanted to be normal. Be the gentle person he dreamed of becoming, his reason for choosing engineering at college. A gentleman's career, a cerebral job that would never require him to use his hands for anything more violent than erasing poorly placed dimension lines.

But Vietnam had spawned a craziness in Jamison's head, and right now, with a late night visitor creaking open his door, the crazy man who reigned in that part of his brain was shouting a basic rule of combat: enemies are destroyed by overwhelming violence.

Two times, and two times only, the crazy man had totally possessed him. Jamison had felt violated then, dirty and used, as much a victim as the men he had killed. He never, ever wanted to relinquish control to the crazy man again, would do anything to keep it from happening.

He closed in on the threat, praying that this was a false alarm. But the door kept moving. He grabbed the handle and slammed the door back against the wall.

Ted Bronovich stood frozen in the doorway, his right leg twitching, trying to move.

"Hey, slow down, it's me!"

Jamison jerked back his hands, his eyes on his boss's face, watching the kind of fear he'd never seen Bronovich show before. Not at work, and certainly not in the off-hours they'd shared together. Bronovich's face mixed fright with resignation, the look of a person who sees some unavoidable disaster hurtling at him like a killer meteor, far-off and small, but closing fast. Some terrible event that he has no power to stop.

"Damn, Ted, why sneak around in the dark? You trying to give me a heart attack?"

Bronovich didn't answer. He just shuffled side to side in the doorway, his sharp nose slicing back and forth through the air in front of him. He looked down the hall in both directions before he stepped inside Jamison's office. He wasn't wearing his jacket, still had the sleeves of his oxford shirt rolled up to the elbows of his thin arms. His Christmas tie drooped from his skinny neck.

Jamison reached to snap on the lights, but Bronovich grabbed his hand. "I've just got a minute. Let's leave the lights off."

Jamison checked the hall then closed the door, leaning against it as Bronovich's silhouette moved into his office. Somewhere over on the other side, completely lost in the darkness, Bronovich's footsteps stopped.

"Okay, Ted, what's up?"

Bronovich took a heavy breath. "Peter, I shouldn't be telling you this, but I wanted to give you a little warning."

Jamison started toward him, but stopped. They were both protected by the darkness, and both had the same advantage. If he moved noiselessly to a new spot farther down the wall, Bronovich wouldn't know where he was.

"Thanks. What is it?" He moved right after speaking, hating that his mind still worked this way.

Bronovich's voice drifted to him from somewhere along the rear wall, near the corner.

"They've taken the Wombat's upgrade off the agenda for tomorrow's board meeting. I just found out. Knew you'd want to know."

Jamison took a noisy step forward, looked hard and tried to find his friend in the darkness, wanting to get a look at what his face said.

"What do you mean, they've taken it off the agenda? What are you saying?"

Bronovich moved too, but he was still speaking and easy to follow. "Simple. They've canceled it."

"Canceled? Why would they cancel it? I had approval fron Casey."

"Maybe you did, but your project is dead, Peter. I'm sorry."

"Damn, Ted, the Navy can't keep flying the Wombat without making a change. Too many pilots have died already. You know that better than anyone. What's their reason?"

"I don't know. Maybe your system didn't measure up. Maybe it was a victim of economics. Maybe it's your old girlfriend's fault. I really can't be sure. It wasn't my idea to kill it, I can tell you that."

"Any word on our jobs? Did they say if my team will be reassigned?"

Bronovich moved again. Jamison tracked him, but still couldn't see him.

"Don't worry, Peter. You're too valuable to let go. You'll be reassigned to modify the heads-up display on the F/A 18C. It's a great opportunity."

"What about my team?"

Bronovich didn't answer.

"Ted, it's almost Christmas. Tell me they're not going to lay them off."

Bronovich walked through the darkness and stopped in front of Jamison. "I'm sorry, but yes. They'll be gone next Friday."

"Friday? Shit! Will they get severance pay?"

"They were contract workers, Peter. There's no severance pay, no guarantees. You know that."

Bronovich opened the door, letting the dim light of the hall drift in.

"Is Casey still upstairs? I want to hear it from him."

Bronovich stopped, lowered his voice as a little panic crept into it. "You can't go up there, Peter. They'd know I was the one who told you. With all the other leaks they'd have my ass. Dillon is too dangerous these days."

"You're telling me."

"Yes. I am telling you. And if you make a stink, they'll just fire you."

Jamison shrugged, thinking that there were lots of things worse than being fired. He stood still for a minute, feeling Bronovich's breath on his cheek. "Ted?"

"Yeah?"

"Why'd you risk this? Why did you come down here and tell me?"

Bronovich winced. "As a friend, I wanted you to know what was coming, give you a little time to prepare, a chance to do something. I doubt it's possible, but I wanted to give you the chance."

"I appreciate it."

"Well, actually, there is something else."

"What's that?"

"You know someone in the F.B.I., don't you? An agent with no connection to the investigation of Dillon's leaks?"

"Sure, Rich Blevins. Known him since the army. Why?"

"You trust him?"

"With my life. With anything."

Bronovich rubbed his eyes. "Can you do me a favor, then? Will you tell him I'd like to talk to him? In confidence."

"About?"

"I've got a small problem, that's all. Nothing urgent, just whenever he gets a chance. Okay?"

"Sure. I'll tell him tomorrow. We box every Friday morning. Soon enough?"

"That'll be fine. Thanks. Our secret?"

"You bet." Jamison looked around his office, then came back to Bronovich. "I'm heading to Jonah's. Why don't you join me? We can talk a little, maybe help with each other's problems. What do you say? I could use your support around my design team."

Bronovich smiled, just slightly, and reached for the door. "No, thanks. I'm anxious to finish my work and get home to the family."

"Understood."

Jamison stepped into the hall and watched Bronovich ease into the darkness, creeping along the shadowy walls until he was invisible, just the sounds of his footsteps coming back. When they faded out, Jamison grabbed his coat and briefcase and ran through the darkened halls. He cleared security and hit the cold air of another winter night in northern Virginia.

He drove along the southern shore of the Potomac, the Washington Monument's reflection bouncing off the black water. It was after eleven when he reached Jonah's Bar, and he was hoping the place would be empty and his team would be gone. But the parking lot was full and he had to park in the back. Trees shrouded this spill-over lot and the spaces weren't marked. It was just a dark little slab of asphalt that had been poured for employee parking.

He turned off his car but sat for a minute before opening the door. He understood his own limits, knew the pressure crowds put on him. This might be a bad night to push the boundaries. And besides, what was he going to say to his coworkers? Sorry, but you've been laid off? Nice working with you, now good-bye? But he'd promised them he would come, so he bolted through the cold and entered the bar without slowing down.

Jonah's was a landmark, a comfortable old bar for people in the aerospace industry. It was the haunt of dedicated engineers who had never developed Potomac Fever. Judging from years of noisy conversations, the men and women who came here to drink didn't care about politics or international affairs or defense initiatives. They just liked to design, and then see their designs produced and working.

Tonight, Jonah's was overcrowded with sport coats and women's suits, and the people wearing them were crushed together, way too tight. They were laughing. Foolishly. Desperately. Jamison stared into the churning mass, into the eyes that met his, and caught them searching, looking for some recognition. They had the same look of hope he'd seen as Saigon fell in '75, that sad plea of people begging to be noticed and saved, to be summoned through the embassy gates and onto the rooftop helicopters—quick salvation in the arms of caring strangers. The desperation was better behaved and nicely dressed, but Jamison saw it for what it was. Saw it clearly.

8

He took a deep breath and pushed himself into the crowd, worked his way to his team's table, smiled and shook his head when he got there. "Okay, wild people, who's the designated driver here?"

Steve Harrison sat at the far end of the table with three men on one side and two women and a man on the other. They'd saved the head of the table for Jamison but had used the spot to store empty glasses. Harrison waved for a waitress then aimed his drunken brown eyes along his nose and squinted Jamison into focus.

"You, Peter. You, sir, are the designated driver." His slurred Southern diction came out loud, rose above the noise of the crowd. "And I should tell you that we're damn glad you finally showed up."

A waitress wriggled up to the table and Jamison ordered a gin and tonic. Then he turned back to Harrison. "No way, Steve. You're not throwing up in my car again."

All of them laughed at the old story, which made Jamison sorry he'd said it. He'd come here wanting to relay a hint of Bronovich's news, give them some kind of a warning that tomorrow would be a bad day. But their laughter made it impossible. He glanced at their faces and thought about their families, then looked into their futures and saw how hard it would be. Defense cutbacks and corporate downsizing had eliminated lots of jobs, and there was no way Dillon would hold onto excess engineers in this tight market. If the Wombat modification project died, it would be impossible for them to find any kind of good work. There was nothing but suffering ahead for them, a sadistic present from Dillon Aerospace.

He couldn't stay seated once that vision hit him. He stood up, dropped five dollars on the table, tried not to rush his words but did anyway. "All right, folks, I've got to run. Just stopped by to tell you not to stay too late or drink too much. Those are the rules, my friends, and now you know them."

9

Seven pairs of eyes locked onto him. Harrison jumped up, wobbled, then sat back down. "My goodness, Peter, what's your hurry?"

"I'm sorry. I just remembered something I need to do at the office. You people have fun, and don't be careless. I'll see you in the morning." He turned and left before they could argue.

He squeezed through the crowd, heading for the front doors, going fast. He was lean, so could slip in and out of spaces others couldn't, and make quick progress for the exit. He covered half the distance, was twisting his way past the bar in the middle of the room, when a woman's arm reached over some shoulders on his right, stretching to touch him as he passed. The arm was lean and muscular. Despite the cold weather outside, there were no sleeves covering the arm. No jewelry, either. Just a brilliant wristwatch encircling a thin wrist. The gold band fit loosely and slid toward the woman's slender hand as she stood on the rail and reached down for him.

Jamison had spent a hundred hours designing the watch, and eleven thousand hard-earned dollars having it handmade. It was more money than he'd spent on all the watches and jewelry he'd ever bought for himself. But he'd spent the money gladly, loved the woman who wore it so much that it had taken that kind of frivolous extravagance and total commitment to express it. Anything less would have been profane. Despite all the women he'd dated over the years, he'd never felt that love for anyone before, and was sure he would never feel it again. It was impossible. All of his love, all of the magical elements that had blended together and matched perfectly to produce it, would belong to this woman for the rest of his life. He had nothing left to give to anyone else, and didn't even want to try again.

He was in slow motion now, moving through the crowded bar and looking at the slender arm scarcely a foot away from him. It took him a long, long time to get there. His heart was jumping, exhilarated, and hurting like hell at the same time. God, how he missed the warmth of that arm, wrapped around his nakedness, snuggling him close on cold nights, her hand caressing his body. This woman had been the one good and honest thing in his life, had filled the spot in his soul that most people had no choice but to leave empty. Even now, as he suffered with the pain of losing her, he felt sorry for the millions of people who would never feel a passion like theirs.

The beautiful arm snaked through a wall of faces, and then her hand touched his shoulder, the electricity from her fingers radiating throughout the right half of his chest, burning holes in his heart which drained him of his strength. He slowed and allowed the hand to stay on him, let the long fingers run across his shoulder and along his neck, feeling like a faithful dog in his master's presence. Trying his very best not to show it.

"Peter." Melissa Corley's voice was soft as gentle rain, almost too quiet to hear over the music, talking, and laughter. But it was the only sound he heard and it stopped him suddenly, glued him in place as her lithe body slid past the men who separated them.

Jamison was stuck, couldn't budge from his tight little space as she moved toward him, her dark blue dress a silky anomaly in the wool and cotton crowd. He saw pleasure crease the faces of two men as she squeezed past them. Jamison tried to ignore it, fought the demon of jealousy who wanted all of those close feelings for himself. He focused on Melissa as she moved through the men. She was absolutely beautiful, at least to him. His precise definition of the word. He was sure he would never see her differently, even though many of his friends didn't see her as he did.

Her skin was slightly dark, Mediterranean, as were the other features of her face. Her dark brown eyes seemed always to look past his face and into his mind. Her thin cheeks tapered to a slightly narrow chin. Thick brown hair framed her face with a soft curl. And behind that face was the best part, a mind he respected. An intelligent mind that had always been a stimulating challenge for him.

11

He didn't speak as she approached, unable to think of anything to say.

"Hello, Peter." The crowd pushed her body into his. "How are you?"

He smiled, trying not to look like a love-struck idiot but knowing he wasn't pulling it off. "Fine, Melissa. I'm fine. Gosh, you look great."

At that instant he wanted to slap himself. Gosh? Had he really just said gosh to the woman he loved? Why had he sounded so stupid? Next time he would say something intelligent, or just keep his mouth shut.

She kept looking at him, smiled a little, tilted her head. "Thank you."

"Sure. You're welcome."

They stood in silence as the crowd jostled them, almost forcing her head against his chest. Jamison knew he couldn't take much more before he would throw his arms around her, so he forced himself to look away, over her head, searching around the bar for a distraction. He noticed things he'd never seen before—aircraft models on a shelf over the bar, a signed photo of the Blue Angels hanging on the wall, a tailhook mounted on a long plaque—but none of it held any chance of helping him. He was in her presence. Nothing else mattered. Except, of course, acting unaffected by her.

"Peter," she said, "I saw you come in a little while ago. I wanted to talk to you before you left. Do you have a minute?"

He leaned back, pushed his shoulders against the man behind him so he could look down into her eyes. "Oh? If you wanted to talk, why didn't you just come back to our table?"

She didn't blink, looking ready to compete with him as she'd always done. "I could have done that. I just thought it would have been rude."

"I didn't think things like that bothered you."

He would never understand how he said those things to her, didn't know where they came from but always hated himself for letting the words out. He watched her eyebrows pinch together, just a little. No one else would have understood how badly he'd hurt her.

"You're right," she said, "I don't. Not really. But I didn't think you'd appreciate it if I interrupted your party."

Melissa's hands were on his arms, squeezing into his biceps. She was trying to keep some separation between them, but failing against the pressures of the crowd. She closed her eyes and shook her head, swirled her brown hair around her face. The scent of IL Bacio stimulated the cinders of his senses like fresh air on a suffocating fire, the fire he had started five years ago and nurtured through the hard times in their relationship. That fire still smoldered, always trying to reignite itself in spite of his best efforts to stomp it out.

He grieved for Melissa and always would. He wanted her and loved her more than he'd ever thought he could possibly love anyone. But he couldn't have her. Not anymore. There wasn't any chance of their relationship surviving. The battle between their employers was building into a war and making them enemies, escalating the conflict every time the papers hit the stands with one of her charges about Dillon's activities. Although he had been the one to draw the line that destroyed them, he was sure she would have done it if he hadn't. The death of their relationship had been inevitable. They had both known it.

Despite his pleas a year ago, she had refused to pass over Dillon Aerospace in her hunt for justice. It was the kind of target she'd been after all her life. Nothing, she'd said, would stop her from destroying it, and companies like it.

Even now, after a year to think about it, he still didn't understand how she could have put her job before their relationship. Sure, he had balked about leaving Dillon, but that was only after she'd decided to go after them. He would have quit if he'd had to, would have found another job if she'd given him a little time. Now, of course, he wished he had. Wished it every night when he went to bed alone and every morning when he woke up the same way. Wished it even more now that she was standing in front of him, her hands touching his body. But at the time, neither of them had been ready to give any ground, so the ground had cracked and shifted under them.

He tried to back away from her but the bar was too crowded. "I guess that was smart, not coming to our table. So, how are things at the Coalition?"

Melissa changed her tone, shifted into her lawyer's voice. "Fine, Peter. Are things okay at Dillon?" She looked down and studied his tie, smoothed it with her fingers.

"Yes, Melissa, everything's fine."

"Hmmm." She lifted her eyes from his tie, licked her lips until her lipstick glistened, making him desperate to kiss her.

"Good, Peter, I'm glad. I heard a rumor about your Wombat project. I was worried about you. Worried about your job."

Jamison drew a deep breath, then exhaled noisily. They had played this game before and Jamison was sure the rules weren't going to change now. She wasn't going to tell him anything so there was no point in pressing her, even if she might know how he could save his project. He stayed silent in the noisy bar. More than a minute passed.

"Well, then, I guess my information was wrong. I'm glad for you. Really." She stretched up on her toes and kissed his cheek, so lightly it almost didn't happen. "Good-bye."

She looked him over once more before she turned and parted the men between her and the bar. She walked through the opening they made, dragging his aching insides along with her. He watched until she was lost in the crowd, not even a sliver of her blue dress showing through the bottles, glasses and elbows. He shook himself out of her spell and turned for the door, rammed his body through the human obstacles.

He ran outside, needing some room to move around. It was colder now, freezing, and he praised the icy wind that numbed his senses and cooled the skin Melissa had touched. He ran full speed to his car, trying to shut her out of his mind. She was the most important story of his life, the most amazing woman he'd ever known. But regardless of how much he wanted to sort through the possible endings again, he had to shake his feelings, or at least hold them in check awhile longer. He had a job to do, an important job. His friends were counting on him. He needed to focus.

He would go to the office. Go over every detail again. Maybe find some way to change the board's decision.

He punched the code into his car's keyless entry system and the lock engaged. He froze, suddenly remembering tripwires and toe-poppers and all the men who had been lost to them because of a casual attitude in situations like this, angry that he still wasted so much of his life thinking about fighting, and staying alive. It wasn't normal, and he knew it. He just couldn't stop himself from doing it.

Could there possibly be a bomb? Was someone lurking around the dark lot? Was he standing on anything that might be pressure-sensitive? Or had he simply forgotten to lock the car earlier?

In less than a second the hairs on his neck prickled against his collar, sent a little shiver along his spine. He had locked the car; remembered doing it. He took a big jump back, anticipating everything, or nothing, then ran around the car next to his. He crouched beside it and waited.

Three or four minutes passed. He didn't move, stayed low beside the next car, his eyes peering through the glass and watching for an attacker to rush from the shadows. But nothing happened. He began to shiver, and shivering always sucked when speed or deftness might be necessary. He stood slowly and scanned the area again. Then he crept to his car, looking for some sign of a break-in. He walked around it, noticing everything, wishing it had snowed so there'd be prints.

There was nothing to indicate a break-in. His CDs were still on the seat, the player still in the dash, his briefcase on the floor.

But he'd learned a lot in the jungle, and the senses that had kept him alive over there were on full alert. He was combat-ready, bladed, as Lt. Blevins had called it.

He crouched beside the passenger door and turned away, covered his head with one arm as he pulled the door's handle, hoping he wouldn't have body parts blown off, or car parts blown into him, or any combination of the two.

The car didn't explode, so he elbowed onto the floor and took a look under the dash for unusual wires or detonation cord. He climbed across the center console to check for a triggering mechanism attached to the driver's door.

Finally, he eased into the driver's seat, shut his eyes, and turned the key. The car sparked to life and the suddenness of it twisted him involuntarily toward the door. He sat there embarrassed for a minute, then drove slowly out of the spooky lot, picking up speed as he hit the highway back to Dillon, wondering who had been in his car, and why.

*　*　*　*　*

Ted Bronovich picked up the phone and called his wife, knowing she'd be upset that he was still at Dillon. He'd promised to come home in time to put their two girls to bed. It was one of hundreds of promises he'd broken since his brother died.

"Hi, Karen. Sorry I'm not home yet. Are the girls asleep?"

"Yes."

He waited, hoping she'd say something else, something that showed she was still on his side, that she hadn't lost her share of his conviction. A security guard walked down the hall toward his office and Bronovich listened to the guard's keys jangling as he waited for his wife to speak. The keys' tinkling grew loud, then soft, and finally faded away. His wife was still silent.

"I'll be home in an hour, honey. Sorry."

"How much longer, Ted? I want to know how much longer this will go on."

"Hang on, sweetheart. Please." He walked to his office door and opened it, looked along the dimly lit halls, listened carefully before closing the door and returning to his desk. "Not much longer, honey," he whispered. "I'm almost done with this. It should be over in two weeks, a month at the most. Then we'll start over, you and I and the girls. Something new and fresh. I promise."

"I'm counting on that, Ted. The girls and I are counting on you."

"I won't let you down. Don't worry. See you in an hour, maybe sooner."

He hung up and picked the gold wings of his younger brother off his desk, the wildcard kid he'd watched over since the day he was born. The Navy wings were a reminder of the last time he'd seen him alive, suited up in his flight gear, grinning as if he owned the entire world, crouched on the boarding ladder of his Wombat aircraft as it sat on the transient line at Naval Air Station Oceana. That was how Bronovich wanted to remember him. Cocksure and ready.

He fondled the wings several times every day, just to cement his brother's grinning face onto his brain, use it to cover up the bloody image he'd imagined from the Naval investigator's finding. The sanitized report said that his brother had ejected safely when his Wombat's weapons system glitched the flight control computer. His parachute had opened, but caught on a mountain ledge during descent. His brother had swung in his harness all night, the high winds smashing his poor body against the rock face until every bone had been pulverized.

*   *   *   *   *

Jack Kane sat in his darkened office on the top floor of Dillon Aerospace, holding pictures of the two men in his hand, imagining his wife and family's last minutes alive. It was part of his ritual, part of what made him so deadly—his willingness to live through the suffering again and again, then focus all of his pain, all of his hatred, all of his vengeance, on whoever was next on the list.

His grief was an affliction he could hardly overcome anymore. As always, tears for his family came to his gray eyes and tried to work their way out. But they never succeeded. His eyes were pinched too tight to let them pass, narrow slits that saw only the evil he wanted to stop.

After staring at the pictures for twenty minutes—imagining what his family had said that night and remembering the gruesome photos that showed exactly what these men had done to them—he put them away and headed out the door, down the hall, ready. The photos had done their job, had started the acid pump and built up the pressure. They'd given him a thirst for blood.

But the executions were getting progressively harder for him, and this one would not be an exception. He just couldn't tell exactly how much more difficult. The surge would still crackle through his big arms and destroy the man's life. There was no doubt about that. But resistance had been growing in his limbs during the last few months. A slowness had begun to govern his stride. His hands would wander a little before the kill. They were all signals of weakness, extra clutter for him to struggle with tonight besides Ted Bronovich.

For nineteen years this work had been a pleasure, a simple act of vengeance played over and over again with a varying cast of characters. It was his way of purging himself of the poison of his family's death, or at least diluting it. It had never mattered if

Kane had known the victims or not. Someone in the organization did, and felt they had to be killed. Kane made the final decision, but he usually agreed with the recommendation. He understood that something had to be done about criminals, those evil men who held good people at psychological gunpoint, causing them to lock their doors and watch their children and patrol their neighborhoods and still know they couldn't stop the violence. Couldn't protect their loved ones. Had to live with the pain and guilt when they failed.

Maybe it was just his age making him soft, his mountain of vengeance weakened and crumbling by the slow erosion of time. Fifty was only a couple of years away. He stopped at a glass panel dividing the long corridor and took in his reflection. He was still big and strong, still handsome. The hair had some gray, sure, and the big face showed the wear. But Kane was still hard and it showed, especially in the reflection of those dead gray eyes, which were lost in the depths of the glass.

He learned nothing new about himself from the image, turned back down the corridor, and stayed in the shadows created by the emergency lighting. He was close to Bronovich's office now, and suddenly wondered whose name would be on the door next week. Strangely, he almost wished the name could stay. After all, Bronovich hadn't done anything to him, and he wasn't even sure his death would plug the leak. Compassion, or at least what he could remember of it, tried to turn him, tried to bubble to the surface for the first time since his family's murder. But he knew this was just weakness and nothing more. Bronovich, by guilt or bad luck, was caught in Dillon's spotlight, and Kane had taken on the task of killing him.

For the first time ever, he tried to think of it as something other than murder, spent a little time twisting around the details. Could he cloak it in some kind of patriotic wrapper? Was there really much difference between this execution and the killing he'd done in uniform, back in the days before college, before Dillon Aerospace?

No, probably not. Killing was killing. A uniform didn't make any difference, and bad people didn't have to live in a foreign country to be his enemies. Hell, there were plenty of enemies right here in Washington, and he was fighting a war against them. Fighting for all Americans. And winning.

He liked thinking that way. He almost smiled, thinking that he could get by just fine with that reasoning. A war, that's what it was. A war he hadn't started, but one he would be more than happy to finish.

At Bronovich's door he stopped and focused on his work, beat back the newborn pacifist crouching at the edge of his power. Jamison had been the last person to leave, about an hour ago. Everyone else had long since coded out and left the building. Everyone, of course, except Casey. He was still here. He would stick around until Kane was finished.

Kane moved his big frame with slow precision, looked through the office door sidelight, saw Bronovich place those stupid gold wings on his desk and go for his coat. It was time to do it. If this got messy he didn't want to be screwing around with Bronovich in the hall. His pulse picked up and his nerves started to jump, his new weakness making it harder than ever before.

But what the hell, it had to be done. Or did it? Maybe the leaks were coming from a different division. Maybe they were all wrong about Bronovich. Was it possible? Could Bronovich be a victim of bad luck, a hardworking engineer who'd just happened to request the wrong files, files that contained information that had been leaked to the press?

He thought about Bronovich's family, probably waiting right now for their daddy to come home from work, the cute little girls who had sat in Kane's lap last month when he'd been there for dinner, asking Kane about his own dead family with shameless innocence.

He didn't know the answer, and would not waste any more time wondering if Bronovich was the leak. He stuffed all of his doubt into his bowels, his hands moving now with the skill of the beast that lived inside every man. But Kane's beast was well trained, mutated by two decades of lethal experiences into a creature of fatal efficiency. He gave the door a push, then pivoted into the opening.

"Bronovich."

The aerospace engineer turned to face Kane, dropping his coat at his feet. His gentle brown eyes snapped steady onto Kane, even as his whole body began to tremble. His small hands shook as he removed his glasses, banging them against his nose in a shaky rhythm. He looked foolish as he set them carefully on his desk, then turned a photo of his family facedown. He squared his skinny body to Kane's, his delicate fingers clenched into tiny fists.

"Hello, Jack. I was afraid you might come to see me."

Kane moved farther into the room, catching every twitch and movement Bronovich made, feeling ridiculously undermatched. Then he shut the door, closed his mind, and advanced silently on the terrified company man.

2

Way out, at the very fringe of his consciousness, Jamison heard the alarm's hands fall into alignment and get ready to ring. He was still asleep but already moving, his hand flicking toward the clock like an uncoiling spring. The alarm didn't stand a chance, was silenced before it rang, beaten by the unwanted reflexes that launched Jamison out of bed.

He was halfway across the room before he began to slow, grudgingly forcing himself awake. He'd worked at Dillon until one-thirty in the morning, had gotten home at two. He needed a couple more hours of sleep, but he wouldn't get that today. He kept moving around the dark room, fighting the temptation of his warm bed on this chilly morning.

He stopped at his dresser and leaned against it, rubbed his eyes into clearer focus, started to make out objects in the blackness. As usual, the first thing he looked for was a picture of Melissa, taken several months before their split. Even though it was right in front of him, there wasn't enough light to see the photo. But the frame was easily distinguishable, directly in his line of sight. He began to stare at it, and through it, his mind tracing the roads of his life that had separated them, trying to eliminate the detours and wrong turns that had led them apart. It was an impossible task and he knew it, but he liked to start each new day like this, begin with some bearing based on where he'd already been, and the mistakes he'd made there. Making sure he didn't repeat those mistakes if life ever gave him another chance.

He dressed and hurried through a light breakfast, then stuffed some clean trunks into his gym bag. He stopped before closing the bag and thought about safety, and how survival depended on being prepared. Then he took his Beretta out of the dresser drawer, checked to make sure it was fully loaded, then laid it among the sweats. He didn't really know why he wanted his pistol, couldn't imagine why the thought had crossed his mind. Maybe it was nervous jitters from working so late in a dead-quiet building. Or that his car had been broken into but nothing taken. More likely, it was a cumulative effect that gave his senses a hangover and told him to pack the weapon. He trusted those instincts completely.

Fifteen minutes later he was at the gym. It was a worn-out facility over a cheesy rent-to-own shop that had iron bars over all the windows and a roll-up gate at the entrance. The dented steel door to the stairs was locked, but yellow light was filtering through the dingy glass of the second floor windows, meaning Rich Blevins was already there. Jamison used one of the keys that the old owner—a feisty little man with a bulbous nose, and arms that still threw mean punches—had given them three years ago when they'd become regulars at the gym. The old man, a boxer who'd turned trainer, had probably figured they'd be safe bets—the F.B.I. agent and the aerospace engineer. They were polar opposites of the hotheaded youths and pasttime punchies who usually hung around the place.

Blevins was rapping on the speed bag when Jamison entered, making the small leather bag dance under the round platform from which it hung. At five feet ten, Blevins weighed a powerful hundred and ninety pounds and looked the way a boxer should. He was thick and stout, hard to knock down. His face was big and round and squared off at the jaw. His large hands were quick, and his brown eyes drew his narrow eyebrows together as they studied the continually moving bag. His crew-cut brown hair stood at attention, like short plumes on a medieval knight's helmet.

Jamison aimed his finger as he headed to the locker room. "Hey! You. I'm gonna kick the crap out of you this morning."

Blevins didn't look away from the speed bag, didn't break his rhythm. The bag took the pounding and snapped back instantly, for more. "You're late, jerk. Take a while to build up some courage?"

"I'll be out in two minutes, get ready to bleed." He smiled at their threats, at the taunts they'd been using against each other for twenty-five years. These were the kind of words that defined their friendship, and Jamison never expected them to change.

He slipped on black shorts over his plastic cup, then locked up his clothes and laced his shoes. He hurried back into the gym, pulling his gloves on with his teeth and stuffing the laces. He was freezing without a shirt, so he ran around the ring a half dozen times, shadow-boxing to get the blood flowing.

The ring's canvas, like the gym's floor, was stained with years of sweat, blood, and spit. Decades of footwork had worn some pretty tricky slick spots on it. The ropes were filthy black in the corners, dark gray toward the middle. The light in the gym was bad, the air stank, and the heater had been broken for as long as they'd been coming. But it was their home gym and Jamison had long ago stopped noticing the scars of brutality. He eyed Blevins as he climbed through the ropes and set the timer. "You ready?"

Blevins was stretching against the ropes with his back turned. "You bet."

Jamison hit the timer with his gloved hand and both men moved to the center of the ring. They smacked their gloves together, then raised their hands, protecting their heads and bodies. As they went into motion, the seconds started to stretch by in long, disjointed ticks.

Blevins went on the attack right away, and looked good doing it. He was moving more smoothly than he normally did, and his timing was excellent. Jamison kept having to adjust, had to change his jabs, needing to work a little harder to find an opening.

In the first few seconds of the third round Blevins landed a big punch on Jamison, ringing his ears like Sunday mass and warning him to expect another one, soon. But Jamison forced his eyes to stay open, was ready when it came again. As Blevins fired his left lead, Jamison blocked it and concentrated on the muscles of Blevins's right arm. The instant they exploded, he feinted and stepped back, drawing Blevins off-center and out of balance.

Blevins looked for a way out of the trap but Jamison had him, used his left to push Blevins's big right hand out of his way, then buried his own right fist into Blevins's face. Once, then with the chance he got as Blevins staggered, again, he connected with both blows coming all the way from his toes, opening a deep gash over Blevins's right eye. Thick, rich blood began to ooze. It was a good cut to work on.

He fired again while Blevins wobbled back. Hit his mark. Then he hit it again. Blevins was getting loose, dazed, his hands looking heavy. Jamison came again, and then again, working on the cut, opening it wider and wider until the blood ran hard, his punches splattering the red juice in a monochromatic shower. The blood was running down the sides of Blevins's nose, filling both his eyes, blinding him, making it impossible for him to fight back. But he stayed silent and kept his fists up. The fight was still on.

Jamison cornered him now, working the cut like Blevins had worked the speed bag earlier, smashing it with his left, then his right, then his left again. Now faster. Again and again and again while Blevins slumped against the ropes.

Jamison spit his mouthpiece onto the floor, started screaming at the best friend he had in the world. "Go down, Rich! Go down!"

A referee would have called the fight, even though Blevins still held his hands up. But there weren't any referees. Only he and Blevins were in the ring. He crashed into the cut again, split the skin in a large arc that ran all the way from the top of Blevins's nose to the corner of his right eye.

"Damn you, Rich! I said, go down!" He was screaming the words, an out-of-control maniac running loose in a civilized world, taking his crazy man out for an early morning walk, doing what he had to do to live with that damned beast. He hit Blevins again, harder than ever before, so hard his whole arm shuddered from the impact. It felt as if his forearm bones might shatter. "Go down, damn you! Go down or I'm going to kill you."

Blevins was wide open, and Jamison smashed into him again, spinning him around until his right knee buckled and he dropped to his left. Jamison stood there, his right arm cocked and ready, hating himself for the words he was screaming but needing to say them anyway. It was a part of his therapy.

"Get up," he yelled, surprised and disappointed that Blevins had actually dropped. "Come on, get on your feet."

Both of Blevins's eyes appeared to be closed, although it was impossible to be sure. There was just too much blood covering Blevins's face to know. But Blevins planted his left foot and tried to stand. Jamison drew back his arm, ready to finish it. Blevins held his head up, even though his hands were barely waist high. He struggled to stand, fell down, struggled some more, tried to push himself off the ground with his hands. Finally, he aimed his bloody face in Jamison's general direction and shook his head—no.

It was over.

But the crazy man hated to see it end. After years of therapy, these matches were the only chance he had to get his pleasure. Win or lose, his pain or someone else's, these precious moments of bloodshed were his very best times. The crazy man dragged Jamison twice around the ring, smacking his hands against each other and crying out in some kind of bestial anguish. He circled back to Blevins, hoping to find him standing and ready for more punishment. But Blevins stayed down, blood-blinded.

Slowly, Jamison gained control. A few minutes ticked by, he got his devil bottled up, and won his second fight of the morning. He sat down in his corner and composed himself, staring across at Blevins while he took deep breaths and worked the tension out of his shoulders. He was sure that lots of other people lived with demons, and wondered what secrets they'd learned about dealing with their own.

A few minutes later he eased back to the person he wanted to be, the person he hoped and prayed would live alone inside his head someday before he died. He pulled off his gloves and dropped them to the canvas, walked over to Blevins and knelt down. "Hey, you okay?"

Blevins had never once hung his head. At the threat of that last blow, so frightening that even Blevins's temporary blindness couldn't have hidden it, Blevins had kept his head up, proud. Jamison admired that raw courage, that belligerent refusal to turn away from the punishment, that insolent look of absolute fearlessness. It was the unshakable foundation of their friendship, the sacred ground on which they'd built their relationship long ago.

Blevins smeared a gloved hand across the gash over his eye, then pushed the leathery palm into his good eye, trying to clear the blood and get it open. "Yeah. I'll be all right."

"You sure?"

Blevins struggled to his feet like a child learning to walk, staggering and unsure. "Uh-huh. Think so. Damn, you sure drew me off-balance. I must have really telegraphed my punch."

Jamison helped his friend to his corner and sat him down, reached into the dirty bucket for a sponge and squeezed yesterday's water out of it. He mopped off the blood, got Blevins to see a little.

"No, it wasn't that. But you caught me with that same combination last week, so I was expecting it. And I was having a good round. Come on, let's get you cleaned up, put some butterflies on that cut and ice on the swelling."

They climbed through the ropes and headed to the locker room. Jamison felt bad about the damage he'd done. He hurt for the pain he'd caused. But last week, he'd been the one to take the beating. He'd won today because of the lesson he'd learned then. That was the way life worked.

After they showered and dressed, Jamison knotted his tie while Blevins checked and holstered his pistol, still a little unsure of his focus. "Today's your big day, isn't it?" Blevins asked. "Don't you do your dog and pony show for the board of directors this morning?"

Jamison adjusted his tie then grabbed his things to go. He checked Blevins's swollen eye once more, made sure the butterfly bandages were going to hold. "No, there's been a change. A bad one. I'll tell you about it later, and I need to ask you something for a friend of mine at work, a guy named Bronovich. But later, okay? Right now I have to get going. You ready?"

Blevins holstered his pistol, gave Jamison a suspicious look with his good eye, picked up his bag. "Let's do it."

Jamison was on the road by seven-fifteen, anxious to get to work. He would be there early, with time to organize his notes and be ready, if given the chance, to defend his work to the board of directors. Dillon had nothing else in the pipeline if he didn't make something happen. There was nowhere else to assign his team, no option but lay-offs if the project died. So it was all the way to the mat on this one.

He parked close to the three-story research facility, double checked the locked doors of his car, and ran to the entrance. People were already filling the halls. The guards and voices and ringing phones had chased away the ghosts of last night, making him feel silly for the fear he had felt here.

He pulled out his presentation and sat it on his desk. Where were the answers hiding? Why had the board killed his project? What had gone wrong? He couldn't envision them thinking that the Wombat didn't need an upgrade of its weapons system. The plane had been in the air as long as the A-6 Intruder, but with only half as many updates. Problems with the current weapons system made it a dangerous plane to fly. Pilots called it The Killer, but didn't laugh when they said it.

He started thinking out loud, his way to slow down and go over things carefully. "Okay, well, maybe that's it, maybe the entire aircraft is slated for replacement, and Dillon just found out about it from the Pentagon."

He liked that idea, rolled it around for a while, thinking maybe Dillon's decision to lay off was just an overreaction, poorly thought out and therefore, maybe, reversible. Maybe his team would just need to redesign their system for another aircraft, maybe one of the next generation fighters. After all, Dillon wouldn't want to scrap all that great technology. They'd just redesign it for something else.

He hoped that was it. His team would just shift to another tactical jet and everything would be fine. But he kept working on other possibilities, because he knew he was wrong. Bronovich had been clear.

At nine-thirty he called a staff meeting. His teammates were smart people, and they had to know something was wrong when he'd missed the board meeting. They deserved to know what he knew.

The people in the conference room looked worried, and sad. All seven of his coworkers were sitting around the table, none of them looking relaxed. They weren't talking, and for the first time Harrison wasn't telling one of his jokes. Their eyes searched Jamison's face as he entered the room, peering out from faces which blended hangovers, fear, and lost sleep into a weird mix of sad squints and tragic little glances, the same kind of looks he'd seen in emergency room lobbies.

"Good morning, everyone."

No one said anything.

"All right, all right. I'm not going to bullshit you guys. I've got bad news and here it comes. Our project is dead. Passed over by management."

Everyone reacted at once, an explosion of language. Some shouted to Jamison and pleaded for reasons. Others turned to whomever sat in the next seat and offered consolation. Jamison didn't say anything, let them live with it for a minute, then held up his hands for quiet.

"Listen. I'm just as confused as all of you, and really want to know why this happened. If the minds on the board can be changed, we're the ones who'll have to do it. It's up to us to justify this project, and we'll need to do it fast."

Harrison stood up. "What do you suggest we do, Peter?"

"Well, first of all, don't bitch about it to anyone outside of Dillon. You all know what's been going on here since the leaks started, so you know Casey won't tolerate any discussion with anyone unauthorized. Period. Just go back to your offices and try to dig up something. Start by looking at the project's costs."

"I don't get it," Harrison said. "Didn't we come in under budget?"

"We did, that's right. But maybe there's some aspect we're missing. Maybe something in the tail of the system. The long-term parts inventory, for instance. Or maintenance schedule, or retro-fit costs. Maybe we presented them poorly. I want everyone to get down in the weeds and take a close look in all those areas."

Harrison kept standing, waiting for more. "Is that it?"

Jamison pushed the hair off his forehead, letting his fingers glide along the scalp and squeeze the long strands at his collar. "No. Understand that this is bad. I think all of you should get your resumes in the hands of your favorite headhunters. I'd be quick about it."

Several heads dropped a notch, the faces looking as though they couldn't believe what he'd said. Jamison didn't want to say it again, and didn't want to lose any more time. He turned and walked out of the room.

He worked all morning, tilting at any possible oversight but discovering nothing. He called Casey's office two times and demanded a meeting, but his access to the vice president seemed to have died with his project.

At eleven o'clock he stood and wandered around his office, trying to think of someone who could help. Casey had the answer, but he wasn't talking. Bronovich probably didn't know any more than he'd said last night. And Jamison couldn't imagine anyone else at Dillon who might know something *and* be willing to talk about it.

He leaned against his office windows, staring out at the bare trees in the courtyard between two wings of the building. His tired mind started to wander, and as always it went straight to Melissa.

"Come on," he said out loud, "stop thinking about her. You don't have time for this."

But his heart defeated his brain, put his feet in motion, and sent him to his desk for her phone number. Then he walked down to the lobby pay phones, hunkered into the phone box as he dialed.

"Citizen's Coalition Against Government Waste. How may I direct your call?"

The sound of the enemy made him flinch. "Melissa Corley, please."

"Just a minute, sir."

He was put on hold, giving him a few seconds to reconsider, realizing that this was a bad idea, that he'd be better off—

"Hello, this is Melissa Corley."

Her voice laced its way through the line and snapped on his lights. He tried to hang up, tried to get rid of the phone which stuck to his hand. But he needed her. Wanted her help. The whole team did.

"Hi, it's Peter. Can you talk?"

There wasn't an answer. Then, finally, "Why, yes, Peter. Of course. I'm glad you called. Surprised, but glad. Hold on a second, okay?"

He heard her cover the telephone with her hand, then tell someone that she would be busy for a few minutes and to please wait in her outer office.

"So, Peter. It's nice to hear your voice."

"You, too. You looked great last night."

She laughed. "That's nice of you to say. So, what can I do for you? Or did you just call to say hello?"

He came straight out with it, didn't wait to see if extra time would make him more certain about what he was doing. "Do you think we could get together today, Melissa? Maybe lunch? I need to talk to you."

The line was silent. He pushed the phone hard against his ear and listened to her breathing.

"Yes. I guess so. What time and where?"

"How about twelve-thirty? You pick the restaurant. Someplace quiet."

She was checking her schedule, he could tell. Could hear her open the leather book she always carried and turn some pages. "Twelve-thirty is fine. There's a Thai restaurant at 401 and the Little River Turnpike that doesn't get too crowded."

"That'll work. See you then. Thanks."

He hung up in a rush, turned toward the lobby, and logged every face within possible earshot. Then he returned to his office, locked up his work and headed to the secretarial pool to check out. He caught Charlotte's attention.

She was a young secretary who'd only started at Dillon a year ago, but had already earned his respect. She had short blonde hair, cheeks that were a little too full, a short but sharp nose and a keen look in her green eyes. A strange mix of round and angular features. She wore suits instead of dresses, as if declaring that she didn't intend to stay on this rung of the ladder for long.

"I'm taking off for a few hours, Charlotte. Need to take care of some personal business. Clock me out, okay?"

Charlotte looked up from her word processor but didn't stop striking the keys, somehow balancing their conversation and the tape's dictation. "Sure, Mr. Jamison. But you'd better go see Mr. Casey before you leave. He tried to call you a few minutes ago, after the board meeting. You weren't in your office."

Jamison grinned and stared while his mind wondered what Casey was up to, if he was actually going to give Jamison a chance to plead his case. Or did Casey already know, somehow, that he was having lunch with the enemy?

He struggled with his nerves, trying like hell not to start any office gossip by acting strange. "Thanks, Charlotte."

He took the elevator up one floor, hurried down the long hall while tossing around what he knew of Ross Casey, trying to find something good to work with. He remembered that before the leaks Casey had been a pretty decent boss, although a no shit kind of guy. His simple motto had always been that this was *his* pond. Do whatever you want away from work, but don't make ripples in his pond. A career naval aviator, Casey had been decorated for every military action from Vietnam to Beirut. When he retired from the Navy and joined Dillon, the only changes were less flying and no uniform. He still demanded obedience from everyone who worked for him, and expected never to have his decisions questioned. Back in the days before Dillon had become so factionalized and fearful, Jamison had actually enjoyed talking to him because Casey had used the types of weapons Jamison engineered, and could accurately account for the human factor that made or broke a design.

The flooring turned from gray tile to burgundy carpet with a deep blue border. All noises were muted by the overstuffed furniture, wood desks, and heavy wallpaper.

"Hello," he said to the aging secretary. "I'm Peter Jamison, here to see Mr. Casey."

She didn't look up. "Well, Mr. Jamison, he has someone in his office right now. If you'll have a seat I'll make sure he knows you're here."

Jamison thanked her, then backed away and pressed himself into the leather couch. He picked up a trade publication and flipped through pages he didn't notice.

After five minutes the old secretary spoke softly into her phone, then hung up and gave him a painful-looking grin that showed no teeth. "Mr. Casey will see you now."

Jamison jumped up and headed toward the large mahogany doors, expecting the previous appointment to leave as he approached. When no one came out, he turned the handle and walked in.

Ross Casey was standing by some shelves behind his desk, speaking to a man who was leaning against the windows. Jamison did not know the man by the window, although he did recognize something about the stranger's face—the severe loss of expression and the thousand-yard stare of the empty gray eyes. Eyes that had seen far too much death. Jamison knew the look well and could spot it two clicks away. He had worn it himself once, back when life was the prize and death was served to all who finished second.

But Jamison had been lucky. Extremely lucky. He'd managed to pry off most of his face after returning to The World. He'd gone to therapy and attended work groups, talked to priests and mothers of dead soldiers. Had healed most of the damage his killing had caused. Some men never managed to do it. Men like the one he faced in Casey's office.

"Come in, Jamison. Thanks for dropping by." Casey motioned for Jamison to sit down, but didn't look like he was going to introduce him to the stranger.

Jamison looked at the two men and had no trouble reading the scene. He knew it wasn't going to be good. And if this was an ass-torching session, he didn't want some stranger watching. He walked past the chair, went over to the stranger, stopped in front of the big man and stuck out his hand. "I'm Peter Jamison."

The stranger did not move. There wasn't a twitch anywhere. He just kept leaning against the window frame as he dug his eyes into Jamison's, his face declaring that he'd seen it all before. Finally, he reached out and gripped Jamison's hand, started squeezing.

"I'm Jack Kane." Kane said his name like it should have meant something, but probably nothing good. He strangled Jamison's hand.

Jamison squeezed back, applied enough pressure to turn coal into diamonds. Then Casey plopped into his seat. "Gentlemen," he said. "Gentlemen, let's get started here."

Kane looked over at Casey and loosened his grip. Jamison went for the fun of wrenching Kane's hand a second longer, just to see pain on Kane's face. It was only a small wrinkle, but at least a reaction. Jamison studied Kane's eyes, tried to show that he knew the address where Kane lived inside himself, and that it didn't scare him. Then he walked over to the chair, turned it so he could watch both men, and sat down.

Casey swiveled in his seat and presented a partial profile. He had an angular face with sharp features; sunken cheeks, and skin so lean that his jaw and skull were clearly outlined. Emerald eyes that looked as if they were always locking on to a target. Jamison had played a lot of basketball with Casey, back before the leaks had started, and knew Casey to be a fierce, unrelenting competitor. His face mirrored that personality.

"Jamison," Casey began. "I just wanted to check with you and make sure you're comfortable with my decision on the Wombat deal." He stopped and waited, made a quick glance at Kane.

Jamison leaned toward Casey, then glanced over to make sure Kane hadn't moved. "No, sir," he said, "I'm not. With all due respect, the Wombat needs a new weapons system more than any other tactical jet in the sky. I can't believe the Pentagon seriously thinks it can keep ignoring the problems of the current system."

Casey shifted his profile, looked calmly at Kane. Then he clicked those green eyes back to Jamison. Any trace of friendliness that might have been there earlier was washed away. "I'm sorry it's such a surprise to you. But I guess I couldn't expect an engineer to understand the business side of our industry." He hesitated, then smiled. "Doesn't matter. Wombat is dead, but we'll find something else for you to work on. Thanks for your hard work."

Casey squared his chair to his desk and stood up. "That's all, Jamison. I just wanted to make sure you were clear on the situation." He produced a shallow smile, which puffed out his flat cheeks. "Thanks for dropping by."

Jamison stood slowly. "Mr. Casey, I have to ask for something more specific. I can't go back to my team and tell them that I'm sorry, that they were hired for this project and did a good job but their contracts were written in pudding. I owe them more than that, sir. And so do you. They deserve to know where they stand."

Casey slapped his hands on the desk. "You listen to me, Jamison. We're in a tough business, and I can't give your people any special privileges. You got that? Your little band of nitnoids is comprised of contract workers and don't deserve shit from me. So don't you dare come in here and make demands."

Jamison was up and moving like he'd been sitting in a pile of red ants. He crossed the room, checking to make sure Jack Kane wasn't moving, too. "They don't deserve shit, Casey? Is that what you think? Well, listen up. Those people you're talking about worked their asses off for you, put in hundreds of hours off the clock to do a great job and then poof, you pull the plug, just like that." He snapped his fingers as he zeroed in on his boss's desk. "You owe us more than that. Come on, Casey, have some guts and give me the truth. What's going to happen to them? Say the words."

Casey looked like a man about to fight, or not, but having to decide either way. He snapped his head to the side, looked over at Kane, then came back and straightened up, leaned away from Jamison. "Get out of here, Jamison."

Jamison stiffened, ready to fight it out, right then and right there. But he understood that there wasn't any sense to it. This fight had already taken place and his team members had lost. He had to retreat, at least for now, with a desperate hope for a counterattack. He whirled around toward the door, thinking he'd better learn how to back down sooner.

Casey spoke again after Jamison took a few steps. "By the way, I understand you have some personal business this afternoon. Is that right?"

Jamison squared himself to Casey's question. "Yes, that's right. Is there some kind of problem with that?"

"Oh, no. No problem. Why would there be a problem? I guess we'll see you later then."

Jamison looked at each man and walked out the door.

* * * * *

Casey watched the door close, then turned to Kane. "What do you think, Jack? Is Jamison a leak, too?"

Kane looked around the room, ramming those gray eyes into all the recesses. Casey flinched when they settled on him.

"I don't know, Ross. Yesterday I'd have said he wasn't. The information he'd requested from closed files was totally justifiable. After all, we paid him to compare the old and new weapon's system, and he needed those files to do his job. The information would've been damaging if disclosed, but . . ."

There it was, Kane's frustrating habit of stopping midsentence to preview what he was about to say. It pissed Casey off, reminded him that Kane's words were always self-censored, even to him. For years he'd tolerated the habit, and not only because Kane scared him. He lived with the annoyance because Kane's immense power required that he put up with it.

"But what, Jack?"

"Well, the truth is that the information he's gathered over the last year is not what's been leaked so far. None of the files Jamison researched for the Wombat modification contained what the Coalition is using against us now."

"What happened yesterday to change your mind?"

Kane lifted his eyebrows, kept his eyes locked onto Casey. "I didn't say I'd changed my mind. I said that until yesterday I'd have said Jamison wasn't the leak. I would appreciate it if you'd keep the distinction clear."

"Right, Jack. Sorry."

Kane continued, but a little more slowly. "Lately, we've had round-the-clock surveillance on several employees who had access to the leaked information. Last night our friend Jamison met someone from the Citizen's Coalition Against Government Waste."

"Really? Doesn't that seem pretty suspicious?"

"We checked Jamison's car, but there wasn't much in it. Just a briefcase with a few innocent documents. We don't know what they discussed. He couldn't have said much because they only talked for a couple of minutes. It was Melissa Corley, the woman he used to date, back before— "

Casey raised his hands. He didn't need Kane's help to remember when his career had started to come apart at the seams. He'd changed every company policy when the Coalition had first begun its attacks. He'd become venomous, even deadly, when he'd discovered that one of his employees was leaking top-secret government information. Whoever was feeding facts to the Coalition was doing one hell of a job, had turned over plenty of information that the newspapers had been anxious to print. The Coalition appeared close to making a public charge of criminal fraud, and that had caused the F.B.I. to begin an investigation into Dillon's leaks of military secrets. Casey was getting skewered by the press, the F.B.I., the Coalition, and his board of directors.

"So Jamison probably is the leak."

Kane took a book from Casey's shelf, opened the cover and read the fly leaf. "No, actually I don't think so."

Casey looked from Kane to the book, then back to Kane. He wished, as he had so many times before, that he was back in his navy uniform, wearing that beautiful captain's eagle on his collar and four stripes on his sleeve, able to demand the answers and actions he wanted.

"Why not? What does Jamison have to do, hold up a sign? He's meeting with the Coalition, for God's sake. That's good enough for me. He must be a leak, too."

The book seemed to have all of Kane's interest now, his conversation with Casey a distant annoyance. "Like I said, the files he read didn't contain the information that has surfaced so far, and I don't think Jamison had any knowledge of some of the leaked data. Maybe he's collaborating with someone else here at Dillon. We just don't know. We'll keep him covered until we find out."

"Damn it, Jack, why don't you just kill the bastard right now and be done with it?"

Kane reached up and rolled an earlobe in his fingers, staring away as though he hadn't heard.

"Okay, I guess that would leave some important questions unanswered, such as who he might be working with. All right, Jack, do it your way. But I'm getting my ass burned, so keep on top of this thing."

Kane had strolled back and leaned against the windows, but at Casey's last words he lurched forward, brought his strong frame erect. He crossed the room silently, with long, noiseless strides. He was impossibly quiet for such a big man.

"I'll do what I have to do, Casey. You know I will." He looked lost, just for a second, then pasted those hateful gray eyes onto Casey. "But I decide who lives and who dies. Remember that."

Casey struggled against the challenge, wanting to fight back. But Kane wielded tremendous power, even if he rarely flexed it. "I'm sure you'll handle it appropriately," was the best riposte Casey could muster.

3

Jamison found the restaurant at a little after one, doubting that Melissa would still be waiting, thinking it would be best if she wasn't. Meeting her for lunch was a mistake and he knew it. He also knew he was going to cross the line and do it anyway.

He parked a block away and jogged to the entrance, pushed the door open and smacked into sensory overload. All of the restaurant's walls were red. The tablecloths, too. The acoustical ceiling had been painted black, and the floor was a checkerboard of black and white linoleum squares. Thick smells of oil and heavy spices burdened the air. Fewer than a dozen people were eating. Melissa stood up beside her table and he went straight to her.

"Hi," she said as he got close. "I was about to give up on you." She touched his left forearm, squeezed it slightly and pulled him toward her.

He leaned over and nearly gave her a hug, wondering if that was what she'd expected. But he couldn't be sure and didn't want to screw up with her again. He erred on the side of caution and stood his ground, his arm tingling at the spot her finger had pressed, his eyes staring at it. He was suddenly lost and a little disoriented. He couldn't really remember why he'd come but was very glad to be here, his stomach churning with the nervous exhilaration of being near the woman he loved.

He put his hand on hers, savored the miraculous feel of her flesh. "I was afraid you'd be gone. Sorry I'm late."

She slid her hand away and sat down, left him feeling like he'd been unplugged.

"That's okay," she said. "Something happen at work?"

He sat down after her. "Oh, yeah. Something definitely happened at work. Maybe we'll talk about it later." He swept his eyes around the restaurant, didn't see anyone he knew. "So, is the food any good here?"

Melissa leaned toward him and hesitated, then spoke in a low voice. "I know I shouldn't bring this up, Peter. But I heard about your project. I'm sorry."

He drew back from her. "How in the world did you find out?"

Melissa shook her head. "I'm just sorry, that's all. No questions, okay?"

He tried to look calm by toying with a menu while stumbling around for an easy question, determined to ease his way across the line. "This place is Thai, right? How hot is the food?"

She grinned. "Well, it depends. If you were Thai, they would make it very hot. Since you aren't, they'll calm it down, make it round-eye hot. Unless, of course, you order it otherwise."

An Asian waitress, short and thin and dark, came to the table. "Take your order now, Ms. Corley?"

"Yes, Pauranee. I'll have the Thai chicken again. Make it Thai hot, please."

Pauranee grinned, then twisted to get Jamison's order, her pencil poised on the little green pad.

"I'll have the same." He shrugged and flipped his menu closed, held it up for her to take.

"Thai hot?" Her eyes widened but she didn't move, stood there frozen, looking down at Jamison. Melissa giggled.

"Jeez, yes. Thai hot, okay?"

Melissa's giggle turned into a laugh. Pauranee raised her hand and hid her mouth.

Jamison looked back and forth between them. "Make it double Thai hot, for crying out loud. Triple, okay? So hot you need asbestos plates."

Pauranee headed for the kitchen, told the story to another waitress, who also giggled.

"It would have killed you, I suppose, to order sweet and sour?"

Melissa hadn't laughed too loud and she hadn't offended him. She had the kind of laugh that made him want to hold her, and join in the fun.

"You know me better than that, Peter. I *love* the hot stuff."

"Yeah." He looked around the restaurant, then leaned toward her cautiously. She leaned in too, her smile fading fast, her face getting serious.

"Melissa," he said, "I have to ask you something."

She cocked her left ear toward him, her eyebrows close together. "Okay. I'll answer it if I can. No guarantees, though."

"Thanks."

"Sure."

"How hot is Thai hot?"

Her eyes filled with sympathy. "Oh, baby, it's hot. I mean, grab-your-ankles-and-hold-on hot."

"That hot, huh?"

"Hot. Very hot."

"Okay, I got it. The chicken's going to be hot. I understand. Really, really hot chicken."

She kept it up, enjoying his worry, looking so natural with him. Happy, comfortable, relaxed, just like she belonged there. He kept looking at her face, thinking that maybe there was a way they could survive the damage she was causing Dillon, a way to get her back. After all, they had survived other hard times, his stint overseas during a bad time in their relationship, and her brief affair with a disreputable congressman. Both had created bad problems, especially since dating the congressman was a real departure for Melissa. She usually avoided anyone of questionable integrity. Jamison had never understood the attraction, and accepted the fact that he never would.

Their relationship had ended prematurely when the congressman died on a D.C. street, murdered outside the restaurant where he was to meet Melissa. She had watched his death from the window by her table. It was, of course, a bad break for the congressman. But Jamison had welcomed the grieving Melissa back, even though he was ashamed of himself for benefiting from the man's death.

"I understand," Melissa said, bringing him back.

He shook the memory. "I'm sorry, what?"

She reached over and pushed some hair away from his face, her fingernails just barely touching the skin on his forehead, electrifying him again. She was still grinning. "I said I understand why you ordered the same as I did. You didn't want to back away from the challenge. Right?"

His eyes were stuck to hers. "You call this food a challenge, a little hot pepper on chicken? Come on, Melissa, you're talking to guy who still eats an occasional hot dog."

"And you think that's more of a challenge?"

"To eat? No. But try thinking about it while you eat and it gets pretty tough. Once when I was younger I stopped by a slaughterhouse before going fishing, trying to get the parts of hog they don't use, for chum. Know what they told me?"

"Yuck. Can't imagine."

"They said there weren't any parts they didn't use."

She looked disgusted. "Oooo, hot dogs?"

Jamison licked his lips. "I doubt they're curing cancer with it. So anyway, how about you? How do you keep busy these days? Aside from work, I mean."

She looked at the ceiling, as if narrowing her choices. "Well, let's see. I'm still running a little, although I haven't competed since we ran the half-marathon. I'm keeping my times down, though. And I'm still fencing."

He rolled his eyes. "That is such an odd sport."

"Oh, Peter, you would love it. It improves your speed, reactions, and balance—all things that are important to you. And besides, it's great fun to poke and stab at other people. I switched from foils to sabers a few months ago, and I really like that. It's all slashing and clanking, instead of just thrust and parry."

The waitress arrived and caught Melissa slicing the air with her knife, chuckled as she set the meals down. The damned chicken was much hotter than Jamison expected. Hell, it was hotter than anything he'd ever eaten before. But he kept quiet about it, drank four glasses of water and wiped just about that much sweat off his face.

He finished when she did, paid as they left, then stepped onto the sidewalk. The sun was bright and the low buildings offered them protection from the cool wind. It was almost pleasant, at least for December.

Jamison touched her arm. "Are you up for a walk? I'd like to talk a little before you go."

"Sure. That sounds nice."

They headed north, away from his car. The sidewalk wasn't crowded, only about twenty people walked the block ahead of them. The street wasn't crowded either. They took a short stroll, then stopped at the entrance of a jewelry store. Melissa looked at something in the window, but when she started to move on, Jamison didn't go with her.

She turned and walked back to him. He shuffled in front of her, then picked up her hands and held them low between them. "Melissa, I don't want to cross the battle line here, but I'm really confused by the cancellation of my project. I think you know what happened and I would appreciate your help."

She smiled, but her lips stayed together. She reached toward his throat, adjusted his tie, then brushed her nails along his neck. "Peter, I can't help you. You know I can't."

"Sure you can. What's stopping you?"

She looked surprised. "Well, ethics, for one thing."

"Come on, Melissa. I know how you feel about ethics, but I also know how you hate to see people victimized. And that's what's happening here. Seven people will lose their jobs unless I get the Wombat back onto the hot sheet. Good people, Melissa. People with families, who need your help. Give me something to go on. Really, that's all I'm asking, some direction."

She had a look on her face that he couldn't decipher. Was it pity? Pain? Whatever it was, she didn't say anything.

"I'm not asking for Coalition secrets, Melissa. Just point me in the right direction. I can take it from there."

"Peter, we shouldn't be having this conversation. Sure, I know some things about Dillon. But you know a whole lot more than I do. I just think we should keep that knowledge separate."

"Well, I don't."

"You don't?"

"No."

She jerked her hands away and stared at nothing in the street. Then she snapped back onto him. "Tough. I'm not doing this, Peter. This is so typical of you. We don't agree so you want me to cave in, even if I don't think it's right."

"I want you to help me. That's all there is to it. I'm not trying to hurt you, or the Coalition. I'm just trying to save jobs. Damn it, Melissa, I need your help. As a friend, I'm asking for some advice."

She rolled onto her toes, moved close to his face. "Okay, *friend*, here goes. Find another employer."

"Oh, that's great advice. Thanks a lot."

"Hey, you asked me as a friend, I'm talking like one. Get out of there."

He opened his mouth but he didn't know what to say, stood there looking at her, then beyond her. His eyes dropped until they were looking at his shoes.

After a minute Melissa shook her head and bit her lower lip. "I'm sorry, Peter. Let's start over, okay?"

"Be glad to."

"Look, I really can't say much, but if you tell me why you think your project was killed, I guess I can tell you if you're hot or cold. It might help a little."

"Except that I don't have a clue."

"They didn't give you a reason?"

"No. Hell, I can't even imagine a decent reason. It's too weird."

"No clues at all?"

"Not really. Although once, several months ago, I had lunch with our director of research, Ted Bronovich. He said that the government still hadn't acknowledged the fatal flaw in the current system, so our new system might not be cheap enough for the government to justify replacing the old one. That was the only objection I ever heard."

"Was he right? Or was it cheap enough?"

"It was cheap enough."

"You sound pretty sure."

"I am sure. After that meeting I spent a week pulling subcontractor bids for assemblage components. I added allowances for retooling, additional training, new distribution, and storage of spare parts. Then I amortized the new system's start-up cost over five years, which is only about a third of the system's life."

"I'm impressed. Then what did you do?"

"I showed the costs and the prototype to Vice President Casey, demonstrated that the system was more accurate, more dependable, and far less expensive than the existing one."

47

A woman came out of the jewelry store, stared at Melissa as she walked past, and turned down the sidewalk. Melissa waited until she was gone.

"And?"

"I was cleared to go ahead. At least until last night." He looked across the street, then around the sidewalk, then, finally, at her. "What do you think?"

She buttoned her coat, lifted her shoulders up around her neck. "That we shouldn't be having this conversation."

"True enough. What else?"

She tapped her right foot, her arms folded across her chest. "Peter, I really hate that you're doing this to me, putting me in this predicament."

"Me, too. It's not right and I know it. But if you can tell me a little, it might help a lot. Don't you think that's a good deal?"

"For you, maybe. Anyway, all I can say is that there are serious legal problems at Dillon. I can't be specific."

"Okay. Thanks for that much. Can you tell me how those problems might have affected the Wombat?"

"No. But . . . I suppose I could look at anything you have and give you my opinion. It'll just be between us, although I'd rather drop this right here and forget we ever had this conversation. I'll let you decide."

He studied a passing car. "Melissa, if you would just look over some of my data, I'd love you for it. Maybe you'll catch something I've missed."

She put her hand over her eyes and shook her head. "Fine. No problem. I'll do it. Are you busy tonight?"

"No. No plans."

"Then come over to my house. Bring whatever you have."

"Okay."

"Good. I'll see you then. Now, are we finished here? Because I really need to get back to work."

Without waiting for his answer she stepped out of the storefront's entrance, headed along the sidewalk toward her car.

He fell in beside her, opened the car door when they got there. She stopped and stepped into him, looked at him for a few long seconds. "I've missed you, Peter. I've missed you a lot."

"Me, too, Melissa. You have no earthly idea how much."

She slid into her car. He closed her door and headed back toward his car.

* * * * *

Jack Kane pulled into traffic as Jamison got close. He drove down the street and found a good spot that faced the sun and provided a concealing glare on the windshield. From there he had an easy view of Jamison and his car. He picked up his cellular phone and pushed a speed dial number. It rang only once.

"Security."

He was busy watching Jamison, didn't answer right away.

"*Security*," the man said again, his voice edgy with suspicion.

"This is Kane."

"Oh. Sorry. Hello, Mr. Kane. What can I do for you, sir?"

"I'm working a case and I need some help."

"Yes, sir. How many men do you want, sir?"

"You and two others. Individual cars. Right away. Head east on the Little River Turnpike, call me ten minutes later."

"Roger that, Mr. Kane. We'll leave now. Be on the road in two minutes, tops."

Kane hung up and dialed again, fighting the urge to straighten in his seat.

"Hello?" The voice on the other end was soft, but strong. Nothing weak about it.

"Are you aware of the problem I'm trying to solve?"

"Yes."

Kane watched Jamison get into his car. "And my actions are approved, in advance?"

"Any measures you think necessary. This is too important, and there's no time to vacillate."

"Thank you. I'll take care of it. Good-bye."

Kane pulled out his map and picked locations for his men. He would start the tail of Jamison, and the others would be here soon to alternate with him. Whether Jamison had leaked information or not, he had met with the Corley woman twice. That made him dangerous to Dillon Aerospace, and Kane's job was the elimination of any threat to the company. He took his work very seriously.

4

Jamison parked in front of Melissa's Georgetown brownstone, lucky to find a spot so close on a Friday night. It was just after eight P.M., and the happy-hour crowd had thinned out. It was still a little early for the dinner and music set.

The darkness made it easy for him to sneak his box of data into her four-story building. Her apartment was on the third floor, accessed by an ornate wooden staircase with small chandeliers at each landing. His steps echoed off the paneled walls as he climbed the polished oak stairs. He could hear shuffling in the apartments he passed, saw peepholes go dark as people watched him from behind closed doors. He was glad to get to her door; shifted the box onto his other hip and knocked.

Melissa swung open the door, holding a small stalk of celery, wearing faded jeans and an oversized sweatshirt. No shoes or socks. Her hair was pulled back and she wasn't wearing any jewelry. His nerves kicked up when he saw her.

"Hi, Peter. Come in."

She leaned against the door as he passed. Her apartment was large, meticulously kept, and nicely decorated with an eclectic mix of pieces. He recognized most of the furniture instantly, set his box down on the floor by the couch, and walked around the few new things, stepping slowly as though this were some kind of museum, trying to get his bearings and feel at home again. He gently touched some of the items, but mostly kept his hands behind his back. He went slowly through the living and dining rooms, didn't see any photos of another man.

She followed a step and a half behind him, looking where he did, keeping quiet for a minute or so. "So, how was your day?"

He picked up an antique dagger and examined it. "Okay, I guess. About what you'd expect. Better now that I've made it here with the data. You wouldn't believe the security at Dillon these days."

"I hear they're acting incredibly paranoid. Is this all the documentation on the Wombat? Everything?"

He looked at her suspiciously. "No. All of it would have filled a small pickup, a little awkward to carry past the guards. This is just the cost data."

He set the dagger down and walked over to the cardboard box, kicked the lid off with his shoe. "I collected most of this stuff over the last six months, before Dillon cracked down so hard. But some is as recent as this afternoon." He turned away from the box and stared at a huge antique bookcase.

She stepped up beside him and looked at the bookcase, too. "I'll never forget how surprised I was when you bought this for me."

His pulse fluttered. He hadn't heard her use that tone in a year. It was a beautiful sound, like a radiant angel calling him home.

"I'll never forget my friends and me sneaking it up your stairs." He arched backward and feigned a bad back.

She rubbed the imaginary sore spot for a few seconds. He was desperate to touch her, and thought this might be a good

52

time to knock down the barrier. But she moved her hand as he turned, walked several feet away.

"Aren't you afraid that Dillon, or the F.B.I., suspects you? The newspaper says the agents have a very short list of suspects. Won't you end up on it?"

Jamison shrugged and looked around some more, wondered if he'd misread her a moment ago. "I doubt it. I've never done anything wrong, at least not until now. The people they suspect have been on the list for some time, I imagine. Probably since the leaks began. Besides, I don't fit the profile." He thought about how fast she'd heard about the Wombat's cancellation. "But it seems pretty likely that the leak is someone who works with me, certainly in my department." He watched her carefully, listened to hear her exact words.

"Oh?"

"Yes, oh."

"Whom do you suspect?"

He gave up, felt stupid trying to trap her. "I don't know. No one in particular."

She nodded, her eyes distant for a second. "What do you think will happen now?"

He had not wanted to deal with this question. He'd spent the afternoon trying like hell to reverse Dillon's decision, but was finally concluding that nothing was going to change without a major fight. So his motivation was simple now. He was in a struggle for his team's survival, and would use whatever weapons he could devise.

"If nothing changes, my team will get lay-off notices next week. Dillon can't carry people without current assignments."

"That's a shame. Will you lose your job, too?"

"No, it doesn't look like it. Dillon loves me because I do a good job."

"You do. No question."

"Yeah? Well, I keep hearing that the Coalition is threatening criminal charges against Dillon. You really think they're corrupt?"

She squirmed a little, reached up and pinched her ear as she walked off. "It's difficult for me to say anything about that, Peter. I'm too far over the line already."

"I suppose. But I'd like to know."

She walked back to him, took him straight on. "How much?"

"What?"

"I said, how much? How much would you really like to know? How serious are you? Where does your comfort zone end?"

He took a step back, wanted to see more than her face, needed the signals her body was sending. "Jeez, Melissa, what are you talking about?"

She put her hands behind her back. "Let me ask you something, Peter. Doesn't it seem to you that Americans tend just to go along with whatever happens in government?"

"You mean that they've quit bitching about the screwups?"

"That's right. Those low expectations are exactly what I'm talking about. Americans don't demand accountability for anything anymore. It's as if they've come to expect that everything's rigged, so why waste time struggling against it."

Jamison nodded, kept quiet, waited to see what this had to do with the Wombat.

"But this country needs accountability. Checks and balances, as originally intended. And people deserve it. The perverse incentives of Washington politics are wrecking this country, but all we citizens do is shake our heads at the excesses and gridlock, get angry for a few minutes, then let it pass."

"You're right. We've all done it."

"Well, I don't do it anymore. Companies like Dillon—who are really just minor players in this game—are in my crosshairs because they're my best starting point. They're corrupt and I'll prove it, then go another step up the ladder, and then another."

"Hey, calm down. I've never seen this side of you before."

She blushed. Smiled. Closed her eyes and breathed deep. "I'm sorry. I shouldn't have said all that. I passed your comfort zone, didn't I?"

"No, it's not that. It's just that it sounds . . . well, hopeless. You're taking on a monster. You can't seriously think you'll win."

She looked patient, as if she hadn't expected him to understand. "I'm not doing this alone. The Coalition believes we can do it."

"Well, good luck. Sounds like a one-way trip to me."

She wanted to argue, he knew that. He also knew she wouldn't. It wasn't her style. She'd fight, sure, but wouldn't waste time arguing.

"I'll get us some coffee, Peter. Make yourself at home and I'll be right back. Instant all right with you?"

He plucked her saber from beside a chair and chased her toward the kitchen, trying to break down the wall he'd just built. "Sure. Need a hand?"

She analyzed his bad form. "No, thanks, Sinbad. But you can close the blinds. Some nosy people just moved into the building across the street."

"Sure." He tossed the saber onto the couch and went to the windows. They filled one entire wall of her apartment and looked down onto 33rd street and across at an old building, which about a hundred years ago had been a warehouse. The new window frames reminded him of the remodeling that Melissa had done two years ago. He'd wanted her to move in with him at the time to avoid the disruption. She, typically, had refused, had stubbornly held on to her independence. They had fought about it.

Now he wished she'd moved to his house, was wondering how different their lives might have been as he rotated the tilt wands of the blinds, incrementally concealing himself from the darkened building across the street. Then Melissa snapped him back and handed him coffee. "Ready to go to work?"

"Sure. Where do you want to start?"

She put her coffee on a table, grabbed a legal pad, and curled up like a cat on the matching loveseat. "I guess at the beginning. Tell me about the Wombat project, right from the day you were assigned. We'll get into your data after we've identified the information we want to target."

He stalled for a second as he organized his thoughts. Her pen was poised over her pad, ready to write. She suddenly looked up at him.

"Peter, we don't have to do this, you know."

"What? Oh, I know. I was just thinking it through, that's all. I'm not having second thoughts."

"You're sure?"

"Yes," he said, trying to sound convincing. Then he began without any more hesitation, told the entire history of the project, including setbacks, successes, and management interferences. Melissa wrote quick notes but never interrupted. Her head bounced gently as she wrote, her beautiful brown hair swinging with the rhythm of his words.

At one o'clock he finished his story and went into the kitchen for some water. When he returned, Melissa was throwing a sheet on the couch, maneuvering the linen as it floated down.

He grabbed a corner and helped her tuck it under a cushion. "Sleeping on the couch tonight?"

She grinned and slapped his arm, hard enough to hurt. "Not likely. But I thought you might rather stay here than make the drive home. We can get a fresh start in the morning."

He tried to get a look at her eyes, see what she was thinking. But she turned away and fluffed a pillow. "Sounds fine to me. Thanks."

She was grinning now. "Not quite like old times, but . . ."

He shuffled his feet. "Uh, yeah. Not quite."

Melissa rubbed her hands together and looked around the living room. "You know where everything is. Help yourself to whatever you need. Use my bathroom, though, because the guest bath is being remodeled. Feel free to shower in the morning if you like. The glass door is opaque, so don't worry. Besides, I've seen it all before."

He felt himself blush.

She rubbed her hands some more, as if they were freezing cold. "Right. Well, I guess I'll see you in the morning."

He fidgeted in front of her, his feet desperate to take the step that separated them, but his heart telling him it wasn't right.

"Good night, Melissa."

* * * * *

Jack Kane used the key he'd been given and opened the door, walked into the large, empty room. It was a storeroom of some kind, or maybe an empty artist's loft. There were no interior walls except for a small room at the far end—probably a bathroom.

Directly ahead of him, about twenty feet away, was a wall of black plastic draped from ceiling to floor and end to end. It divided the huge room in half, lengthwise, allowing the area by the windows to stay dark.

A man with a nice smile, friendly eyes, and a big handgun walked up to him with a cup of coffee. "Good evening, Mr. Kane."

Kane took the coffee, sniffed at it before he sipped. "What are they doing over there, Corderman?"

Corderman snickered. "Well, sir, they're getting ready for bed right now. We were in her apartment earlier, so Martin's got their entire evening on tape. We're betting they'll be bumping butts soon, so I left. You know I hate watching that stuff when I'm stuck on surveillance. It makes me miss my wife too much."

Kane chuckled. "I thought you hated your wife. I've never heard you do anything but complain about her."

"Doesn't matter, sir. You listen to enough of some other couple's heavy action, anybody would miss his wife." His eyes popped open and he stiffened. "Oh, jeez, Mr. Kane, I'm sorry. I didn't mean to say that."

Kane stood solid, turned his face to stone, refused to give up any of the pain or sorrow or anger. Saving it all for himself. Still aching, feeling guilty that it had taken half a day before the tragedy of his family's deaths had really affected him.

He was a technical representative on cruise, liaison between the Navy and Dillon Aerospace when tough problems came up with one of their planes. He was aboard the Carrier Constellation when the ship's captain called him to his quarters. "Mr. Kane," he began in a voice that tried not to hesitate. "I have some terrible news for you. Terrible news."

Kane remembered standing in front of the captain, noticing the way his eyes flicked back and forth, feeling each second force its way to the next, waiting quietly for the captain to finish. Terrified.

"Your home was broken into last night, Mr. Kane. I'm sorry to say that your wife was killed. Both your children, too. You'll be launched stateside as soon as you're ready. I'm very sorry. If there's anything I can do . . ."

The captain's words couldn't be true. They didn't sound as if they could possibly be real. But then, his family didn't seem real, either, not out here on a ship in the middle of the Mediterranean. He hadn't held them in his arms for six months. Six long months without hearing his wife's voice, or her enthusiasm as she planned their future. If his family was gone now, it was hard to feel. He stood there knowing the captain was still talking, hating himself for not suffering more intensely.

For not collapsing, or crying, the second he'd heard. Totally unaware of how much pain would settle on him later.

By the time he got back to Washington the police had moved on to the next day's murders, leaving his family's deaths behind until someone jumped up and confessed. The detectives had to move on, they'd said. If a murder in Washington wasn't solved within forty-eight hours, it might never be solved. They didn't have the man-hours to spend on something that might not end in an arrest. It was over, they'd told him. Try to forget about it.

Like hell. Kane worked the case himself and talked to everyone who knew anything. He pieced together tiny shreds of information until he had some leads, chased the leads until he had suspects, chased the suspects until he had . . . nothing.

They were gone. His family's murderers were hiding, fearing the vengeful husband and father who was out to get them. The word of Kane's obsession had filtered back to them from the hundreds of people he'd interviewed.

That was when he found out about Dillon Security. Two men approached him—not at the office but at the pistol range. Two men with F.B.I. credentials, a piece of paper with an address, and two photos of the men who'd killed his family. Two men who said nothing except, "Dillon Security wanted to help."

Kane accepted the photos and the addresses without speaking.

A few weeks later, after he'd gone to the addresses and killed the men, another man he did not know came to see him. Would Kane be interested in shifting career paths at Dillon? They could use a man like him, he'd said. In security. Dillon's security.

And use him they had, with every one of his victims wearing the faces of his family's murderers. They'd gone down easily at first, then easier. It was his pleasure, and for nineteen years he had been venting his rage on whomever Dillon wanted dead, waiting for the meanness to drain out.

Kane shook the memory, tried to move past it, save it for the right time. "What has Jamison been saying over there?"

Corderman exhaled the air he'd held for more than a minute. "He's telling her all about his project, has told her a bunch of classified information and has a pretty big stack of data with him to support it."

Kane stepped to the black plastic and passed through the overlap. He walked to the spot where another man sat at a card table, monitoring video and audio recorders. Nothing else occupied the large room other than roaches.

"How's the signal, Martin?"

Martin shifted the headphones off one ear of his massive head. The thick fingers of his weightlifter's body were awkward, but surprisingly gentle as he adjusted the small knobs of the equipment. "Good, Mr. Kane."

"Audio and video?"

"Yes, sir. You should hear the crap I'm taping. They sound like a couple of awkward teenagers over there. You know what I mean? Not understanding anything about love, yet absolutely certain that they're in it."

"Really?"

"Yeah, sure. But they don't love each other, Mr. Kane. I know love and this ain't it."

"You're the expert, huh?"

Martin shifted his giant's body around and pretended to pick up a microphone. "Yes, sir. And this is the Love Connection. Tonight we have Peter Jamison and Melissa Corley, two starcrossed—"

"Are all the rooms covered?"

Martin straightened up, set the pretend microphone on the card table. "Yes, sir. We've got a small blackout in the hallway, but that's all."

"Good. Stay on it."

"Mr. Kane, there's some Dillon material in there. You want me to go in and get it?" The huge man smiled, his big blue eyes looking like they belonged to a salesman who really needed a sale.

Kane knew Martin well, knew he wanted to take Jamison down and pick up the bonus money for a killing. And Martin probably had the right idea. Just go ahead and do it. Get Dillon's data back, nice and simple. Clean.

But Jamison was an amateur. The Corley woman was, too. Kane could take them down whenever he wanted. He could wait a little while without paying a price. Maybe, just maybe, there was a better way to use Jamison, a way to stop the leaks and retrieve the data without having to kill people.

Kane stuck his gray eyes onto Martin and watched his massive body wiggle around in his seat. "Do you think we should, Martin?"

"No, sir. I mean, I don't know, sir. Just a thought, that's all."

"Thank you, Martin. If I decide to send Corderman in to get the data, you can stay here and guide him around Jamison and Corley."

A huge muscle bumped up on Martin's right shoulder, looked as if it might burst the seam of his shirt. "Yes, sir, Mr. Kane. Whatever you say."

Jamison slept until six, a very late start for him. But he knew how Melissa hated mornings, and knew he'd still have time to get things organized before she woke up. He headed to her bathroom to shower, checking on her as he passed through her room. She was lying on her stomach, twisted in the sheets, her T-shirt up to her waist, revealing her black panties. He stood over her for several minutes wanting, more than anything else, to lay down and hug her. Rub her back and smell her hair. Nothing else mattered at that moment. He would give anything to hold her again, to wrap her up in his arms one more time.

But he pulled himself away from her bed, climbed into the shower and tried to forget that the woman he loved was half naked on the bed in the next room. He dried, then dressed in the bathroom, forced himself through her room without looking toward the bed, made coffee and went to work in the living room. When she stumbled out an hour later, blurry-eyed and beautiful, he was standing beside five piles of data.

"Hi. How did you sleep?"

She shuffled up and hugged him, hung on spaghetti-armed. "Good. You?"

He had trouble letting his arms go around her, afraid he would wake her up fully and she'd realize they were hugging. "I slept well. Care for some coffee?"

She nudged her head against his neck, then tossed herself erect and rubbed focus into her eyes. "That would be nice. Thanks."

"I'll be back in a minute."

She waved over her shoulder, then fell into the chair by the documents.

He stopped in the kitchen and stored all the pleasure of the hug, just in case it never happened again. He poured the coffee and returned, found her with a piece of paper funneled into her left hand. Her right hand clutched her robe closed. Delicate, wire-rimmed glasses added to her intense look of intelligence.

She reached for the coffee without looking up. "Thanks, Peter. I hope you don't mind that I started."

"I don't mind. Why don't I make us some breakfast while you get up to speed?"

"Sounds wonderful."

She picked up some copies and went to her bedroom. Jamison headed to the kitchen and searched for a skillet. In fifteen minutes she was dressed and in the kitchen, toweling the hair that dampened the back of her T-shirt, all the way to her jeans. She leaned against the counter, holding some of his documents.

"Peter, why does Dillon use such old technology for the Wombat's targeting system? Microprocessor technology has advanced so much that I can't imagine where you get this old circuitry manufactured."

"That's a good question. The fact is, we pay a fortune for it." He waved a spatula in the direction of the living room. "Copies of the accounting invoices are in another stack out there. Shoot, the savings from converting that item alone would more than offset the retooling expense, and make the current system much safer for the pilots."

"I would think so. Hasn't anyone ever suggested that before?" She went to another page, asked the question without looking up.

"If someone did, they were about as successful as I was. Of course, you're going to find a whole lot of reasons to convert to a new system as you wade through that stuff, and I can't imagine I'm the first to ask about any of it."

He slid the omelettes onto plates. "How about grabbing some silverware, and the pitcher. I made orange juice."

Melissa put down the documents and finished setting the table. "Peter, I've already seen lots of things I'd like to check against the information in my computer. Would it be all right if I went over your stuff in my office? You can come along, or I could call you when I have a question."

"I'll pass, but you can do that. Just be careful about who you tell, okay?"

"I won't tell a soul. Hardly anyone works on Saturday anyway, so the place will be quiet. The building has great security."

"Good. You'll call me later?"

"Sure."

Thirty minutes later he gathered his things to leave. Melissa approached him as he stepped to the door, looked around the room to make sure he had everything.

"What are your plans today?"

"I'm going to the gym, and then out for a run. Maybe we can get together after you finish."

She picked up his hand and traced a finger across his palm. "Sounds nice. We'll set it up when I call."

"Great. Good luck today." He watched her finger working on his palm. It was driving him nuts, making him struggle to stay in control. His arms twitched to wrap her up in them.

She let go but didn't look up, opened the door and leaned against the jamb. "Have a good workout. Bye."

She closed the door behind him. Then, as he hit the stairs, he heard her bolt it.

Jamison spent most of the day working out, dealing with the pain and frustration of dying careers. At four o'clock he began to wonder when Melissa would call about their plans for tonight. He was counting on her, knew that if anyone could find a way to save those jobs, she was the one.

He stopped in the kitchen on his way to the shower, sweating from a ten mile run. The phone rang and he answered it, dripping sweat all over the floor. "Hello?"

"Hi, it's me. Can you talk?"

He grabbed a roll of paper towels and snapped some off, wiped the burning sweat from his eyes. "Sure. What's up?"

"Peter, I've been here all day going over your stuff, and I don't know how to tell you this without just blurting it out. It's really good news. Or really bad news, depending on your viewpoint."

He wiped sweat off his right shoulder, then switched the phone to that ear. "Go."

"I analyzed all of your information and came to the same conclusions you drew in your synopsis. But Peter, your Wombat project doesn't even matter anymore."

"What? Why? What do you mean?"

"Well, first let me admit that I haven't finished yet, so some of what I say might change slightly."

"Understood."

"Good. Now, remember those bids and invoices you had for the old system, the ones you got from accounting?"

"Sure."

"I cross-checked them with the information we have on file from those same subcontractors, most of it obtained through the Freedom of Information Act, tax returns, annual reports, and disclosure statements. We hacked into the Pentagon's computer to get some of it."

"And?"

"There's no question about it now. Dillon has been committing criminal fraud against the government for years. Decades. Just like we suspected, but honestly, it could have taken another year for us to prove it without your help. It looks like Dillon has defrauded American taxpayers out of . . . oh, I don't know exactly, but over a billion dollars since that weapons system first went into use. We can get criminal convictions with this information. Maybe restitution."

Sweat started running down his face again and he grabbed another towel. "Are you sure?"

"I won't have the actual numbers finalized until tomorrow. But am I sure about the fraud? Yes. Absolutely."

He wanted to ask again, maybe phrase his question differently. But he didn't. If Melissa said she was sure, she was sure. "All right, so what happens next?"

"Well," she started, then interrupted herself. "Peter, I thought you might need to digest this a little first."

"No, I'm all right."

"Okay. But if you want me to clarify anything, just say so."

"Thanks, but it's pretty clear what you're saying. What do we do now?"

She was excited and he could hear it. She was closing in on her prey, and loving it.

"There are two ways to approach this. One, the Coalition could make a full disclosure and pursue prosecution, get the fraud out in the open and put pressure on Dillon and the

65

Defense Department administrators who must have gone along with them. The only problem is that it puts you in a really bad spot. You could be charged criminally for passing along classified information, unless we get you some whistleblower protection."

She paused and waited, but Jamison was not about to speak until he'd heard both options.

"But I think the better choice is for me to give you the facts *we* have, and let you take it to Capitol Hill. That would protect you, because there'd be no proof you ever told us anything."

"To whom would I take it? I doubt there's a complaint department for this sort of thing."

"Senator Drummond, on the Senate Armed Services Committee. I've known him all my life and have worked with him before. He's a real bulldog. He's always ready to jump down someone's throat so I can pretty much guarantee he'll open a senate investigation, and probably push for the appointment of a special prosecutor."

Jamison didn't put much faith in politicians. He'd fought McNamara's ridiculous war because of them and had never forgotten how far removed they could be from real-life values. But he wanted to trust Melissa's advice. After all, this was her job, and she was good at it. Besides, it wasn't like he had any other plan. "How soon can your guys have the facts detailed in a way that Drummond can understand?"

"I want to move quickly on this. I'll call my people right now, bring them into work tomorrow. Then I'll call Drummond at home and set up your appointment for Monday. Are you ready to move that fast?"

"Yes. I guess so. Should I go into Dillon this weekend and look for anything else?"

"Absolutely not. This is dangerous enough already. There have been rumors for years about how ruthlessly Dillon retaliates. Don't cross them until we're ready. Promise?"

"Yes."

"We've got everything we need. Don't do anything else. I'll call Drummond right now. Okay?"

Jamison hesitated long enough to think about his team members. Would this help them? No, probably not. Could it hurt them anymore than they were already going to be hurt? No, again. They would be all right, or not, regardless of what he did now. He would do the right thing, and trust in that.

"That all sounds fine. Can we meet later to clear up some details?"

"Sure. Why don't you come over to my house. Think about this between now and then, Peter, because it'll get pretty ugly."

"Not much to think about."

"Okay. As long as you're sure."

"I'm sure."

*　*　*　*　*

Martin couldn't get comfortable on the hard chair in the cold warehouse across from Corley's apartment. His muscular body wasn't designed for long hours of sitting. He was too big, too powerful, and too used to pushing things around. Things like weights, people, and anything that annoyed him

And right now, Peter Jamison was annoying the hell out of him. Martin had sat on his ass all day waiting for the little prick to show up. Sat here reading magazines and playing stupid mind games while he ate junk food he would normally avoid. It was all Jamison's fault. And Kane's. If Kane had given him his way, he would have finished it last night, killed Jamison and maybe the Corley woman. Cut their throats and left with the stuff Jamison had stolen from Dillon. He would be out in the bars now, his favorite places on a Saturday night, using his raw power to force himself on young girls, and daring anyone to challenge his right to do it.

Jamison had come back to her apartment about six o'clock, right after dark, carrying a small suitcase as though he planned to stay for awhile. Corley had arrived just after that. They'd been sitting on the floor of her living room since then, going over a bunch of boring damn receipts and talking about how incriminating those silly pieces of paper would be once they put their case together.

As if Martin found any of it interesting. Throughout the long evening, nothing those two lovebirds said had sparked anything in him except the desire to get out of this dark, roach-infested building and get cleaned up. Put on a tight shirt that showed all of his muscles and go out drinking.

About midnight he tried to take things into his own hands, took a chance and called Kane, even though his instructions had been specific.

"Mr. Kane, this is Martin. Did you know that Jamison and that woman are planning an attack over there. He's definitely joined up with her, and is giving her lots more information for the Coalition to use against Dillon. I think I should do something, Mr. Kane."

Kane breathed into the phone, didn't speak for half a minute. "Martin?"

Martin cringed at the way Kane said his name, knew this wasn't going to be good.

"Yes, Mr. Kane?"

"Didn't you understand what I said earlier?"

"Yes, sir. You said not to do anything unless it was absolutely necessary. But I just thought this might be—"

"Martin?"

"Yes, sir."

"Don't push me on this."

"Yes, sir, Mr. Kane. I understand."

"Are you sure?"

"Yes, sir, Mr. Kane."

"Good."

Kane hung up and Martin was glad to be rid of him. He checked and tweaked his monitors, watched as Jamison laughed and gave the woman a hug. This was all Jamison's fault, the little bastard. Martin couldn't wait, was actually longing for the chance to even the score with him. Until then, he would have to keep sitting on his crappy metal chair, listening to the bugs scurrying across the floor in the dark. Let Saturday night slip away without him.

5

Jamison woke up on Melissa's couch, feeling great, far better than he'd felt on any of the other three hundred and eighty-two mornings since their breakup. He'd spent the last two evenings close to her, roaming her apartment, sleeping one room away from her, listening to her breathe throughout the night, thrilled to be so close.

But even more exciting was the fact that she seemed to enjoy having him here. She'd given him a key again. He could feel the fire of their relationship starting to give off some heat. Not much yet, but a little. If they kept fanning it, and he didn't douse her feelings or smother her, they had a decent chance of regaining the white-hot intensity of a year ago.

He pulled his jeans on, then sat in the early morning light for an hour, fondling a headband she'd left on the table and looking through her open bedroom door, watching her sleep, fascinated by every little movement of her body and knowing he was way-over-his-head in love with her, far beyond the bounds of good sense. He was addicted to her. He had to have her and could barely think of anything else.

She rolled over in her bed, twisting the sheets around her slender legs. Twice she pushed the hair out of her eyes without opening them, then said something in her sleep that he couldn't make out. Mostly, though, she'd just lain there, still as could be, her chest rising and falling with a sensual, intoxicating rhythm.

He loved her too much and he knew it. More than she loved him and far more than he dared show her. The air she breathed —the oxygen she had sucked down her mouth, taken in for nourishment, then pushed out past her lips—was precious to him. The stroke of her fingers was magical and arousing. He loved everything about her, from the hypnotizing way she walked to the quiet confidence with which she looked into his eyes when asking questions. He couldn't imagine ever letting her go again, and would do anything to win her back.

He was almost glad the Wombat had been canceled. The project's death had been the catalyst that rebonded them, had given their relationship new strength. And even if it didn't matter now, it had been the right thing for him to do at the time, joining forces with her and fighting for his teammates. That was his original motive and it had been an honorable one. But nothing he did now would save those poor souls.

However, Melissa would be proud of him if he helped her clean out Dillon, and that might make her feelings for him return. Why wouldn't they? She'd loved him once before. It could happen again. There was no reason to believe she was in love with anyone else.

But until he believed she loved him back he would keep his feelings to himself. He could scare her away if he weren't careful.

She woke up about seven-thirty, which for her was early. She didn't like mornings, which was something else he found adorable about her. She staggered into the living room and sat down beside him, her T-shirt just covering her panties.

He didn't say anything at first, just sat there and watched her. Couldn't believe he was here again, with her sitting so close.

She opened those eyes that could make him do anything, looked directly at him and pulled the trigger on his passion. "Hi," was all she said before she closed them again and leaned against his shoulder.

He wanted so badly to put his arm around her and squeeze her shoulders, wrap her up in his arms. But he didn't. He did turn his face into her hair, though, and breathed in her scent. "Good morning. Sleep okay?"

She nodded her head up and down against his shoulder.

"Hungry?"

She sat up slowly, rubbed her face with both hands. "Yes." Then, with a burst of energy she scooted away from him, swiveled around on the couch and grabbed his arm with her right hand, her left tugging her T-shirt down a little. "Peter, let's go out for bagels and coffee, like we used to do! Get the Sunday paper, spend a little time loafing over breakfast. What do you say?"

She was so excited there was no way he could refuse, even if he wanted to. Which he didn't. "You're on. Get ready."

She jumped off the couch with so much enthusiasm that a stranger might have thought he was taking her to Cannes, or Monaco. That was Melissa's way. It didn't take big things to thrill her. Just the right things.

Thirty minutes later they were sitting at a front table of Einstein's Bagels, right under a poster that said, "I wish I was the bagel baker." Melissa couldn't seem to stop grinning as she split the paper the way she always had, took the business section for herself then gave him all the rest.

He sipped his coffee, took a bite of bagel, and tried like hell to sound unaffected by her presence. "This was a good idea."

Melissa kept her lips together, still grinning. "Oh, Peter, it feels so good to be with you again."

He tucked that little gem away for safekeeping, opened the *Washington Post* and glanced at it, tried very hard to notice something other than Melissa. "Sure does."

She smiled, but hid it quickly as she buried her face in the paper. He did the same, was immediately jolted by Dillon's name in the headline on the front page.

"Oh, shit," he said.

"What?"

"There's a big article here about the leaks at Dillon Aerospace."

She lowered the business section but kept it in her hands. "Really? What does it say?"

Jamison scanned the article, flipped to page A5 and read some more. "It gives a recap of every bit of information that's been leaked, the date it was first reported, and the criminal implications if the information is ever verified. From what I know, they're dead-on in what they say, too. Whoever the leak is, he provided reliable information. The allegations appear completely accurate."

"I wish they'd stop," she said, "before someone gets hurt. Or killed."

He folded up the article, would read it some other time when they weren't having fun. "Come on, those are just wild rumors, circulated to keep people in line. I don't believe Dillon has a retaliation team, or anything of the sort. You don't seriously think Dillon would ever go that far, do you?"

She didn't blink, her eyes scrutinizing something a hundred miles away. "You tell me, Peter. If you were Dillon Aerospace, would there be a limit to what you'd do to protect yourself?"

"Sure. I wouldn't kill people, or anything close to it."

"They would. They have."

"Go on. Killed people?"

"Yes."

"Who?"

Melissa looked away from him, then back. "A few years back. A woman who was helping another of the Coalition's investigators. We believe Dillon killed her. We're pretty sure of it, but never got the proof. At the time, it was a matter of survival for them. They survived. She didn't."

"And you think this article might get someone else killed?"

"It could. Every time the *Post* prints that stuff, they help someone at Dillon narrow down his list of suspects. One day the list will be down to one. And what will happen then?"

He watched the concern in her eyes, understood right then that she knew who the leak was. And not only did she know the leak, she cared a lot about her, or him.

"I don't know what will happen then, but at least there are two of us attacking Dillon. Maybe that will confuse them a little. Hopefully, one of us will be able to take them down."

She grabbed his hand with a jerk. "Peter, I'm not asking you to provide a diversion for someone else's protection, and I sure don't want to sacrifice you over this."

"No argument there."

She stared at him, studied his face until he began to blush. "We've got to go," she said. "I've got a ton of work to do before your meeting with Senator Drummond tomorrow. Are you ready?"

He looked at their bagels, only his one bite taken. Their coffee cups were still full. "Sure. Let's go."

Monday morning. 6:05. Jamison watched the clock flick to 6:06, then threw his legs over the edge of Melissa's couch. He made himself do it, forced himself to move fast so he would get to work on time.

In that same little slice of time he thought up a hundred reasons why he shouldn't go back to Dillon. Given any choice at all, he would never go back there again. He would rather stay away and wait for the war to begin, make his accusations loud and clear, then stand ready to defend them. But he had to go to the office this morning. His teammates had to be told that there was no hope. It would be cruel and cowardly to let them wait around until Friday.

Melissa was already in the shower. He was surprised she had beaten him out of bed. He entered her bathroom slowly and a little embarrassed, started to shave, tried not to stare at the blurry image of her naked body through the opaque glass.

"Peter," she said over the noise of the water. "Do you want to go over your presentation again this morning? We can take the time if you think it's necessary."

He finished shaving, washed off the excess lather and turned around, leaned against the sink and looked boldly at her body. "No, I feel pretty good about it. A little nervous, but that will pass once I get started. We'll go over it at lunch, like we planned. That'll be enough."

"Okay." She turned off the water, pulled her towel down over the door, wrapped it around her and stepped out. She squeezed some water out of her hair, then motioned him into the shower with a sweep of her hand. "All yours."

She started brushing out her hair, and he suddenly felt embarrassed to pull his boxers down in the bright light of the bathroom. When he finally did, she looked. It was just a quick glance at his reflection in the mirror, but he caught her. "Hey, what are you looking at?"

She turned around and crossed her hands over her chest, stared right at him. "Nothing I haven't looked at before."

He started doing a weird sort of dance, an embarrassed shuffle toward her, then a hop toward the shower, then a funny little squeeze of his knees, not knowing which way to go with this and not wanting to look stupid. Or at least not any more stupid than he already did, flopping around indecisively in front of her, wanting to go to her if she wanted him, yet anxious to get out of her stare if she didn't. She seemed to enjoy his panic, watching him with one eyebrow up and a tiny smile on her lips.

Finally, he thought about how late it was, and his team members and Senator Drummond, and he went for the shower. Knew he'd made the wrong choice when she wandered off to her bedroom. He showered and dressed quickly, but when he came out of the bathroom she was completely dressed, waiting to send him out the door with a cup of coffee. He took the coffee, reminded himself of what an idiot he'd been, promised himself not to be a moron again, then stood in front of her. She was beautiful, standing there in a dark blue dress, looking almost as awkward as he felt.

"Maybe tonight," she said, looking at his shirt buttons, "well, I thought, maybe you'd like to sleep in my room. I know that couch isn't very comfortable."

Blood rushed to his head, felt like it might spout from his ears. He knew he was blushing, but didn't care. Just wanted to sound cool. Keep his enthusiasm to himself. Didn't want to chase her off. "Sure," he said, giving in to the urge to smile. "I think that would be . . . fun."

She grinned, too. A burst of air came from her mouth as she tilted her head toward him, acting as if she hadn't heard correctly. "Fun?"

He wouldn't have thought it possible, but his blood pressure jumped another notch and percolated at the top of his head. He fidgeted in front of her. "You know what I'm trying to say. Not fun, but—"

"So it wouldn't be fun?"

"No, no, that's not it, either. Come on, Melissa, you know what I'm trying to say."

She put her right hand on his waist, slid it around his back and stepped close to him. Slowly, she rose up to his face, pressed her lips against his and pulled herself into him.

He strangled her body with his arms, heard her gasp as some of the energy he'd been storing for her got loose. He pulled her so tight their bodies melded together, only their clothing and the wrong angle keeping him from penetration.

She stayed in his arms for a minute, grinding against him in a rhythm that matched his. Then she stepped away, turned him around, put her hand on his back, and pushed him through the door. "Good-bye, Fun-Boy. See you at lunch."

He shuffled out the door, wondering if she would always be able to thrill him like that.

He parked in Dillon's huge lot, in the space with his name on it. Dillon was big on putting a good employee's name on things. Doors, plaques, parking places. Tombstones, too, if what Melissa said was true. He stared at his sign, knew it would be the last time he'd ever see it.

Everything he did this morning seemed inherently dangerous. Handing his coded card to the guard, walking down the crowded hall, opening his office door. He felt like a burglar, prowling the darkness in someone's home, hoping to take what he wanted and get away before they woke up and discovered him. Anxious to get out the door without taking a bullet.

At ten o'clock he quietly met with his team and told them to expect the end. This time none of them seemed to be caught off guard. They'd seen other engineers escorted out the door, their personal possessions jammed pathetically into old cardboard boxes. They all wished each other well, promised to keep the news secret until Dillon made the announcement, then slipped out of the conference room, one at a time. Steve Harrison was the last to walk out. He stopped in front of Jamison and shook hands.

"It's been a pleasure, Peter."

"I'm sorry, Steve. If I could have done something—"

Harrison shook his head for Jamison to stop. "If anything could have been done, I know you would have done it. Believe me, I know. We all do."

Jamison stepped close and hugged him. "Take care. Stay in touch."

"Will do. Same with you." Then he peered into the hallway, looked both ways, and left.

At eleven-thirty Jamison walked around and removed his personal pictures and certificates from the walls, jigsawed them into his empty briefcase. He stopped at the door and looked back, then headed to the secretarial pool to check out. Charlotte looked up when he approached.

"Hello, Mr. Jamison. Going somewhere?"

"Mark me out to lunch, please."

She changed screens and made the entry. "Yes, sir. Do you want me to enter a return time?"

He looked behind him, just to see if anyone was lurking there. "No thanks, Charlotte. I don't know when I'll be back."

She'd caught a scent of something, he could tell. But she hardly betrayed it, made the entry without changing her tone. "No problem, Mr. Jamison. Have a nice day."

"You, too, Charlotte."

She looked at him in a way she'd never done before. Sad, sort of. But understanding. He'd always suspected that she was a sensitive woman.

He stared down the long, long corridor. It seemed to stretch to Montana, maybe Oregon, and have a hundred checkpoints along the way, with a thousand armed guards. He would never clear them all, could never summon enough strength to make that long trip down the hall and out the door and all the way to his meeting with Senator Drummond, to his moment of defection.

But he took a step. Then another. All the way to the first checkpoint. The guard there just monitored travel from one secured area to another. In the quirky world of armed security guards, he wasn't too intimidating. Of course, all of Dillon's guards were former federal agents, most of them earning more than a senior engineer. They were trained to notice anything that wasn't quite right. They were armed and deadly and looking for an excuse to prove it. So how could any one of them *not* be intimidating. It wasn't possible.

Jamison's shoulder blades were shifting as he left the first guard, scrunching up as if they were about to stop a bullet. But he forced his jumpy nerves into submission, walked away without tripping or dropping his briefcase, or his sweat glands flooding the floor.

Two more checkpoints and two more successes, only a few standard questions and a hard stare from the last guard. Then he was out the door, the cold air feeling clean and fresh as he walked away from Dillon for the last time.

Forty-five minutes later he was at the Chamber Restaurant, an old power-lunch place five blocks from the Capitol. He saw Melissa sitting at a corner table, staring at the wall, waiting to go over the finer details with him one more time—a refresher before his meeting. But he didn't go to her right away. His senses were more active now than they'd been in a long time, flooding his brain with warning alarms and contingency battle plans. He'd heard too many rumors about Dillon in the past, and Melissa had convinced him to believe that Dillon would kill him as soon as they found out what he was doing.

The restaurant was busy and felt dangerous. Was the man standing over there the same one he'd seen earlier on the street, a block or so away? He had looked suspicious then, walking toward Jamison then stopping short, turning into a store, pretending to look at something on the counter. It sure looked like the same man. But maybe not. Same type of blue suit, could be the same shoes. But something about the jaw was different, maybe.

Jamison suddenly realized he'd been watching the man too long, had left his back completely unguarded. He turned as quickly as possible without attracting attention. His back was clear. He went to Melissa's table, reading her body language as he approached.

"Hello," he said as he got within whisper distance. "What's wrong?"

He sat down, scooted his chair closer to her. She kept staring at the wall. Didn't speak.

He asked again while he turned his head, still studying the man in the blue suit. "What's wrong, Melissa?"

She took a staggered breath, as if she were struggling to keep from crying. She unlaced her fingers and reached for him, wrapping his hands up in hers, pulling the whole bundle of fingers up against her face.

"Peter, the leak at Dillon, the one you've been reading about, is . . . gone." She lifted the clump of fingers, used the back of his hand to swipe at her wet cheeks. She stretched her eyes open and tilted her head back, as if trying to call back the rest of the tears.

Jamison didn't want to say anything. He just sat there, trying to guess what she meant. Gone? He waited for a minute without an answer.

"What do you mean? Dead?"

"I mean gone, as in vanished. Maybe . . . maybe he's dead. His wife hasn't heard from him since he called from work, late Thursday evening

Jamison ran through faces, trying to remember who he hadn't seen at work on Friday. "So you think someone figured out he was the leak?"

"Yes. He's been our primary source all along. Like I said, all of those newspaper articles kept narrowing the field. . . ."

She closed her eyes and breathed deeply. Held it. Exhaled.

"Someone finally found him. I knew it would happen. I warned him, Peter, I really did. I told him he should get some government protection. But he refused. And now it's too late."

"Are you're sure he's not just out of town for a few days? After all, I've read all the papers, too, but I couldn't tell you who the leak was. Not for certain, anyway. Maybe it's just because you know him that the articles seemed to strike so close to home."

She rolled her eyes. "Oh? Really? Well, who would you guess my informant was, if you had to, based on what you've read?"

He didn't want to get into this, didn't want to look across the battlefield at her again, and didn't really want to know who the leak was. He didn't need to know, and didn't want to be responsible for the knowledge. But she was waiting.

"Hell, I don't know. Based on the quality of the information, I guess it would have been someone pretty high up, a grade-five engineer or higher, probably in the Development Division. It wasn't me. I just saw Harrison, so it wasn't him. That just leaves Bronovich, if my assumptions are all correct."

She spooked when he said the name, turned back to the wall, traced a wallpaper seam with her finger. She nodded her head, almost crying, as if she'd lost something important. A sudden shiver moved her in the cool restaurant. "Peter, maybe we should stop what we're doing. We could destroy your files and act like none of this ever happened. I can tell the people at work that you've decided not to cooperate, then go after Dillon on my own. No one ever has to know you were involved."

Jamison listened to her, or at least tried to as he thought about Ted Bronovich. Guilt wrapped him up like a mummy. Was Ted's death his fault? He was a friend, and he'd asked for Jamison's help, had asked to talk to Rich Blevins. How could Jamison have deferred Bronovich's simple request? What had he been waiting for? Had Bronovich died because of his stupidity, or laziness? He damned himself, already knowing he would drag this cross around with him for a long time, probably forever.

He shook his head, trying to imagine how and when they might have taken him. Had Bronovich struggled, maybe even hurt them a little bit? Had they killed the little aerospace engineer quickly, the way everyone wants to die? Or had they made him pay slowly for what he'd done, recounting the specific information he'd leaked in tortured details?

81

Quick or slow, dead was dead. Only the length of the trip mattered. Maybe it was a car bomb, like the one Jamison had looked for the other night. Not a particularly bad way to go. Maybe he'd started his car and blown a big damned chunk of D.C. asphalt into the cosmos.

Either way, Jamison wanted revenge. Maybe Melissa could turn over the rock under which Ted's killer lived. "No, Melissa. I'm not quitting, and I won't run from this. I'm not made that way and you aren't either. So let's quit pretending we are and get down to work. We'll be more careful as we go after them, but we're going after them. Agreed?"

She didn't answer.

"Come on, Melissa. We'll think this through and determine how much danger we're really in. Then we'll plan for it, take appropriate security measures. And we'd better get started because I'm about to meet Senator Drummond, and all hell is going to break loose."

"Have they been following you, Peter?"

He nodded his head. "Yes, some, I think."

"Me, too."

"When?"

"I'm not sure when, or how many times. I couldn't really swear that I've been followed. But Saturday, when I went to the office to study your data, there was a car behind me all the way."

"Right behind you?"

"No, back about half a block. As I said, I'm not even positive. But it sure gave me a creepy feeling."

Jamison checked the room again, his senses crackling the way they had when he'd arrived. The man and woman two tables away probably were not a threat. They were too loud. But beyond them, angled off to the right, was a lone man in a booth. Lean and hard and paying attention as if this were all business.

Or maybe it was someone in the small clutch of suits at the round table in the middle of the large room. Congressional staffers? Maybe. But weren't they looking over here an awful lot. And where was the other one, the one who'd stood and left a few minutes ago?

"Melissa, if Dillon got Bronovich, we have to keep you safe until Drummond gives you some protection." He checked the restaurant again, found the missing man returning to the table with his wallet open. Lots of other people still seemed to be looking his way.

Melissa met his eyes when they came back to her. "The Coalition has excellent security. I could stay there if necessary."

"That's a good idea. Are you sure you'll be safe?"

"Yes. So many companies are angry at us that we really had to bolster security. A new system, and armed guards. I'll be safe; I'll go back there when I leave here. You'll come to my office after meeting with Senator Drummond, won't you?"

"I don't know, it depends on what happens. But I'll try." He pulled out a pen, then snatched a paper coaster from under a glass. "Here's Rich Blevins's number at home. Just in case something happens."

She gripped his arm as she took the napkin. "Nothing's going to happen, Peter. Promise?"

"I promise. But let's be careful anyway. Okay?"

She looked around the room, never came back to his eyes. "Yes."

Senator Drummond's secretary led Jamison into his office. The room was nearly as large as Jamison's condo. It was a mess and smelled of cigarettes. Files were stacked on several tables, which had been set up in a haphazard maze running through the office. The only tidy area was the top of Drummond's desk, evidently the only place where the hardworking senator didn't do any work.

Drummond rose when the senator's scheduler opened the door, then he limped awkwardly across the room to shake hands and help Jamison with the box he carried. After the information was on the desk, Drummond waved toward a chair, then painfully lowered himself into the chair next to Jamison—in front of his desk instead of behind it. It was a good gesture, Jamison thought, to sit so close. Probably not genuine, but a useful performance anyway, most likely perfected by years of practice.

Jamison had studied Drummond's media photo as he'd waited in the outer office for his two-thirty appointment. But now he had a little trouble recognizing the old man who sat next to him. The wrinkled face, bald head, and bony arms seemed an odd parody of the active senator portrayed in the campaign literature. Reality versus hype. But Senator Drummond's eyes were definitely the same. Bright green friendly eyes. Probably his best asset on the campaign trail.

Drummond began in a comfortable voice. "Mr. Jamison, I want to thank you for coming by today. Since I received Miss Corley's call this weekend I've been most anxious to hear what you have to say. By the way, would you like some coffee?"

"No, thank you. But you go ahead."

Drummond rose and hobbled to a service bar while Jamison looked around his office. The walls were decorated with pictures of Drummond shaking hands with other political leaders from around the world. There was an Honorable Discharge from the Marines, and several pictures of a grown daughter on his desk—turned so that Drummond's visitors would see them. It was nice imagery, Jamison thought, although it suffered for lack of a wife's photo.

Drummond sat down with a sigh. "Now, how can I help you today, Mr. Jamison?"

The words were polished and natural and made Drummond sound like an old priest offering absolution for the millionth time. Jamison began with the lead-off sentence he'd practiced, and the facts rolled out smoothly. The documentation came out in perfect order and he sounded convincing that Dillon was corrupt. Several times he gave credit to Melissa. He wanted to make Drummond proud of what his young friend had been doing.

Drummond listened to every word with an intense look on his shriveled face. The information obviously bothered him. His face flushed several times but he never interrupted, never vented his anger or frustration. He just sat there and listened, his eyes almost hidden, his teeth grating together. When Jamison finished, Drummond stood up, hobbled to his desk, and picked up the phone.

"You just sit right there," he said as he dialed. "We're going to get some answers on this right now. There's no way I'm going to . . . hello? Bostwick? What the hell are you guys doing over there?"

Jamison leaned forward, tried to hear the other half of the conversation but couldn't. He was beginning to understand why Melissa trusted Drummond. He was fearless. Scary.

"What do I mean? Hell, Bostwick, I'll tell you exactly what I mean. I've got a nice young man in my office who says Dillon Aerospace has been defrauding you people for decades. Personally, I don't believe it's possible unless you, or somebody who works for you, is in on it. Yes, that's right. Uh-huh. Yeah, you're damned right it's illegal!"

Jamison cocked his left ear toward Drummond, leaning farther out of his chair, trying to hear the secretary of defense's response.

"Damn it, Bostwick, you'll be doing some big-time explaining if this information proves to be correct. So you'd better start digging around right now, because I'm calling President Albright next, and I'm going to recommend a full F.B.I. investigation."

Drummond slammed the phone down. "That son of a bitch. I never have trusted him."

"Are you going to call President Albright, Senator?"

Drummond grinned, hobbled over, and put a bony hand on Jamison's shoulder. "Yes. Give me a few minutes to cool down, though. It would be a bad idea for me to call him when I'm this angry. I can handle Bostwick, but I have to show Albright more respect. You know what I mean?"

"Yes, sir."

"Good." Drummond shuffled back around the desk, stopped at the pile of data, and reached for a cigarette. "Can I keep these documents, Mr. Jamison?"

"Yes, sir. Those are your copies."

"Fine. Can I assume that the originals are in a safe place?"

"Yes, they are."

"Are you sure?"

"Yes."

"Good. Well, then, Mr. Jamison, thanks for coming by today. If what you say is true, I'm going to tear the butts off a few people in this government. But I have to tell you that this whole situation, if it's as bad as you suspect, will get dangerous. I'd like to assign a security detail to protect you. I can do that, you know. It's not a problem."

Jamison smiled, stood up and shook Drummond's hand. "I don't think that will be necessary, sir."

"Don't be too sure, son. I've been up on this Hill for a long time. It's a dangerous place, even for a nice old guy like me." He grinned as he lit his cigarette. "If you *are* right, you're going to be in danger. Simple as that. I'd feel a whole lot better making sure you're safe."

"I'll be safe."

Drummond squinted one eye against the smoke and looked Jamison over carefully. "Yes, well, you young people always think you're bulletproof."

"Just careful, sir."

Drummond narrowed his squint. His other eye didn't close a bit. "All right. But I want you to stay in touch with me. Here's my card. Call me anytime, night or day. My home number's on the back. Don't hesitate. Let me know if you need anything, and I mean anything. Be very careful. Fraud against the government, on this level, is a very serious crime. Lots of people could go to jail. They'll fight like hell to avoid it."

"Thanks for your concern, Senator."

"No problem. Give my best to Miss Corley."

"I will. Good-bye."

Jamison turned and left, feeling more confident than when he'd come. In the lobby he called Melissa.

"How'd it go?" She sounded better than she had in the restaurant.

"Good, I guess. I don't know the guy like you do, but he sure got steamed. I think you were right, he's probably the best man to go after Dillon."

She laughed, still not anywhere near happy, but getting better. "That's why we call him a bulldog."

"I can see that."

"Did he give you any suggestions, or instructions?"

"Not really. He made an excellent point about keeping the evidence in a safe place though."

"Safer than here at the Coalition?"

"Maybe. I think I've got a better place. I'd like Rich Blevins to keep it, if that's all right with you?"

"Yes, sure. I'll trust Rich with it. In fact, that's a good idea. It keeps the Coalition a little farther out of it, which helps protect you from charges of disclosing classified secrets."

"Then do me a favor. Put all of my research and all of your notes in a box. Seal it and leave it at the desk in the front lobby. Don't put my name on it, but tell the receptionist that I'll get it shortly. Can you do that right away?"

"Sure."

"Good. I'll call you after I've given it to Blevins. I've got to go now. Thanks. Bye."

"Good-bye, Peter."

6

Jamison rushed out of Senator Drummond's building, moving fast, understanding that he'd passed some point of no return, and sure that Dillon would find out and come after him. Ted Bronovich flashed across his mind, their last meeting before he disappeared, the moment in his dark office when Bronovich had asked for help. Now it was Jamison's turn in the line of fire. It was just a matter of time. And time was something Dillon didn't waste. Their retribution would be swift. He'd done the deed and the price had to be paid.

He wasn't going to pay it without a fight.

Tourists in jeans and staffers in suits crowded the sidewalk in front of the Hart Senate Office Building. They parted for Jamison as he got close, used the good judgment God had given them, and got out of the way of the running man. He stopped at the curb and scanned the street.

"Careful observation," he murmured to himself. "Memorize everything that pops up on radar."

He didn't see any danger, so double-timed across the street where there was more cover. He kept looking around, constantly figuring where he'd go if there were trouble—an escape and evasion plan if attacked. He got to his car and climbed in, still watching for an assault.

He pulled into traffic and stayed in the outside lane as he stopped at the light, the first car at the line. He sat there, waiting for the light to change, looking everywhere, wondering how long it would take for them to find him.

A blue Ford pulled up beside him. Two men in suits—one fat, one ugly—sat in the front seat. The fat passenger must have felt Jamison's stare because he looked over and smiled at him, then turned to the Ford's driver. The driver leaned forward and both men grinned, looked over at Jamison, and bobbed their heads back and forth. Jamison smiled back as he watched the light, thinking maybe he'd seen them somewhere before, maybe passed them in the corridors at work. That would be just his luck; the one time he'd see people he might know in this big-ass city, it had to be right after he'd defected from Dillon. What were the odds? When the light turned green, he looked back and smiled again, trying hard not to look like someone who'd just turned in his employer for committing a crime.

This time the passenger had a short-barreled assault rifle in his hand. The man's window was down and the gun was coming out in a hurry.

Jamison stomped the gas and fired his car off the line, rolled a right turn and accelerated hard, watching the Ford cut off a car and do the same thing. The next light was red. Traffic in his lane was stopping three hundred feet ahead, and there would be room for the guys in the Ford to pull alongside and shoot him. The oncoming traffic was slow, but there was a small gap in the inside lane. Jamison kept his foot nailed to the floor until he got parallel with the opening, then jumped on the brakes and started sliding, arced a tight U-turn into the opposite lane just as the Ford finished jostling its way off Constitution Avenue.

The Ford skidded to a stop as Jamison finished his maneuver and passed them in the opposite direction. The Ford's driver glared at Jamison while his partner clambered into the backseat. Jamison laughed at their confusion, at the stupid look of failure, big and angry on the driver's face. Then the rear window opened and the gun barrel poked out into the crisp winter air. Jamison stopped laughing, felt the aim, knew the flash was coming. He sped up, braked hard, sped up again, trying to be the hardest target possible while stuck on a busy street.

He didn't hear the muzzle blast. But the metal of his car went *tang, tang* as two bullets struck the rear door and rattled into the dash as their cars separated like boxers moving to their own corners. Round one had begun, just seconds after he'd left Drummond. And now, just as quickly, it was over.

Jamison turned back onto Constitution and made a U-turn, wanting to know if the Ford would come back for round two. He waited in a bus zone for twenty seconds, looking forward and back and all around, searching for people who looked like they might be planning to kill him.

Enough time passed. He gunned his engine just as the light turned red, shot through the intersection as the cross-traffic blew their horns. At the next corner he turned again, stopped, waited another minute before believing he'd lost them.

At the Citizen's Coalition Against Government Waste he locked up his brakes and slid into the loading zone, jumped out, and charged up the steps. He ran through the lobby to the receptionist's desk. Although she was on the phone she understood when he pointed to the box and motioned him around to get it.

Outside, he put the box in his trunk and ran to a pay phone at the corner. He pulled out his wallet to find Rich's card, then stabbed at the buttons.

"F.B.I., Washington field office."

"Special Agent Blevins. Make it quick."

"Stand by."

He waited, checked the sidewalk, checked the street.

"This is Blevins. Who is this?"

"Rich, it's Peter."

Blevins's voice lost some of its growl. "Hey, Peter, how are you? You're not worried about me, are you? That little scratch over my eye isn't—"

"Rich, I'm in trouble. It's hard to explain quickly and I don't have time to tell you anyway." He rotated his body like a turret, checking his back, watching his car. "Could you meet me outside your building in ten minutes?"

Blevins started talking like an agent again, using the official government monotone. "Absolutely. But don't stop in front. Pull to the curb at the end of Half Street, the fire zone. I'll wait there for you, then jump into your car. We'll talk while we ride."

Jamison felt someone closing in on his back, spun around to see a teenager walking toward him with a camera in one hand and change in the other.

"See you in ten minutes."

"I'll be there in four."

Jamison ran back to his car and stuck a quick finger in the two bullet holes. They were large-caliber rounds and, judging by the clean penetration, full metal jackets. A strange choice for urban warfare, the kind of round that could penetrate an engine block but would only whistle a very clean hole through a man's body.

He rushed downtown, cursing the traffic and the men in the Ford. But mostly he cursed himself for not having a cellular phone to call Melissa. It was hard to guess what might happen next, but he didn't want to underestimate, didn't want to take a chance on getting her hurt. She was too important, too precious. Always had been.

Jamison slowed and Blevins stepped to the curb. His thick hands grabbed the door and he flung his stocky body into the car before it stopped. "Drive, Peter. Go."

Jamison jerked back into traffic, felt Blevins staring at him.

"So, how are you doing?" Blevins scraped his right palm across the bristles of his short hair.

"Damned if I know, Rich. You won't believe what I'm about to tell you."

Blevins stopped, didn't move a muscle, just sat there with his back against his door, staring. "I think I might."

Jamison glanced over as he turned the corner. "Huh? What do you mean?"

Blevins glanced at the dash, shifted around and caught the shredded backseat upholstery without comment. "My supervisor stopped me as I headed out to meet you. He wanted to tell me personally since you and I go back a long way."

"Tell you what?"

"The F.C.I. squad just opened a case against you, Peter. They have a tip you've been stealing government secrets, maybe for a foreign government."

"What? You've got to be kidding!"

"Am I laughing?"

"No."

"Then I'm not kidding."

Jamison studied Blevins's eyes, turned to check the road, then came back and stared at Blevins some more. "So, what does that mean? You going to arrest me?"

"Hey, don't act like it couldn't happen. You know damn well our friendship won't get in my way if you've crossed the line."

"You think I have?"

"I don't know. Why don't you tell me your story?"

"Okay, here it is, quick and dirty. Remember eleven months back when Dillon thought about scrapping my project?"

Blevins didn't answer.

"Well, in building a case for keeping the project alive, I uncovered some evidence of criminal fraud by Dillon. I'm really condensing here, Rich, but I have proof that Dillon has been defrauding the U.S. government for years. Decades."

"Have you been sharing this information with the press?"

"What? Hell, no, Rich. Man, I'm not the leak. But I know who is. He's a guy in my department who's been missing since Thursday. Nobody's seen him."

"You're talking about Jason Bronovich?"

"Jeez, yes. How did you know?"

"His wife was in today, asking for our help. She was pretty upset."

"No shit? That's tough. I'm the guy who's responsible if he's dead, too. He asked for your help, but didn't make it sound urgent." Jamison strangled the steering wheel.

"Don't beat yourself up until we find him. He may have run off with a woman or something."

"I doubt that, he's a family man who—"

"Let's go back to your story. What have you been doing with your evidence?"

"I took it to Senator Drummond this morning. He heads the Senate Armed Services Committee. He's going to look into my allegations."

Blevins pinched the bridge of his nose, squeezed his eyes closed. "Is that all that's going on?"

"Hell, no, that's not all. Some yahoo just blew two rounds through my car, and your foreign counterintelligence agents are out to arrest me. There. I think that pretty well covers it."

"You're not doing anything illegal? Nothing that would give these charges some merit?"

"No. Damn, Rich. Back off a little."

"Hey, don't tell me to backoff. You want my help? You got it. It's that simple, nothing else to it. But I've got to know what I'm dealing with here. If you're clean, I'll back you up a thousand percent. If you're dirty, I'll be the one to take you in. Either way, I'll fight for you. But you've got to be straight with me. Every word. You read me?"

"I am being straight, Rich. Dillon Aerospace is corrupt. I have a box of evidence in the trunk that proves it. I want you to take it for safekeeping. If you'd like to look through it, go ahead. But right now I have to get going. I'm worried about Melissa." Jamison rounded the block and turned into the curb at the Federal Building. He stopped, shifted in his seat and squared up with his friend.

Blevins nodded, didn't look happy. "I should have known she was a part of this."

Jamison tried to look cocky. "Hey, you think I could do this all by myself, get people mad enough to shoot at me?"

"I've seen it happen."

"Well, this time I had help. And I don't want to take chances with her."

"Then this is what we'll do. First, I'm going to open you as a 137—an informant. Everything you tell me will be filed normally on an FD-302 as evidence for your defense if you end up on trial. But your identity will be extremely well protected, even by Bureau standards. As soon as I've done that, I'll meet with the F.C.I. supervisor and tell him you're a source for me, promise to bring you in next week."

"What should I be doing?"

"You'd better keep your head down or someone's going to blow it off. I'm not kidding. It looks like you've got some powerful people pulling strings here, and that makes me very nervous. Especially in this city. Don't go home, or any place familiar. Check into a hotel under an alias then let me know where you are. Do you have some cash?"

"Cash? Yeah. About four hundred bucks."

"Let me know if you need more."

"I will. You'll take that box out of the trunk?"

"As good as done. Call me tonight at home to let me know you're okay. But make the call from a remote location. Since the F.B.I. knows we're friends, a wire-tap would be a logical move on their part."

"Will it cause you a problem if I call?"

"Don't worry about me, you've got your hands full already. Do you have any kind of weapon?"

"I brought my Beretta."

"Good. Keep it close."

"I will."

Blevins split his lips open and showed some teeth, but couldn't seem to manage anything more. He was the smiling policeman, almost. All crew-cut and clean-shaven and smiling, because that's the way he'd always done things. It was his way. When trouble came, you smiled at it.

He went to the trunk and got the box, then came back to the open window. "Stay low, brother. We'll get you through this. Just don't go fugazi on me."

"Not to worry, Rich. I won't let the monster out of the box."

"Good. D.C. doesn't need the body count, and I don't need the paperwork. Now go, get out of here."

Jamison wheeled his car away from the curb and onto the street. He checked the mirror, saw the blue Ford pull into traffic several cars back.

"Shit."

It was ten o'clock before Jamison was safely checked into the Red Roof Inn near Ronald Reagan Washington Airport. He'd tried two other motels but they'd insisted on seeing identification, so he'd gone to the counter of the Red Roof just before a crowd unloaded from a bus in the lot. He took his time with the clerk, let the long line pressure her into accepting cash payment and his story of a lost license and early departure.

He sat on the bed in the motel room and thought about Melissa, tried to decide if he could call her. Had Dillon or the F.B.I. tapped her phone? He doubted it, but wasn't sure, so he got in his car and drove to a convenience store ten miles away.

He called her on the phone outside, knowing she'd be mad, hoping it wouldn't set their relationship back too far.

"Damn it, Peter, where are you?"

Actually, she sounded more concerned than angry, and the sound of her worry made him happy. But still, she was plenty sore.

"I've been waiting forever. You said you'd call right back."

"I'm sorry, but I've been busy. Some men were following me. I just lost them a little while ago."

"They just followed you around? That's all? You drove around all night and they didn't do anything?"

He felt a little stupid as she described his evening. "Yeah. That's all, just followed me. I tried to draw them close once, just to get another look at them, but even then they hung back. It started getting irritating."

"Well, at least they sound harmless."

"They do now. Earlier today they shot at me."

"They *shot* at you?"

"Yeah. Can you believe that? Must not have liked the way I drove."

"Peter, this is too dangerous too soon. Did you talk to Rich?"

"Yes. He had good and bad news. I'll fill you in later."

"Where are you?"

"At a pay phone. Are you okay, Melissa? Is anyone still there with you?"

"Only the security guys. Everyone else left hours ago."

"But you feel safe?"

"Yes, of course."

"That's good. I was worried."

"Peter, the car that followed you wasn't dark blue, was it? Four doors? A Ford?"

Jamison felt muscles tighten all over his body. "Yes! How did you know?"

"It's parked outside. I noticed it a few minutes ago when the guard and I went to get something from my car. There's a man sitting in it."

"Just one man?"

"Well, I didn't actually walk up and take a head count, but yes, it looked like just one man. Someone else could have been lying down in the back, I suppose."

"Melissa, can I call you right back?"

"Why?"

"I need to find out whose car that is."

"Sure, okay. But *right* back. You understand what I'm saying? No more of this all night bullshit."

"I promise."

He struck the phone with two fingers, cutting the connection and getting a dial tone. He called Blevins at home.

"Hello?" The woman's voice was nice and fresh and easy. Jamison had so much energy coursing through him that, by comparison, she sounded sedated.

"Hello, Elaine, it's me, Peter. Is Rich home?"

"Hi, Peter. Yes, he's right here." He heard her pass the phone.

"Hey, Peter. I'm glad you called. Where are you?"

"Someplace safe. But a blue Ford has been following me around all afternoon. It's the same one that shot up my car earlier. You know anything about it?"

"The one that picked you up when you left Drummond's office?"

"That's the one."

"When did it start again? How soon after we met?"

"Right after. They knew I was at your office, Rich. Damn it, they knew to find me there."

"Hey, I know what you're thinking, Peter, but it wasn't us. At least I don't see how it could be. F.C.I. didn't move on you until after we talked. They sent agents to your home and office."

"I don't care about that. I just want to know who's in the Ford. It's important now."

"Maybe it's some of Dillon's security guys keeping tabs on you."

Two men, one black and one white, came out of the store and walked off in the other direction. Jamison lowered his voice, watched them until they'd gotten into their car and driven out of sight. "That's about what I was thinking."

"Where was the last place you saw them? Where can I find them?"

"They, or maybe just one of them, are over at Melissa's office. At least they were a minute ago."

"Do you want me to send someone over there? If you're worried about Melissa, we could pick her up and keep her safe until we identify those guys. She could spend the night on the boss's couch."

Jamison kept checking the street. "No, I don't think so. She feels safe there, so why expose her to danger by moving her? Besides, I don't think she'd go for the idea."

"It's your call, whatever you say. But we found your friend Bronovich this afternoon. It was a grisly sight, too. Somebody shattered his neck, Peter. The way you and I were trained in Ranger school, but with a hell of a lot more power. Spun his head halfway around."

"Damn it! I knew I'd gotten him killed. Any idea who did it?"

"Nope. We know absolutely nothing except that the hit was professional. European quality. But I'll tell you something. If you'd seen Bronovich you'd probably want to give my idea about Melissa another run-through. I could call her and try to talk her into it."

"Do you think these guys in the Ford are the same ones who killed Bronovich?"

"Don't know. Probably not."

"Why not? They shot at me."

"Earlier, sure. But they didn't shoot after you left me. Why the change?"

Jamison watched a pretty woman climb into her car, wondered why she didn't look nervous in this rough neighborhood. "Out of bullets?"

"Very funny. No, I think they might have different orders now. But I can't guess why. But if they are the same guys, and they did pick up your tail again, I think they would have taken you down. Unless they were just watching."

"Maybe they saw you take the box. Maybe that's really what they're after."

"Could be. Maybe not. At any rate I don't think they'll bother Melissa. They're only watching her so they can pick you up again. But I would like to bring her in, just to be safe."

Jamison shook his head, ran his left hand through his hair. "Okay, Rich. Go ahead and call her. See what she wants to do. She makes her own decisions; I'm sure you know that."

"Who doesn't know that?"

"Good point."

"Then you and I need to meet. How about tomorrow morning? The Smithsonian, Museum of Natural History. Dinosaur exhibit. Ten o'clock? Be careful, just in case they're listening now."

"Sure."

"One last thing, Peter. The F.C.I. supervisor refused to back off, even when I promised to bring you in. He still wants his boys to arrest you, so we're going to have to develop plan B."

"Let's talk about that tomorrow. Right now I want you to call Melissa."

*　*　*　*　*

Blevins hung up and speed-dialed the squad room. He wanted to get an agent moving Melissa's way before he called her.

"Okay, new Agent Davidson," he murmured as the phone rang, "you've wanted your chance to do something on your own. Graduated from the Academy a month ago and haven't even checked out a car yet. Well, this is your lucky night, pal. I'm calling you because you're new, you're green, and therefore, you're there. Just like all new agents are always there, afraid they're going to miss the Big One. Don't ever want to leave, or sleep. Can't get enough of the ego trip."

SA Davidson answered the phone as though he were responding to the crime of the century. "F.B.I., Squad Seven, Special Agent Robert Davidson."

"Hey, Davidson, how's it going down there tonight? You keeping the world safe while I take it easy?"

"Yes, sir, Mr. Blevins. I'm in complete control. The world lies in obedient silence."

"Great, cowboy. That's great. You have no idea how good that makes me feel. Listen, I've got a little mission for you. Not much to it, I'm afraid. A little tame for a grizzled old veteran like yourself, but hell, a chance to burn some fuel. You want it?"

"Yes, sir. Absolutely. What do I do?"

"A woman named Melissa Corley is at her office a few minutes from you, at the Citizen's Coalition Against Government Waste. Some shit in a blue Ford is set up on the street in front, and I'm kind of thinking we should get her out of there."

"Should I take backup?"

Blevins shook his head, hoping the freshly minted agent would sense his disappointment. "Don't ask me. This is your mission, rookie. You decide if you need backup or not, and how many. Don't they teach you fellas anything at Quantico anymore?"

"Sorry. Has the guy in the Ford done anything to her?"

"No. He might have shot at someone earlier, but he's done nothing to her. Keep in mind, though, that this woman might have some association, and I mean way out on the tangent, with the body we identified today. I'm not sure about that, but maybe."

Davidson gasped, and Blevins knew that the nightmare of Bronovich's body would haunt him for a while. Blevins gave him a quiet moment, some time for a quick appraisal of his courage and talents, as honest as possible.

"Sir, if it's just a taxi ride she needs, I think my sixteen hollow-point brothers and I can help her out."

Blevins laughed. He liked Davidson much better than the other agents he'd trained because this guy understood that the job was mostly bullshit, bluster, and bravado. That's what they were paid for. That, and some deadly business on very rare occasions.

"You should have been a cowboy, cowboy. If that's your call, get on it. There's an alley behind her building. I'll phone her right now and ask her to meet you there. Leave now, Davidson, because I want you waiting for her the second her toes hit fresh air."

"Yes, sir."

"Go!"

Blevins hung up, then fumbled a minute to find Melissa's private office number. It had been a while since he'd called her; hadn't had a reason since she and Jamison broke up.

"Melissa, it's Rich Blevins. Is everything okay there?"

"My goodness, Rich, how nice to hear your voice. Yes, of course, everything's fine."

"It's great to hear your voice again, too. My heart flipped to a new year when Peter mentioned you earlier. I hope everything works out. Not, of course, that it's any of my business, but . . . ah, hell, Melissa, you know what I mean."

"I know what you mean, Rich. Thank you."

"You're welcome. Look, Melissa, Peter and I would like you to come down to my office, just until we find out what's going on with that Ford."

"That's ridiculous, Rich. They haven't done anything at all. They're just watching my building."

Blevins thought about Bronovich's face, the thick, swollen tongue and wide awake eyes. He started to worry that he'd minimized her danger. "We both know that, Melissa. But I'm coming in early tomorrow and I was hoping we could go down for breakfast together. There's a great couch in the boss's office where you could sleep. What do you say?"

"You are too smooth, Rich."

"Yeah, I know. So . . . great! Go out the back of your building to the alley. I have an agent named Robert Davidson on his way, and he'll meet you there in a typical Bureau roadster. He's a good-looking guy, like me, you know, with short brown hair and brown eyes. And he'll be grinning, I believe, like he's just been promoted to top doggie. Ten minutes. Okay?"

"Wait a minute. Is Peter all right? Why didn't he call me himself?"

Blevins was feeling it now, too, the same anxiety she had in her voice, the little fear nibbling a good-size hole in his confidence. "Sure, he's fine. Now, get your stuff together, please. Ten minutes. The alley. Got it?"

"Yes."

Blevins hung up, but stared at the phone for half a minute, then stood and walked over to where Elaine was reading a book. He bent over and kissed her cheek. "Got to go, honey. Make sure the boys finish their homework."

She stopped reading, looked up at him with a thousand questions on her worried face. "I will, baby. Be careful. You know I love you."

"I know. Love you, too."

* * * * *

New Agent Robert Davidson was pumped. He was glad to have Blevins the Legend as his field training agent, the man who'd dropped the top-ten fugitive with a long, clean head shot while a hostage struggled two inches away from impact. Tonight he would make Blevins proud.

On his second lap around the Coalition he jerked into the alley from the south end, so that Melissa wouldn't have to walk around the car to get in. He screeched to a stop as she came out of the building, looked deep into the rearview mirror and felt the butterflies flutter off with his stomach.

"Get in," he yelled. "Come on, get in!"

She opened the door and jumped. When her butt hit the seat he flattened the accelerator. He rocketed the car toward the other end of the alley. The blue Ford that had followed him into the alley stopped a few hundred feet behind him.

Davidson barreled down the narrow chasm, putting more distance between him and the Ford. Melissa was bracing one hand against the dash and groping for a seat belt with her other hand. They were halfway to the open street and building speed.

Suddenly a brown Dodge sedan bounced through the gutter and blocked their exit. Davidson jammed on the brakes and slid to a stop. Then he cursed himself, thinking he'd been stupid, that he should have crashed into that guy, rammed his car into the street while he had the speed. Now he was really screwed.

He thought about grabbing the mike and calling for help, but there was no time. He had to get away from these guys. What about that blue car? Was it still back there? Shit, yes. Davidson's choices were suddenly down to two, merely a matter of which car to start with. "All right, you sons-a-bitches," he said as he dropped the car into reverse. "Want to play rough? Let's do it."

"Hold on to something," he yelled to Melissa as he twisted around and blasted backward down the narrow alley.

The driver jumped out of the Ford and ran for a doorway. Another man, short and heavy in a loose-fitting suit, came from the passenger side and ran around in front of the Ford with some kind of an assault rifle in his hands.

"Lady, if something happens and you get a chance to run, go south, past this car we're about to smash into, away from the Dodge!"

He heard her start to say something but stopped listening when the fat man fired his weapon, blasting the rear window into shards of glass but missing both of them. It pissed Davidson off and he started yelling, his foot burying the gas, his car screaming through the chute, the tires churning up an acrid smoke that curled over the rear fenders and streamed through the hole where the rear window had been. "I'm going to get you for that, you shit! Stay right there, Fatso, and catch the ass-end of this two-ton weapon."

The fat man understood. He stopped aiming and started to run. But Davidson caught him, hit him so hard that his stubby body flew through the shattered back glass of the Bureau car with a surprised look on its just-dead face.

"Okay, that's one. Where's the other guy? Lady, you see the other guy? He headed over to my side!"

"I don't see him! It's too dark. I don't!"

Davidson looked everywhere but didn't see the other man. "Okay, lady, I'm going to barrel-ass out of here, launch us into that other car like a big, bad bolt from hell. Ready? Let's go."

The transmission bucked as Davidson jammed it into drive and tromped on the gas. His eyes were still jumping around, still desperate to find the Ford's driver. Davidson was barely moving when the gunfire started again. More glass shattered. Davidson raised his pistol, or at least struggled to, as the bullets slammed into his body, burning their way through his flesh and muscle, ripping big pieces of him away. The wheel twisted out of his grip. He couldn't hold it anymore. He couldn't see, couldn't hear, couldn't . . . do . . . anything.

*   *   *   *   *

Melissa snapped around to face Davidson when the shooting resumed. She heard the sickening noise of the bullets as they slammed into his body, felt the car veer, then idle into her building while the young man's body twitched and jumped from the trauma. She sat in concentrated horror as a large ugly man in a nicely tailored suit stepped from a doorway and walked toward the car, firing carefully aimed shots into Davidson's head with every step, splattering chunks of Davidson's skull all over the inside of the car.

Someone pried her door open but she didn't turn, couldn't stop staring at the ugly man shooting Davidson. He walked slowly until he was beside the car, then reached in and took Davidson's pistol, calmly checked the pockets of his blood-soaked clothes.

A hand grabbed Melissa's shoulder and dragged her out. Her mind was beginning to come back now, telling her to follow the man's orders until her feet hit the pavement. The second they did she scraped her right heel against the man's shin, digging hard, going for oil, gouging as though she was jump-starting a motorcycle.

"Aaagh," he screamed. "Sonofabitch!" He let go of her and fell away.

Melissa whipped around and pushed her hands into his face, raked some deep furrows into his cheeks with her nails, then grabbed his head with her hands. She dug her thumbnails hard into his closed eyes. The flesh of his upper eyelids stretched back into his head, much farther than she would have expected. But then the lids shredded open, making slits for her long-nailed thumbs to sink deeper into his head, gouging at the back of his eyeballs, not stopping until she'd completely buried her thumbs into the spongy material at the back of his sockets, his blood and tears squirting onto his face, the diluted red mixture pouring out of his head and running down her wrists, soaking the sleeves of her dress.

He screamed in a terrified voice and lurched backward. She pulled her thumbs out; the suction broke with a disgusting pop. He fell to the ground, whimpering and writhing. She ran like hell for the street.

She was screaming as she rushed down the dark alley, wiping her bloody thumbs on the front of her dress. "Help! Somebody help me, please." She headed toward the streetlight at the end of the alley, wide-eyed and watching carefully for potholes or slick spots. A man was chasing her. She could hear him, feel him. He was getting closer, gaining on her.

She burst into the spotty light of the street and made a hard right turn toward an all-night drugstore, hoping to open up enough of a lead to reach safety. But her shoes didn't hold the turn and she fell. The man crashed into her falling body and went down with her, giving her a whisper of a chance to get up and run again.

He was the ugly man, the one who had shot and killed Davidson. He stretched out his hands as he flew through the air, did a quick parachute roll, then landed on his feet in front of her, his gun back in his hand.

She collapsed onto the pavement, silent, planning to stay there and delay him for as long as possible. Maybe the police would come. Maybe someone had heard the noise and called them.

Above all else, she would not cower. She held her head up, defiantly, as the man walked to her. His steps seemed cautious, as if she frightened him a little, even as he aimed his pistol at her head. Three steps away he reached into his suit coat pocket and pulled out a leather wallet.

"Melissa Corley, you are under arrest for espionage. You have the right . . . ."

Melissa could barely hear the man, and she couldn't see him at all. Her eyes were stuck to the F.B.I. credentials he held in his left hand.

7

Jamison hadn't slept, hadn't really even tried. He'd spent most of Monday night rattling around the Red Roof Inn, worrying about Melissa, hoping she wouldn't be angry that he'd asked Blevins to pick her up. She liked to make her own decisions, and didn't like being told what to do. If she thought he was trying to control her she'd be gone, out of reach again. She was that independent.

During the few moments of the long night when he wasn't worrying about her, he had tried to think through everything that had happened since Thursday, hoping to tie it all together and figure out how to keep her safe. Assuming he hadn't pissed her off, he still hoped that they could work through their problems after this was over. Get back together, where they both belonged.

He'd started with Dillon's cancellation of his project, although that hardly seemed to matter anymore. After all, Melissa was positive that Dillon was evil. Bronovich's death was pretty convincing proof that she was right. Add the facts that he'd been shot at after giving Senator Drummond his evidence, and that Blevins was worried enough about the blue Ford to send an agent to get Melissa, and it got pretty easy to buy her criminal corruption theory.

His teammates were actually beginning to look like the lucky ones. They were only losing their jobs. As far as he knew they weren't being followed, or shot at, or investigated. He tried to forget, at least for a while, that Bronovich's neck had been broken over this. He wished he didn't have to hold himself responsible for Bronovich's death, wished he'd told Blevins right away that Bronovich wanted to talk to him. Why hadn't he called Blevins at home? What had he been thinking? Several times during the night he'd thought about the way Blevins had described Bronovich's body, then immediately tried to forget what he'd heard. It just made him worry more about Melissa, made it even less likely that he'd fall asleep. He didn't usually make those kinds of mistakes, and wasn't used to failing people who counted on him. If only he'd done what he'd promised and put Bronovich and Blevins together, maybe the little engineer with the two sweet kids would still be alive.

He remembered the day Bronovich had brought his girls to the office on Take Your Daughter to Work Day. Jamison had been touched by the way his proud friend had roamed the halls with his daughters, introducing them to Jamison's team and everyone else they met in the halls, the little girls polite as debutantes, dressed in frilly Easter outfits and carrying patent leather purses.

But Bronovich was gone now and his daughters were fatherless. Most of Jamison's team was gone now, too, or soon would be. It was just him and Melissa. He couldn't save Dillon from the penalty of its own crimes and that was fine with him. He didn't care about Dillon anymore. In truth, he didn't care much about the corruption Melissa hated, either. He was one of the ambivalent people she had described Friday night, programmed to expect the government to act foolishly, or criminally. But pursuing them was important to her, so he would make it important to him. He loved her and would do anything to prove it.

At five-thirty he gave up on sleep, showered, dressed in some clothes he'd bought on his way back from calling Blevins and Melissa, then walked to an all-night diner for coffee and breakfast. Time was crawling by; there were still too many hours left before his ten o'clock meeting with Blevins. He didn't see how he could wait that long for answers, wanted to know right now that Melissa was safe.

Was she at the F.B.I. office, sleeping on the SAC's couch? Had everything gone okay? Or had there been trouble? He thought about their last morning together—had it been only yesterday?—sneaking glances at her naked body as she showered. Bashful as a little boy when she'd done the same to him. He wanted to live those few minutes again, wanted to travel back in time and disengage the safety catch from his feelings, forget his insecurities and press his bare body against her wet towel, see if she was as ready to pick up their relationship as he was. He loved her so much; had never stopped loving her. All he wanted now was a chance to tell her.

He said a prayer that she was safe, even though he was lousy at praying. He'd never given it much of a try, and would never think to pray for his own safety. But Melissa was different. For her, he would pray. Make all the standard promises he'd heard his buddies make during the war, with the very best intentions of keeping every one of them, respecting the possibility of a supreme being too much to take the obligation lightly.

He made no promises to God about killing, though, because trouble was coming. There wasn't much doubt about it. He was expecting it. Could feel it. He'd danced on this stage before and knew the choreography intimately. He understood that Bronovich wouldn't be the last to die.

And he was glad he saw it coming. Expecting more deaths actually made it easier, helped him step up his defenses, switched his survival over to instincts and training.

* * * * *

It was too early in the morning for Blevins to be pushing this hard, but he stalked the assistant special agent in charge anyway, backing him around the steel furniture and demanding more information. He wanted every single detail, wanted to know exactly how he'd gotten Special Agent Davidson killed.

"What were those other guys doing out there anyway, Strick? And what about Melissa Corley?"

ASAC Leo Strick was acting as the Squad Seven supervisor until the regular supervisor recovered from surgery. Blevins considered him to be a weasely little prick. He had a ferret face and a woman's hand gestures, had survived the dangers of being an agent by finding an endless string of chores to keep him in the office. Therefore he deserved no respect from a street agent. Strick, a petty man with a scheming personality, had made his career by stealing glory from other agents, or successfully destroying the careers of agents ahead of him. Throughout the entire Bureau he was known as Strick the Prick.

Blevins didn't trust Strick. He was pretty sure his boss, SAC Sackett, felt the same way. It was a normal reaction, the same wrench of the guts people had when a cockroach raced across a dinner table.

Strick backed away from Blevins and shrugged like he'd just spilled coffee. "It was just some kind of a damned mix-up, Blevins. Those agents went to ask Corley some questions and Davidson overreacted, threatened them, I guess. Jeez, Blevins, it's not like they knew he was an agent."

Blevins kept advancing, glaring into Strick's face, wanting to kick his ass. But he was hurting, too. Hurting bad. He had gotten a young man killed and no amount of ass-busting would change that.

"So Davidson was gunned down by F.B.I. agents? Is that what you're telling me? Who, Strick? Who was it?"

Strick rabbited to his desk, his pointy face away from Blevins's glare, his eyes searching for something else to catch his attention. "Don't start with me, Blevins. It was just a mistake. A horrible one, but a mistake nonetheless. That's all there is to it. It wasn't anyone's fault."

"Hey, when agents die in gun battles with fellow agents, it's someone's fault. Mostly mine, I know. But who else? Who shot him?"

Strick looked up as the squad secretary stepped silently to the door and watched for an opening. Strick greased his smile and focused on her. "Yes? What can I help you with?"

Blevins turned to her, too. She immediately began to fidget in his crosshairs.

"I . . . gee, I'm sorry to interrupt. But Mr. Sackett wants Special Agent Blevins in his office right away."

"Good," Blevins said, "I'll get the story from him." He left Strick's office so fast that the secretary had to jump out of the doorway to avoid being knocked down.

William Sackett was the special agent in charge of the F.B.I.'s Washington field office. His was a political position, the powerful liaison between the F.B.I. and the media, other law enforcement agencies, and the community. He didn't normally work cases, but Blevins expected him to be working this one.

All things considered, Sackett wasn't a bad investigator. At least, not for a desk pilot. Unlike the fool Strick, Sackett had worked the streets hard while coming up, had stayed out there in the line of fire longer than most. He'd made some good arrests and obtained solid convictions of a slew of organized crime figures. That gave him honor in Blevins's eyes.

Blevins charged past Sackett's secretary without breaking speed, opened the door and stormed in, tried to catch his boss off-guard and tilt the advantage in his favor. Two other agents were in the room, quietly standing away from Sackett. Blevins had met one of them before, briefly. A big, ugly bastard named Pate.

Sackett sat at his desk, his family's pictures on the bookshelf behind him—a wife, son and daughter, both the kids nearly grown, about college age. Blevins figured Sackett to be about fifty-one, maybe fifty-three. A little softer now, sure, but still showing plenty of physical power. His brown eyes were steady and calm, framed by silver wire-framed glasses and a gray mustache.

He was reading a file, but rose as Blevins kept coming. He walked around and intercepted him. "Good morning, Blevins. How are you doing?"

Blevins went right into it, animating a short countdown with two fingers. "Well, let's see. One: an agent I was training is dead. Fresh and green and dead, right out of Quantico. Two: I don't know who killed him, but I'm told it was our guys. I'll tell you what, Sackett, I'll feel a whole lot better when I find out who dropped the hammer on him."

Blevins pivoted on the balls of his feet until he faced the other men. Pate held most of their power, it was obvious by the easy shift of his ugly face as he followed Blevins's movements, and the squint that studied Blevins's hands when he moved close. Blevins chose him as contestant number one, stepped over to him, and jammed a hard finger into his chest. "Was it you? Did you kill Robert Davidson?"

Pate rocked back from the pressure of Blevins's finger, looked down slowly, stared at Blevins's finger with cold eyes.

Sackett stayed back and kept quiet, allowed Pate time for his own defense. When Pate's head came up like a snarling dog's, pushing emotions farther toward critical mass, Sackett hurried over and stepped between them. "Ease up a little, Blevins.

Nothing we do here can bring Davidson back. It was just a damned awful mistake."

"So I've been told."

"And it's the truth. Hell, you contributed to it. Didn't you send him there without backup."

"Yes, I did. Absolutely my mistake and I'll accept it. But right now I want to know who killed him."

Pate took a little step toward Blevins. He was a big man, meaner-looking than most, and genuinely ugly. Not just bad-skin, bad-features ugly, either, but warped and twisted so badly that his face had a burned-in look of evil. He almost looked like he'd been scarred in a fire. Blevins would have normally found him hard to look at, but right now he was staring.

"I'm very sorry about your partner," Pate said, looking down into Blevins's eyes. "And I know exactly how you feel. Davidson killed my partner first, while we were attempting our routine traffic stop. I guess he just overreacted. Took us completely by surprise. I barely got off my shots before he tried to run me down, just like he ran down my partner. We didn't know he was an agent until later." He took a step back.

Sackett spoke to Pate and the other agent. "Will you gentlemen please excuse us?"

The two of them hesitated, then walked out slowly, showing that they hadn't been thrown out but had been asked nicely to leave and were moving on their own, leaving Blevins to decide how things stood with them. They headed toward the door while Blevins stayed balanced, knowing that one more push, the slightest error by either man, might start a game of bleeding.

Sackett picked up a file and slipped on his glasses. "Blevins, come over here. I've got more bad news for you."

Blevins took another quick look at the departing men then crossed to Sackett's desk, leaned on it and hovered over the file.

"Have a seat," Sackett said, then waited.

"I'll stand."

Sackett glared up at him, waited ten or fifteen seconds. Blevins didn't budge. So Sackett stood up, his eyes even with Blevins's. "I've opened another administrative inquiry on you, Blevins, regarding your association with this fellow Jamison. Apparently you two are good friends, old war buddies and all that. Since he's the subject of a national security case I have to make sure you haven't acted criminally with him. If he turns out to be a foreign agent, this could end your career."

Blevins threw up his hands. Sackett jumped, started to go defensive.

"He's no more a foreign agent than you are, Sackett. It's ridiculous that F.C.I. would even call him a suspect."

Sackett's glasses came off. "Dillon's a high profile case, Blevins. If Jamison's part of it and is selling those secrets, it would be a terrible embarrassment to the F.B.I. So regardless of what you say, I'm having your cases reassigned until we can accurately gauge your criminal involvement, if any, with Jamison. As of right now you are on administrative leave, pending the outcome of the investigation."

Blevins said nothing. He looked at his watch and saw Sackett do the same. "Fine. I'll be gone by eight-thirty. But I want last night's shooting covered in absolute detail. I'll take every dose of my blame, and know I've got a lot coming. But I want to know the hows and the whys. Everything that went wrong."

Sackett replaced his glasses, seemed to shift off ready-alert. "Will do, Blevins. You have my word on it. And I'll keep you updated on the inquiry, as much as possible."

Blevins turned and left. In the secretary's office he stopped in front of Special Agent Pate and memorized the hard look of his face. Then he stepped into him, eye to eye and toe to toe, his clothing brushing against Pate's, his nose locking in the scent of the man who'd killed his young partner. He stayed there, staring, waiting for Pate to take a step back. It took a long, long time.

By the time Blevins got back to his squad room a black agent was already removing Blevins's files. Every other agent was rushing for Strick's office.

"Hey, Thomas," Blevins said to the agent at his desk, "what's going on with Strick?"

Thomas didn't look up. He spoke quietly and didn't give away anything by his eye or body movements. "While you were in Sackett's office some agents brought your buddy's girlfriend through here, the one involved in that firefight at the Coalition."

"Was she all right?"

"Yeah, she looked okay to me. Good-looking lady. Anyway, it must have been shit for the fan because now we're all assigned to the case. Nobody's exempt. We're going to prosecute her, arrest your friend, and save the planet. You know, all the normal jerk-off things, but in double time."

"Sorry I won't be here to help. I'm also sorry you're getting stuck with my cases."

"That's all right, Blevins. This whole process aggravates the shit out of me, though. If you work for the F.B.I. and one of your friends gets in trouble, well, it's whoops, sorry, and bend over, chump. They'll drag you through months of mud just to prove you're clean. In case someone should ever ask. It's degrading. Insulting."

"I know what you mean, Thomas."

"Man, I'm sure you know exactly what I mean. They've probably autographed a copy of that playbook for you."

"If they haven't, they should. This is my third inquiry."

Thomas dropped another stack of files on the desk. "You see? That's a crock, man. You're the best man here. If you're not clean, no one is."

"They feel they've got to check."

"It's still a crock."

Blevins filled in his three-card, acted like he was ignoring Thomas as he whispered, "Thanks. Listen, Thomas, one other thing. I was going to do an FD-302 today but, obviously, won't have time. There's some evidence in the locker that I promised a guy I'd get released. The case is weak and ready to be closed. It's a white, file-sized storage box logged in under a twenty-six-new case number. Can you take care of it?"

Thomas played it coy, made no movement that might attract Strick's attention. "Man, I don't know. Strick and Sackett will want access to everything you've been working on."

Blevins straightened up, bobbed his head as he checked what he'd written on his card. "Yeah, sure, you're right. I just didn't want to screw this guy if I didn't have to. He didn't want to part with the stuff, but decided to be a cooperative citizen. I hate making it hard on good guys like that."

Thomas leaned over and looked all the way to the back of the file drawer, then slammed it shut. "Well, Rich, if I can do it, I'll shake it free for him."

"Thanks, Thomas. But be cool about it. I don't want you to end up like me."

"What do you mean, brother? Ending up like you is my career goal."

Blevins picked up his briefcase, looked around one last time. "Thanks, Thomas."

"Don't mention it. I'll see you around."

"Yeah. Be back when the ice melts."

*　*　*　*　*

Jamison sat in the diner until the hardware store opened up across the street, then walked over and bought a roll of duct tape, a standard telephone with an RJ11 plug, and a multipurpose tool with pliers, knife, and an assortment of screwdrivers. By eight-thirty he was back in his room, dumping everything out of his gym bag then refilling it with the items he expected to need: Some deodorant, a razor, a change of

117

underwear and socks, the stuff from the hardware store, a roll of quarters he'd gotten at the diner, a box of nine-millimeter ammunition from his trunk, and his Beretta. After he finished, he stuck the suit he'd worn yesterday, along with everything else from his gym bag, into the trunk of his car, locked it, and headed to the corner where he caught a cab for the twenty-minute ride downtown.

He made the driver go down every street within ten blocks of the Museum of Natural History, kept a keen lookout for the blue Ford or anything else that looked like a threat. But he saw nothing and started feeling a little silly, thinking that his imagination might be overstimulated. He paid the driver and got out four blocks from the museum, walked a few minutes, then stopped in the chilly shadows of the post office depot. He watched the museum's entrance and every car that passed in front of it.

At nine-thirty he entered from the north side, rode the escalator up to the main hallway, and stayed at the edges of the rotunda. He kept his distance from the African elephant in the center of the huge round room because people couldn't help but look in the direction of that big-eared beast.

He edged toward the dinosaur exhibit, his eyes and ears set at highest sensitivity, his hands open, his fingers together and rigid. He was creeping through a minor hall—a series of displays depicting ancient hunting techniques—when he heard a slight squeak of a shoe, quiet as a sparrow flapping its wings. The noise had come from behind him, a little to the right and closing fast.

Jamison whipped around, guts up, ready for whatever level of threat awaited him. He recognized Blevins immediately but couldn't abandon his attack, only managed to decelerate to a ridiculous-looking slow motion.

Blevins stepped back and put a hand to his chin, his raised left eyebrow bending the butterfly strips that held his ripped flesh together.

"Pretty slow there," he said. "I could have had you, easy. Paid you back for this eye. Are you on medication or something?"

Jamison dug his hands into his pockets, looked up and down the hall. "That's funny, Rich. Anybody ever tell you what a funny guy you are? Come on, let's get to someplace safer." He led him down a smaller hallway, stopped as soon as they were alone.

"So tell me, is Melissa all right?"

"I knew that would be your first question. Yes, she's all right. At least she was earlier this morning. I don't know what's happened since then because I'm on the bricks again. But she was in the office today. Some F.C.I. guys were sent to pick her up."

"What are you talking about? I thought *you* sent an agent to get her. Did you send foreign counterintelligence guys? And if so, why? Aren't they the ones trying to arrest me?"

Blevins had tried to interrupt, but now he was slow with his answer. "No, I did not send them to get her. I sent my new partner, Davidson. Apparently the F.C.I. guys went there to question her." Blevins lowered his eyes a little. "In the confusion, my partner got gunned down. Another agent was killed, too."

"Holy shit. Man, I'm sorry."

"Yeah."

"But Melissa's all right?"

"Yes."

Jamison squeezed Blevins's shoulder and checked his eyes, remembered seeing that same look the day he'd led their squad into the ambush, a mistake that had cost five lives and given birth to the crazy man. "That sucks about your partner."

"Yeah."

"I caught the morning news, but didn't hear anything about it."

"Maybe the media didn't get the story yet."

"Sure, I guess that's possible. You think?"

"I don't know. It is a little strange. We usually hit the news right after a muzzle flash."

"Seems that way. And even in Washington, F.B.I. agents killing each other should be a big story, shouldn't it?"

"You'd think so."

"What do you know about the dead agent?"

Blevins glanced around, seemed to answer without thinking. "Theirs or ours?"

"Huh? What the hell does that mean? Aren't all of you guys supposed to be on our side?"

Blevins looked puzzled for a second, then seemed to understand what Jamison was asking. "Sure. Of course we are. I didn't mean that like it sounded. It's just that I met two agents this morning in the SAC's office that were, well . . . different. They're still on my mind. That's all."

"Different in what way?"

"I don't know exactly. You've got to understand that all agents are a little different in how they work. Organized crime guys work differently than white collar crime guys. Reactive agents handle things differently than drug guys. So, differences are kind of expected and come with the territories. But these guys seemed like they had an entirely different set of marching orders."

"No kidding?"

Blevins narrowed his brown eyes, his bristle of crew-cut hair creeping forward a little. "Yeah. No kidding. Sometimes that happens. I've seen it. A few guys work together awhile as a team, develop their own, oh, I guess you could call it consciousness or direction. Whatever. Sometimes they kind of forget about the law. They just become more careful, less open."

"Like what happened in Houston?"

120

Jamison watched the pain streak across Blevins's face. But he had to know if this situation was similar. Melissa was involved.

"Damn, Peter, you said you'd never bring that up again."

Jamison kept his eyes steady, even though he ached to drop them. "I'm sorry," he said. But he still wanted an answer. After all, hadn't those agents intentionally set out to kill a man, and gunned him down in cold blood? And hadn't Blevins gone along with their story?

"Hey, Peter, you know it's real easy to stand here, all safe and snug, and judge me for what I did. You weren't there, you can't possibly gauge the pucker factor when it takes a high-speed chase to catch your suspect. It was late, dark, and scary. The guy was supposed to be A and D. They said he went for a gun, which forced them to shoot him. Case closed."

Jamison bit his lip, then looked away from Blevins. "Uh-huh. If you say so."

"Damn you, I just said so!"

Jamison watched Blevins's face, the squinting eyes and sealed-up mouth, good warning signals that Peter knew to heed. "I'm sorry, Rich. I'm a little upset, that's all. I'm pissed off that the F.B.I. picked up Melissa."

Blevins took a deep breath, then exhaled and wrenched a kink out of his neck. "Ah, hell, you're right, anyway. About Houston. I wish you weren't, but there wasn't a reason in the world for us to kill that guy. We had him easy. Man, they just gave that poor bastard a quick vote and decided he was a blight on society. Which, of course, he was."

"Even so, I'm surprised you went along."

Blevins's eyebrows went up as his eyes went down. "The other agents were convincing with their story, Peter. Swore that they thought the man had gone for a weapon. I never saw it and, as it turned out, no gun or knife was there. But they stuck to their story and I backed them up. Or, more correctly, I didn't dispute them. It was wrong, I know. Would I do it today? No. Absolutely not."

"Good."

"It sucks, too, Peter, but that's the very best and worst part of my character, and definitely the part that causes the most problems in my work. I trust people too damn much. When they said they saw a gun, I wanted to believe them. I've always had trouble believing that people lie as often as they do."

"Strange problem for a criminal investigator."

"I fight it all the time. Can't tell you how many times I'm disappointed by people."

"And you think the guys that got Melissa might be working like the agents in Houston?"

"Did I say that? No, I did not say that. I said they were different. That's all."

"What do you know about them?"

"Not much. As I said, I think they were F.C.I. types, and that makes them a different breed right off the bat. I've seen one of them before, at Quantico. He's a big, ugly guy that might have been on the S.O.A.R. team."

"Sore team?"

"Special Operations and Rescue. Kind of like S.W.A.T. but a notch up. But I'm not sure about that. I've barely even spoken to him until today."

Three men in suits headed down the hall. Jamison's training made him split from Blevins, giving the interlopers harder targets if they were looking for trouble. He studied them for weapons. There were no straps from shoulder holsters bending the men's jackets. No bulges around their waists. The cuffs of their pants wrapped smoothly around their calves as they stepped, so no ankle holsters. But even though there wasn't an indication of weapons, he stayed on guard until the intruders passed.

"Rich, how often do you think agents cross the line?"

"Jeez, Peter, what kind of question is that? And how should I know anyway?"

"But you think it does happen?"

"Sure, it happens. There's temptation out there, fueled mostly by frustration. Once in a while, sure, somebody goes over to the other side."

"Could there be more than one. More than just a couple?"

"What are you getting at?"

"I'm just wondering. Something seems strange to me, that's all."

"What?"

"Rich, a dozen F.B.I. agents have been ripping Dillon apart for months, looking everywhere for the person leaking classified secrets. But they never could find him, at least as far as I know."

"So?"

"So, the leak was Jason Bronovich. Melissa told me that. Now he's dead, and I'm trying to figure out how it happened. It just seems weird to me that the F.B.I., with all its resources, couldn't finger him, but someone else managed to do it secretly."

Blevins grew about an inch. "Are you thinking *we* killed Bronovich? Is that what you believe?"

"I don't know. Maybe. Or maybe your guys sold the results of their investigation to someone at Dillon. But, and this is where it gets pretty scary, it would have to be all of them, all of the agents assigned to Dillon would have to be involved. Otherwise the honest agents would have jumped up and made some noise when their suspect was killed. Don't you think?"

"Makes sense."

"And what about your partner getting gunned down. Isn't that pretty unusual?"

"Sure it's unusual. But again, those things do happen. It was my own fault."

"Okay, but why were those other agents there to pick up Melissa? What could they have wanted from her unless they were working with the guys from Dillon? Maybe they knew your partner was going to get Melissa and followed him there. Maybe they were afraid she still had more data from Bronovich. Did anyone check to see if her apartment had been searched?"

"Don't know. But I do know some agents are executing a search warrant at the Coalition. Makes sense it would be her office."

"Can they do that? Do they have the right? She hasn't done anything."

"Oh, they can do it all right. Hell, yes. All they have to do is convince some judge to sign off on the warrant, and that's not a hard thing to do. Once they get the evidence out of there, even if they never use it in a trial, it could get, you know, lost. And Bronovich certainly couldn't provide it again, so—"

"So the case he was helping her build goes right down the drain."

"Exactly. But what about your stuff, Peter, the data you gave Senator Drummond? Wouldn't they need to get that, too, if they wanted to shut her down?"

"Sure. All three sets. Hers, Drummond's, and the copies I gave you."

Blevins rubbed his chin. "I might need to get Drummond some extra protection, before he ends up on someone's list, too."

"Sounds like a good idea."

Blevins looked him over, as if sizing up Peter's chance of survival. "If your suspicions are even partially correct, this mess is going to turn into a downhill shitball, fast. I know our guys are very serious about arresting your ass. I'd expect them to stake out your car, Melissa's apartment, your condo, your office. Man, the whole stinking office was called in on this."

"No kidding. Should I be flattered?"

"No! You should be scared to death. Let's just assume for a moment that you're right, that F.B.I. agents had something to do with Bronovich's death. That means you're pissing off the same people who killed him. And I'll tell you that whoever they are, they're very well connected. They got us working a full-blown case against you in a matter of hours. And we're the good guys, at least as far as I know. Have you ever stopped to think about who else may be after you?"

"No."

"Well, if I were you I'd start thinking along those lines, while I was still breathing and everything."

"No time. I'm too worried about Melissa. If we're right, who's going to protect her? Those agents who arrested her are probably part of the corruption."

"She'll be all right, I promise. Don't worry about her."

"Can't help it. And you know better than to expect me to sit around and wait to see if you're right, unless you can absolutely guarantee her safety."

Blevins looked around, came back shaking his head. "There are no guarantees, Peter. You know that. But I'm sure she'll be safe."

Jamison wanted to shout at him, feared that it might come out despite his best effort to hold it in. A family was walking toward them so he pulled Blevins against the wall and spoke in low tones. "Don't expect me to stand around and watch her get hurt, Rich. You have no way of making sure she's safe, probably don't even know where she is right now. If you believe I'm in danger, then I have to think that she's in just as much danger. I'm going after her."

"You can't, Peter. Please, leave it to me. Damn it, I'm already under investigation because of you. Don't make things worse. I'll make sure she's protected."

"And just how are you going to do that? People are dying because of Melissa's charges against Dillon. Bronovich is dead, and so is the agent you were training and the other agent who died with him. I'm not about to stand around and let some asshole put Melissa's name on that list. I'm going to get her."

"You're going to turn your world to shit, Peter."

"Nope. If my world is turning to shit, Rich, it's going to happen regardless of what I do. I'm not the cause. I'm just getting ready."

"My guess is you're getting ready to get killed."

Jamison cut his eyes over to the family walking by, the parents and three kids smiling and laughing, living proof that he was already missing out on the best parts of life. Without the hope of winning Melissa back there wouldn't be much left anyway. "I wouldn't bet against you. But I wouldn't bet against me, either. I'll get her back. If I die trying, that's just the way things work out sometimes. It's not a tough choice."

Blevins's pug face made another weird contortion, half grimace and half grin. "You're an asshole, Jamison."

"Uh-huh. Thanks for noticing."

Blevins pushed his hand against Jamison's chest, a friendly way of moving him out of his way. "I've got to go, want to start checking this out. Call me at this number, three o'clock sharp." He handed Jamison a piece of paper.

"Will do. Have some answers when I call."

8

John Butler was the very best, the one most often called and the highest priced. He had done this kind of work since Vietnam, a wonderful war he'd enjoyed very much and missed terribly. After three tours and the fall of Saigon, he'd slipped over to Cambodia in order to stay in a killing environment.

The Rhodesians hired him in 1976 to fight in their civil war, and he'd stayed there perfecting his craft until Zimbabwe statehood ended the strife in 1979. He liked the Dark Continent, with its harsh pockets of isolation, and had returned there often. Recently he'd helped the Boers fighting in South Africa, but quit when the proud heritage of the A.W.B. demanded that soldiers work for the glory of the Volkstaat, instead of just a paycheck.

His home was simple and remote, a two-room shack far out in the dusty-bumps thirty miles north of Roswell, New Mexico. He could relax there, the isolation being his most basic need. The millions of dollars he'd earned over the last twenty years were buried in jars, spread around his property. Money held no fascination for him, and he couldn't remember where he'd buried most of it. It just didn't matter, except as a way to measure his worth to the people who employed him. As long as no one ever visited him and his only calls were about work, he was completely content. Didn't need anything else.

Jack Kane's call had come before dawn, while Butler had been running the ridge line with a pack full of rocks—a challenge he loved since a little misstep in the dark or an unexpected shift of the pack's weight could send him over the edge of a sheer rock wall. He'd played the tape twice, watching the sun come up, listening for any extra meaning, hating Kane's voice and surprised to hear it again. He had recognized it instantly, knew it belonged to one of the few killers who could best him. Maybe the only one. He hated admitting that, and would never, ever say it out loud. But in his line of work, it paid to be brutally honest with yourself about where you stood with your enemies.

"So, Kane, you need me again, huh? Need my help? Well, screw you, you shit. You should know better than to call me. What are you thinking, that maybe I've forgotten the last time, that I'd overlook your refusal to pay me? No chance, man. Your age must be making you stupid."

He slid out of his climbing shorts and stood naked at the mirror. The desert sun, already intense as it began its path across New Mexico's sky, threw harsh light on all of his scars. He caressed each of them, touched them with respect, ran his fingers along the jagged healing of his favorites: the horizontal scar across the center of his face where a Namibian bushman had sliced through his nose during their civil war, the ragged patch on his chest where the Khmer Rouge had tried to skin him, and the one on his stomach that had healed with his skin folded over, leaving a lump of flesh on his left side that he'd pierced and hung through with earrings. Each scar was a tribute, a medal for beating circumstances that would have killed anyone else. He knew the injuries were hideous, even more ugly because he'd never gotten medical care for any of them. But he wouldn't trade them for anything. Looked forward to getting more. He gloried in his defects, felt proud of them as he headed to the shower. He was addicted to the challenge of killing people. The adventure. The rush. He was a danger junky, and bloodshed was his fix.

The shower water was so cold it hurt, the only thing in the desert that stayed cold without refrigeration. It came from deep in the earth, unspoiled by the sunlight that bleached everything else. He washed his legs, scrubbing hard to get off the sweat and desert dust, watching the dirty water swirl down the drain and onto the sand below his shack, not even noticing when his fingernails snagged the scab of last week's wound—the stab of a knife that had passed through his calf. Before he could stop, his nails had peeled back the skin flap and torn the healed edges loose, sent the white puss of infection running down his leg.

Butler hardened to the pain, hating its power and refusing to give in to it. He grabbed the big stainless-steel knife that always hung in the shower and took a wild, arcing swipe at his leg, just missing the calf and slashing off the loose chunk of meat. He threw down the knife and the chunk of meat, then jammed his thumb into the wound until it poked out the other side of his leg —a simple matter of honor over enemies. He screamed. It was a war cry, not a whimper.

He twisted his thumb around in the wound, made the nerves tingle and twitch, then popped out his thumb in a quick movement that produced a loud, sucking sound. He screamed louder, enjoying the pure sound that pain produced. Even if it was his own.

Once out of the shower, he wrapped his leg with a dirty T-shirt, a halfhearted effort to slow the bleeding. His curiosity forced him to pick up the cellular phone he'd leased under a series of credible aliases. Then, while the hot breeze dried his naked body and his leg gushed blood onto his raw pine floor, he poured a glass of water and returned Kane's call, leaving a thick trail of blood as he moved to the chrome and plastic dinette table for a pen and some paper.

And then, there it was. The voice that kept coming back to challenge and aggravate him. "Hello," Kane said.

Butler was silent for more than a minute, knowing Kane would let the silence last forever. Finally, he spoke. "What the hell do you want?"

More silence now, pissing him off even more, tilting the power away and making him do the asking. Again. "I *said*, what do you want?"

Kane's gentle voice chilled Butler, reminded him that this was a man who could kill him whenever he wanted. "Don't be a shit to me. Do you understand?"

More time down the drain, lost to bravado that could turn deadly. Butler would normally rush to a plane and fly straight to anyone who'd said that to him, go for all the marbles, life or death, over an insult like that. Except that with Kane, he knew he would lose. He squeezed his water glass until it shattered, driving a sharp glass wedge deep into the meat of his left palm. "Yes. I understand."

"Good."

There were a few seconds of silence, enough time to let the significance sink in that Kane ruled the battlefield.

"I've got some exigent circumstances, would like you here as soon as possible. Your standard fee, two hundred thousand."

Butler tried to mimic, tried to sound calm and unhurried. "All right. Same drop zone as last time. Same signal. Nine o'clock tonight, your time. Agreed?"

"Agreed."

Butler hung up and stepped over to the full-length mirror. He admired his naked body until he began to feel better. Then he combed his hair precisely, and went to dress.

*   *   *   *   *

Kane hung up and looked at Ross Casey before he redialed.

"How soon before he's here, Jack?"

"Nine o'clock tonight. I've got a lot of work to do before then, but at least this should finish it. Jamison won't be a problem after tomorrow."

"Do you think it will work as well this time as before?"

Kane silenced Casey by holding up his hand, needing to pay attention to his phone conversation and make sure he was talking to the right person.

He nodded to Casey, showed that it was the right voice. "It's me again," he said into the phone while watching the seconds tick past on his watch. "Twenty-four hours. No more."

Casey watched with his mouth open.

"Right," Kane said, then hung up.

Casey sat down and leaned back into his power pose, hands behind his head. "You're sure Butler will come through for us and kill Jamison."

"Butler's a good man and a tough predator. He'll get the job done, no problem. And he'll recover the evidence if that's possible, assuming our guys don't get Jamison first."

"How many have you assigned?"

"Five of our men. And Butler. I'll send more if necessary. But right now I've got to get going."

"Good luck, Jack."

Kane ignored it and walked out of the office, short on time. He needed to sort through all the information he'd collected on Jamison and determine what was significant and what wasn't. Make sure all the information was still accurate.

He knew he was shirking his responsibilities by hiring Butler; knew he should be the one to kill Jamison. But it was getting so much harder now. Bronovich's eyes—the panic, the terror, the frantic glance toward his family's picture as he died. The tragedy of his little girls, which stroked the loss of Kane's own family. Kane was having trouble carrying the load. There were so many of them now.

So he would work on it from this side, sorting and selecting information about Jamison as if putting together a puzzle, forgetting, at least for the moment, that another life would end when the puzzle was complete.

*   *   *   *   *

SAC Sackett wasn't taking any chances. Not this time. Too many other times the F.B.I. had earned a black eye for allowing spies to operate with impunity. He wasn't about to let that happen on his watch.

So he'd detailed two hundred agents and sent them out to arrest Peter Jamison, would assign more if they didn't bring him in soon. Dead or alive, he wanted Jamison off the streets, wanted his days of selling secrets to end.

But catching Jamison was proving to be very difficult, even with the emergency wire-taps and mail covers. Jamison had not used a credit card, tried to buy a weapon, been involved in a traffic stop, rented a car, bought an airline, bus, or train ticket, charged a phone call, or been seen anywhere. He had vanished. There were no clues out there, at least none that the F.B.I. had turned up. His disappearance was compelling evidence that the F.C.I. supervisor was right. Jamison was a highly trained foreign agent.

Sackett had worked all through Monday night, had poured so much coffee down his throat that the burnt smell was coming out his pores. His head hurt and his eyes ached, his stomach felt as if gasoline sloshed around inside of it, burning the lining and sending bitter fumes up his throat. But he ignored it all as he closed his door and stalked the White House counsel who'd arrived at ten-thirty this morning, insisting they meet right away.

"Aughton, I don't give a tinker's damn about what President Albright wants today. It was just yesterday afternoon that the U.S. Attorney stormed in here with the F.C.I. supervisor, twitching like a cat and repeating President Albright's demands that I pursue this case. Now that I'm in it up to my sphincter, you want me to call off this manhunt?"

Aughton didn't move, just sat in his chair, dressed like he'd come straight from a country club, too comfortable in a golf shirt and sport coat, soft-skinned but tan. He picked at something under his left thumbnail. "That's right, Sackett. I want you to call it off."

Sackett looked out his window, watched Aughton's reflection in the glass. "I told you earlier, and now I'm telling you again, unless the Attorney General closes this case, it's staying open until Jamison goes down. Hell, two agents have died already, and another one was totally blinded by that crazy Corley woman, who right this minute is screaming about unlawful arrest. I've had to put my very best agent under an administrative inquiry, then divert agents from every other case this office is supposed to be working. With all due respect, counselor, if you think I'm going to let a political appointee like yourself close down this investigation before I get some solid answers, you're pissing up a drain pipe."

The White House lawyer sat quietly in one of Sackett's leather chairs, looking nervous as he glanced around Sackett's office, as if expecting trouble to jump at him from a shelf or crawl toward him from under the desk. His sharp, lean face had a natural urgency to it. He nodded at Sackett, as if agreeing, then smiled with only one corner of his mouth.

"This is a bad case, Sackett. It never should have been opened. Clearly, President Albright overreacted to Senator Drummond's information. He worried too much about Jamison, and didn't want to take a chance that he'd sell our military secrets to the world. No question, the President prematurely labeled Jamison as a threat to our national security. He was just afraid—"

Sackett stomped over to the lawyer's chair, leaned down, and used the oak arms for support. "Afraid? Now we're getting somewhere. Tell me what scared Albright?"

The attorney stretched out his thin neck and wiggled his body to attention, explained away his poorly chosen word by changing it. "He was just . . . concerned. That's all."

"And that concern made him too quick on the trigger?"

"I wouldn't say that. Between you and me, I think President Albright was perfectly justified in demanding Jamison's arrest. His information was too classified to allow him to run all over town with it. Considering the number of military secrets that have already been leaked out of Dillon, I think he acted prudently. But now it's gone too far. The President wants you to back off before other people get hurt. That's all."

Sackett sat in a nearby chair and glanced at the closed door, hoping that Aughton had more than simple marching orders. "Come on," he said in a low, easy voice, "tell me what's really going on here? If I knew the truth, I might be inclined to cooperate."

The lawyer shifted as far away as possible. "It's just as I said, Sackett. Although President Albright's decision was made in good faith, in retrospect it appears to have been a mistake. We're simply trying to remedy it before any more people suffer."

Sackett sprang out of the chair and went straight for the door. "That's a load of crap, Aughton, and we both know it. This case is still open. "I'll let *you* know when it's ready to close." He snatched the door open.

Aughton stood, looking just for an instant like a failure. But by the time he moved the look was gone, replaced by the cocky confidence of someone who believed himself to be untouchable. Sackett had seen the look before, and knew to worry about it.

Nixon had looked like that. So had Alexander Haig. George Bush had tried to get the hang of it during investigations into his relationship with Saddam Hussein before the Gulf War, but he'd never quite managed to pull it off.

Sackett stepped to his secretary's desk as the lawyer cleared security. "Do me a favor. I need an update from the case agent on Peter Jamison. Get him in here right away. I also want Pate and the other agents who arrested Melissa Corley to stay in the area until the arraignment. They can go back to Quantico but no farther than that. Make sure they know those are my orders. I also need complete service jackets on all of them, including the one killed this morning by Robert Davidson."

"Yes, sir."

The White House lawyer's affidavit was still on Sackett's desk, and he picked it up as he sat down. He reread it, worried about what it might really mean, thinking about the way things used to be done, and the agents he suspected of still doing things that way. He knew it went on, but he usually turned away without looking for evidence, hoping that, somehow, he was wrong. But there were times when special assignments were just too political, and the agents who worked them were a little too insulated from F.B.I. guidelines. He knew he should start looking harder at them, but as long as justice was done in the end, he didn't really want to interfere.

So where did that put him? Was he culpable for turning a blind eye, even if the country was probably better off for what had been done? Had he been an accomplice to conspiracy simply because he'd allowed his agents to do the job they'd been paid to do, the job Americans expected them to do? Would his career end when the truth, if such a thing really existed, came out?

He read the affidavit once more, absolutely certain that this was another one of those times, but less certain about what he should do.

* * * * *

Kane examined the stack one last time before he left, made sure there was nothing that could be traced back to him. He'd cut off every letterhead and removed all references to anyone but Jamison. On his way to interview the Corley woman, he stopped in to see Casey.

Casey looked worn down and almost out. "Jack, I've just found out that the F.B.I. won't close their case against Jamison. Damn, Kane, it was stupid of you to bring in the Bureau. Stupid."

Kane wouldn't apologize. He would just explain it calmly, again. "We thought Jamison would be an easier target, Casey. Our guys from Quantico thought it was him picking up the Corley woman. They had no way of knowing the guy at the Coalition was an agent."

"Well, he was. And killing an F.B.I. agent is kind of bad business, don't you think?"

Kane strolled over to Casey and parked his big frame right in front of him. "You just hold up your end, Casey. I'll take care of mine. Jamison is a little smarter, maybe a little better than I expected. But Butler will be here tonight and Jamison isn't that smart, or that good, or that lucky."

"I hope you're right, Kane. I sincerely hope you are."

* * * * *

Melissa's prison wasn't what she'd expected. When the Federal Marshals had come to transport her from the F.B.I. office, she thought she would be going to jail. And jail meant bars, dingy bunks, and filthy toilets.

But there were no bars. The walls were concrete, white, and freshly painted. She had a small, clean toilet/sink combination and a clean bed. All of it was in good shape. The door was solid steel with a small window of wire-embedded glass. A person on the outside could take in her whole room from that window.

She sat on the bed, thinking about the shooting of Special Agent Davidson. It broke her heart that she couldn't remember his first name. A handsome young man had died last night. Maybe not because of her, but certainly for her. At the very least, she should know his full name.

And the name of the man who'd killed him, too. She couldn't recall if he'd identified himself or not, but she could remember him without a name. Even the darkness of the alley couldn't hide the man's ugly features. She would remember him forever, stepping carefully toward Davidson and firing over and over into his young face, the blood and tissue spraying all over the car and covering her dress.

But she could not remember anything about Davidson's face before it was totally destroyed. Nothing at all. So she wanted his name. Wanted it desperately.

A stranger looked through the window of her cell door, but she caught herself before she showed any fear. A key clanged as it twisted the lock open. Two men stepped inside then locked the door behind them. The ugly man was not one of them. She was glad for that.

One of the men was hyperactive, his deranged-looking eyes wide open and shooting around the room, his head twitching and his hands moving constantly, messing with his thin, curly red hair. He was lean, but strong-looking in a stringy sort of way. His face was thin with sharp angles at the nose and chin. Razor-sharp lips that hardly moved when he said to the other man, " —and that's all she's told them so far."

The second man was almost the exact opposite. Big and fluid, but with sharp lines in his face, too. Sad gray eyes. Intelligent, too, you could see that a mile away. Both of them smart, she figured. No undergrads in this room, no sir. All advanced degrees. She wanted to know, right away, how smart they were.

The big man responded to the other's statement. "That certainly isn't much. Maybe we won't have a problem with her after all."

She started right in on them. She would begin by challenging the skinny man with the twitch, the man she would call Jitters. After all, this is the United States of America. She had rights that had been denied. There were plenty of safeguards in the legal system to protect her.

"You should learn what the Miranda warning means, moron. I asked for an attorney during the last questioning. I am demanding one now. If you don't—"

Jitter's hands had been moving since he'd entered, so it was a little hard to tell exactly when he'd sent one of them in her direction, blasting at her head like some old style interrogator. But she did see it in time to snap her head back from the danger, understanding instantly that this was going to be a different game than she'd expected to play.

His hand flashed by her face, close enough for her to reach him, just for a second. Close enough to make her mad, too, remembering what it had felt like to be victimized by a violent man. With the speed and accuracy she'd learned in fencing, she reached out and grabbed a handful of his thinning hair, knotted it into the fingers of her left hand, then jerked that scarecrow close to her, spinning him around with her other hand as she backed into the corner with him, reaching under his coat—fast as a saber slash—and grabbing . . . nothing. An empty holster. No gun in there.

Jitters was grunting, trying to untangle his hair from her hand. But when their bodies smacked into the wall he backed into her, then slammed his right elbow into her ribs. She held on to his hair as his elbow knocked the wind out of her, her weight dragging both of them toward the floor. He jammed his pointy elbow into her ribs again, and then again. Six times, fast as the snap of a rat trap. She heard some ribs crack on her left side and felt the muscles deflate in that arm.

He struggled against her grip until the hair ripped out of his head. Then he spun around to face her from five feet away. Drops of blood formed a connect-the-dot pattern on his scalp where the hair had been. His eyes were wet and tears were streaming down his outraged face. She stayed on her feet, cornered, but managing to smile as she reached out slowly and dropped the handful of red hair on the floor.

She looked straight into his eyes and laughed as the hair fell. It almost killed her to do it, her ribs screaming with every breath. But she wanted both of the men to be uncertain about her and was willing to pay for it. She wasn't going to be anyone's easy victim again. Not ever again.

Jitters went into motion before the hair hit the ground. Her laughing had done it, she could see that. She had leaned toward him and laughed at his falling clump of hair, and he'd gone nuts. Jitters wanted his revenge. He was coming, and she had nothing left.

"Stop it!" The big man intercepted Jitter's lunge and held him back easily, like a grown man with a small child. Jitters had exploded, but Big Man had stopped it. Stopped it in a second.

"Yeah, that's right, Jitters," Melissa said, enjoying the chance to use the moniker out loud. "You'd better stop, like your friend says. It's anybody's guess what I'll rip off and throw away next time."

Big Man shot her a dirty look, then pushed Jitters past her while both men watched her carefully. She started for the door when Big Man opened it, but he was too fast and too ready. He shoved Jitters out of the cell then locked the door and backed into the opposite corner, at the head of her bed. He sat down, nice and gently.

"You should get the prison doctor to look at your ribs, Melissa. My friend—what did you call him, Jitters?—is pretty good at his work. He might have done some internal damage. It could be serious."

She sat down at the foot of the bed, watching him, knowing he still had the key and waiting for her chance. "Next time I'll play rougher," she said, "do some serious damage to him."

Big Man seemed to like that. His eyes opened up as he made an avuncular smile. "My, my, Melissa. You are everything I expected. Absolutely everything."

"Based on what?"

"Why, based on who you are, of course." Big Man's smile faded a little. "You see, I knew your father."

What little strength she still had spilled out, emptying her for a minute of everything except grief. And guilt. And anger. But she wouldn't let it control her for long; had learned to deal with it years ago.

"Big deal. My father was an important man. Lots of people knew him. You think that makes you special?"

Big Man leaned back, pushed down on the bed as if checking the springs. "Oh, no, Melissa. I think that makes *you* special. My question for today is, how special? How much do you know?"

The muscles around her ribs spasmed and pulled at the cracked pieces. But she allowed no sound of pain to come from her mouth. "I know all the things I was taught in school. There's a lot of stuff I've learned since. Some things I've know since birth. You want to be a little more specific?"

Big Man laughed and stood up.

She wrapped an arm around her ribs and held on, stood up with him, almost as tall as his chin.

Big Man took a small, slow lap around his end of the cell. Then he sat back down, a little closer to her but still out of easy range. "What do you know about your father's profession, what he did for a living?"

"He was an engineer. If you'd known him you wouldn't be asking."

"Yes, of course. He was an engineer. And an excellent one, too. Do you recall how rapidly he was promoted, the great fortune he amassed?"

"He worked hard. The company appreciated it. It's not a big mystery."

Big Man was losing patience. It showed up first in his eyes, but then his hands started moving, too.

"What do you know?"

"About what?"

"You know what! I want you to tell me how much you've found out."

Melissa suddenly jerked in his direction, not attacking, but just testing to see if she should.

It was a bad idea. Big Man was lightning, way too fast and much too smart, too good at reading her mind. She could never come close to matching his speed, much less beating it.

"Whatever I know, it's staying with me. You must be an idiot to think I'm going to sit here and chat with you about my father's business."

He shifted on the bed and got a little closer to her. She knew he wasn't worried. She'd shown her speed and he'd done the same. She had nothing for a man like him to worry about.

"Look, Melissa. I may be trying to help you. Or I may be your worst enemy. You'll have to decide that for yourself, then follow my suggestion or not."

She moved closer, just to keep him in doubt, maybe. He did not move away. "And what is your suggestion?"

"Keep what you know about your father private. I've been watching you for years, thinking you might be out for some kind of revenge. So far, I haven't seen you use what you might know. I suggest you do not start now."

She stared at him, thinking about his face, thinking that maybe she'd seen it somewhere before. Maybe in a store, or a congressman's office, or her father's living room. Or, maybe not.

"Is that all?"

141

He stood up, kept his distance as he moved toward the door. "One last thing. Has your investigation, or your heritage, made you aware of anyone trying to take control of your father's business? I'm sure you know that rumors have been circulating for years."

She took two steps in his direction. Two of the five steps necessary to cross the distance. "If I knew anything, do you think I'd tell you?"

He scratched his head, looked as if he'd been caught with his zipper down. "No. I suppose not."

"You're not too stupid, then. Maybe even smart enough to understand that I'm going to destroy you, and all those despicable cretins who work with you. There won't be anything left of my father's business when I'm done. So if I were you I wouldn't lose any sleep over someone else taking power."

He smiled at her. It was a nice face. "Pretty big talk."

"You bet. Can I go now?"

Big Man opened the door, opened it all the way like it was an invitation to leave. "No." He stepped out and started to close it. But he stopped and looked back, as though he expected her to beg.

Melissa turned away and looked at the wall. Could he possibly think that she was the begging type?

* * * * *

Jack Kane caught up to Jitters outside the men's room. He had dried his eyes and combed some hair over his scabbing scalp. He was still twitching, though, overflowing with explosive vengeance.

"Step in here a minute, Jitters."

Kane smiled when he said it. Jitters followed him into the bathroom.

142

"Don't *you* start calling me that. Damn! And don't you ever, ever touch me like that again. You hear me? I don't care who you are. If you put your hands on me again, I'll—"

Kane turned and grabbed Jitters, twisted him just the way he wanted. Then he uncupped his fingers from his knife and buried it deep into the side of Jitter's sinewy body while covering Jitter's mouth with his left hand. Jitter's eyes went still and stared up at him. His whole body went rigid. First time for everything.

Kane moved his hand, like always, to hear his victim's last words.

"Why," Jitters gurgled. "Why, Jack?"

Kane knew why, even though Jitters would never understand. He was making his own decisions now. Who was good, and who wasn't. It wasn't based on assignment, or Dillon's worries, or a politician's paranoia. It was strictly his call.

"Because it's your time, Jitters. That's why."

Jitters slid off the knife and slumped to the floor. Kane stepped away and washed his hands, got the specks of blood off his sleeve. He called Dillon Security from his cell phone, then waited twenty seconds before stepping out into the hall. Two uniformed prison guards were running toward him with their guns drawn. Kane waited until they were close.

"Put those weapons away. Do not enter this room. There'll be an emergency unit here soon. Let no one else in. Do you understand completely?"

They didn't. Kane knew that. And he didn't really want them to understand. He just wanted them to stand in front of the door, stupid and cocky and doing what they'd been told to do, guarding the crime scene until experts arrived.

"Yes, sir."

"Good. Thank you."

He left and walked to the exit of the Federal Detention Center. At the sign-in desk he picked up Jitters's F.B.I. credentials and gun, along with his own weapon.

9

Jamison had held back after Blevins left, stayed in the Smithsonian another hour and wandered around, setting up ambushes for anyone who might have intercepted his phone call to Blevins last night, or followed Blevins this morning. Kids with cheap cameras walked through his kill zone. So did fat-bellied men in sweatshirts and overweight moms in running shoes and fanny packs. None of them triggered his warning sensors, and the display of out-of-shape humanity tempted him to drop his defenses, made him wonder again if he was exaggerating the potential for danger. So far, he hadn't seen anyone who could ever make him worry.

But that was how people got killed, and he knew it. Just let your guard down a little, boy, and that's when you trip the wire, or miss the small warning detail that could have saved your life. He rode down the escalator and walked out onto Constitution Avenue, joined the Tuesday crush of tourists and federal workers.

But he ignored their presence and took no comfort in being among the living. He was spiraling into some kind of war, as surely as he had years before. He knew it intuitively. And war meant casualties. The city's buildings were big and concrete instead of squatty and bamboo, but his role was exactly the same. He was armed, edgy, and confused, ready to kill whomever hoped to kill him. It was war wherever it occurred, and the innocent people around him were nothing but incidental soft targets for the sniper who might lie ahead, or the bomber who could be across the street with a transmitter.

He had hid last night, caught up in the escape, baffled by what was happening around him and waiting to see which way this was going to play out. But now he knew they'd taken Melissa, and that was a step too far. F.B.I. agents, maybe the same men who'd killed Bronovich, had arrested her and killed Blevins's partner. There was no way he would assume the best and pretend she was safe just because the Bureau had custody of her. No, sir, he wanted her back. He kept thinking about yesterday morning, her coming out of the shower with wet hair and a sexy smile, looking him over and driving him nuts.

He was hunting humans, searching for whomever might keep her from him, and not caring what badge or uniform or alias they were hiding behind. He walked big down the street, looking for trouble, wanting the answers he would beat out of his victims once the fight was over. Making himself an easy target, hoping they'd crack one off at him.

The walking increased his anger, pissed him off that no one was coming after him. Where were they? He crossed streets against the lights, walked at the edge of the gutter, did everything he could to attract attention. All the while he ground his teeth, almost to the point of shattering. He was mad, but not crazy. He still had the crazy man by the tail, holding him back. Twice before he'd seen the uncontrollable fury of the crazy man, and he never wanted to see it again.

Melissa, thank God, had never seen the crazy man, even though she'd been nearby the one time crazy man had escaped on American soil. But Blevins had seen him. He'd seen what that wild animal could do, and Jamison was sure he hadn't forgotten. Who could?

They had been out on patrol. It had been another hot, smelly, rain-soaked day in Southeast Asia, and they were patrolling, far out in the boonies. Humping. Humping through the tangles of vines with all of their gear and all of their fears, carrying forty pounds of deadly tools that intimidated them with their own destructive power. Carrying letters from home and photos and bug spray and smokes and water and grenades. Humping foot powder and dry socks and a sidearm and knife and an M16. Pushing themselves through the dense bamboo, wanting so badly to live through this day, but knowing that some of them probably would not.

It wasn't anything like the movies. There was no soundtrack, no John Wayne, and no sweet endings. Just land leeches and itching and sweating and worrying that your next step through the brush might pick up a wire and drag an armed grenade out of a tin can nailed to a tree across the path.

In some sense, though, it was boring. Walking alongside the trails and daydreaming about home, about eating with clean hands and sleeping in a dry bed. Or kissing a girl and touching her breast. Starting the day with a hot breakfast. Going to a job where you didn't have to kill strangers to earn your pay. Simple things.

How many times had they humped their way through this jungle, waiting to attract enemy fire? And why didn't the Army just let them go kill the Viet Cong? Hell, every grunt was sure he knew where to find them. Only the REMFs back at Headquarters seemed to be in the dark.

But they crept along in split columns, staying off the trail for safety reasons, but close enough to it to find their way. Rich Blevins was their new Second Lieutenant, a nugget who'd just

147

arrived from the World, given the assignment after Lieutenant Trask diddy-bopped into some V.C. tanglefoot, had been shot to pieces as he struggled against the thorny wire. Jamison's squad had fired back at the V.C., emptying magazine after magazine while Trask's shredded body danced hideously between them and the enemy.

No one trusted Blevins. He was a new guy, and F.N.G.s knew nothing. Especially the officers. Where were they supposed to have learned, anyway? College? OCS? No sir, you learned the rules of this game by playing it, and this was Second Lieutenant Blevins's first time at bat. But they would walk his patrol and follow his orders, as long as Blevins's commands followed their own formula for survival.

Jamison was nineteen. He'd spent the first part of his life bouncing around America with his parents, his father a pioneer in the consulting business. City management type of stuff, with six months to a year per location. There had been lots of schools, lots of missed lessons, and lots of trouble. They'd settled in Virginia Beach long enough for him to finish high school, but he was far behind his classmates and barely made it through.

After graduation, the army had requested his attendance, and it was his first real chance to be a part of something permanent. He was thinking about that now, and thinking that he would try to write his parents tonight, if he lived that long. Where were they living? Portland? No, that contract had ended. Maybe—

Blevins hadn't done anything wrong. It was just one of those days when bad things happened in the Zoo. He'd led them as well as anyone, using all the training he'd been given, looking pretty sharp up there in his newly pressed uniform and giving perfect hand signals. Jamison and a couple others had just finished laughing at him, at how worried he looked pushing away the giant leaves of the banana plants and peering into the wall of jungle, looking for a hole big enough to allow a patrol of men to pass through. Blevins was the first one hit—it looked like two rounds in the stomach—but he turned, grabbed his guts, and signaled his men toward their target before he went down.

Automatic weapons began popping at them from the trees. Five or six of them, Jamison figured, with all the advantages—high ground, cover, concealment, and surprise. He was the very last man, covering the rear, and was barely in the V.C.'s kill zone.

Everyone blasted away with whatever weapons they had in their hands. Shotguns, M-79 grenade launchers, M16's, and the ubiquitous M60. A jet could have screamed by and no one would have heard it. The high-tech chatter of their M-16's laid down good fire against the mechanical stutter of the communists' AK-47's. You could tell from the sounds how many were shooting. How many GIs and how many V.C. Scary statistics. Lt. Blevins's squad was already down by half, maybe more. It had been less than a minute, hell, less than half a minute, and they were down by 50 percent.

Once the primary kill zone had been worked over, the fire began raking in Jamison's direction. Up until now he had been taking carefully aimed shots into the overgrowth, shooting at targets just behind the dancing leaves. But now all the leaves were starting to flip toward him. This was going to be bad. Real bad. There was very little fire from the M-16's anymore, maybe he and one other GI shooting back. Still lots of it from the Kalashnikovs. Had anyone called in air support? Or artillery? Was help coming?

He listened for aircraft, longing for the bittersweet smell of Napalm dropped Danger Close by some clean-shaven, God-love-you, A-4 driver. But all he heard were the screams and crying of the men in his squad, gruesome proof that you really could die out here.

And that's when his water broke and Jamison felt another person born inside of him. A person so powerful that he was barely controllable. Recklessly powerful. Crazy.

Crazy man didn't care about anything. He was fearless and frightening as he jumped up, taking, of course, Jamison with him. There was a second of absolute silence in the steamy heat of the jungle, as if the whole world stopped and said, "Oh, shit. Do you see the look in that guy's eyes?"

Then the AKs starting clacking at him again.

Crazy man walled over Jamison's face. He could feel it changing, toughening. He could feel the change all over his body—the jump in blood pressure, the cotton spit in his mouth, the swelling of his muscles and his mind's new obsession with brutality. He became unstoppable. Murderous. He jumped up and ran straight into the brushline, firing his weapon, flipping the clip, firing some more. Running hard and fast and . . . couldn't wait. What a strange feeling. Crazy man was absolutely exhilarated by the near future, by the chance to run straight into the foliage, right up to the damned Gooks, smashing their pumpkins with the butt of his weapon and hearing the ripe thump of a shattered skull.

He angled across the trail and moved into the brush at a trot. He got shot right away, then hit again. But crazy man didn't care; paid absolutely no attention. Couldn't even tell for sure where the bullets had entered his body. Crazy man was screaming, scaring the shit out of Jamison. Scaring the shit out of the V.C., too, because look, there goes one now, right in front of him. Crazy man wished for a bayonet so he could stab the little bastard right through the back. But he had to settle for a quick burst to the man's head, his V.C. noggin ripped apart like a paper target while his wobbly legs kept his body moving.

Crazy man had not broken stride yet, hadn't even staggered when he'd been hit. He was a bullet himself and could not be hurt by them. Terrain didn't matter. Thick vegetation didn't matter. He would fly over it, through it, straight to his enemies, straight for their hearts.

Gunfire behind him now. Crazy man spun around, arms first, so close to the other muzzle that Jamison wanted to jump back

150

to get away from it. But crazy man would not allow it. He stepped into his enemy, inside the tip of the AK's barrel. He pressed his weapon against the forehead of the communist's face and fired a short burst, then turned and fired again, bringing down another one who had jumped up and ran.

Jamison started running again. Hit once more but so what? Who's next? Which one of you little bastards goes on my list next?

The jungle suddenly went quiet. He started noticing his own sounds for the first time, as loud as a battle tank crashing through the jungle.

No. Please, God, no. Crazy man shattered the silence like it was glass. "Noooo! Get back here you sonsofbitches!"

But the enemy was moving out. Crazy man had to settle for long shots at the last of them, the two V.C. who'd seen the crazy man, had heard the crazy man, and didn't want to fight the crazy man. They'd seen up close what he could do. Saw firsthand that they had absolutely no power to stop him.

Jamison tucked himself into the jungle for a long time after that, as long as it took to learn how to lock the crazy man away. He wanted to hurry, to get back to his squad and give first aid. But he didn't want the crazy man to lead the way. Not again. Not twice in one day.

He waited to be the last man medivac'd from the firefight, listening for the thump of the last chopper. After two Dust-Offs he walked to where they'd been ambushed and sat down beside Blevins, who looked totally shocked to see him. The lieutenant was holding his guts but showing little pain. Morphine, probably.

"What's your name, again?"

Jamison didn't want to talk. He was still coming back, trying to be ready to recognize normality when it hit. Figured he'd know he was there when his wounds started to hurt. "Jamison, Peter."

"Well, Jamison, that was really something. You're one brave mother."

"It was stupid."

Blevins grimaced with pain but fought it back and didn't say anything about it. "Maybe so. I'm too green to really know. But I can tell you one thing, I'm putting you in for a citation."

"Don't."

Blevins flung his chest and head forward, threw up a smelly mixture of blood and food. Jamison supported his lieutenant's head until the wretching stopped.

Blevins leaned back against the tree. "Huh? Why not? You deserve a medal. They would have killed us all. We'd be in body bags now, every last one of us."

"Just don't. Okay? I don't ever want to hear about it again."

Blevins kept staring. But Jamison had learned, just in that brief slice of time, what it was like to live with the crazy man. It was going to be hard, and would be almost impossible back in the World. He didn't need people honoring the guy. That much he knew for sure.

This D.C. street was no place for the crazy man. Still, even without him taking charge, Jamison was ready to go at it. Right here, right now, thinking a little bit about torture and a place to administer it. He'd take any odds as long as they offered close-in fighting. No long shots that could drop him or his enemy. No sir. Up close and personal, that's where the answers would be found. Answers that would get Melissa back, and rescue her life from the fire.

*   *   *   *   *

Dillon Security man Samual Martin had his orders. Kane had not been very specific that night in the warehouse by Melissa Corley's apartment, but they were orders all the same. Watch

Peter Jamison, but don't kill him unless it becomes absolutely necessary.

So Martin's problem was a simple one. Although he liked security work, he loathed being on surveillance. He preferred things face-to-face. Rough and tumble. Bloodied knuckles and broken noses.

He was a pugilist. His huge body was perfect for it. He loved to hurt people more than anything else in the world, except maybe getting teenage girls out of their silky panties. Even that would be a tough choice.

His propensity for violence had cost him his job on the Metro Police Department, and probably would have kept him off Dillon's force except for that big favor they owed him. He had killed one of their traitors when he'd been a cop, and made it look like self-defense. There was the routine traffic stop, followed by his frantic radio call for backup. By the time other cops showed up, he'd already shot the suspect four times in the face and stuck a freshly fired throw-down weapon in his hand. Martin's story had held, even against the gentle backdrop of the traitor's peaceful reputation.

That job had been easy. A short hunt, then straight to the kill. Just the way Martin liked it. But this bullshit going on now was cat and mouse, the kind of thing that really hacked at his nerves. Because of Peter Jamison, Martin had spent an entire night in a dark, roach-infested warehouse, spying on Corley's apartment. It was Jamison's fault that Martin spent long hours in his car, glaring at curious pedestrians while he kept his surveillance log and shot rolls and rolls of pictures. Things he hated to do. Things he could stop doing as soon as Jamison was dead.

He'd followed Jamison to the museum, wondering how Kane knew he'd go there. Kane was truly amazing. He had informants everywhere, and they enabled him to maintain his status as the organization's ultimate enforcer. Martin fantasized sometimes—not often, but in the middle of the night, maybe, alone in some car—fantasized about being like Kane. Intelligent. Impossibly efficient. Unrelenting. Quick and silent and deadly.

Martin didn't idolize him, of course. Martin had no idols. He was his own. Kane was just an inspiration. That's all.

Suddenly, Martin saw Jamison walking in his direction. "Not very smart," he muttered to no one. "Jamison came out of the museum the same way he entered. I'd have gone out the back, or maybe a window. I don't know why Kane is giving him all this special attention, he ain't showing me nothing. I could take him down anytime, whenever I wanted. Get off this lousy detail."

All of a sudden that seemed like a pretty good idea. Sure, he'd been up all night drinking coffee. Most of the previous night and day, too. He knew his thinking might not be perfect, so he gave it another run-through. What were his orders again? Don't kill Jamison unless it was absolutely necessary? Yeah, that's right. Absolutely necessary.

He opened the door of the company car and heaved his weightlifter's body out, then started down the sidewalk after Jamison. He was about a half block behind, but damn if Jamison didn't already have him. Martin had seen it, seen Jamison's head turn around and take in all the faces for half a second. He'd caught Martin. Martin felt Jamison's stare for a long time. A long, long time in the context of hunting. Maybe two seconds. Long enough and bold enough to show that the terms of their meeting, whatever they might be, were perfectly acceptable to Jamison.

Martin was impressed. Actually impressed by Jamison's bravery. And excited. This might be, if he were really lucky, an actual contest. Not another boring mismatch between him and some pencil neck. But a fair fight, if such a thing existed for him, between him and a guy who was as ready as he was. Jamison sure looked ready. Martin would get his chance to show off a little. It would be fun.

"What the hell? Has Jamison lost his mind? What's he think he's doing?"

* * * * *

Jamison had no idea who the big bastard was but figured he was on the other team, and therefore might have the other team's playbook. He would take the man down and beat out whatever answers he could, then use them to get Melissa free.

The guy was huge, that's why he'd been so easy to spot. Six feet seven, eight maybe. Pushing three hundred pounds. Solid. A giant by most standards. But Jamison thought he could take him. Could take him all by himself, with no help from the crazy man. Take him straight on, but careful as a surgeon.

In the middle of the crowded sidewalk, Jamison turned around and stopped, just like that. It was a noisy spot where a brick building was being torn down. As good a place as any to make a scene. Other people on the sidewalk muttered and scowled as they squeezed around him, but they quickly formed a flow, like a fast-moving stream around a large rock. He waited.

The giant stopped and flashed a stupid look when Jamison stared at him. He glared back as the two of them held their ground, separated by a hundred feet and several hundred people, jackhammers and car horns filling out the soundtrack. Finally, the man's stupid look lifted, replaced by something else, something mean and simple. The giant started coming for him.

Jamison waited, watched the man's hands and his walk, looked for any kind of weapon or weakness but saw neither. He came close, then closer. The giant slowed. Ten feet away, the stupid look—or was it surprise?—trying to work its way back onto the giant's face as Jamison stood his ground. Slower now. Eight feet. Six. Four. Three. The giant stopped. Three feet away. An arm's throw. Jamison looked at the man's arms. His biceps had to measure twenty-five inches. Maybe thirty. Hell, it didn't matter. A full blow from those arms could kill him. So he did the only logical thing and stepped into the man, almost against his chest, closed the gap to less than a foot.

The look—it was definitely surprise now, not stupidity—was big on the giant's face. His chest was as large as a reclining chair and sucked air like a huge pump, robbing half the block of oxygen then blowing it into Jamison's face.

Jamison was on his tiptoes, trying to stay balanced as he rose up to the giant, trying to get close to eye level. "Where's Melissa?"

The giant must have spent one of his past lives as a chameleon, his face changed so often from surprised to stupid. Now it was set on stupid again. "Huh?"

"Don't 'huh' me, dumbass. Where's Melissa?"

The giant smiled, and damn if he wasn't fast for such a big man. He threw his right leg back, found his range, and snapped up his fists. Started to swing.

But Jamison didn't let it happen. Like a shadow, he stepped with the guy and stayed within a foot, then smashed his right elbow across the bridge of the giant's nose, sharp and hard and quick as electricity. Crack! Then he came back from the opposite side, not wanting to leave his ribs open for long. Crack again.

The giant's nose squirted blood and the crowd shoved back. Giant was hurt a little, but didn't seem to mind. He smiled, then took a slow swipe across his face with his monster hand, smeared blood all over his fingers and left four clean streaks along his bloody cheek. Then he came like a bear, those huge arms closing around Jamison like a clamp.

Jamison shoved his open palm up at the big face, driving hard, hoping to cram the giant's broken nose deep into his head. But he missed and the clamping arms closed around him, pinning his own arms by his sides, dragging his face into the giant's smelly shirt. There was hardly any time left now. The big arms had him. He had to do something quick or he would be crushed. His lungs gave up air and his organs shifted higher into his chest, squeezed out of position by the powerful grip.

He raised up his right foot, then drove it hard onto the giant's size sixteen, or whatever, sneaker, smashing the giant's toes. He ground his heel into the toes, feeling like he was standing on five large mice.

Giant's arms stopped closing, but Jamison knew he wasn't hurt. He had a curious look on his face, as if he wanted to look down and see what had happened. He let Jamison slip, just a little, so he could see his foot.

As soon as he had room, Jamison fired his fist like a rocket, launched from way down low and close. It traveled the straight path from the giant's belt to the bottom of his massive chin, hitting home, rocking the big bony jaw skyward and throwing the giant a little off-balance. Jamison swept his right leg behind the giant's calf and drove himself against the hardened chest. The man was unbelievably solid. Even with the giant leaning back, it was like ramming an elephant's rump. Jamison pushed as hard as he could, kept his right leg locked behind the giant to keep him from stepping back. Gradually, big boy began to fall.

Jamison was on him as he hit the pavement, grabbing his head and banging it onto the concrete, pummeling it with his fist, smashing the nose so many times that it became unrecognizable, a flattened slab of bloody mush. But it wasn't enough. He tried to crack the giant's head on the concrete and break it open. But the giant's neck muscles were too strong to allow him a good blow.

Giant pulled his hands up and covered his face. He didn't seem to know what to do, and acted as though he'd never been on the losing side before. How could things go so wrong so fast?

Jamison heard sirens several blocks away, trying to make their way through the workday traffic. No time to question this guy, but time enough to put him away for a few days.

People were screaming. The construction workers were yelling at each other to stop the fight, each offering an excuse as to why he wasn't going to do it. Jamison jumped off the giant, who was bleeding from his nose and ears and eyes. But still, he wasn't badly injured. Jamison knew he would see him again if he left him like this. He knew the giant would be more careful next time. More deadly.

Crazy man started screaming in Jamison's head, the only voice he could hear now, shouting that the giant must have a gun and that Jamison should grab it and shoot him. Shoot him now, before the police came. There was still time.

Jamison flipped open the giant's jacket and reached for the big handgun. But just as his fingers touched the grips he stopped, begged crazy man not to kill this man, screamed that it was way too much. Crazy man hesitated, and Jamison did the same, his fingers wrapped around the butt of the weapon, but not pulling it from the holster. Crazy man stunned Jamison by agreeing, as long as the giant was hurt badly enough. Crazy man backed down, but stayed very close.

Jamison saw the loose bricks by the construction area twenty feet away. He ran and grabbed one, came back to the giant – who had watched through the cracks in his fingers – and started breaking ribs. Two of them there, now a couple more over here. He listened to them snap as the giant's massive body twitched on the sidewalk. One more wild swing at his sternum. Ugh, that was a good one. Okay, that's all the time.

He jumped up and held the brick like a football, threatened the crowd opposite the sirens. They immediately split apart, couldn't seem to do it fast enough to suit themselves. He threw the brick down and ran through the hole, turned the corner and slowed down, started walking. One of hundreds of people in the Tuesday crush, heading back to work.

10

Jamison walked into the Grand Hyatt Hotel at three o'clock, checked the lobby, then went to the phones by the restrooms. He dialed the number Blevins had given him, sure that it would belong to a pay phone, knowing that Blevins liked to be in a busy area when he spoke secrets.

Blevins was out of breath and panting when he answered. "Hello."

Jamison looked around to make sure he was alone. "Rich, is everything all right?"

"Yeah, yeah, I'm fine. I'm just a little tired from dodging the Bureau's surveillance teams, that's all."

"What? The F.B.I. is following you?"

"Hey, don't sound so surprised. I'm a suspect now, just like you. That's how it goes with the Bureau, you're either in or you're out. Right now, I'm out. And I know the guy they're trying to arrest. So they'll follow me. Why shouldn't they?"

"I guess. Did you find out about Melissa? Is she safe?"

"Yes. I did and she is. The Bureau turned her over to the marshals. They'll be responsible for her until the arraignment."

"You sound like that's supposed to make me feel better."

"It's good news, under the circumstances. She'll be fine. I'm sure of it."

"Yeah. Right. She's under arrest and facing trial. You'll excuse me if I don't share your confidence."

"You've got to have faith in the system, Peter. They don't have much on her. Maybe a little disclosure violation, maybe some computer hacking, but nothing they'll waste much time on."

"What has she told them so far?"

"From what I hear, she told them about Dillon, the same story you told me. She speculated, along the same lines we did, as to what it might mean in a larger sense. But the agents didn't buy a word of it."

"Why not?"

"Come on, Peter. She was just talking. She had no evidence. I'm sure it sounded ridiculous for her to make charges of high level corruption without some kind of proof."

"Those agents are idiots, Rich. Why wouldn't they check out her story? They could have called Drummond and looked at the evidence before they decided."

"I can't answer that. What was interesting, though, is that my buddy Thomas told me that a guy from the National Security Agency was there when they questioned her. He reminded the agents who interviewed Melissa that her allegations, even though they couldn't possibly be true, were still of a highly sensitive nature, and that the information was not to be disseminated in any form. Not one word."

"Is it normal for the N.S.A. to show up like that?"

"No. Actually, it's really weird, and set my mind to thinking in strange ways. So I visited a friend of mine who's a middle echelon guy at Langley."

"And?"

"First we just crabbed about old times for awhile, talked about things that affected both the F.B.I. and the C.I.A., just to get the conversation rolling. But then I asked him what you asked me, made the question very specific—Is there a rogue element in the F.B.I?"

"That was bold. What did he say?"

"He was reluctant to talk at first. Very reluctant. But I stayed after him, kept breaking down the walls. Eventually he told me some pretty strange things. What was kind of surprising was that he didn't seem bothered at all by the things he said, even though they sounded terrible to me."

"Really? What kind of things?"

"Some pretty way-out stuff about corrupt politicians and businessmen. Apparently, a long time ago—and I don't have any idea when it started—some rich beltway bandit with a big scheme and the right connections formed a very select group of politicians and warriors, then armed them with the power to do things secretly, without a lot of fuss or fanfare."

Jamison checked his watch and wondered what Melissa was doing. Was there any chance she was thinking of him? "How did they do that? And how is this going to help me get Melissa back?"

"Don't know. But to answer the first question, they did it with money. Supposedly, there was a secret fund. Whoever controlled the cash could do whatever he wanted."

"Like what?"

"Like . . . I don't know really. But suppose . . . okay, here's one. Suppose you were the President of the United States and you thought some country was a threat to an ally. But Congress doesn't buy it and won't approve military action, and the threat doesn't merit the President's use of his war powers."

"I guess, under those circumstances, there wouldn't be much a president could do."

"Wrong. Remember, if you're in on the game you've got a big damn pot of gold. You can hire your own men and send them in to kick some ass. Then keep quiet about it."

"What are you saying, that America uses mercenaries?"

"Jeez, Peter, I don't really know. I'm just thinking this through myself, based on the examples my C.I.A. guy used."

"Which were? Any specifics?"

"Not at first. But I've known him a long time, and once he started talking it was like opening a tap. One story just led into another. These guys go all their lives with secrets jammed into their brains. But they're just like the rest of us, they like to brag when they can."

"So what did he say?"

Blevins's voice began to echo, as if he were hunkering deeper into his phone booth. "Are you ready for this? My friend started off by laughing at my ignorance, then asking me how in the world I thought the Speaker of the House had managed to keep American hostages held in Iran until their imprisonment turned the tide of the presidential election."

"Jeez, what did you say?"

"I just stumbled, you know. Confused. And I wanted him to do the talking, so I said I couldn't imagine how that was pulled off. Then the guy laughed again and said, 'Okay, here's a softball. How were the Contras really funded, aside from Ollie North's little contribution?' "

"And you said?"

"Nothing. Man, the guy was starting to perform."

"Did he have other examples?"

"Oh, yeah. He kept skipping around, reminding me about all those weapons shipped to Saddam Hussein before he invaded Kuwait. They never showed up on any government balance sheet, and George Bush always denied we'd sent them. He asked me where I thought the money came from to pull that off."

"This fund, I guess."

"Yup. Same place as the money that bought the cooperation of criminals like Noriega and Ferdinand Marcos. And covered up a presidential assassination. And shipped arms to Iran."

"No kidding. He said all that?"

"Yeah, and more. Hell, he talked for an hour or so, detailing crap like the windfall channeled into this fund by scrapping all one hundred and ten of the military's Atlas missile sites after just three years instead of the scheduled fifteen. That program was fully funded at the front end, so the early shutdown meant—"

"Big dollars to work with."

"Bingo. But here's the kicker. When I decided to risk asking him about the Wombat, he said that companies like Dillon Aerospace were what Eisenhower had in mind when he gave that speech about the danger of a military/industrial complex."

Three men came out of the bathroom and Jamison memorized all of their faces, compared them to the other faces he'd already logged into his brain today. "What? What's he talking about, this military and industrial complex?"

"Not sure. I guess some kind of illegal cooperation between the military and American business. From what he said, I would probably define business pretty narrowly. He probably just meant defense contractors."

"They would have the motivation, that's for sure."

"You bet. My man said that between 1980 and 1990, the U.S. Navy alone spent ten billion, *billion*, dollars producing aircraft they'll never, ever use. The F-14D, the ADVCAP, the A-12 Avenger, the A-6F."

"I wondered how those programs survived. So you believe this guy?"

"Yes, I think I do, although I hate to admit it. I'll tell you something else, too. He seemed to think this fund was a very good thing, the one and only way for this country to stay powerful. He was a flaming zealot."

"You're kidding."

"Nooooo. Not at all. You have to remember that those guys in Spookville get very cynical about public opinion, and how it hinders their range of options. They'd prefer to conduct their slice of America's business without any oversight at all. That's why they'd support just about anyone, in anything they could pull off that would further their goals."

"Can you go back and get more out of this guy?"

"Doubt it. When he stopped, he knew he'd gone too far."

"Damn."

"Yeah. But he did mention one other thing. He suggested that anyone, and feel free to take this personally, who was thinking about confronting the guys who controlled this fund had better be well-informed, ruthless, and here's the tough one, invincible."

"Great. I hate it when people use hyperbole where my life is concerned."

"He didn't say it to insult your abilities, Peter. I never told him anything about you, or that you even existed. But he believed one hundred percent that anyone challenging these guys and their . . . whatever the hell you want to call their organization, should expect to be dead within a few days. Fewer if he hadn't been professionally trained. There have been rumors for years about someone trying to organize a takeover of this cozy little group by getting rid of the top layer of leaders. Apparently, it's made the current leaders very paranoid and dangerous. They feel threatened by the Coalition, so there's a couple of good reasons for you to expect them to be deadly."

"Hey, I'm not challenging these guys! And I sure don't want to take over their little fraternity. I tried to save some jobs, that's all. Now I'm trying to get Melissa back. It's as simple as that." Jamison realized he'd sounded weak and hated that the words had gotten by him. "But if it's a fight they want, by God, I'll sure give them one."

"You may have to. Here's the last thing he said. He told me that the F.B.I. had always been pretty clean, whatever that means. Your guess is as good as mine. But at one time he did know of a group of dirty agents working around D.C. I guess that would mean Washington Field Office, Headquarters, Baltimore Field Office—"

"And Quantico! Rich, you said you recognized the agent in Sackett's office yesterday. He was from Quantico, the SOAR team, remember? Do you have any idea why he was assigned to this case?"

"No, not yet. But I'm thinking like you. I'm calling Headquarters as soon as we hang up, going to find out the whole story about him and the dead agent. Although it's not unusual for an agent to show up at an office for a brief, special assignment, it's usually at the SAC's request, or because the case relates to something he's already working on. I don't see how that could apply here. You and Melissa weren't even a case until yesterday. Unless you two dovetailed into something he already had open."

"That makes sense. Either that, or Sackett's in on it, too. No matter how you slice it, I still hate that the government has Melissa."

"Try not to worry. As I told you earlier, if they wanted to kill her she would have died in the shootout at her office. Once they brought her in she was pretty much out of harm's way. At least that's the way I see it. My guess is that they just want to use her to catch you, either by piecing together the information she supplies trying to defend you or, if they let her go, by following her. Either way, your play is to back off until this is over. For her sake."

"That's probably good advice, Rich. But it sucks and I won't do it. I'm going to try getting her back. Help me if you can, but I'm going after her."

"I knew you'd say that, but had to try. Sure, I'll help you. Got a plan of what you're going to do?"

"There's not a lot I can do, short of marching into the federal building with a ransom note and a bomb."

"You're kidding, right? About the bomb?"

"Just barely. Actually, I'm thinking that there's a secretary named Charlotte who might be willing to monitor activities around Casey's office, if I can still get to her. I'd like to find out what Dillon's security men are doing, then pick them off one at a time, get a little information from each of them."

"Not a bad idea. Where will you be staying?"

Jamison's warning lights popped on. A face nearby matched one of those in his brain's data banks. It had taken a couple of seconds to make the match, and now the face was gone. Where was he?

"I've got to go, Rich. Remember the hotel where you and Elaine stayed during New Year's Eve, three or four years ago? I'll be there if they have room, using the name . . . using your cat's name."

"Okay, I'll call you at eleven o'clock, tonight. Be there, damn it, or I'll assume you're dead and take over responsibility for Melissa."

"Right. Good thinking. Thanks."

*   *   *   *   *

SAC Sackett was talking out loud, just as he'd done through lunch and dinner, telling himself that it was way past time to figure out what was really going on.

"Okay," he said, "one more time through these personnel files. First the dead agent from Quantico, then his ugly partner, Pate. What is it? What's wrong with this dead guy's service record. Something at the most basic level, where simple things can be so elusive. Once more now. Slow down, Sackett. Concentrate."

The agent's file was not impressive, and Sackett was hardpressed to see any reason why headquarters had been reluctant to release it. But they'd kept it locked down until he'd shown up personally and shoved his demands down a clerk's throat. He'd been plenty pissed by that time and his anger had sent all but one of them scurrying for cover. The slow mover had finally gotten him the file he wanted.

It contained all of the information he expected: the background checks, the grade increases, a couple of "aw shit" letters offset by several "atta boys." Eight years in the Bureau and all of them at Quantico. It was weird that he'd been held there after his sixteen weeks of New Agents Training, all of his other field assignments being TDY, temporary. In Sackett's twenty-six years he'd never seen anyone permanently assigned, but it was a new F.B.I. these days, and things like that surprised him less and less.

Toward the end of his third pass the snake jumped up and bit him, just the way he had hoped it would. The file contained no mention of case assignments. There wasn't a single arrest or conviction statistic. No case numbers cross-referenced by the indices clerk. Nothing. It was as if the man had served eight years as an F.B.I. agent without ever enforcing a law or investigating a crime. Sackett was shaking his head as he picked up the phone and called the Academy.

"Get me Special Agent Warden."

Sackett waited, thinking about Amos Warden, looking forward to hearing his old friend's voice again, hoping he would learn something from him. They had shared a dorm room during New Agents Class 71-9, then been assigned to WFO together. Five years ago, Warden had been gut-shot during a raid at a biker's clubhouse outside of Houston. He had recovered pretty well and now lived at Quantico, training the SWAT teams that cycled through from the various offices.

His voice boomed out of the phone. "Warden."

"Hey. Jeez, take it easy on my ears."

"Bill! How the hell you doing?"

"I'm good. You?"

"Me? Damn, I'm exhausted from this hard work down here."

Sackett leaned back in his chair. "Sure, Amos. Don't forget I spent some time at Quantico, too. I've got a pretty good idea how hard you're working. Were you in the bar?"

Warden didn't let up on the volume. "No. Absolutely not. Truth is, there's a bunch of National Academy guys up there tonight, so I passed. Even this early in the evening, there's too much tension up there for a guy like me to have any fun."

"Hasn't changed much, has it?"

"Never will. Those cops think they know all there is about police work. Our boys, of course, are on home turf and more than a little smug about their advanced degrees and higher salaries. And after all, they're F.B.I. agents. Mixing those two groups in a small barroom with discounted booze is just a bad idea. Always has been."

"You're right."

"Of course I'm right."

Sackett leaned toward his desk, turned the file sideways so he could read the agent's complete name off the tab. "Look, Amos, I've got a dead agent here—"

"Yeah, I know. I was briefed right after it happened. Hell of a tragedy. But at least there isn't any family, no grieving widow."

"You knew him?"

"Hell, yes, I knew him. Trained him. A good trooper, too. Not as good as his partner, Pate, but still a great agent. Skillful, intelligent, resourceful—"

"And dead."

"And dead. That's right."

"What was his job at Quantico? Was he a member of the Hostage Rescue Team?"

Warden laughed, way too loud for a guy in his line of work. "No way. He was much too independent for H.R.T. Too individual in the way he worked. Not a team player at all. He didn't even like having Pate as a partner until they got to be friends."

"So what did he do?"

There was a little silence on the line, an unusual element when talking with Warden. "Sorry, Bill. Can't tell you."

"Don't bullshit me. I'm not in the mood."

"Then get in the mood. Or go ask your question someplace else, 'cause I can't help you. By now you probably know those guys were working under a Group I status. After the shooting, security clamped down even harder. I can't tell you more than that."

"Who directed the increased security? At least tell me that. I'll go to him with my questions."

Warden cleared his throat. "Ah, hell, it was an ADIC, all right? I won't tell you which assistant director, though. Why are you bothering me, anyway? Who put the gerbil up your drainpipe?"

"Who put the gerbil—damn you, Warden! Something illegal is going on around here, and I'm in charge of finding answers."

"Then I'm really sorry. But as I told you, I can't help. And while I'm at it I might as well tell you something else that's going to piss you off."

"Which is?"

"The other agents involved in Corley's arrest have been prohibited from talking to you. Or anyone else."

"They *what*? They damn well better talk to me! I'll have their credentials if they don't. Hell, I'll prosecute them for obstruction of a criminal investigation. I don't give a damn if they are agents!"

Warden chuckled, as though someone had told a dirty joke in mixed company. "I know you would if you could, Bill. But the simple truth is, you can't. The orders came down from above. Top floor. My boss, their boss . . . your boss. You won't override them. Besides, the espionage charges against Peter Jamison are being dropped, so there's no investigation for the agents to obstruct. There will be no arraignment of the Corley woman, and no prosecution of either of them. You'll probably get word in the morning."

"Damn you, Warden. How come you know so much?"

"Come on, Bill, don't act high and mighty with me."

"What?"

"You've played along before, you've done your share. Don't pretend you haven't, at least not with me. You went with me on my first time, remember? What's it been, twenty years? Twenty-five?"

"Hey, I didn't know it was wrong at the time."

"Liar."

Sackett squirmed in his seat, checked to make sure he was on his private line. "Warden, why are you doing this?"

"I'm trying to save your life, that's why. Don't make me destroy you. You know too much to let you roll over."

There was a crack, then the phone went dead. Sackett sat there for a long time, confused and a little worried. Finally, his frustration drove his fingers back to the phone. He called Blevins's home number, left a message, then paged him.

* * * * *

Blevins got the page as he rolled down his own street, heading home for the first time since sending Robert Davidson to pick up Melissa, and getting him killed. Had that only been last night? It seemed like a week ago. Maybe more.

He waited until he got inside the house to call. "This is Blevins. Let me talk to Sackett."

There was perfect silence on the line. Blevins reminded himself of the large spool recorder that turned slowly in a back room, taping every word of incoming calls. Its presence had never bothered him, but he never forgot it either.

Sackett sounded like he already had a head of steam going when he took the call. "Thanks for calling back, Blevins. Look, I'm going to be working a lot this evening, going over your administrative inquiry, Jamison's espionage case and hell, just about everything that revolves around them. I think you and I should talk. How soon can you be here?"

Blevins had spent most of the afternoon sneaking in and out of Headquarters. He knew the case against Jamison was being closed and was glad to hear it, even though he knew it wouldn't be the end of Jamison's problems. It might even make things worse for him, if it caused Jamison to drop his guard.

"I'm an hour away. Soon enough?"

"Get here earlier if you can. Expect it to be a long night."

Blevins hung up and headed for a quick shower and a change of clothes, thinking about what he'd found out today, and wondering how much of it Sackett already knew.

He had called in every favor he was owed by anyone who might be helpful, and had learned that at least one contract was out on Jamison. But he didn't know any of the details. Jamison was still alive, though, or at least he had been a few hours ago. The agent who'd killed Davidson had returned to Quantico. And Melissa was doing all right at the Federal Detention Center. Things could be a lot worse.

After dressing, he picked up his nine-millimeter pistol, released the magazine and snapped the action open, sent an unspent round somersaulting onto the bed. He checked the breech, counted the rounds in the magazine, then slipped it into the handle. He pulled back on the slide and let it slam forward, seating a new round. Then he flipped the decocking lever, dumped the magazine, and topped it off. This was the procedure he had established back in the war and it never varied. Whenever the weapon had been out of his sight he would empty, check, and reload it before holstering. With all the other uncertainties in the world, he wanted no doubts about the readiness of his personal firepower.

* * * * *

The District Drug Store, near the corner of Fourteenth and K streets, had always worked out well for Kane. The copier was in a back corner, out of easy view. But it was still a public copier, muddling the usefulness of any clues from paper type or toner analysis if the copies were ever discovered and tied to the crime.

Kane rolled in his quarters and copied all of the material for John Butler. He made two sets, just in case Butler somehow failed and another man had to be assigned. He doubted it could happen, but it was a possibility. He was not going to underestimate Peter Jamison a second time, wasn't going to look as foolish as the men who'd tried to shoot Jamison after his meeting with Senator Drummond.

He wore his driving gloves as he bought a large envelope and tape. Then he drove to Ronald Reagan Washington Airport and went directly to Delta ticketing. He found the bench they'd used before, unoccupied as usual in this little stretch of hallway. There was no long view to this place, so there was no way to set up surveillance from a safe distance away. Someone would have to be close to see him, and that made it a good drop zone.

Kane checked the envelope, held in the center of his briefcase by a wad of putty. He slipped a gloved hand under it, then pushed it up under the bench and stuck it to the bottom.

Now to signal that the drop had been filled. Kane headed down the main corridor and followed the crowd to a small incline in the hall. As he started up the grade he slipped his hand into his pocket and squeezed a slick of petroleum jelly out of a tube and onto the tips of his fingers. He glided the palm of his hand along the rail until he reached the designated spot, directly under the overhead sign. At that point he curled his greasy fingertips around to the bottom of the aluminum handrail and lubricated a foot of it with a thin streak of gel.

* * * * *

Butler's plane had arrived at eighteen minutes after eight and he'd been the first passenger off. It was a convenience of first class that there were usually seats available for last-minute ticketing. The short flight to Albuquerque in his own helicopter had made the schedule easy to keep.

The pressing crowds of the airport reminded him of why he lived where he did, and how he did. Almost everyone coming toward him stared at his face. Some turned away when he looked at them. Others couldn't seem to do it, although it looked like they were trying hard. His scars and ugliness made him special and he liked the feeling. Some of those same people bumped into him and stepped rudely in front of him, but he didn't like that. Their assaults made his fingers twitch. But he was a professional, and could control himself. He walked through the terminal, looking for the ramp he'd used once before, a little uneasy at the idea of using the same drop zone twice.

Butler shifted the shoulder strap of his canvas carry-on bag as he headed up the incline. The bag was his only luggage and contained everything he might need. He was quirky about firearms, and condemned them as noisy, sloppy devices that were laden with evidence, used by amateurs who couldn't differentiate between a killing and an assassination. His weapons were no less deadly, but silent. Perfectly legal to carry onboard a commercial aircraft, too.

He headed up the ramp, sliding his fingers along the bottom of the handrail for the entire length, not trusting in anyone's accuracy but his own. His fingers hit the slick of gel right where it should be, a greasy skid of goo. At one time in his life he would have looked around suddenly, or at least wanted to look around, to see who might have left this signal, or to see if anyone had noticed him getting it. But that curiosity had been cut away years ago, thrown into the scrap heap of weak parts that didn't fit his profession.

He went to the bench near Delta ticketing and recovered the envelope, rented a car, and was out of the airport in fifteen minutes.

11

Jamison hated leaving the hunt, and resented every step to One Washington Circle, a wonderfully private hotel with lots of comforts he wouldn't use. He couldn't wait to talk to Blevins and find out what he'd learned, then get back on the street. A few more minutes, then he could get going again. Blevins was a man of accuracy, and would call at eleven o'clock.

He stretched out on the hotel bed, a short reach from the phone. He closed his eyes and tried to rest, tried to make good use of the downtime. But his mind wouldn't relax. There were too many unsolvable questions washing around in it, too much that would not compute until his brain's program was upgraded. He hoped Blevins would provide the information he needed to solve the tough question: how to get Melissa back?

He'd called Senator Drummond after his street fight, hoping for help in identifying the giant. Drummond was furious with him for putting himself at risk, demanded that he come in immediately and take advantage of the protection his office could provide. He wanted Jamison alive, at least long enough to testify at a senate hearing. Jamison had tried to explain that it was impossible. He couldn't do that now. When he was sure Melissa was safe, maybe. They might even come in together. But not one second before he had her back in his arms and away from danger. He could still hear her begging for help the last time she'd counted on him, her tortured plea was still ringing in his ears. He had no intention of spending the rest of his life with another failure like that.

They had gone down the coast together, hidden themselves away on a golden fall weekend. They'd hoped to work out the hurt they'd caused each other, to forget the painful things they'd done to their relationship. They spent two days longer than planned because it had been a wonderful time, a healing time. He had never wanted to leave. Until the attack.

It happened on their last night, a beautiful evening that was cold enough for a jacket but warm enough for bare feet. A perfect night for an easy stroll along the Delaware beach. There had been no reason to suspect the men who had walked up to them, although in hundreds and hundreds of shameful replays, Jamison *had* suspected them, had not allowed himself to be so careless. He had seen the men coming and watched them carefully, ready. After all, he was bigger, stronger, and better trained. They were just a couple of local toughs out for a thrill. When they'd made their move, he'd made them regret it.

But the reality was different, and time stubbornly refused to rewrite it.

The men had come up while he and Melissa were walking slowly, sharing secrets and good feelings on the isolated beach just south of the Cape Lewes ferry. The men were easy and friendly in their approach, said something nice and polite, then hosed Jamison's face with pepper spray. Instantly, his eyes turned to flames and his face heated up.

Through the itching and burning he heard Melissa scream, "Peter, help, please help!" It was a terrifying, shrieking sentence that ended in a muffled garble. Jamison went right to attack, hastily dragged the crazy man out of his dark cell and threw him into action, allowed him to burst out blindly with everything he had, even as Jamison felt the knife slip in-between the ribs of his lower back. Then one of the men clubbed the side of his head and sent him toward the sand.

But the hand that delivered the blow was too slow. The crazy man caught his attacker's hand and wrenched it around, snapped it back and broke it at the wrist. He twisted the limp thing a few times, listening to the man scream and liking the sound of it. But still he couldn't see, and had no idea where Melissa was anymore.

He grabbed the man's forearm with his other hand, then yanked the dangling hand back toward the man's body. His attacker's horrible scream almost deafened him with its pitiful plea for mercy. "Please, mister, don't! I'm sorry!"

But the crazy man wasn't finished. Even without eyes, Jamison's crazy man could feel the man dropping. He followed the man's arm to the ground, then stomped down with his foot, braced himself against the man's body and gave the arm a violent twist, rotated it until the shoulder separated and the arm rolled out of the socket. Then he cranked it again while the man twitched around, crying and screaming and swearing. The floppy appendage led Jamison to the man's neck, which he grabbed and broke with a Ranger's twist.

No more than thirty seconds could have passed. Not much time, but at least ten seconds longer than it should have taken. Ten extra seconds that might have cost Melissa her life. Where was she? Calm down. Stop. Listen. Where?

There! He heard a scream over the dunes, or at least in that direction—away from the sound of the breakers. It was high-pitched and terrified like Jamison was expecting to hear. But it wasn't Melissa. It had to be the second man. He must have pulled Melissa away, and now, God bless her, she was hurting him.

He started running, but there weren't any more noises. He ran blindly all over the beach, blocking the pain of the wound in his back. He ran and fell and ran and fell. More time passed. How long had it been? Ten minutes? Twelve, maybe? He stopped and listened, then ran some more, falling and bleeding, then running—the crazy man loose the whole time and wanting a victim. Wanting to get his hands on the son of a bitch who'd taken her.

Finally, he heard crying, and this time he knew it was Melissa. It was the only time he would ever hear her cry. He followed the sound and worked his way to her, forced his burning eyes open and sat down to hold her, the crazy man having no idea what to do now but sticking around just in case he got his turn on the animal who had done this.

Her jeans and panties had been stripped off. Her blouse had been ripped like a rag. She was lying in the sand, naked except for her bra, which was unsnapped and loose up against her neck. Her feet were spread apart but her knees were together and flopped over to one side. Her left arm covered her eyes and her head was turned away from him. She was sobbing.

He wanted to pick her up, wanted to carry her off and call an ambulance. Wanted to get the police looking for her assailant. Waited for some sign that she was ready.

She stifled her crying, seemed to lock away her suffering and force herself into a conversational voice.

"Peter," she said as she sat up and reached her left hand for the sandy panties, her right arm across her naked breasts, "I . . I want to forget this. Okay? Will you help me. Please? Don't call the police. I don't want to relive this just so the cops can get their jollies. I feel so dirty already."

He closed his eyes and bit his lip, hating that the bastard would get away with what he'd done. "Shouldn't you see a doctor?"

She shuddered. "I can't. The thought of another strange man inside of me—"

"I understand," he said quickly, then held out her jeans and looked away. He didn't understand, not really. But he wanted to stop her because he couldn't bear to hear any more. He knew she was strong enough to live with this. He'd watched her carry her father's suicide for years without the slightest stumble, knew she had an enormous capacity for suffering. He would respect her wishes and keep her secret, understanding that some people preferred to suffer quietly, and alone. He would learn to do the same.

They walked back to their hotel. She took the shower she wanted, insisting that they never talk about this again. Forget it had ever happened.

But he had never forgotten. He heard her begging for help all the time, had never forgiven himself for letting the man take her. He should have been ready for the attack. He should have been quicker to kill his attacker, and therefore, quicker to get to Melissa. Why had he taken so long, wasted those ten extra seconds and given her rapist the extra time he needed to drag her away? Was it fear? Had it entered his mind, even for a second, that he might get hurt helping her, that he'd been less anxious to get to her than he pretended? He loathed thinking about it, preferring to believe that it wasn't possible. But he'd wasted ten precious seconds, and he'd spent the last two years trying to figure out why.

He despised himself for the possibility, regardless of how remote, that fear might have held him back or slowed him down. He was conscious of fear all the time now, and would never again give it a toehold on his actions. It was why he'd fought so hard for his coworkers' futures. It was the reason he would do anything, and kill anyone, to get Melissa back. He was never going to shame himself again. And this motivation, he knew, was selfishness. He hadn't been out to save his coworkers' jobs. Not really. Even today, right now, he was only trying to preserve himself, wasn't really trying to save Melissa. Everything he did was selfish, because every action created a personal record, for better or worse, which he would later scrutinize harshly. He could not live a life that might shame him later.

He stared at the ceiling of the hotel room, remembering Vietnam and his murderous run through the jungle. But he couldn't take pride in what he'd done there, either. A thousand times he'd looked back and tried to convince himself that he'd been completely unselfish, that it was loyalty to his squad that had sent him dashing into the deadly foliage. He tried to believe it was the one pure act of his life. But he knew he couldn't take credit for what he'd done, so there was no way to take pride in it. The crazy man had saved those men. Jamison had just gone along for the ride, and hadn't even done it willingly.

Jamison sat up on the bed and rubbed the sides of his head, struggled to think about something else. He began to wonder if his secretary, Charlotte, would actually be able to help him. He'd met her earlier at a small coffee shop. She told him how jumpy everyone at Dillon was, how Jamison's name was being spoken with the same hushed worry as Bronovich's. She said she would try to help him, even though he made it clear he would not be able to repay her. At least not in the way she wanted. She liked him, she had said right away, before they'd really even started talking. Liked him a lot and understood him pretty well. She wasn't really that much younger than him, and she hoped he would learn to like her the same way. For that she would help him, even though he had told her how much he loved Melissa.

The phone rang and he caught it instantly. "Yes?"

"Mr. Caligo?"

Jamison shook his head, felt himself blush. It was a stupid cat's name, assigned to the poor beast before Blevins's sons were old enough to say calico. "Yeah. How you doing, Rich?"

"Good, buddy. You?"

"Okay. Confused. But alive and kicking. Small favors, you know. Where the hell are you, anyway, a bomb shelter?"

"Almost. I'm down in the F.B.I. garage, calling from my car phone. I've been upstairs with SAC Sackett for the last few hours. He paged me earlier and called me in."

"Did you ask him about Melissa?"

"More than that. I demanded that he tell me about Melissa."

"And?"

"Nothing new. She's still under the marshal's custody, doing okay."

"I guess I'm supposed to interpret that as good news."

"I would. Anyway, Sackett and I have been working out our differences, getting closer to trusting each other. He had a question he wanted me to ask you, so that's why I'm in the garage. Obviously I didn't want to call on his phone."

Jamison moved to the table in front of the sliding glass doors. He looked out and saw his reflection in the glass, then saw the statue of George Washington on horseback in the traffic circle beyond. There was nothing else in the darkness. He picked up a pen, pulled out a pad, and got ready to write. "What's the question?"

"It's off the wall."

"Perfect. It'll fit right in with the rest of my day."

"That's true enough."

"What's he want?"

"Ready for this? He wants to talk to you."

Jamison flipped the pen in the air, watched it pinwheel to the floor. "Oh, sure. That sounds like fun. Let's see, a little polite conversation, a few minutes of kid and giggle, and then, oh, yeah . . . my arrest! Sorry, Rich. No can do."

"Kind of thought you'd say that."

"I'm kind of surprised you'd even ask."

"It does sound stupid, doesn't it? The entire F.B.I. is looking to take your ass down and I want to bring the boss by for a visit."

"I'm glad you didn't miss the irony. It was the best part."

"No. Here's the best part. I think it's a good idea."

"You do? Well, I don't. And since it's my life that'll slide down the drain, I'll pass. That is, if you don't mind."

"I don't mind. But Sackett is starting to have some doubts about what's happening around here. He's a smart guy, Peter, and this case looks funky to him. He took me off administrative leave to help him sort through it. Things aren't adding up in his book and he's not accepting anything as truth that he doesn't check out himself."

"What will keep him from trying to arrest me? And how will this help me find Melissa?"

"He's promised to talk only. If he tries to arrest you, I'll restrain him myself."

"If he tries to arrest me, Rich, I'll stop him before you ever get the chance."

"Fair enough. Can we come by?"

Jamison kept staring at George Washington on horseback, something in the statue's beleaguered look of determination making him realize how far he really was from Melissa.

"I don't like this, Rich."

"I know. But if you can convince him you're clean, that's a big step. He'll probably assume Melissa's clean, too. Gets you a lot closer to getting her back."

"Think so?"

"Yes."

Jamison looked around the hotel room, trying to size it up for an interview, or a fight.

"Okay. I'm trusting your judgment here. Room 318. Warn him that he might get hurt."

"I will. Good-bye."

* * * * *

John Butler had hidden in the shadows of the F.B.I. garage. Although he'd listened hard, he hadn't heard anything clearly. But he was willing to bet that Blevins was talking to Peter Jamison, or making plans that involved Jamison. The short biography that Kane had provided on Blevins had identified him as Jamison's best friend. Kane had even suggested that Blevins might lead Butler to his victim. It looked as if Kane might be right, as usual.

He kept silent, watching as Blevins hung up and tossed the phone back into his car. All of a sudden Blevins looked edgy, like he'd just realized his senses had missed something lethal in the dark recesses of the underground garage. Blevins slid into the shadows, too, and started moving among the concrete columns. Butler watched him pull out his pistol and probe around the parked cars, making hilarious lunges and quick steps.

Butler had to work like hell to keep from laughing. This was just too damn funny. He always wanted to laugh when he held the trump card. And he held it now, with that stupid F.B.I. agent bumping around in the dark, afraid of something he couldn't see and hadn't heard.

And why? Because Special Agent Blevins could *feel* Butler's presence, that's why. He felt it pushing against his chest like the bony finger of Satan. Felt the spiritual presence and knew it could kill him whenever it wanted.

But it wouldn't. At least not now. Agent Blevins had a mission first. He needed to take Butler to Jamison. Then, maybe he would kill him.

"Go on now, Blevins," he whispered in the dark as Blevins started to leave. "Go to the elevator with your gun drawn. Stand there in the light like an easy target as you wait for the doors to close and take you out of here. Point your weapon into these shadows if it makes you feel better. I won't hurt you now. You'll live through this engagement. But, my friend, I make no promises about next time."

The elevator doors closed and Blevins was gone. Butler bent down over the dead guard who'd failed to protect the garage. He cut off his left ear, put it in a plastic bag, and admired it. A nice addition to his collection.

* * * * *

Thirty-six minutes after Blevins's call, Jamison heard the stairwell door shut differently than ever before. Alarming, because it hadn't slammed like a dozen other times tonight. This time it closed quietly with a rub and a click, barely loud enough to hear, but enough noise to switch on his instincts and send him flying.

He launched out of bed, grabbed his Beretta, proned out on the floor, and listened carefully to the steps in the hall. Two pairs, light. The hotel walls were hiding nothing. Jamison had his Beretta up, the hammer back, his kill zone selected. He was ready to light this place up and cut down anyone who smashed open his door.

There was a gentle knock.

"Who is it?"

He was far enough back in the room. Any shots through the door would probably not hit him.

"It's me," said a loud whisper. "Rich. I've got Sackett."

Jamison rose and crept slowly, noiselessly, toward the door. He wrapped his left hand silently around the doorknob, then flung it open, flashed through the doorway and stuck his Beretta right into Sackett's face.

"Don't move a muscle."

Sackett's eyes crossed as they followed the muzzle to the tip of his nose. "You kidding? You think I'm stupid?"

"You are if you think you're going to breeze in here with a weapon."

Sackett was lifting his arms in slow-motion surrender. "I left it in the car. Blevins made me."

Blevins raised his hands, too, just about halfway. "That's the truth, Peter. He's unarmed. I searched him before we came up."

Jamison didn't say anything as he stepped back, his pistol still trained on Sackett as the two F.B.I. agents entered the room. Blevins closed the door and the three of them stood there as if none of them knew what to do next. There was a small table by the sliding glass doors, and Jamison motioned Sackett to sit.

"Can I put my hands down?"

"As long as I can see them. In the air or on the table. Your choice. Nowhere else."

"Thank you."

Jamison leaned against the dresser, his pistol low but both hands holding it, ready to do some quick combat shooting if Sackett came up with a weapon.

"Let's get on with it. What do you want?"

Sackett eased into a chair and made a dry smile. "I just want to ask you a few questions, Mr. Jamison."

"About?"

Sackett chuckled, as though it was a private matter he was embarrassed to reveal. "I've got a problem."

"Makes two of us."

"It does, doesn't it?"

Blevins wiggled uncomfortably and glanced over at Jamison's pistol.

"Peter, Mr. Sackett would like to know what you discovered in your research of the Wombat."

Jamison shot a look at Blevins to show he didn't like the question. Even if he decided to answer it, how much should he tell? Sure, he could let this guy into his room and make nice with him. But they—the government—had Melissa, and Sackett was one of them. Blevins, too, although it was Sackett's turn under Jamison's microscope.

He decided to give up a little information. Tell Sackett some of what he wanted to know and see if that got him closer to Melissa. Tell a little about his research, the meeting with Senator Drummond, the shots at his car, and the giant on the sidewalk. Then ask about the agents who'd arrested Melissa, and where was she now?

It seemed like a fair trade and he started talking, cautiously. Turning over his part of the deal. Sackett interrupted with questions, always asking Jamison to clarify a little more than he wanted. As he finished, Sackett stood up.

"Where is your evidence, Jamison?"

Jamison pushed himself away from the dresser, was fully erect at least a second before Sackett.

"Where's Melissa?"

"She's safe."

"I bet. So is my evidence."

"I'll need to see it."

"Tough. Get it from Senator Drummond."

"Oh, that's helpful."

"Listen, Rich says I should trust you, Sackett, so I'm trying. But right now you're just a big question mark in my book. You're responsible for men arresting Melissa, and coming after me. I'm not giving you any more advantages."

Sackett dug the pads of his fingertips into his eyes, lowered himself back into his chair, and glanced over at Blevins.

"Drummond's a hothead, Mr. Jamison. If he thinks something criminal's going on, he'll suspect everyone and tear this city apart. He won't even trust the F.B.I., so I doubt he'll give me copies of your data."

"Then I guess you're out of luck."

"Just wait a minute, not so fast. How about if I had Melissa brought over here? Would that change your mind, help you become more cooperative?"

Jamison felt his glare soften and knew he'd already sent his answer. Could it possibly be that easy to get her back? He looked at Blevins.

"What do you think?"

"It's worth a try. I'll go get her myself. I can have her back here in an hour."

"I won't be here. Sackett knows I'm here, so I have to leave after he does."

"I think you can trust him."

"It's not your life if you're wrong. It's mine. And Melissa's. Besides, what's to keep him from having agents pick us up right after he gets what he wants."

Sackett nodded, as if it was a logical concern and easily understood.

"I'll tell you what, Jamison. How about if I let Blevins send some men up here, men he trusts completely, operating strictly under his orders to keep you and her safe? Would that do it? Remember, you have to think about Melissa, too. How would you feel if she got hurt while you two were on the run?"

"We can take care of ourselves."

"Maybe. But I'll need you to testify. I need you both alive."

Jamison turned to Blevins. "Rich, call the odds. Good or bad?"

Blevins stood up and stretched, then spoke easily.

"I've told you before, Peter. Agents build up loyalties to other agents. I've sure got my share of brothers who are loyal to me. You can trust them as much as you can trust me. I'm sure. Good odds."

Melissa. Just an hour away. This whole ugly thing could be over tonight. Blevins could give Sackett the data, and he and Melissa would slip off someplace and start over, if she would allow it.

Or maybe this was a trap. What was the additional risk? His life? Hell, Melissa's neck was already on the block, so this was a chance worth taking.

"Okay, Sackett, the data for Melissa. I'll give it up after Blevins brings her here."

Sackett spun toward Blevins and took command. "Pick any six agents you trust, any office close by. Use my authority to get them here on the double. Use our planes if you need them. I want that information right away." He turned back to Jamison. "Does anyone else know you're here?"

"No."

"Are you sure? Because I'm about to turn the heat up, maybe scald a few people in high places. You're going to be right in the thick of it, so I'll ask you again, are you sure no one else knows you're here? Sure you don't want us to move you?"

"I'm sure. As long as you didn't tell anyone and weren't followed."

Sackett ignored him and didn't answer. He kept staring at Jamison as if looking for doubt to creep across his face.

"All right, then. Blevins, how long before your men get here?"

Blevins was just hanging up the phone. "Fifty minutes."

Sackett smiled. "There you have it, Mr. Jamison. Fifty minutes. Try to stay alive until then."

"I wish you wouldn't say it like that."

Sackett laughed, touched him on the arm, then walked out. Blevins lagged behind and whispered to Jamison, "My guys will identify themselves by asking if you ordered champagne."

"Thanks."

Jamison followed as far as the elevators, then watched the doors shut before heading back to his room. He closed and locked the door, then headed to the bathroom. He wanted to clean up before Melissa came to him.

12

John Butler watched the two agents go into Jamison's room, then spent two hours resting his butt on the metal steps of the stairwell. He passed the time admiring the smudge he'd made on the small window of the stairwell door, staring at its intricacies, looking for some kind of pattern in his work. When he heard the three men step into the hall, he stood up, took three steps to the door, and wiped a clean spot in the corner of the glass. The agents left, then Jamison walked back to his room and closed the door.

The dirty window had hid Butler well. Even his gloriously scarred face hadn't attracted attention through the dirty smear.

He checked the time, decided to give the agents a few minutes to leave before he struck. Maybe tomorrow he would send Blevins a thank you note for getting him here. Ten minutes passed. More than enough time. If the agents had planned on circling back, they'd have done it by now. He walked out of the stairwell and crept down the hall, worked Jamison's lock with his pick and rake. He cracked the door open but was stopped by the gentle creak of its hinges. He stood absolutely still and listened, ready to fly into the room and start the bleeding.

He heard water running in the bathroom, but heard no other sounds. He slipped into the room, ready, just in case Jamison was still undressing.

He searched the room thoroughly, but didn't find the box of evidence Kane had described. He knew it wouldn't be that easy to earn the bonus money. If this guy was that much of an amateur, Kane would have taken him down himself.

Butler decided to wait before starting the games. If Jamison didn't take too long, he would allow him to come out of the bathroom and get dressed before he killed him. There was no need to do it in the shower, torturing Jamison's naked body to find out where the evidence was hidden, ending up soaked himself. He'd done that before and hated it, slopping around afterward like he'd fallen into a fountain. No, he would let Jamison get some clothes on and give him a chance to cooperate. Then let him die with a little dignity. Maybe earn the same privilege when his turn to die came around.

He removed the magazine from Jamison's pistol and emptied out the cartridges, put them in his bag along with the extra magazines he'd found. Then he stuck Jamison's Beretta back on the dresser, where he'd found it. He was ready.

$$* \quad * \quad * \quad * \quad *$$

Jamison stepped out of the bathroom, naked. He dried quickly, then combed his wet hair straight back, walked over to the bed and dragged the socks and clean underwear out of his gym bag.

He dressed, then checked himself in the mirror, hoping he would look okay for Melissa. The mirror's reflection was shocking. His eyes had become hard, painful-looking discs. Until last Monday, he had still managed to hold onto some of the luster of his youth. But now there was nothing left. None of that innocent glow from when a new bike or peek at a girl's bra would make them shine. Even the small, bright flecks he'd thought would last his whole life were gone, replaced by a dull flatness. He stood there and stared at himself, wondering if it would be possible to find the lights again when this was over.

He was still staring at the mirror when he noticed the small movement of the closet door. It was almost imperceptible, but riveted his attention. He whirled around, grabbing his gun and aiming it in the same motion, knowing that he should have been expecting this, that it had been stupid to trust Sackett.

The door swung open with a bold sweep. Jamison focused on his pistol's front sight, anxious to train it on whoever stepped out of the dark closet.

"Who's there?"

He was stunned to see the face that emerged. He knew it. Understood it. Recognized it immediately, so suddenly it took his breath away. God, it was the ravaged face of his crazy man, fleshed out and scabbed over, no longer a specter of his conscience but a low-order life form standing across the room. Jamison gawked at the face, had always wondered what it would look like, had never expected evil to look this terrible. It sickened him to think that this same creature lived in him, an alien eating his insides, always trying to gnaw its way out.

The face looked like a burned marshmallow, except that it was smiling, all quiet and calm. But threatening as hell. Relaxed, but moving with deadly precision. The jagged mouth spoke without any emotion.

"Mr. Jamison, I'm John Butler."

Butler grinned as he said his name, as though the mere mention of it should intimidate.

"I'm sorry to intrude on you like this, but we have a little business to conduct. You have some papers, I believe. Your copies of the documents you gave Senator Drummond. I've been sent to get them. Will you tell me where they are?"

Jamison was dead-on ready with a head shot, but his finger was stuck in uncertainty. Not that he was afraid to kill, hell no. He had done his share of killing. More than his share. But it had never been like this. Every other time there had been a clear-cut reason for killing. Uniforms, flags, battle lines, or self-defense had identified the enemy, making the decision to kill an automatic one. But this man showed no weapon. He made no overt threat. Was he even a threat? And wasn't he really, in some strange way, family?

Jamison was stuck briefly in this doubt. Then he decided, lined up the sights of his Beretta and squeezed the double action trigger, feeling the smooth movements of the pistol engaging the case-hardened parts that would cause the weapon to fire. He aimed directly at Butler's gnarled head as the butt-ugly thing took a step toward him.

The hammer extended fully, then slammed down with a powerful snap. Jamison steadied his aim, allowed himself no distraction while waiting for the explosion and messy spectacle of bloody tissue spraying across the room.

Click

The simple mechanical sound was terrifying. Butler was only five feet away now, stalled in the Beretta's sights. Jamison threw down his gun and charged, his eyes searching for a gun to muzzle up, or a knife to flash.

Butler fell onto his back, out of range, his feet pointing at Jamison. He scissored his legs around Jamison's shins, one in front and one behind. The foot that snuck behind Jamison jammed into the back of his knee joint and shoved it forward. The leg in front kept him locked in place, unable to move and compensate. He fell hard and landed on the floor next to Butler, who was already on his way up.

Jamison jinked around, trying to get out from under the mountain boot that hovered over him. But in less time than it took to flinch, Butler launched his right foot at Jamison's head, smashing it against the floor and grinding the boot into the flesh above his right cheek. Then Butler kicked him, a full, well-trained blow to the chest. Then one to the stomach, and finally, the groin, each kick harder than the one that preceded it.

Jamison was stunned, but that didn't keep his body from convulsing. His stomach heaved a big wad of bloody juice out of his mouth and onto the carpet. He couldn't see it very well because his right eye had filled with blood. His head whirled from being stomped and crushed. The paralyzing fear had done something to the crazy man, and Jamison felt alone.

He struggled to his knees, his stomach still pitching bloody phlegm balls, his testicles swelling in his clean drawers. He caught a glance of Butler strolling around the room and watched for an opening, knowing he had to find one soon or die, recognizing that he was dealing with a crazy man. He struggled to his feet, protecting his organs with his arms, expecting Butler's mule kicks to knock him down again.

Butler leaned against the dresser and spoke calmly. He sounded almost kind. "Mr. Jamison, please don't attack me again. I cannot continue to be patient unless you cooperate. Do you understand?"

Jamison made it to his feet, briefly celebrating the fact that he and Butler were at eye level again. But his brain had lost its gyro and he had trouble standing. He could feel blood flooding into his ear and down his neck. How bad had he been hurt? Did it matter? He would die if he wasted time thinking about it. He used his left hand to cover his blood-soaked eye, struggled to focus on the blurry image pacing the room.

"The evidence isn't here."

Butler slipped into an eerie, conversational tone. "I know it's not here. Don't take me for a fool because I'm not one. I do, however, tend to run a little short on patience." He moved to Jamison's blind side and disappeared. "Where is it?"

"Who hired you? What are you going to do with the evidence?"

"Come now, Mr. Jamison, are you trying to stall?"

"I'm trying to figure out what's happening. That's not much to ask."

"Does it really make any difference?"

Jamison knew Butler was close, most likely within his striking range. But fear held Jamison back and kept the crazy man from attacking. There was no way to win if he had to guess where Butler was. It would be hard enough if he could see him.

But it was fear, nevertheless, that kept his hands by his side. Jamison recognized it, and hated it. If he lived through this, he would chalk his hesitation up to the crazy man's terror and good judgment when coming face-to-face with himself. Try to live with that excuse.

"Probably doesn't make any difference to you, freak. But it's important to me. So humor me and maybe you'll get what you want."

"I'll get what I want regardless, Mr. Jamison."

"Oh yeah? You going to kill me?"

Butler stepped in front of him, just out of range, and grinned. He seemed to like the idea.

"Yes."

"Then screw you, scab-man. I'm not telling you anything."

Butler disappeared behind him. Then he snuck up on his blind side, patted his back as he passed, made Jamison jump and wish he'd known Butler was coming.

"Oh, Mr. Jamison. So foolish of you. But if that's your wish, I will comply. Ready?"

"Go to hell."

"Maybe later. But right now, here is the way our little story will go. In a few minutes you will be dead. Sad, isn't it? But as unfortunate as that news is, you need to remember that the data I seek will do you absolutely no good afterward. I should mention, however, that it could have done Melissa Corley quite a bit of good, because your cooperation would have allowed her to avoid this same line of questioning."

He cracked his chapped lips into a smile.

Jamison didn't move. He just stared. Not afraid anymore. Angry, though, and getting worse. It was building from his deep guts, from the place he usually locked up the crazy man, and flushing through him like bad medicine. He'd seen Melissa attacked once, had sworn that it would never happen to her again. He had never, ever broken a promise to her. The thought of failing made him straighten up, snapped all of his senses into alignment, focused everything he had on killing Butler. He was sure he could do it. He had no earthly idea how.

Butler sauntered around the room.

"I must admit, Mr. Jamison, that I am a little excited about that prospect. Umm, the idea of having that beautiful woman to myself is very stimulating. As you can imagine, with a face like mine I get very few opportunities to be intimate with beautiful women. I could have quite a pleasant time with her."

He grinned as he rubbed his left hand up and down his crotch.

"You are some piece of work, freak. She hasn't done anything."

"Of course not. But she will be my pleasure unless you give me your research data. I'll give you one last chance. Where is it?"

A film of Melissa suffering at Butler's scarred hands jumped right in front of Jamison's good eye. But strangely, it didn't hurt. Not even a little. And the crazy man—where was he?—didn't even seem to notice. What the film did, though, was splice his hatred of Butler's threat with his love for Melissa, giving him a sharp image of what he had to do.

"Tell me who hired you. I'll give you the data."

"I'm bored with this game, Mr. Jamison, I've already—"

Jamison lurched forward, caused Butler's reflexes to snatch him back.

"Who hired you? Answer me!"

Butler stiffened. His face seemed to jump off his skull as he narrowed his focus on Jamison. Just for a second, his jaw muscles chiseled anger onto his face. But then, just as quickly, he smiled. It was a hideous look on him.

"Kane sent me."

"Jack Kane?"

"How many Kanes do you know? Now, where is your data?"

Jamison started making plans for Kane. He just needed to get rid of this guy first. "I buried it. I'll draw you a map, but you've got to promise not to hurt Melissa."

"Fine. There's no money in it, anyway. A bonus for the data, sure, but nothing for killing her."

Jamison tried not to listen. He didn't want to hear the economic considerations of the killing business.

"There's a pen and some paper on the table by the patio doors. Mind if I go over there?"

Butler slid along the dresser until he was close to the table, never looking away from Jamison and never giving him an opening. Once there, he motioned Jamison over.

Jamison was pretty well stabilized now, his mind had reset the controls. His balance was returning and his movements were more fluid. He knew Butler was studying him as he hobbled to the table, then leaned over and began to write. Butler stayed too far away to attack.

"It's buried, like I said. By the boathouse on the west side of the Key Bridge. The Georgetown side of the river. As you go down this little private road, look left, toward the bridge."

Butler moved a step closer. Jamison could see Butler's reflection in the patio doors, set off against the dark statue of George Washington riding his horse through the chilly night. Butler's face looked intent, as though he were trying to catch all of the details Jamison was giving, certain that a buried object would be difficult to find, even with wonderful directions. His eyes strained at the paper from a distance.

Jamison watched his reflection in the glass, but kept his body turned so that Butler couldn't see him. Twice Butler checked the glass, too, but Jamison was fast enough to get his eyes back to the paper in time.

He slid his fingers along the plastic pen until his thumb corked the end of it. He pointed his left hand at the map while he checked their reflections once more. This was as close as Butler would get, but it wasn't close enough. There was more than an arm's length separating them and it was clear that Butler's interest had not dissolved his caution. Butler kept his hands open, like a wrestler.

"Now here," Jamison continued, "you'll have to watch very carefully or you'll miss the marker. There is a fallen tree right about here. . . ."

Butler leaned a little closer. Only two inches, maybe three. But close enough to try.

Jamison exploded, pivoted his left foot around, then rotated his body like a discus thrower. His right arm, the last thing to take flight, absorbed all of the speed and momentum, racing around in a wide arc toward Butler's head.

But Butler was quick and ready. He struck Jamison twice in his bad eye and once across the throat. Then he casually stepped back, heading out of Jamison's range with mild disappointment on his face.

Jamison ignored the pain, although his windpipe felt like it had been crushed and his bad eye throbbed from the pounding. He boxed away the hurt, would not give into it. His arm was still in flight. He still had his good eye. He still had a chance.

Butler had taken one step back, and began to take a second. But then he jerked to a stop. The bed was blocking his retreat. Suddenly, Butler's face lit up with an interesting look. Maybe it was fear. He raised his hands again.

Jamison's right arm had picked up incredible speed, his hand holding the pen like a knife, flying it sideways through the air. He grimaced as the last second ticked off, no variables left to either of them in the piece of time that remained. The pen would hit its mark, and there was nothing to do now but watch.

Butler stopped moving. He just stopped and waited for impact, must have recognized destiny when he saw it coming. He looked queerly at Jamison and relaxed his hands. All of it in a tenth of a second. So quick, yet plenty of time to see it, and to understand. Surrender. It was almost as if Butler wanted to do it

The point of the pen struck Butler on the left side of his neck, almost directly below the ear. It slid through tissue and muscle and slurped its way into Butler's skull with much more ease than Jamison had expected. The exposed meat of his palm screamed as he jammed the pen into the lower part of Butler's head, the pressure driving through the soft skin of his hand. But he kept pushing, giving his arm all the gas he had.

Butler cried out, a mixture of gurgling air and bloody blockage. Almost as if they were involuntary actions, he reached for Jamison's throat with his right hand while his left grabbed the wrist that drove the punishing instrument. He smiled as Jamison watched the point of the pen come out the other side of his neck.

Jamison tripped Butler with his feet, then pushed the short end of the pen toward the carpet, using it as a tiny lever to crank Butler's head around to the floor. He let go, jumped on Butler's back and reached for his chin. He yanked Butler's ugly head backward until his neck reached full extension, so far back that he could see Butler's eyes looking up and watching him, far enough to keep Butler's skull from catching on his Atlas vertebrae. Then he snapped the head sideways with every bit of strength God had ever given him. The sickening pop, coupled with a fleshy, tearing sound, made Jamison's wrenching stomach puke more of the bloody juice, which landed on Butler's back. It was the first time he'd ever gotten sick killing. Was this a good sign? He savored the taste of the vomit, realizing he'd never killed without the crazy man before. He was disgusted by what he'd done; would do it all over again to save Melissa.

He jumped up onto the bed and stayed there a minute, ventilating. Then he started moving, gaining speed with each action. He searched Butler's pockets for a weapon or identification, but found nothing. He stumbled toward the closet and snatched the bag he'd seen lying on the floor. It contained a large assortment of small, peculiar items: a man's ear in a plastic bag, two full magazines for his Beretta, an empty magazine, and a bunch of loose, nine-millimeter rounds that Jamison knew were his own. He scooped them up, lifted his pistol from the floor, and reloaded it.

Should he wait for Melissa? Hell, was she even coming? Had Sackett told Kane where Butler could find him? Why had he stepped into this trap, and how could he avoid the next one?

He thought it all through quickly, knowing from the very start that he couldn't stay here and wait. If Sackett actually did let Blevins bring Melissa here, Blevins would read the scene and get her away. He would trust his friend to do that.

He washed his own blood off his face, and Butler's blood off his hand. Then he slipped into the hallway and left, went down the stairwell and out into the late night. Hunting.

13

Rich Blevins sweated the entire twenty-eight minutes it took to drop Sackett off then race to the Federal Detention Center, hauling ass down deserted streets in the middle of the night, wanting to get back to Jamison's hotel as soon as possible. He squealed into the parking lot and skidded into a space marked RESERVED FOR LAW ENFORCEMENT PERSONNEL TRANSPORTING PRISONERS, then ran into the three story building through the prisoner's entrance.

Once inside, he was slowed to a frustrating pace by several sets of security doors, then forced to stand around and wait for an escort to take his weapon and lead him to the transfer pen. He was completely out of patience by the time a buzzer opened the last two sets of doors that separated him from the processing officers.

Blevins charged to the counter and pounded on the bulletproof glass, made enough racket to wake up the prisoners in the first cell block. Two uniformed guards were isolated behind the counter. They jumped out of their seats and one of them dumped coffee on the broad beam of his belly. He cussed as he flicked the hot brown liquid from his fingers, but stopped the instant he saw Blevins's face.

Blevins couldn't stop glaring at them, didn't find anything they did funny. He just wanted to get Melissa and take her out of here. These boys had already wasted forty or fifty seconds of his time.

"I'm Special Agent Blevins, F.B.I., here to pick up a prisoner." He stuck his credentials against the inch-thick glass, steadied them while the other guard wrote down his number. The guard finished writing and stepped away, made room for the heavier guard to saunter over. The coffee was soaking into his T-shirt, wicking out from the original spill and nearly covering his belly. "Okay, Special Agent Blevins. I guess I can help you with that. Where's your paperwork?"

"It's being processed. You'll have it within an hour."

The guard did a slow roll of his head, looked at his partner as if in love, then gave Blevins a stupid grin.

"Well, don't that beat all, Sam. I'll be damned if it ain't another one of them hotshot agents come to get one of our guests without the proper paperwork."

He leaned over, dug his right elbow on the counter, and used that hand to support his head. Hiding behind the glass.

"I suppose you know, Special Agent Blevins, that we can't just go around handing out prisoners to every agent who asks for one. They ain't free, you know."

He smiled as he looked at Sam for congratulations.

"So I'm afraid you'll need to run on along, Mr. Blevins. Go back to your office and get the proper forms filled out. Then, shoot, I'll be more'n happy to give you your prisoner." He stepped back and smiled big, folded his arms across his chest.

Blevins knew the guard was right. So he'd kept quiet as long as he could and let the man play his silly game. But enough was enough. He leaned toward the glass with such force that both guards reeled back a little.

"Look, pal, I really don't care how this goes down. But as of right now, I'm out of time. I'm going to walk around the corner and order your boss to open this door. Then I'm going to beat on your stupid skull until my arms get tired. You've still got a choice, I'll give you five seconds. Call the paramedics or get my prisoner. But decide right now." Blevins lined his watch up with the guard's face and studied them both closely.

A short silence followed, then Blevins moved, just a little. The guard had wasted three seconds conjuring up his toughest look, but it withered right there in front of Blevins. He snatched a couple of forms and dropped them into the slot.

"You've got to fill these out, Special Agent Blevins. It's the very minimum. I'd lose my job if I released someone without these forms in the file. Court's orders."

Blevins took the forms as he yanked a pen from his pocket. "Fine. How about getting my prisoner while I write?"

The second guard was all elbows, moving quickly to the computer keyboard then looking up at Blevins with cooperation written all over his face.

"What's the prisoner's name, sir? I'll locate him and have him brought down right away."

"A woman," Blevins said, without looking up from the papers. "Melissa Corley."

Both of the guards' heads snapped, drawing Blevins's head up, too.

"What? What's the problem?"

The guards looked at each other in a silence. Then Sam, the smaller guard at the terminal, said, "She's not here, sir. One of your agents came for her earlier. She left about . . . let's see," he scrolled down the screen, "an hour, well, almost two hours ago."

Blevins pressed his face against the thick glass and tried to see the screen.

"What? Who came for her? Give me a name."

The guard jumped to the file cabinet. "Here it is, right on top. Brewer, Special Agent Phillip Brewer. Credential number 1282. Paperwork is . . . yeah, it all looks in order." The guard stuffed the forms into the slot like they were on fire.

Blevins didn't recognize the agent's name, and he should if the guy was working this case. He ran across the room to a bank of payphones and called Sackett, studying Brewer's paperwork while he waited.

"Yes, Blevins, what is it?"

"Melissa Corley's gone. Taken from the Detention Center by an agent named Phillip Brewer. Credential number 1282. They left about two hours ago."

"Brewer? Brewer? You know him?"

"No. Never heard of him. How about calling Headquarters and getting his office assignment."

"All right, good as done. Blevins, something else has happened, too."

"What?"

"One of our security men was killed in the garage tonight, about the time you called Jamison from your car. Very professional. No bleeding at all, except for a little bit where his ear had been cut off."

"His ear was missing?"

"Yeah, that's right. Mean something to you?"

"Uh-huh, but nothing good. Go on."

"It's just a guess, but I'm thinking it had something to do with you, and your relationship with Jamison. Whoever killed the guard might have put a positioning transmitter on your car, or might have followed us to the hotel. I don't know for sure, but I suspect it's a real bad omen."

"Shit yes, it's a bad omen!"

"Are you going back to Jamison's hotel?"

"Got a better idea?"

"No. I'll send some agents to guard the room until you get there?"

"Don't. My men should be there any minute, if they're not there already. If Jamison's still alive, they won't let anything happen to him."

"I hope they're not too late. What do you want me to do?"

"Tell the switchboard to route all of my calls to you, in case he calls the office for me."

"Done. Then, after you clear from the hotel I want you to hook up with the SWAT team. With any luck, we're going to serve some warrants later and you'll want first look at any evidence seized."

"Got it. But one last thing, boss. If Jamison does call, expect him to be real suspicious of you. He told you what you wanted and a killer came knocking. Now Melissa's gone. You're not looking good to him."

"I can understand that. How about you, Rich? Are you suspicious of me?"

"Trying not to be, boss. But not sure. If you turn out to be dirty, you and I will spend some time talking about it. Got to go."

* * * * *

Melissa Corley sized up Special Agent Phillip Brewer as he led her up the back stairs of a two-story building and into a nicely furnished apartment. He was a regular looking guy, about five feet eleven. Medium build, but strong. Brown eyes with a goofy sort of look, like they were always focused on two different things.

Her wristwatch was still in the property envelope, so she had no idea what time it was. Maybe two A.M. Maybe three. It didn't really matter. But she did wish she had some idea of where she was. She'd tried to get some bearings after leaving the jail, but Brewer had been too careful, had kept her down on the floor and hadn't let her see anything that could serve as a landmark. Brewer hadn't spoken since they'd left the Detention Center, and she hadn't either. She was just watching him, and waiting. Waiting for her chance. It would come, she was sure, and she would take it. She wouldn't even think about this guy, whose side he was on, whether he was good or bad. He had the power to abuse her, and that made him bad. It was as simple as that. But she did worry that the Big Man would come again. The Big Man who had sat down in her cell and spoken with gentle words and a killer's movements. The Big Man who probably suspected what she was going to do, and had given her something else to think about. The Big Man who had her visiting the ghost of her father.

Her damaged ribs flared up and she tightened, but she was not about to show Brewer that she was hurt. It would just give him an advantage when the music started and the dance began. She hid the pain while watching for her chance, praying that it would come.

* * * * *

Rich Blevins met his agents in Jamison's hotel room, then quickly assigned most of them to guarding every one of the hotel's entrances. They did as he told them, protecting the crime scene as best they could while groping around for any information about the dead man in Jamison's room.

When he came down from the room he went over to one of the agents and spoke casually as he headed to his car.

"What do you think, Roland?"

Roland straightened his lanky frame, then rubbed his big hand over his mouth to wipe away a frown. His sharkish black eyes scanned the area as he grabbed Blevins by the arm, bringing him to an abrupt stop.

205

"Rich, your man lived through this one, don't you think? We didn't find any evidence that his wounds were life-threatening. Did you?"

Most of Blevins's mind was on Melissa. Part of it was trying to remember an agent named Phillip Brewer. The rest was celebrating the fact that Jamison had killed the assassin in his hotel room. His friend could still take care of himself.

"No."

Roland went to a whisper. "You want my opinion here, Rich? Because I've sure got one."

"Let's have it."

Roland glanced around, lowered his voice another notch. "Okay. I hate to say it, but I think another assassin might already be hunting your friend."

Blevins pushed Special Agent Brewer out of his brain, gave Jamison's situation his total concentration.

"Damn, Roland, what makes you think so? It's only been an hour."

Roland nodded, as if he'd expected those exact words.

"You're right, it would be pretty quick. But if that dead guy is any indication, he was being hunted by experts. You see the stuff in that bag of his?"

"True enough, he was a pro."

"And professionals usually have access to police information, right? Maybe the police themselves?"

Blevins looked around, then stepped closer.

"Maybe. I don't know. What's your point?"

Roland's eyes swept the area for the fifth or sixth time, then he leaned close to Blevins's ear.

"A hotel guest saw the hitter working Jamison's lock. The guest was in a room down the hall, some kind of insomniac. He called the Metro P.D."

"That's right."

"And then the cops arrived before we did, worked the room pretty thoroughly. They found the dead man and his bag. That the way you see it?"

"Yeah. So?"

"Well, I'm not sure, but I think the police department knows who the dead guy is, and has a positive I.D. on him. Of course, *we* haven't got a clue who he was. There's no record of the guy anywhere, based on what we know about him."

"Did you ask the P.D. for an ident?"

"Yup. And they stonewalled me."

"What makes you think so? Maybe they honestly don't know."

"It's possible. But listen to this before you believe it. Somebody called the hotel right after the first patrol unit arrived here. The desk clerk switched the call up to the police officers at the crime scene because the caller asked for Jamison's room, used Jamison's real name."

"So, somebody knew he was here. Maybe it was someone from the precinct."

"I think it's worse than that. Ask yourself how the desk clerk knew Jamison's name. How did *he* know what room the caller was asking for? I would have expected him to check his computer when the call came in, then tell the caller that there was no one registered by the name of Jamison. But he didn't."

"Damn, you're right. I wasn't thinking."

"Neither was I at first. But I just couldn't figure out how he could have known, so I asked him. Know what he said?"

"That he's psychic?"

"No, something even more unbelievable. He said the police told him about Jamison when they arrived. They told him Jamison's name, if you can believe that. Well at first I thought, fair enough, they just did something stupid, that's all. We've all made mistakes like that. But—"

"But there's no way the police should have known Jamison's name. He signed in under the name of Caligo. Paid cash, didn't use a phone card or anything else dumb. What little evidence he left—fingerprints, some blood, hairs, and fibers—are still being collected, and hours away from processing."

"Now you see my point. If the P.D. knew who he was, they had the information before they arrived. There's nothing here that would have enlightened them. That makes me think some of them are playing from the other end of the field. Assuming that, I have to conclude that the caller was another assassin, scrambling to pick up Jamison's trail. He called here hoping the P.D. would save him time."

"If you're right, Roland . . . damn! Any idea who the caller was?"

"No. The clerk remembers the call and the approximate time, but nothing else."

"Shit!"

"You can say that twice if we don't find Jamison pretty quick."

"True enough. Okay, clear the P.D. from the scene, now! It'll probably mean a fight, but throw their asses out. Have the SWAT team roll over them if they won't leave peacefully. Then get the hitter examined, head to toe, fingertip to fingertip. Analyze everything he had with him. Get the lab running laser tests. I want an I.D. and I want it soon. Maybe we can track this guy back to whoever hired him, then work the trail in both directions to find the caller."

"I'm on it."

Roland waved for six other agents to join him, then headed into the building.

Blevins stood there watching while the seven of them ran into the lobby, their pistols in hands. He waited another four minutes without hearing gunfire, began to believe the P.D. might leave without a fight. He ran to his car and took off.

* * * * *

Jamison kept his head cocked so he could use his good eye. He saw Blevins run out of the hotel, stop and talk to another man for a few minutes, then run to his car and leave. He wished he could have gotten his attention, spoken with him for a moment. But it just wasn't possible.

He watched the cops and agents from across Washington Circle, hunkered down at the edge of a cold-ass alley, his feet in a half-frozen puddle. His head and body ached. The damage Butler had done was intensified by the uncontrollable shaking he'd been doing for more than an hour.

But he suffered through it, stood in his frozen puddle and memorized everything: faces, vehicles, uniforms, gestures. Everything. It was always good to know your enemy, and what better place to see a whole bunch of them than right here. Only Sackett and Kane were missing.

He was also looking for someone in particular, he just didn't know who it was yet. Jack Kane was at the very top of Jamison's suspect list, but it could just as easily be someone from the Coalition. Or it might be someone who had passed through his field of vision once too often to be a coincidence. Whatever the circumstances, if the mystery person showed up he could turn this frosty vigil into a chance to get some real answers, get the tools to pry Melissa away from their enemies.

But so far, nothing.

Four hours passed, slow and icy. The activity in front of the hotel had slowed considerably once the body was carted off, and there wasn't much left to watch. He walked to the other end of the alley and checked the sidewalks of L Street before stepping out of the alley's shadows. The sun's light was just making its move and the street was beginning to carry a few pedestrians. Jamison walked down to a coffee shop near the corner.

The little shop was nothing much, hardly more than a counter with stools on one side, a grill on the other, and an old man staring at Jamison's bloody face. Bagels and donuts were displayed in a glass case beside the register. The smell of hot coffee was overwhelming and he ordered a cup and a bagel. As he paid, he bought one of the phone cards that were for sale behind the counter, took his coffee with him to the pay phone in the back.

He was trying to remember how he'd seen Blevins do it, once at the gym and once at his condo. He'd only watched those two times, but if he could at least get most of the words right, maybe that would be enough to cover up some of his nervousness. He practiced his lines to himself several times, then looked around before whispering them out loud. He had already gotten the number from long distance information.

A woman answered and sounded all business.

"F.B.I., Houston field office."

Jamison's hands started to sweat. Probably the coffee. He sat it down on the flat top of the black pay phone.

"This is Special Agent Forbus," Jamison began. "I'm here in Houston on a special assignment. I need an FTS line to WFO."

The phone was quiet. He fought the desire to hang up. If the operator in Houston was at all suspicious, she could be tracing him right now. He turned, took in all the cars and all the faces he could see on the street. Locked them into memory. Held his ground. Waited. Worried. Thirty seconds. A minute. He had hoped to be done already.

Suddenly, she was back.

"I'm sorry for the delay, Agent Forbus. I was waiting for an FTS line to clear. I'll connect you now." There was a click, and then another, and then a ring.

"F.B.I., Washington field office."

He was in. As long as they didn't check back down the line, he was safe.

"I need to speak to Sackett, your SAC."

"Who's calling, please?"

"I'm a friend. It's personal."

The operator asked nothing else.

Jamison took a quick sip of his coffee as Sackett picked up his phone. He sounded angry.

"Who is this?"

"You set me up."

Sackett's voice turned to feathers, all soft and fluffy. "Jamison, jeez, are you all right? Where are you?"

"No chance, Sackett. I don't trust you anymore."

"No? Well, I guess I can't blame you. I probably wouldn't either."

"Now there's a nice answer."

"It's the truth, Jamison. In your situation, you can't afford to trust anyone."

"I still want Melissa, Sackett. Do you still want my research data?"

"Yes."

"Then let's stop bullshitting and trade. You give me Melissa and—"

"I can't."

"Then you'll never get—"

"I'd like to, Jamison. Really. But I can't. Melissa was taken from the Detention Center a couple of hours before Blevins got there. We're doing our best to find her, but so far we've come up empty."

"That's just great. You lying bastard. Nice work. We're finished talking."

"Wait! Jamison, don't hang up. I may not be able to give you Melissa, but you and I both know that whoever is holding her is acting out of fear, or self-preservation. They're afraid of you, of whatever evidence you might have against them. Give me your data, Jamison. Let me use it. Give me the tools to get Melissa free. I promise you I'll find her."

"Forget it."

211

"It's not doing you one bit of good. Use your head, give it to me!"

"It's the only leverage I've got."

"On who?"

"On you. And people like you."

"Listen you hardheaded jerk, I'm trying to help you. But you're making my job—"

"You want to help me? Huh? Give me Jack Kane's home address."

"What did you say? Who?"

"Jack Kane. He's a security man at Dillon. I want his home address. It's not in any public records. I checked."

"What good do you think it will do you?"

"I don't think you want to know."

"You'll trade for the data?"

"Yes. You give me Kane's address, I'll give you the data. But no agents go to his house, Sackett. I'll kill any of your men I find there, won't even think twice about it."

Sackett didn't say anything. Was he really thinking about giving up the address, or just stalling for time? Jamison was about to break the connection when he heard Sackett talk to someone on a speaker, asking for the address. Less than a minute later the voice on the speaker came back with the information, and confirmed it was reliable.

"You get that, Jamison?"

Jamison didn't answer until he had the address scribbled down.

"Yeah. Thanks."

"Don't mention it. Good luck. Try not to do anything I'll have to arrest you for."

"I'll try. Can't guarantee anything."

"And your data?"

Jamison reread Kane's address, just to be sure it made sense, tried to remember if he'd heard of the street before.

"Blevins locked it in your evidence vault. I hope it helps you. Be careful with it, it's the last set of copies."

"I'll be careful with it. So, I guess I'll see you around."

"I plan on being around."

* * * * *

Sackett had initiated the trace the second he'd heard Jamison's voice. He called WFO's communications room immediately after hanging up.

"Where did he call from?"

"Houston, sir. Our field office there."

"That's impossible."

The sound tech didn't say anything, didn't waste any breath defending himself.

"Are you sure?"

"Yes, sir, I'm sure. His signal came in on our FTS system."

"Well, I'll be damned. Jamison is either a very smart guy, or he's been well-trained in this business."

"Or he's both, a smart guy who's been well-trained in this business."

"Good point. Contact Headquarters. For the next seventy-two hours I want a trap and trace on every FTS call, Bureau-wide, effective now. I want all the logs on my desk, updated every ten minutes. Got it?"

"Yes, sir. I've got it."

Sackett hung up the phone and stared at it. "I'll be damned," he said again. Then he hurried to the evidence vault, wondering how much Jamison knew about Jack Kane, and where he'd learned it.

14

Sackett brought Jamison's data from the evidence locker, set it on his desk, and reached for his coffee. It was his first cup since the sun had come up, probably his fifteenth cup since he'd eaten anything that hadn't dropped from a vending machine. The bitter Bureau coffee made his stomach grind, made him work fast to get this mess behind him. He recognized that he was getting careless, had overstepped himself by giving Jamison the address he wanted. If Jamison went over there and killed Kane, or was killed by Kane, his career could be over.

Sackett had called the United States Attorney's office right after Blevins told him Melissa Corley was gone, left a message for him to come down the instant he got to work. He wasn't sure exactly what he would ask the U.S. Attorney to do, but he knew he had to start making some decisions, and some arrests. Earn his pay. Since Monday, the situation had gone from bad to worse to terrible. He didn't want to sit around waiting for it to get disastrous.

He'd already decided to start with Special Agent Pate, the man who'd killed Robert Davidson. No part of his sworn statement had held up under scrutiny, so he was Sackett's chief target. The fact that Amos Warden and some F.B.I. assistant directors were covering for him made Sackett want him even more.

Oscar Riley, United States Attorney for the District of Columbia, popped into Sackett's doorway just as Sackett's lips touched the rim of his cup. Riley leaned into the room, his hands hooking onto the door's frame and his body hanging forty-five degrees to the floor.

Riley was a young man, midthirties, with brilliant, flashing features. His hair was dark and cut like a fashion model's, the top just a little too long and the sides cut short. His tailored clothes matched the look. He had bright green eyes. There was no way to mistake this guy for normal. He was much too young, way too powerful, and far too good-looking.

"I got your message, Sackett, so here I am, first case this morning. What have you got? I'm on a real tight schedule with lots to do before lunch." He grinned like a kid and chewed gum the same way.

Sackett waved Riley in. "Sit down. I'll make it brief."

Riley fidgeted his way into the room and dropped into a seat, stretching and twisting a rubber band around his fingers. His assistant, a tall woman who hid her gangly legs under a long print dress, followed him in, glanced around Sackett's large office, sat down next to Riley and nailed her pen to her legal pad.

"I need an arrest warrant for one of our agents," Sackett said, "and search warrants for three locations at Quantico."

Riley leaned back in his chair, brought the front legs an inch or two off the floor, and stretched his arms behind his head.

"No kidding. What are the charges?"

"Murder. And conspiracy to commit murder. Here's my complaint detailing the probable cause."

215

Sackett slid the affidavit across the desk. Riley didn't move as his assistant leaned forward and picked it up, adjusted her round glasses on her narrow nose, and studied it.

Riley ignored the document, never even glanced at it. He just leaned farther back in his chair, right to the balance point, and smiled as he checked out Sackett's ceiling.

"I might be able to do something with a conspiracy charge, Sackett. But murder? It isn't even a violation of federal law. You know that. We have no jurisdiction unless it happened on federal property"

"It didn't."

Riley pounded the front legs of the chair onto the floor and leaped out of it. "Well, then, I guess we're finished. Nice seeing you again."

"Wait just a damned minute, Riley. We're talking about a man who killed one of my agents, a nice young man named Robert Davidson who had a Constitutional right *not* to be gunned down. So call it a violation of his civil rights if you want. That's federal. The point is, I want his killer arrested today, and I don't want to trust local jurisdiction with it because the overriding case is federal."

Riley gave a sly smile and started pacing, still working his gum and his rubber band. "Okay, Sackett, you win. I'll work something out on the arrest. Now, what about the search warrants? What's your probable cause there?"

"That's a little tougher."

"Yeah, it usually is. Are you working with information provided by an informed source, something that would sound credible?" He turned so his assistant couldn't see his face, then narrowed his eyes and cut them to Sackett.

"Uh, yes. I have an allegation made by an informed but confidential source in the C.I.A. regarding the conspiracy. He told Special Agent Rich Blevins about some unlawful activities now or formerly conducted by a group of agents assigned to Quantico. Special Agent Blevins confirmed these facts, to the

216

best of his ability, by cross-checking the allegations with another source, a 137 informant who, until Monday, was an engineer at Dillon Aerospace." Sackett stated the information in a way that he hoped would be upheld as probable cause in a trial that wouldn't take place for months, or years, if ever. He watched to see if the assistant looked convinced.

"Sounds kind of weak to me, Sackett. You have anything else?"

"No. At least nothing I can disclose at this time."

Riley suddenly stopped pacing and turned with a big smile on his thin lips, as though he and Sackett were planning a practical joke on the legal system.

"Are you looking for a conviction based on the evidence gathered during these searches, or are you willing to have any seized evidence thrown out once you get a chance to look at it? You know, of course, that if the search is deemed unlawful because of insufficient probable cause, none of the resulting evidence can be used as grounds for any other arrests, or in any related trial, unless subsequently obtained through a separate, legal search, or through the confession of a suspect legally arrested without using the fruits of the illegal search."

Riley popped his gum and blinked his eyelids, seemed to love the sound of his own voice and looked like he wanted to say it all over again.

"Riley, the charge against Pate for Robert Davidson's death has to stick. That's important to me. As far as the search goes, I have other information that will not be tainted if the resulting evidence is thrown out. I can live without the search warrants being upheld. At least the search will confirm the suspicions I already have."

"Hold on, Sackett, not so fast. Would a sharp defense attorney be able to show that your other information, without the confirmations obtained through the tainted search, would have been too vague or broad to uphold the final arrest warrants?"

"I don't think so."

"Sure?"

"No. But pretty confident."

"Okay."

Riley worked the floor again, giving the rubber band a real workout. He stopped behind his assistant and looked over her bony shoulder at Sackett's document.

"How does the complaint look?"

The assistant frowned, then shrugged. "Not great. But I think it will stand up all right."

Riley seemed satisfied and didn't read the affidavit. "All right, Sackett, you're on. You know how it works from here. Do you swear that the information you are providing in this affidavit is the truth, to the best of your knowledge?"

"I do."

Riley spun around and headed for the door, like a ghost with lots to do before he vaporized. The assistant scribbled as he spoke to her.

"Give Sackett his arrest warrant. Carefully identify the three locations for the searches and give him those warrants, too. Sackett, good luck to you. Tell me the rest of the story when you can. I'll see you later." And then he was gone.

The assistant sighed. "You can have these in thirty minutes, Mr. Sackett. I just need the locations at Quantico."

Sackett sat down, closed his eyes, couldn't believe what he was about to do.

"The SOAR's office, F.B.I. Academy, Quantico, Virginia. The living quarters of the arrestee, Pate. And the living quarters of Special Agent Amos Warden. Both of their addresses are F.B.I. Academy, Quantico, Virginia."

She was still writing as she rose and headed out the door. Sackett reached for his coffee, which was stone-cold, and drank it anyway. He picked up the phone and asked his secretary to get Blevins.

Blevins was in Sackett's office immediately, had been back and forth a dozen times since returning from Jamison's hotel room. He sat on the arm of a chair but looked ready to fly out again.

"Any word from the crime scene guys, Blevins?"

"No, boss. Nothing."

Sackett walked over and stood behind him, put a hand on his shoulder.

"Well, I've got some good news for you. Jamison is still alive. He just called me, about twenty minutes ago. An FTS call from our Houston office, if you can believe that. I wonder where he learned that trick."

"What did you talk about?"

Sackett turned away. "Sorry. Can't tell you."

"Why not?"

"I made a promise, that's all. Told Jamison he could go somewhere without us hassling him. If I tell you, someone may end up going out there, and I don't need another dead agent."

"You sound like you might have broken the law."

Sackett kept his back to Blevins. "I did what I had to do. Let's move on."

"Sure. Whatever you say."

Sackett sat down at his desk, but didn't look Blevins in the eyes.

"I'm about to hand you a live grenade with a missing pin, Blevins, so try not to let it blow up in your face."

"Sounds like a plan."

Sackett slid a personnel file to Blevins, a credential photo of Special Agent Pate clipped to the top. "You remember this man from yesterday?"

"You're kidding, right? Of course I do."

"Good. The U.S. Attorney has just issued an arrest warrant for him. I want this ugly bastard taken down this morning, at Quantico if at all possible. You'll also have a search warrant for his domicile, as well as Amos Warden's domicile and the

219

SOAR's office. But if you arrest Pate somewhere else, search that location for evidence, too. As thoroughly as possible without exceeding the legal standard."

"Evidence of what?"

"He killed Davidson, I believe, as part of a conspiracy. I'm looking for evidence to support that charge."

"It takes more than one person for a conspiracy, boss. Who else am I going to take down? This Warden fellow?"

"To be honest with you, I don't really know. Depends on what you find searching his room. By the way, has Jamison ever mentioned a man named Kane?"

"Kane? Not that I recall."

"Well, get going then. Be careful. As you can imagine, everyone at Quantico will be acting like your favorite brother. Sort through them carefully. My advice is that anyone who acts like he might get in your way is probably part of the conspiracy, so react accordingly."

"Will do. Is that it?"

"For now, yes. Try not to get any of your guys hurt. You'll need them later when we arrest Phillip Brewer. Assuming we ever find him."

Blevins eyes brightened up. "Can't wait for that."

"I'm sure. Especially if he still has the Corley woman. Questions?"

"None."

"Then that's it. I'm assigning this whole mess to you. You'll be the overall case agent, and will have responsibility for every other case that spins off from here. I'm closing your administrative inquiry, too, and transferring all the files on my desk to you."

Blevins looked at the stacks of files. "Thanks, I think."

"Good luck. Blevins. Be careful."

"You got it."

Blevins started out of the office, but stopped and turned when he got to the door. "Are you all right, boss? Anything else we should talk about?"

"I'm fine. Too much coffee, but I'll be all right."

Sackett walked over and closed the door of his office, sat down on the couch, plopped his face into his hands, and watched his career swirling down the drain. Amos Warden had been right, and both of them knew it. Sackett had done his share of going along.

He wondered if he'd fooled Jamison. Or had the sound of Kane's name made his voice falter?

Jack Kane. Twenty years ago, when Sackett was a nugget agent, he'd had no idea Kane was going to be so powerful. He was just a broken man with a lot of hate and friends with the power to help him, friends who sent Sackett and Warden on their first real assignment after new agent's training. They had checked out a Bureau car and driven to a gun range in northern Virginia, found Jack Kane, and given him an envelope. Said their lines exactly: "Dillon Security wanted to help." It was simple at the time, almost innocent. For all Sackett knew, he might have been handing Kane a subpoena, or job application.

After Kane killed the two men, the Metro P.D. came to Sackett and asked why he'd gone to the gun range that day, wanted to know how Kane had managed to find the killers when they couldn't. They didn't buy his story, and Sackett—young and cornered and alone in an interrogation room—had lied to convince them, had lied about who'd sent him to meet Kane, and why.

His career took off from there. He had worked hard and made more arrests than anyone else. But the men who'd asked him to deliver the envelope had always had a hand in his promotions. He could never be sure of their reasons.

He knew Warden had been wandering back and forth across the line ever since. Sackett hadn't done anything to stop him. In truth, Sackett had crossed the line with him a few more times.

Not in any big way, of course, and certainly not like Warden. Nothing that had gotten anyone hurt, or incarcerated, or killed.

But he'd passed along some information from time to time, provided valuable assistance to high-powered people who could advance his career. It hadn't seemed so bad at the time, and didn't really seem that bad now.

But it was wrong. Now that it looked as if he might get caught, he wished he hadn't done it. Just like every criminal he'd ever arrested, he was experiencing the Pragmatic Repentance. That's what he liked to call it.

But all of his justifications for violating the law evaporated the second he assigned Blevins to arrest Warden. Warden knew the truth and could bring Sackett down, could dime him out if he decided to make a deal with U.S. Attorney Riley. Sackett had sacrificed his honor for his career, and now he might lose that, too.

* * * * *

Jamison rushed out of the coffee shop after getting Kane's address, didn't stopped to finish his bagel, left his coffee sitting on top of the pay phone. Several cabs were at the corner so he ran down and climbed into one, gave the driver an address five hundred numbers higher than Kane's, then slumped into the backseat for the twenty-minute ride.

He rubbed his tired eyes, flinched when he hit the bloody scrape on his right cheek and the sore spots on his neck. He had forgotten all about the injuries. But the cabdriver must have seen them, which was probably why he kept checking his mirror.

In less than forty-eight hours, from Monday afternoon until this early on Wednesday morning, he'd taken a long slide from aerospace engineer to killer. No wonder people looked at him funny. It was impossible to make that kind of trip without it showing on his face, even if he didn't have scabs from a recent conflict. And it wasn't over yet, either. How much farther would he slip?

And why? Why had he done this to himself?

The cab hit a pothole and took a bad bounce. Jamison's sore muscles tightened, stiffened his body all the way up to his neck. Made him think about poor Ted Bronovich. His skinny little neck must have hurt, too. Not even allowing for fear and terror, it must have been agonizingly painful for him when his killer grabbed his tiny head, angled it just right, then twisted his head until the neck and skull separated, the spinal cord stretched until it ripped apart like hard taffy. That poor, honest bastard. Who would have ever thought he had so much courage?

Jamison might have been able to save Bronovich. Maybe he could have kept it from happening. Bronovich hadn't had to die. He'd asked Jamison to contact Blevins when he thought he needed help, before he actually did need it. But Jamison, being the lazy bastard he was, hadn't done the one simple favor his friend had asked of him. He'd put off telling Blevins about Bronovich until it was more convenient. The only problem was, Bronovich hadn't had the time.

Jamison had to do something to redeem himself now, kill someone who'd had a hand in Bronovich's murder, make some attempt to settle the score. This whole ugly deal was decaying into a simple, bloody math problem. Would one John Butler and one Jack Kane equal one Ted Bronovich? What would one Sackett be worth in trade?

He didn't know, had no idea, would have to wait to find out.

But he knew that Melissa was an unfathomable number. Nothing equaled her value. He would kill as many people as necessary to get her back. There was an infinity sign in the equation of her worth.

He slumped down in the cab and closed his eyes, vowed again—for the hundredth time since the F.B.I. arrested her—that he would not fail her. He had let her get raped on a Delaware beach, hadn't done nearly enough to help her when she'd needed him that night, and had wasted ten precious seconds that might have saved her, might have allowed him to stop her assailant before he'd dragged her off into the dunes.

But he would not let anything else bad happen to her. He would go the whole distance for her, do anything and everything to make up for what he'd failed to stop before.

The cab careened around a corner, a tight turn that almost threw Jamison across the seat. But he kept his eyes shut, found that he was staring at himself, and his real reasons for what he was doing right now. For the first time he was looking at a part of his soul that he had never wanted to be examined. A little cell of truth, a filthy dungeon where honesty reigned as pure and unencumbered as a Tibetan monk, only a door or two away from the crazy man's cell. The door to this intimidating room was marked with the question: Was he really doing this for her? He jerked his closed eyes away from the dingy room, didn't even want to think about looking inside. Afraid, suddenly he was so afraid. His hands started to shake and his throat clogged up. But the truth kept calling him, louder and louder, like a siren's song, telling him he had to understand, someday, what his motives were. Why not today?

He floated into the room and felt pain immediately, as if God had reached a big hand into his chest and squeezed his heart like a wet sponge. Melissa was in the room, waiting for him, lying with her clothes shredded and her legs squeezed together at her knees, watching as he approached. He looked at her, and . . . God, what was he feeling now? Something entirely different than ever before, something that felt so terribly wrong, but yet, so natural and understandable. Something unspeakable, but honest. Was it hate? It was so intense that he wanted to spit the bitter taste out of his mouth. It was definitely hatred, he was sure now. Nothing else tasted that foul.

224

How was it possible? How could he ever hate Melissa for what had happened? She was a victim, had been completely powerless to stop the attack. It was totally irrational to feel otherwise, to hate her for letting it happen.

But he did hate her. God help him, he was actually holding her responsible for the attack, for letting something happen that would destroy their relationship. He had lied, pretending they'd split up over their careers, a convenient excuse for their friends and themselves. It was obvious to him now. The rape was the reason. He hadn't been able to live with it, couldn't accept the fact that he'd been worthless when she'd really needed him, couldn't get past the pain of failing her. Couldn't escape the guilt.

The terrifying room had more to tell and wouldn't let him go. He tried to open his eyes, tried to get away, but he was trapped in a web, feeling the woven strands tremble as the truth crawled to get him. He was crying now, his shoulders lurching up and down in staggered rhythm with his sobbing. He thought briefly about where his body was, thought about the cabby who, he was sure, had regretted picking him up. But he hardly felt the cab around him anymore, and he surely didn't care about the driver.

Guilt was his worst enemy, he saw that now. It had been for two years. It wasn't the guilt of allowing the rape, either. It was the guilt that he felt about his own feelings, the ones which he could repress no longer.

He had stayed strong for her after the attack, had been patient and loving and understanding for as long as she'd needed, because that was what she had asked of him. Support, while she regained control of her life.

And that's what he'd done for her. He'd held her while she cried, tried not to treat her any differently than he had before, and reminded her over and over again that she deserved none of the responsibility for what had happened to her. He had done exactly what she'd asked, standing quietly by her, remaining patient and understanding.

But he wasn't patient. And he sure as hell didn't understand why he had to contain his vengeance. He was mad as hell, wanted to move to Delaware and spend all his time hunting that animal down, delighting in the pleasures of his tortured death.

But she'd said no, absolutely not. She was worried that she might need to confront the man herself some day, if the opportunity ever arose, and that Jamison would be victimizing her again if he eliminated that option.

So he'd shut up about it and didn't say anything more, did nothing to heal his own pain. He kept wearing the mask of a patient lover. He began to hate her because he loved her so much, was willing to do what she needed even if it cut him off from his own emotions. Whenever he thought about his own needs he felt ashamed and self-indulgent, and that completed a nasty circuit that made him hate her even more.

As he bumped along in the cab, he understood that he was not out to save Melissa. Not really. The truth from the scary room was this: he had to prove something to himself. Prove that he had the power to help her. Prove that she could count on him, and that he would not fail her.

His feelings for Melissa changed that very second. He saw her as a timid, frightened woman who needed his help, stripped of her clothes. Raped and helpless, just like he'd seen her that night on the beach, back before the pain and guilt and shame of living with the crime had descended on him.

His love for her coursed through him now, as suddenly as a lightning strike, and it occurred to him that, maybe, he really had saved her after all. If nothing else, he'd done a lot to help her save herself. Maybe he had failed her on the beach, but in the months and months that followed he had been her soldier. Her strength. He had sacrificed for her. Sacrificed his good, natural feelings about sex. Sacrificed the chance ever to make love again without thinking of that night. He had done the things she'd needed and put her healing far ahead of his own sanity, had suffered for her in ways she would never understand, had done more for her than he'd ever done for anyone else in his life. Right now, for the first time, he felt pretty good about all that.

The cab slid to a stop and the door to the room slammed shut, locking him out. He opened his eyes and blinked. Somehow, everything seemed a little different.

He paid and jumped out, feeling lighter and faster than he had in years. He still felt like crying, but he didn't have all that much trouble holding the tears back. He was nearly happy. He'd seen the truth and it had truly set him free. For the first time since Delaware, he realized how much he really did love Melissa. Loved her the way he used to, loved her for who she was and what she meant to him. A deep love that was, once again, unfettered by guilt for a past mistake.

He headed down the sidewalk, about four blocks from Kane's address, almost breaking into a run. He was forgiving himself, and enjoying atonement. Forgiving himself for letting the rape happen. Forgiving himself for the shame he'd felt about his self-centered whining. And most of all, forgiving himself for the guilt that had driven her away. While he was at it, he forgave himself for Ted Bronovich, for being a normal human being who'd made a very bad mistake.

His motives were pure now and he understood them completely. He loved Melissa Corley more than anything else on this earth. God have mercy on anyone who stood between them.

15

Melissa sat across from Special Agent Brewer and waited. Neither she nor Brewer had left the living room of the second floor apartment since they'd arrived, not even to go to the bathroom. They had stared at each other for several hours, separated by a dozen feet of hardwood floor and the silent suspicions of two enemies.

Anytime now, she figured. It wouldn't be long. Brewer had sat there since the middle of last night but had said hardly anything, hadn't moved, hadn't even gotten up to make coffee when the sun rose an hour ago. He was waiting for someone, she was sure. Probably the Big Man who'd come with Jitters to her cell at the Detention Center. Her chances of getting away from Brewer were slim, but would never be better. She wouldn't have a chance at all once Big Man arrived. If only Brewer would come closer, then maybe she could do something. He had to be tired of sitting there staring at her legs. Anytime. Come on, let's get on with it. She'd tried getting him to adjust the cuffs that chained her right hand to the arm of the couch. But he was sure he'd left plenty of room and locked them so they wouldn't constrict, and that was that. Nothing else happening. So what now? She waited and planned. And thought about Peter. About how he had no idea what he was up against, had no concept of the power of the organization her father had started.

It was her second year of law school when she'd figured it out. For as long as she could remember, since she was a very little girl, she'd heard her father having odd, low-volume conversations. Sometimes on the phone, sometimes with the important men who came to their home. Talks about foreign accounts, reliable sources, and necessary actions. Necessary, that was the word that glued all their conversations together. Whatever the men decided to do, they did because it was necessary. It was all very strange talk for an aeronautical engineer.

During that same law school year of 1975, one of her professors, a sixties radical who still wore his frizzy hair a little too long, was lecturing on the illegal impact big business had on the policies of American government. He was an intelligent man who seemed to have all the answers. After the lecture she stayed to talk with him. In an effort to contribute something to their discussion she asked him about some shreds of information she'd carried from childhood, things she'd overhead her father say, things that had never made sense to her but refused to be forgotten. What did he think they meant?

The professor had thought a long time before answering, had watched her carefully as he formulated his response, made it clear that he could only speculate. He answered delicately, skirted the issue of corruption and fraud while he made vague allegations. She could still remember his look, the suspicious way he'd eyed her as if she'd read a very rare book that made her smarter than him. A book he would never be able to get his own hands on, but would give up his tenure to possess.

That weekend she had gone home and talked to her father, quietly, while her mother was out. She came right out with her professor's allegations, respecting her dad too much to do otherwise. She asked if he and his friends had committed crimes against the United States government. And then she waited, said nothing more, positive he would laugh and deny it and clear away her doubts.

But he did not deny it, and did not look upset at her charges, either. He did not say a single word in his own defense. Instead he walked over to her, slowly, and put his hand on her head, very gently. Then he looked up, the same way he often looked into a starry sky on a clear night, and stroked her long hair

"You are a very smart woman," he said, "and I am extremely proud of you. I'm sorry that I've disappointed you, hope you're not too ashamed of me. You know how much I love you, don't you?"

"Yes."

"Good. I'm glad."

Then he kissed the top of her head, wandered to his bedroom, and shot himself to death.

Melissa's body shuddered as she shook herself out of her past, and her sudden movement attracted Brewer's attention. Her father—God how she missed him—was gone. But one of his creations was standing up now, stretching. If she were ever going to accomplish the goal she'd set the night her father died, she might as well start with him.

"So, who's in charge of you guys now?"

Brewer looked a little shocked. "What do you mean?"

"What part didn't you understand? It was a simple question. I asked who's pulling your strings these days? President Albright? That would be my guess. I know it was once the Speaker of the House, because nobody trusted Carter with the power. But Albright is probably playing along just fine with you guys."

Brewer had a kid's look on his face, as if he wanted to stick out his tongue and call her stupid. But he didn't. Melissa studied his look and tried to decide how much ridicule she could put into her voice without sending him over the edge.

"What's wrong, Brewer? Afraid to talk? Afraid you might say something you shouldn't and get yourself into trouble with the big boys who really have some power?"

"Shut up."

"You're afraid, aren't you?"

She laughed and tried to sound like she really enjoyed his situation, convince him that he was playing the fool.

"How's it feel, being a grown man who can't even think for himself? Being stumped because no one's told you how to answer a simple question. I'd be ashamed if it happened to me."

"Shut up!"

She was close to making him talk or driving him nuts. Of course, either way it went, he would try to kill her afterward. She understood that, but she would make the deal. She had to be sure who was in charge of the fund, who sat at the point of the pinnacle. Wanted to make sure she took him down, and anyone else who could ascend to power. Assuming she got out of this apartment alive.

"It is President Albright, isn't it? Come on, little boy, you can tell me."

Brewer lurched toward her and she flinched, just a little, not enough for him to see. His face was angry as he hovered over her.

"You want to know who's got the power? I'll tell you. But it's a trade kind of thing between us. First I get something I want, then I'll answer your question. After that, I'll kill you. We'll wait a few more hours, just to be sure they don't change my orders. Then I'll take what I want, and give you your answer."

She rose as far as she could into his face, gave him his look right back.

"Deal."

* * * * *

Jamison was shivering in the shade of Ross Casey's mansion, but the stabbing wind couldn't dull his anger toward Sackett. The bastard had tricked him again. The address he'd given for Jack Kane did not exist, was just a missing set of digits between two row houses. A worthless trip and a waste of time. He had traded his data for nothing.

So although he wanted Kane and hated Sackett, he huddled under a window of Casey's home, wishing the telephone interface device was on the sunny side. That would have been nice, the feeling of bright, warming sunshine beating down on his frozen body. Maybe it would help his feelings of isolation, all alone out here, following his own orders, doing everything he could to get Melissa back.

His plan was to break into Casey's home and go through his closets, desk, and dresser, find anything that would lead him to Kane. See if Kane would lead him to Melissa. If not, he would go after that lying prick Sackett. Then he would go wherever that led him, taking his suspects in order, going straight up the list without looking back. Nothing was unthinkable. There were absolutely no limits.

Casey's house was impressive, a huge home on a large estate surrounded by lush landscaping. A tight line of evergreens concealed him from the next door neighbors, a thousand feet away. Jamison was pretty sure no one had seen him sneak up to the house through the backyard, if that's what an acre or more of perfectly manicured winter grass was called. If someone had seen him, the cops would have responded by now.

He'd seen only one person moving inside the house, an attractive blonde woman about his own age. He'd watched her through the window for half an hour, waiting for her to leave so he could go in. She was going out soon, he could tell by the way she'd dressed. He would wait a little longer. The cold wouldn't kill him. Bad timing might.

He dabbed a finger at his swollen, scabbing eye, ran today's plan through his head once again. It wasn't much, a flimsy scheme based on the hope that he could trust his secretary, Charlotte. She'd seemed trustworthy when they'd met on an obscure sidewalk last night, a little before Blevins and Sackett had come to his hotel room. She'd said she would keep her ear to the ground and let him know what was going on at Dillon.

But he was having trouble trusting anyone now. Sackett had tricked him twice, had done a pretty good job of it. He could be wrong about Charlotte, too. She could be one of the enemy.

The woman he assumed to be Casey's wife put on her coat, set the alarm, then left. He saw the alarm code, was pretty sure he'd gotten it correct. 9407#. He stayed in the bushes until she pulled away.

Time to go to work.

He dug into his gym bag for the multitool he'd bought at the hardware store, then used it to open the interface box. He unplugged the house phone line from the jack, then plugged in the cheap phone he'd brought with him. He dialed Dillon Aerospace and asked for Charlotte.

"Good morning," she said, "Dillon Aerospace, Research and Development."

Jamison could hear her fingers dancing on the keyboard.

"Hi, it's me." He listened closely, wanting to hear her recognize the sound of his voice. Not wanting to hear surprise. Or nervousness.

Her voice didn't carry anything but words. Some happiness maybe, but nothing really measurable.

"Yes, sir. How are you?"

"Fine. Can you talk?"

"Yes. Wait a minute."

The keyboard went silent, Charlotte giving him all of her attention, probably shifting away from the other women in the secretarial pool.

"Okay, go ahead."

"Have you found out anything? Heard them say anything about me?"

"Nothing." Her voice dropped to a whisper. "I checked the computer when I came in this morning. You're still down as being on vacation."

"Who made the entry?"

"Don't know. There's no record."

"That's all?"

"Sorry, yes. Haven't heard a whisper about you. I think, with the way things are going around here now, people suspect you're in trouble but don't want to mention your name. I'm sure that's what everybody's guessing. But no one is talking."

"Well, thanks anyway. I'll let you go before anyone gets suspicious. Can I call you back in a hour? You're still ready to help?"

"Anytime. Yes, of course."

"Be careful, Charlotte. Don't take any big chances on my account."

"Don't worry." Her fingers shifted over to her word processor, her voice moving back to normal as the rhythm of her keystrokes picked up.

"Thanks for calling, sir. I'll make sure he gets the message."

"Good-bye."

Now it was time to wait. See if anyone showed up, find out if Charlotte was good or bad. If she was good, into Casey's house he'd go. Find Kane's address, then call Charlotte and put his plan into action.

* * * * *

Jack Kane felt good today. He enjoyed the walk down the long corridor, watching Charlotte, way down in the distance, take off her headset and place it in her lap, getting ready for him. He walked right up to her desk and stepped close. He kept his voice low.

"You did a nice job, Charlotte. Remember, this is strictly between us."

"I will." She dropped her head toward her chest.

"I know you will."

Kane turned away, heard her breathe a little as he headed toward Casey's office. He walked right in, caught Casey pouring scotch.

"A little early in the day isn't it?"

Casey tossed back the scotch without setting down the bottle, refilled the shot glass but didn't drink it. He set the bottle and the full glass on the bar, took two steps toward Kane.

"It's none of your business. Did you trace the call?"

"I did."

"And? Find out where he is?"

"Yes."

"Well, don't just stand there, send someone after him. I've got to get rid of Jamison today. You have no idea the pressure I'm under."

"Sure, Casey, sure. We'll get right on it. As it turns out, we have some men near where Jamison made the call. Right across the street, in fact."

Casey jutted his chin out. "You're kidding. How is that possible?"

"Just lucky, I guess. After he killed Butler, I realized how badly I was underestimating Jamison. He's really quite good, could be a professional if he wanted to be. Since I couldn't figure out what to expect from him I covered all the bases.

Hired several more independent contractors, and upped the reward to seven hundred and fifty thousand dollars. Then I had our security men set up on every place he would logically think of going. Dillon offices, favorite company bars, executive's homes, places like that."

"And Jamison called from one of them?"

"Yes."

"Which one?"

Kane smiled, turned to walk out the door. "He called from your house, Ross. Funny, huh?"

He spun around quickly to catch Casey's reaction.

Casey had gone back to the bar while waiting for Kane's answer, was raising the shot glass he'd poured. He stopped with his drink halfway to his lips and stared at Kane with his eyes wide open.

"Oh, shit."

Kane laughed. It slipped out and felt strange, his first real laugh in years. He'd tried to choke it back down his throat, but couldn't. He had forgotten what it was like to have something feel deep down funny, how hard it was to keep laughter from forcing its way out. His life was beginning to seem a little more enjoyable these days, even with the disaster he faced over Jamison. His blood was warming, melting the ice in his veins. The watered-down fuel was barely sufficient to power his hatred. He worried what his wife would think if she'd seen him laugh like that.

He always kept his last glimpse of her and their daughters on one side of his scale, their bloody nightgowns pulled down and straightened out before the cops had taken their last pictures. They were his sacred victims. His poor, beautiful family. They deserved that place of their own, away from the savages he'd killed and piled haphazardly on the other side.

But weren't they all starting to look like victims now? What about the families of the men he'd killed? Didn't they also suffer for their loss of loved ones? Had those men's deaths done one damned thing to help his own suffering, or brought his family closer to him? Was vengeance helping him, or killing him?

* * * * *

Dillon Security man Richard Murray led his partner, Hamel, up Casey's porch, then smashed open the front door. They'd been across the street, surveilling the house from the home of a neighbor who wintered in the islands. Dillon's data sheet provided them with Casey's alarm code and keypad locations, but no key. After busting down the door, they turned off the alarm during the thirty-second delay.

How had they missed Jamison's approach? They had been watching like peepers at a nudist camp. The sun was shining and the streets were quiet. Everything should have caught their attention, even the stirring of bare tree branches, or a bird's fluttering; certainly the approach of the man they'd been told to kill with extreme prejudice.

Was Jamison really that good? Had he been in the house with Mrs. Casey all along, hiding in some unused room? Or had he gone in and made the call after she left? And if so, why was the alarm still on when they smashed in the door?

It didn't matter. Their job was to find Jamison, right now, and kill him. Or pay Kane his pound of flesh for letting him slip away. Kane's price for failure was steep.

Murray was the older of the two men. He'd joined Dillon after freelancing for too many years. At forty-one, the strain of independent contracting had almost caught up with him. As good as he was—and some told him he was the closest thing around to Kane—the bullshit of self-employment had bled away his singularity of purpose. While waiting in a man's house on his last job before joining Dillon, he had gotten so involved in budgeting his expenses that his mark had almost slipped up on him. That kind of mistake could be lethal, and would not do in this line of work. It was much easier working for Dillon and taking home a regular paycheck with the occasional bonus, being a team player with others on his side, and having someone else worrying about expenses and payments. He'd started wearing suits then, Armani suits, and having his hair cut once a week. Those were his only diversions. He concentrated everything else on his missions. He smiled a lot these days, a wide-open grin that turned up the ends of his thick eyebrows and pushed them together above his nose.

Hamel was much younger, maybe twenty-eight. A kid, really. Murray always suspected that Hamel knew someone pretty high up at Dillon Security, otherwise he wouldn't have been hired. He was too fast and too messy. Of course, no one learned the finer points of this job in his twenties. It couldn't be done. At Hamel's age, it was still a fun game. Catch the guy then whack him. Hamel didn't seem to worry about evidence left behind, or getting hurt himself. For him, it was just a deadly game of tag.

As the door crashed open, Murray crouched low, just inside, and aimed his pistol down the hallway that went through the center of the house. Hamel strolled past him, standing straight up, moving easily with a big smile on his face and an automatic weapon in his hands.

*   *   *   *   *

Jamison had hoped he could trust Charlotte, had really wanted to have someone inside Dillon to help him. He'd hoped for the best but expected the worst, hiding in Casey's shrubbery and waiting to write down plates if anyone showed up. Part of him hoped it wouldn't happen, but part of him wanted the street to fill with Dillon cars. One of them might be Kane's.

238

He was plenty surprised when two men came running from across the street and broke into Casey's house. He worked his way to the porch, lying low and listening as the two men hesitated at the broken door. When they entered the house he crept up the steps, just behind them, quiet as a ghost. He didn't want to be left outside where he'd have to open the door and go through it once they were inside. Besides, he needed to know where they were in the big house. He pressed himself against the wall outside the front door and listened hard, waited for the two men to move away from it.

He heard them split up. Neither of them closed the door. The younger man headed upstairs while the older guy whispered that he would search the first floor. Jamison decided to go after the guy on the first floor because the young guy was just too hard to read.

The man stepped slowly away, but Jamison waited, wanting him out of the hallway. It would be bad news for him to be caught in the foyer where the young gun could look down from the balcony and shoot him.

Finally, Jamison stepped through the foyer with his eyes going up the stairs, then straight ahead, then back up the stairs. He stopped at the living room, peeked in, and advanced. In the dining room he waited for the man to come out of the kitchen.

He didn't have to wait long. The man came out quickly and strolled back into the dining room as if this were familiar ground now. Jamison was standing right beside the door, and stuck his gun against the man's head, pushed so hard the man nearly fell over sideways.

"Shhh."

The man started to swing around, but Jamison kept the gun to his head and pulled back the hammer of his double-action Beretta. It was unnecessary, the pistol would have fired without cocking. But the sound sent a clear message. The man stopped instantly, as though his life had been one long study in good judgment.

Jamison reached over and took the gun from the man's hand. Second chance was written all over the guy's face, like, Okay, I'm not dead yet, so I'll have a second chance at this guy. This isn't over yet.

Jamison concentrated on not giving the man any advantage. "Over here," he whispered, then added, "and you know I'll kill you if you make noise. I'll need you dead so I can concentrate on the guy upstairs. Don't force my hand."

The man seemed to understand, like it all made perfect sense. Jamison pointed to a dining room chair that faced the hall, then pushed the man over to it. The man started to sit down.

"Wait a minute." Jamison was still whispering, even though he could hear the young man clomping around upstairs at the far end of the house. He still had some time. He grabbed the man's coat at the collar and pulled it down to his waist, leaving the man's arms in the holes, a kind of makeshift strait jacket. "Now sit."

The man sat.

Jamison stood behind him, facing out toward the hall. He checked to make sure the man's hands hadn't wriggled out, made sure the coat had pinned them behind him.

"I want two things from you. One, the location of a friend of mine named Melissa Corley. Two, where to find Jack Kane. Start talking."

"I –"

"Shh. Keep your voice down."

The man tried again, low, and gave Jamison an earnest look.

"I don't know."

Jamison got his whiskers right against the man's face and whispered into his ear.

"All right. I knew you would say that, and you knew you would say that. But now that game is over and we get to start a new one. Where's Melissa?"

Jamison pulled the multitool from his pocket and flipped out the scratch awl. He stuck it into the man's ear canal and pushed. The man's head made a violent jerk when the point hit his eardrum. It punctured, and a stream of blood ran down the side of the man's head. Jamison moved to the other side, still watching the doorway, his hand reaching around his victim's head and pushing hard on the tool.

He spoke into the man's good ear, the one that didn't have a sharp instrument buried two inches into it. "If you don't tell me where she is, I'm going to drive this blade right into your brain. Don't want to do it, but will need to move on to contestant number two. You understand? You've got five seconds."

The man was going to answer. His face lit up like a pinball game, lights flashing and bells ringing. The truth was coming, and Jamison wouldn't have to kill him for it. Surprisingly, even the crazy man seemed satisfied with that, just watching from the bleachers with bored disinterest.

But then it happened. That damned kid from upstairs jumped into the doorway, spraying the room with gunfire. Jamison caught a round in his side. His skin ripped and blood began to flow. But it didn't feel serious. If he could avoid the rest of the kid's bullets, he'd be all right.

Jamison had barely heard him coming, or maybe he hadn't heard him at all. Maybe he'd seen it in the other man's face. Either way, his reactions had taken over and thrown him toward the doorway, right at the kid with the automatic weapon. Jamison hit the floor and rolled forward while the kid rushed backward, trying to get Jamison in his sights but unable to move the long-barreled weapon fast enough.

Jamison was at the kid's feet now, at least a foot inside of the barrel's tip, the silenced rounds tapping into the floor behind him, each one just missing his head and going past his ear with a *pffft* and a crack. He raised his Beretta, jammed it into the kid's stomach, and fired. The blast lifted him off his feet and sent him

241

backward. Jamison fired twice more before the kid's body hit the ground.

Now, quick, where was the other man? Jamison couldn't see him from where he was, lying on the ground. Had he gotten away, or worse, taken a position of advantage? Jamison jumped up just as the man came charging at him, empty-handed.

"Stop!"

The man kept charging. Jamison hesitated, didn't want to kill the man, wanted him alive to answer questions. But the man kept coming, almost on top of him now.

"Stop, damn you!"

No change. The man sprang off the floor and flew through the air toward him.

Jamison fired twice at the man's head and watched it snap back as his body went down. The polished wood floor shuddered as it caught the man's dead weight.

The gunshots had sounded like cannons going off in the dining room, but Jamison convinced himself that no one had heard. Expensive neighborhood. Big open spaces between houses. Calm down. Make the call.

He picked up the phone in Casey's kitchen and dialed the office number that was taped to it.

"Hey," Casey said, as if he expected a friend, or maybe his wife. Someone special enough to have direct access.

"They're both dead, Casey. Are you next?"

"What? Who is this?"

Then Jamison heard him gasp. There was a little stagger to it.

"Oh my God. Is that you, Peter?"

"You got it, Casey. I had no choice out here. But you? You're a different story. It's your fault Melissa's gone. Tell me where she is or I'm coming for you next."

"I don't know."

"Don't even start with that. You want me to ask you these questions in person?"

"No. But Peter, it's the truth. I honestly don't know. Kane had her picked up. Kane sent those men to kill you. This whole operation is Kane's. He hasn't told me anything. Really. Never has."

"Where can I find him? Where does he live?"

"He's gone. Left right after you called your secretary. And he's never said where he lives. I'm not sure anyone knows."

"Don't dick with me, Casey."

"I wouldn't. Honest. It's the truth, and that's all I know."

"You tell him I'm going to find him, Casey. Tell him I'm going to take Melissa from him. Tell him!"

"I will, Peter. I hope you do get her back. Really."

"Go to hell."

16

Blevins returned from the Quantico raids with blood on his hands. His team had killed Pate in the woods around Quantico. Pate had taken a hostage, a new agent working her way through the obstacle course, and hurt her pretty bad. He'd tried to ransom his way out with her, but the negotiations were cut short when a sniper's .223 round whistled through the tip of Pate's nose. The small, high-velocity projectile had rattled around in Pate's skull until it ran out of gas, and had shredded his brain into rice.

They almost spilled more blood when they raided the office of the SOAR team, a nasty group of men who weren't used to being ordered around. The black-suited SOARs agents made a short stand and refused to leave the building or give up their weapons. But they added up the odds, counted the number of gunmen Blevins had with him and compared it to their own number. Doing the mathematics of life, they finally decided to cooperate.

Blevins killed Amos Warden. He'd had no choice. Warden rushed into his room while Blevins's agents were tossing it, pulled his weapon and started to fire. Blevins was working security during the search, so he'd been the one with a quick double-tap, two fast rounds fired into the K5 area of Warden's upper chest.

Warden died slowly, writhing on the floor, worrying about a diary and telling Blevins he wanted him to understand. Blevins used his fingers to plug the holes in his chest while Warden demanded that Blevins respect him for what he'd done for his country, even if he didn't understand the reasons.

Agents found the diary in a small personal safe. They'd handed it to Blevins as if it were the silver chalice, all of them speculating about what it might reveal. Blevins skimmed it quickly, learning just enough to know that Warden and some other agents were dirty. He started wondering how it could happen, how the Bureau could have gotten so corrupt that his men would need to get into the SWAT van, drive an hour to Quantico, then kill two of their own agents. Was the line between good and bad that poorly drawn? If so, was he one of the good guys? Hell, he was just a grunt following Sackett's orders. How would he know which side of the fence he was on?

Now that he was back in the office, he huddled in a corner of the squad room with Warden's diary, like a little boy with his daddy's *Playboy*. He read it carefully, started feeling ashamed of himself and the F.B.I. According to the diary, Sackett had allowed Warden's crimes to go on under his nose, had even conspired with Warden at times. But others had to have known, too. Were there that many bad F.B.I. agents?

Sackett walked into the squad room and strolled in Blevins's direction. Blevins set the diary down, watched the way Sackett walked, and wondered what kind of a man he really was.

Sackett sat down beside him, nodded at the diary, then reached over and picked it up.

"Anything good in here?"

Blevins took the small book out of Sackett's hands. "No. Enough covert crime to bring down a government, but nothing I would call good."

Sackett put his hands on his knees and stared at them, but didn't look anywhere near Blevins. "Did Warden mention me?"

Blevins breathed deeply, held it as long as he could, took a hard look at the side of Sackett's head. He made sure no one could hear them, then looked away as he spoke. "You want an attorney, boss? It might be a good idea."

Sackett made a nervous laugh, kept staring at his knees. "You think I need one?"

Blevins offered the diary to him. "I think you might."

Sackett turned his head enough to see the small book in Blevins's hand. "Thanks, but I don't need to read what's in there. I don't want an attorney, either."

Blevins set it down and put his hands in his lap. There was lots of hustle farther away in the squad room, and agents kept glancing their way. But no one stepped closer than twenty feet. Blevins kept quiet for a long time, pissed off, lost in some kind of trance as he and Sackett sat like stones while the rest of the agents bounced off the walls. Finally he dug his right elbow into his leg, held that hand upright, and cradled his face in it. He didn't look away from his knees and he spoke as though he were bored.

"Boss, Peter Jamison saved my life once. A bunch of other men's lives, too. Now he's out there fighting to save Melissa and not giving two shits about his own survival. The last time I spoke to him he said he wouldn't fail her. It was a threat and a promise, so I wouldn't want to stand in his way."

"Neither would I."

Blevins still didn't look at him, kept his head down, like his voice. "Maybe not, but it might be too late for that. While he's been out there catching fire, you've been sending me on bullshit details that haven't helped him one bit. I've wasted time at the Detention Center, and then running the raids at Quantico. Now

I'm sitting here like an idiot, out of ideas. What I want from you, right now, is one good lead. Something solid. I'm a pretty good investigator, Sackett. Just give me something worth a damn."

"You think I'm tied in with Warden, don't you? You think I'm privy to information you don't have."

Blevins didn't answer.

"Do you think I'm part of the corruption Jamison and Corley were uncovering?"

"A lead, boss. One lead, that's all I'm asking. So I can help my friend. Right now, I don't care about anything else."

Sackett stood and paced back and forth, doing small laps, both hands lined up alongside his nose. He stopped, and looked down at Blevins.

Blevins didn't look up as he waited.

"Jack Kane."

Blevins wanted to jump up and shake Sackett for more information. But he didn't. Just kept his mouth shut and waited some more.

"Jack Kane is the man in charge of killing Jamison. He probably has Melissa, too, or knows where she is. If Jamison's as good as I believe he is, by now he'll be getting close to Kane, so you'll probably find them in the same vicinity. But keep something in mind, Blevins."

Blevins didn't realize he was staring at Sackett until he heard his name.

"Yes?"

"If Jamison gets too close, Kane will kill him. He hasn't got a chance, not against Kane. I doubt anyone does."

Blevins thought about a day long ago on a jungle trail. He remembered Jamison performing the most savage acts Blevins had ever witnessed, and caught himself praying that Jamison still had what it took to do that kind of work.

"We'll see. My money's on Jamison."

Sackett didn't say anything, just stood there, as if waiting for more. Blevins stood up and started to walk toward the computer, thinking of every possible spelling of the name Kane.

"Blevins?"

He turned around. Sackett looked lost. Frightened. Blevins really didn't care.

"You going to arrest me, Blevins? I would, if I were you."

Blevins had already thought about it. But he still didn't know who was good, or who was bad. All he knew was that the body count of agents was rising. And Phillip Brewer was still out there, waiting to become dead agent number five.

"Pick a team, Sackett. I can't waste any more time on you. Just let me know where you stand."

Sackett glanced at the spot where he'd said Kane's name, then stepped in front of Blevins. "I just did."

The other agents were twitching around the room but keeping their distance. Blevins hoped none of them knew what was happening as he made the call.

"All right, Sackett, I'll take your sworn statement later. Do you have an address on Kane?"

Sackett smiled a little, sighed, put a hand on Blevins's shoulder.

"That's something I can help you with. I can take you there. I'm probably the only person around who can. Had to go there once when he'd been hurt, took one of our doctors to do some confidential work, remove a bullet from his chest."

Blevins didn't care and he didn't smile back. "Yeah? Well, how about Phillip Brewer? You know where I can find him, too?"

"No. Sorry. I was telling the truth when I said I didn't know him."

Blevins started walking away, switching back onto combat status. Then he stopped and turned back to Sackett, made a little snicker, coupled it to a very small grin. "Get the SWAT team ready, then meet me in the assembly area. I want Kane."

Blevins left to lock the diary in a security vault before anyone else read it. He passed the lobby on his way. Reporters were elbow to elbow, and cameramen held their bulky equipment over their heads because that was the only space left. Their numbers had increased exponentially since the evening news had broken the story that F.B.I. agents were still killing each other, that it hadn't stopped with the shoot-out at the Coalition. It looked as if every newsperson in Washington was in the lobby, trying to jump on the lead. Blevins glanced at the crowd through the bulletproof glass, turned away when the cameramen snapped on their floodlights.

Leo Strick stepped out of the SAC's office, his pocked and pointy face smiling at the cameras. He held up his hands like a preacher, waiting for Blevins to move through, and was startled when Blevins grabbed him in front of everyone, dragged him back into Sackett's office, and slammed the door closed.

Blevins threw him against the wall, took a little bit of his frustration out on Strick the Prick.

"Before you do your Hollywood celebrity thing, I want to tell you something. Listening?"

Strick did his best to look mean, but his hands were pressed together in front of his chest and he made no threats with them. He looked like a small, cornered animal, overmatched, just hoping to get away.

Blevins felt like thunking him on the head, disgusted that the F.B.I. had actually promoted this frightened rodent to ASAC.

"I've got twenty agents looking for Melissa Corley and Special Agent Brewer. I'm going to be gone for a while, Strick, but I want continued updates on their progress. Every thirty minutes, then an immediate call when they find either one. Understand?"

Strick muttered something, then did a little sniff with his nose and went back to rehearsing his lines.

Blevins was close to his limit. He slammed Strick into the wall again. "You hear me, Strick? I want an update on Melissa Corley every thirty minutes! No excuses."

Strick looked at the door, seemed worried that the spotlight of attention might move away before he had a chance to glory in it.

"Right, Blevins. Corley. Sure, sure, I got it. Let go of me."

Strick squirmed around in Blevins's grip, finally pulled away, and walked out, immediately smiling and talking to the reporters. Blevins didn't stick around to hear whatever stupidity would slosh from his mouth. He locked the diary in the gun vault, then ran down the hall and swung into the main assembly area. It was a large room, almost fifty feet by sixty feet, but it felt like a five by six closet. Agents were crammed into every inch of it, talking and breaking down their weapons and rechecking their gear. The unity of their voices mixed well with the mechanized clicks and snaps of magazines being loaded.

The room went silent when he entered and everyone turned to watch him. Sackett stared, too, one question lighting up his face, something he seemed to want answered before anything else happened. Was he a leader, a follower, or a suspect?

Blevins nodded at him, showed that he would wait for him to get started.

Sackett nodded back, and hurried to the center of the room. "Okay, men, real quick, here's the deal, all down and dirty. We're going to the residence of a man named Jack Kane. You all have his picture. We will arrest Mr. Kane if he's there, search the premises either way. If he's not there, some of you will head to Dillon Aerospace to search for him there. If anyone gets in our way, we will arrest him. If anyone fires on us, we will kill him. Questions?"

No one spoke. The crowded room was so quiet that when someone shuffled a boot, half of them flinched and reached for their weapons.

"Blevins will be the team leader. I will coordinate and control the search. You've all been briefed on what we're looking for, so grab anything that looks like it might tie in to this corruption. We'll deal with any sticky legal issues later. Expect resistance, men. Respond with deadly force. And gentlemen, you may not like some of what you find tonight. You may discover some traitors among us, some people you know very well. Be ready for that." He looked at Blevins, gave it a second, shrugged. "Ready? Let's go."

Blevins headed toward the stairwell with his men, sneaking out to avoid most of the media. They stomped down the stairs, heading for the bowels of the garage, heavily armed and ready to fight a small war. They carried fully automatic weapons, shotguns, night vision equipment, gas masks, and M-79 grenade launchers with high explosive rounds. Blevins carried some extra CN tear gas. There was no way they were going to be caught unprepared or outgunned tonight. It was the F.B.I. way, a long tradition of using overwhelming force.

*   *   *   *   *

Jamison headed to Melissa's Georgetown apartment, needing a chance to recharge, to be around her things, to be in her home. It was also a chance to think up some new strategy while he sewed up his bullet wound.

That damned kid at Casey's house had sent one round burning through him. The bullet had hit him in his side by his waist, slightly below the tip of his lower ribs. It hadn't done any real damage, considering that a few inches over might have killed him. No organs were hit. But the bullet had torn a two-inch gap between his ribs and his pelvis, ripped the flesh wide open. No guts were squeezing out, and there was surprisingly little pain. But the damned thing would not stop bleeding, had soaked the dish towel he'd taken from Casey's kitchen and stuck in the hole. The blood had soaked his shirt and the inside of his jacket, and was running down his leg in a sticky stream. It wouldn't be long before people would start pointing and staring as he walked among them.

He knew there was a chance that his enemies would be at Melissa's, waiting for him to show up, paid to kill him if he did. If Jamison had been in charge of the other team, he would have stationed someone there. He hoped Kane was thinking the same way, that he'd get a chance to capture an opponent and interrogate him in the quiet solitude of her apartment. Take his time, torture him as long as it took to get the answers he wanted. Find out where Melissa was, and how to get her back.

He hobbled down the street, holding his side, glad that it got dark so early in the winter. He was lightheaded from the loss of blood, so he focused on simple things, kept testing his judgment and acumen in small ways. What day is it? Wednesday. When's Melissa's birthday? April fourteenth. How many rounds does my Beretta hold? Sixteen, including one in the pipe. Each right answer made him stronger, gave him the confidence he needed to keep going, through the front door of her building and up the stairs, stumbling a little and making lots of racket, not even trying to surprise someone behind the door, suspecting now that if they were really there, he would die. The trip here had cost him too much, left him little with which to fight.

If he died here, it was as close to dying in her arms as he could hope. He would be glad for that. It would offset some of the sadness of knowing he'd failed her miserably both times she'd needed him.

He banged up the last flight of steps, somehow keeping himself from falling back down them as he passed the last door, then wrestled his Beretta out of his waistband. He unlocked her door with the key she'd given him, flung it back, stood smack in the middle of the opening and waited for the flash of light that would blow him away.

It didn't happen. The room stayed dark, with no light at all inside. He kept his Beretta in his hand, parallel with the floor, and waited some more, listening like hell for a sound in the darkness, and not afraid to hear it, either. He wanted to hear it, wanted someone to be there, needing to get information from them, then take another enemy out of the game.

He stepped in, kicked the door closed with his foot, and leaned back against it, realizing how exhausted he really was. He started slumping down the door, wanting to fold into a neat little puddle on the hardwood floor, sit there and close his eyes, pass out, and sleep. But he didn't. He pushed himself away from the door and turned on a light.

Melissa's apartment had been destroyed. He stood there with his fingers on the lightswitch, looking around her apartment, thinking it couldn't have been damaged any more by an earthquake. He let his hand drop off the switch, started wandering through the debris, wondering how someone could have done all this without alerting the neighbors. Or had they told the neighbors, given them a good story that convinced them? Maybe showed them some credentials and a warrant?

Nothing had been overlooked. Every item on the shelves had been flung down and broken. The furniture had been dumped over and gutted, the stuffing shredded and the drawers emptied into several piles. The antique bookcase he'd humped up the stairs as a birthday surprise had been smashed to pieces. Holes had been punched in the walls, as if someone had been looking for a hidden safe. Boards had been pried up from the hardwood floor.

As Jamison picked his way through the rooms, his strength began to come back, chasing away the weak resignation he'd felt a few moments earlier. His anger returned with his strength, or maybe it was the other way around. Either way, he was building power he needed to keep moving, to do more than he'd believed was still possible when he'd first arrived.

He walked to her bathroom, trying to avoid the piles of her clothes on the bedroom floor that were already heavily trampled by an army of dirty shoes. He picked up some of the cleaner items and laid them over a chair, hoping Melissa would live here again and need them.

He lifted the dress she'd worn last Thursday when they'd met by accident at Jonah's Bar. The silky blue dress still carried the scent of IL Bacio, which worked its way into his nose and forced him to press the dress against his face.

Everything in Melissa's medicine cabinet looked to have been swept out by the quick flick of a hurried hand. He found her small sewing kit on the vanity, half buried under the fallout that covered every flat surface. Jamison picked it up and took out a large needle, selected white thread because it looked clean, sat down on the commode and wrapped a towel over his hip, above his jeans, just below the jagged edges of his flesh.

He wasn't going to sew up the wound, hell, he had no idea how to do that. He just needed to close it a little, bring four edges together in the middle to give him a solid foundation for a field dressing which would stop the bleeding. The loss of blood was making him too weak, and too obvious. He had to bring it under control. He studied the hole for a minute, picked around it with his fingers, and found four skin flaps that would stretch the distance. He punched the needle through the piece of ragged skin farthest away, came in from the outside so the knot would rest against the epidermis, planning to stretch the skin as far as it would go and use that to determine where the four pieces of flesh would meet.

He felt only a mild tingle as the silver needle and white thread passed through the meat. When the knot snugged up against his skin he jerked it tight, tugged on it several times, checked to make sure it wouldn't pull through the hole. Then he came straight up with the needle and stuck it through the underside of the flesh dangling under the tip of his rib, pulled the thread tight, then stretched the two pieces together. They fit pretty well, and made him sort of proud of his sewing. He pulled six more stitches to hold these pieces together, then knotted it off, cut the thread, retied it, and repeated the same procedure with pieces from his front and back.

The patch slowed the bleeding to a trickle, but Jamison didn't kid himself. He knew infection would set in. Blood might pool inside him. He could die without proper medical care. He had to go to a hospital, but knew he wouldn't take the time to do it. Not unless he got Melissa back first. He would ignore every twitch of agony, every signal of pain that tried to work its way into his brain. He would pretend he was dead already, or at least sentenced to death. With that attitude, it would be easy to ignore anything else.

He searched around for an antiseptic. Something, anything. Alcohol, peroxide, iodine. Couldn't find any, remembered the army teaching him that urine was sterile and could be used in an emergency. He hated the idea of doing that, and searched some more. Held his side and went to the kitchen where he found a bottle of antibiotics. He took four, and they gave him hope. The hope gave rise to pain, which he quickly converted into anger that he would unleash on Jack Kane.

He pressed a hand towel against his patch job and tied it in place with one of Melissa's stockings, then changed into some clothes he'd left there. Felt pretty good actually, relieved as much as recharged. His anger had been energized by the sight of her apartment. The touch of her clothes had fueled his determination. The smell of her perfume had refreshed his senses, brought her closer than she'd been since Monday.

He'd called Drummond earlier and said he needed help in finding a very elusive man named Jack Kane. Drummond had begged Jamison to come into his office and hide behind a security detail, to let the trained professionals get Melissa back. Drummond reminded him that he'd known Melissa all her life, loved her as much as Jamison did, and understood his motives completely. But the F.B.I. would get her back, he'd said. Jamison didn't have to get himself killed in the process.

Drummond must have heard the pain in Jamison's voice. Not the pain of injuries but the pain of panic, of knowing he had a loved one out there needing his help, but Jamison not quite able to provide it. He sounded like a hysterical parent whose child has been kidnapped.

Drummond had agreed to help. Both of them valued Melissa's life more than Jamison's. So Jamison had tried to sneak into Drummond's building an hour ago, straight from Casey's house, but he'd found too many Secret Service agents camped out to allow a bleeding man with a handgun to get near the building. So he had searched her apartment for an address book or Christmas card list, and found one under a kitchen drawer which had been dumped, then dropped on the floor. Opened it to D, wrote down Drummond's home address. He took one more look around Melissa's apartment, then left. Back to work.

17

Jack Kane turned off all the lights except for a small brass lamp his wife had given him the last Christmas she was alive. Although the lamp wasn't an antique, it had the worn look of one. He had rewired it twice over the years, polished it a dozen times and replaced the switch over and over. He would keep the inexpensive gift working until he took it to his grave.

By the fragile light of its little bulb he pulled the spindled envelope from his bottom desk drawer. He held it gently in his hands, stared at it for a long, long time. All of Dillon's offices were quiet this late in the evening, and quiet times were never good times for Kane. Silence always took him back to when the lady in the envelope was real, a beautiful, graceful lady who'd shared his life, raised his children, and loved him like he would never be loved again.

He pulled out her picture and held it in one of his big hands. Held pictures of his two sweet daughters in the other. Suddenly, without any warning, he started to cry. The tears came immediately and surprised him terribly. Not one drop had ever leaked out before, much less flooded out like this. They had never been strong enough to penetrate his barrier of hate.

But he was crying now, sobbing like a small child. His lower lip quivered as he remembered her sweetness, the way she was so loving to everyone, and worried about every person on earth except herself. Knowing her the way he did, he suspected she'd been nice to the men who'd killed her and his family that night, concerned about those men getting into such serious trouble, genuinely offering to help them if they were allowed to live.

He savored her memory as long as he could before pulling out her killers' pictures. He always waited like this, holding on to his family as long as his anger would allow, shutting off the venom until its pressure became overwhelming, his big hands snatching the killers' pictures as he remembered the wonderful sounds of their painful deaths.

But something strange happened tonight, an aberration, an anomaly, a miracle. His anger did not come. He held onto the pictures of his wife and daughters longer than he'd ever managed before, and the anger still did not come. He was still crying, even worse than before. Yet somehow better. The sobs made him ache and drew him into a knot, curled him up in his big leather chair with his hands fidgeting over his mouth, shaking in staggered rhythm with the rest of his body.

Some of their personal things were in the envelope. Kane hadn't been able to touch them in twenty years. But now he gently tipped the envelope over, let the sacred items spill onto his desk. Her wedding ring, and the inexpensive charms he'd given his daughters to wear around their necks. He picked them up and caressed them, held them against his face and stained them with his tears. Tears that kept coming like never before. Tears that might never stop. Two decades worth.

He could not stop trembling. His lips, hands, and legs twitched with the rest of his body. The shaking was uncontrollable, like his tears. Like his sobbing.

He saw his family alive, for the first time since they'd been murdered. Saw them laughing and giggling and rolling on the floor with him, playing games and tickling each other. Having more fun than he could believe had ever been possible. The haunting, full-color morgue photos began to fade from his mind, and his ears began to hear laughter. He heard his daughters teasing him about his clothes, about how out of style they were. Saw his beautiful wife join them, put an arm around each of his girls, stand in loving solidarity and give him a hard time, too. He watched himself chase them out the door of their comfortable home and take them to McDonald's, then miniature golf.

Kane was afraid to move, wanted to live in the past as long as the ghosts would stay with him, to enjoy his memories as if they were rare old movies only recently rescued from some dusty shelf. Gradually he began to understand that the pleasant ghosts were not going to leave, that his family was back to live with him again. Even if they were confined to his mind and heart, he was happier than he could describe, felt as though he'd come out of a long, dark coma.

He saw his life as something entirely different than what it had been a week ago, and couldn't wait to get on with it. There was no desire left in him to look at the men who'd taken his family away. He picked up their photos and dropped them into the garbage.

He hurried down the hall, but moved slowly into Casey's office, not wanting to scare him, letting his eyes adjust to Casey's darkness. Casey jumped anyway, although Kane didn't actually see it. Casey snapped to attention while Kane located him and analyzed his changing position, all from the sound of a flinch. That sort of thing came automatically to Kane, a sadly normal part of his day to day life, as natural as breathing.

He flipped on the lights and watched Casey squint, his eyes streaked with red from booze or crying. Kane imagined a wicked combination of the two.

"What, Jack? What have you found out? What is the F.B.I. doing? Are they coming here?"

Kane sat down and smoothed the crease of his trousers. "I received another call from one of our men inside. He said that F.B.I. agents have gone to my home. Sackett has rolled over and is leading the way. They'll be coming here next."

Casey's hand went to his lips, then made a fist, then went back to his lips. He jerked his eyes around the room in no particular direction. They ended up back on Kane.

"Okay, Jack. We're still okay, I think. They won't find much at your place, will they?"

"No. Nothing."

Casey slumped in his seat, probably the position he'd been in when Kane entered.

"But they won't stop there, Casey. They've got Jamison's data. That friend of his, Blevins, has copies of all the stuff Corley and Jamison put together."

"So what. That won't be a problem once they're dead. But how far will they go? That's the real question."

"Frankly, Casey, I don't think they'll quit until they find everything. We're not going to dodge this one. It's over."

"All the stuff in the storage vault, Kane? Is that what you mean? I've never seen it, but you have. What's in there?"

Kane walked to his spot at the window, wondering where Casey had heard about the storage vault. Casey stood up and followed him, trailing like a kid begging for candy.

"Yes, I think there's a decent chance they'll find it. And it's all there, Casey. Everything. It's a big walk-in safe that was built for military secrets sixty years ago. It's jammed with records of everything our group has ever done, back to the beginning of the Vietnam War. By tomorrow the F.B.I. could know what's there, which will justify search warrants for hundreds of locations. Maybe thousands."

Casey's eyes and mouth were wide open, staring like Kane's head had just spun around.

"Then . . . then we're finished, Kane. All of us. After all this time, why does it have to end now?"

Kane checked his nails. "It's probably just as well."

Casey slammed his hands against Kane's chest. "What's that supposed to mean?" He quickly jumped back with a terrified look and stood there waiting for a second. Then he came at him again and hit him with a clenched fist.

Kane took it, let Casey get some of it out, let it continue until Casey started to rage. At that point he stepped back and gave him the Look, but had a little trouble getting it onto his face.

Casey stopped, then came again, ran at him with a panicky kind of terror in his eyes. Kane waited until he got close, then grabbed his arms and twisted him around, pinned him against the glass and spoke quietly in his ear. "Listen, Casey, you need to cool down."

Casey struggled. He wriggled and squirmed in Kane's big embrace. But he couldn't work anything loose and calmed down pretty quickly. Kane let him go.

"Sorry, Jack. Really. I'm just. . .shit, they're going to find out everything. And I'm the one that's going to take the fall for Dillon."

"Maybe."

"But you'll go down, too! Hey, at least I haven't been going around killing people. I might have contributed to a little corruption, but jeez, you killed people!"

Kane was losing his good feeling. If Casey brought his weak-ass shit again, he might actually hurt him, just to shut him up, to preserve the pleasure he felt for his family.

"You're right, Casey. But it doesn't matter. If all the F.B.I. had was Jamison's evidence, hell, we could get past that. Pay a fine, maybe. Be cut off from contracts for a year. But to go any further with that evidence, the Justice Department would just be wasting time, chasing vapors. Once they open the safe, though, our world is going to cave in. America is going to come down hard on people like us."

"Not so fast, Kane. We're not the ones who started this cozy little relationship. So I'm going to take all of them down with me. You hear me? Everybody. I won't look so bad if I drag a long parade of corrupt politicians and corporate leaders into court behind me."

Kane laughed, because Casey was right. Richard Corley had married the defense industry to the Hill long before either of them had come along. He'd shown the way to finance their missions through cost overruns, and it was a tribute to his genius that they'd lasted this long. Except for a couple of small issues that blew up in their faces—six-hundred-dollar hammers and thousand-dollar toilet seats—they'd managed to divert billions of dollars and nobody had ever gotten wise. And that was just Dillon's contribution.

Casey paced to the window and looked out, then walked back to Kane. "Well, it never had to end. You should have killed Jamison when I told you to. But no, you said. Just kill the project, you said. Lay off the whole division. That would stop the leaks. Well, guess what, pal. You failed. Failed Dillon, failed all of us. You're the reason this is happening."

"I suppose you're right. I guess that would have ended it, at least for the time being. But we all knew it would end someday. We couldn't last forever. Eventually, someone would have caught on to the deal. If it hadn't been Jamison, it would have been someone else. Anyway, I'm about finished with it."

Casey looked up quickly, as though this sounded pretty good, an option he hadn't known existed. He looked like he wanted to come along and be finished with it, too. "What do you mean?"

Kane was at the service bar, pouring himself a cola. "I'm going to turn myself in to the F.B.I. and make a full confession. I've got a few things to do first, but I'm heading there in the morning. If you can make it out of this, fine. But you'd better start moving."

Casey stared at the drink fizzing in the glass. "Why, Kane? Why would you do that? We're not really criminals, neither of us. Sure, some things have gone on that we participated in, but we can say it was blackmail. It was those guys controlling the fund. They made us cooperate, would have cut us off from government contracts otherwise. The F.B.I. would believe that. Our attorneys can make us out to be victims. You know that."

"You're probably right, Casey. Problem is, if I don't confess to hiring those men to kill Jamison, no one will be looking to stop them, or know who they're looking for if they do. Hell, *I* can't even find them, so I know the F.B.I. won't without my help. As you can see, I'm not holding much of a hand."

"Why would you care about Jamison? Hell, he's the cause of all this. Let him get picked off, I say. I sure wouldn't lose any sleep over it."

Kane stretched out his big, dangerous hand, held it in front of Casey's stomach. "I know you wouldn't. Listen, good luck to you." He squeezed Casey's hand, then turned to leave

"Yeah. Same to you, Jack. Same right back to you."

* * * * *

Special Agent Brewer had stayed calm, had struggled with his temper each and every time Melissa Corley had taunted him, had spent the entire day waiting for orders to kill her, or move her, or release her. But no orders had come, and her words were really starting to bug him, creating some genuine fear about what he'd done. The darkness outside made him feel more alone than he had during the day.

He knew the F.B.I. assistant director who'd given him this assignment would quash any criminal charges filed against him for taking her. He, hell, all of them, would probably avoid prosecution, just as certainly as they had in the past. But Brewer had never been so blatant before, signing out the prisoner with his own credentials. And that was the part that really worried him.

"What are you waiting for, Brewer? What are you going to do with me?"

The Corley woman had not spoken since their most recent clash, more than two hours ago. Her voice startled him a little.

"I'm sure they know you have me. What do you think will happen when they find us?"

Brewer peered out of the safehouse window then walked to where she sat on the couch. He already had plenty of worries and he didn't need her to start antagonizing him again. He checked to make sure her right hand was still cuffed to the couch, then sat down beside her, looked at her for about a minute, trying to make his goofy eyes show that he'd crossed the line once, years ago, and decided to stay on the wrong side. Just in case she wondered where it stood with them.

"They won't find you, Corley, so I don't have to worry about what happens. You and Jamison have no idea what we're doing, or how capable we are of doing it. But to answer your first question, you are going to die, just as I told you this morning. I've waited as long as I was supposed to and no one has called to rescind or amend the orders. So your time is up. Sorry."

He'd hoped the news would make her beg. It certainly would have made him beg if the roles were reversed. He watched her closely but was disappointed. She gave back nothing, looked absolutely fearless. It pissed him off.

"Second, I don't think anything will happen when they find out I've killed you. It's the way we do things. You, obviously, should know that."

Corley's free hand reached for her forehead, as if rubbing away a headache. "Tell me about your work, okay? Tell me some details."

"I think you already know how our government really works."

"Only the way it's supposed to work."

He chuckled but didn't smile. "Oh, I see. All that good investigative work you've done at the Coalition hasn't enlightened you at all?"

"Enlightened? In what respect?"

He moved closer, tried to make her squirm. She was stalling for time and he knew it. But it didn't matter. He could give up the time. Nothing was going to change.

"Come on, you expect me to believe that the daughter of the great Richard Corley doesn't know how we operate?"

"I didn't say that. I know you don't mind distorting the system of justice we have in America. I know you don't care about rights. Or laws."

"See, I knew you understood. You're exactly right. Surely, then, you understand that we only work this way because our legal system is so badly busted. If people like me, and your father, and others like us didn't work outside of the system, who would defend the regular, honest guy. How else can citizens' rights be protected when the courts are obsessing over the rights of criminals?"

Brewer felt his engine building pressure, straining his control. But he would kill her shortly, so he could afford some indiscretion.

"Do you know, Corley, jeez, do you have any idea how hard it is to bring someone to trial in America, let alone get a conviction? The defense attorneys manipulate the law, the prosecutors have no choice but to plea-bargain everything they can, the ACLU wants every single right—never mind the cost to past and future victims—protected with a vengeance. The criminal breezes in and out of court like a celebrity."

"It's American justice, Brewer. It's not perfect, but it's the best thing going."

"It stinks! Everyone is afraid of incarcerating an innocent man, worried to death about the possibility of making him a victim. Well, lady, they're right, there's always a chance an innocent man might go to jail. But there's a war going on in our streets. There has to be victims! If one innocent guy goes to prison along with a thousand criminals, sure, he's a victim, and it's a damn shame, no question. But the justice system is so afraid of that happening that they let the thousand criminals go free with him, just to avoid the risk. So what happens then? Huh?"

Melissa was staring at him. She looked like a teenager being lectured about cleaning her room.

"I'll tell you what happens then. Those criminals who *weren't* sent to jail in order to save the one-in-a-thousand innocent guy, well, they go out and create their own pool of victims. Maybe hundreds of them. Maybe thousands. Thousands of victims instead of one. Now you tell me, where's the justice in that? Who protected the rights of all of those victims?"

Corley shook her head, still didn't seem to get it, didn't looked like she understood. "A criminal's rights have to be protected, Brewer. I suppose the ACLU would argue that all of our rights are protected along with the criminal's."

Brewer had heard that argument hundreds of times, but still couldn't believe the stupidity of it.

"That's bullshit and you know it. The fact is that honest, law-abiding Americans don't even need, or want, most of those rights. Why? Because they're not breaking the law! They've got nothing to be afraid of and they're not hiding anything. You stop an honest man and ask him to open his trunk, you know what he says? He says, 'Sure, Mr. Policeman. What's the problem?' So you take a quick look inside his trunk, thank him, then go on to the next guy who matches the description and drives a similar car.

"But try stopping a criminal and the story is big-time different. He knows his rights 'cause he's some kind of a half-ass jailbird lawyer and he says, 'Screw you, get a warrant.' Drives off laughing, with maybe a dead body or a kilo of heroin back there. Those, lady, are the rights the courts are protecting. I think those great men who wrote the Bill of Rights were brilliant, no question, but they'd never want to see the protection of individual rights lead to the collapse of this nation."

"And so that's where you guys come in, huh? You level the playing field?"

Brewer was going good now, couldn't even get his hands unclenched.

"You bet your sweet ass we do. We didn't take this job to be judge, jury, and executioner, but no one else seems willing to do it. The courts, hell, they aren't any kind of deterrent to crime. Ask anyone, any of those career criminals who've been through the revolving door. They laugh their heads off at it, couldn't care less what the law says. But you can take it to the bank that I'm a deterrent. And others like me. We deter crime by eliminating the criminals who perpetrate the majority of it, the ones who would already be in prison if they'd done their crimes in any other country in the world. And I don't mean just harsh, third-world countries, either. *Any* other country."

Corley checked her nails, had a little trouble doing it with the handcuffs. "Does President Albright authorize all of your actions? Is he your leader?"

Brewer was up and pacing now, feeling the inspiration of the truly converted. "You're shitting me, right? You don't know, really?"

"Don't know what?"

Brewer shook his head as if this was just too funny. "President Albright is just a figurehead, like the queen of England. He's not smart enough or tough enough to handle this kind of power. We're running this country from the background, and Albright is just fancy scenery that—"

Corley laughed, damn her. But it made her breasts move and he liked seeing that. Felt a twinge in his groin.

"You're kidding," she said, still laughing. "You're telling me that someone with more power than the president spends his days worrying about petty criminals?"

Brewer hit his head, hard enough to hurt, sort of liking the feel of it.

"No, damn, of course not. He hardly has time to worry about our justice system at all. He's far too busy with world affairs. But don't you see, the same types of problems exist in world politics. Just think about it, some second-rate shit running a third-world nation starts creating problems for America, and everybody talks about using sanctions to weaken his power, or diplomacy to placate him. But what we really should do is smack the crap out of the little bastard. Know what I mean?" He slammed his right fist into his left palm, then looked at her for some signal of understanding.

"Oh, sure," she said. "I guess it makes sense. I can believe that some of the leaders around the world are just, well. . . plain old criminals."

Brewer made a hallelujah with his arms. "Well thank you ma'am, and you're exactly right. So what we're all really trying to do, to the very best of our abilities, is . . . our jobs. Exactly what we're paid to do. Protect this country from all enemies, foreign and domestic, just like we promised when we took the oath of office."

Corley looked at her dress, smoothed it out a little with her free left hand. "I see. And how many people in the Bureau, and on Capitol Hill, understand and support your efforts?"

Brewer's stop sign went up. His zeal had not overtaken his F.B.I. training.

"You wouldn't be playing me for stupid, would you?"

She turned her hands up and shrugged her shoulders.

"I wouldn't if you weren't."

* * * * *

Melissa held onto her nerve and waited with what she hoped was a fearless look while Brewer hovered over her. A second later he lunged at her and grabbed her shoulders. She struggled, but he held her tight with his left hand, ripped her blouse down with his right. One of her bra straps got tangled in his grip and was jerked down with her blouse, exposing her left breast. The brown nipple must have gassed his jets because he climbed onto her and straddled her legs, his heavy weight pinning her legs down as he kissed the left side of her neck. Then he slid off her legs, kept kissing her neck while he pinched her nipple and groped around under her dress, moving up her legs until he reached her panties. The ribs that Jitters had injured were screaming for him to get off, but she fought the pain.

She didn't struggle, not even a little. She waited, thinking, planning. After all, this was what she'd wanted. His rough face was grating her skin but she didn't resist. He was too close and too strong to push away with her one free hand so she gasped lightly, as if this was something she hated herself for enjoying but didn't want to stop. Then she slid her left arm around his head and pulled him in, close, and tight. A lover's embrace.

He followed her lead, grinding his body up and down hers, pinching her nipple harder, squeezing her breast too hard. He slid down her and licked her nipple, then started sucking her breast, hard enough to hurt. He kept rubbing his body against hers, grinding his crotch against her hip, faster and faster, the blood pumping up the veins of his neck as his hand slipped under her panties and into her body, his mouth moving back to her neck as she squeezed her legs together and locked his hand in her crotch.

When her teeth first penetrated the skin of his neck he went rigid, just for a second. Then he screamed, a frantic, desperate,

269

hopeless scream, the agonized cry of one human being eaten alive by another. The horrible screams grew worse and worse, then turned pathetic as she sunk her teeth all the way into the left side of his neck, as far as they could go, so deep that her jaws hurt from the strain. Then she clamped down hard, ripping and tearing the flesh, shaking her head like a hungry shark trying to shred away the loose meat. The bite was too big and wouldn't come away in one piece, but Brewer's carotid artery popped and gushed blood all over both of them. She almost gagged when Brewer's blood filled her mouth and flooded her throat. But she swallowed it, gulped it down with the rhythm of his heart, holding onto him with her teeth and left arm while her stomach engorged.

Brewer rocked and jumped but she'd clamped down hard, held him in this awkward position and gave him little leverage, knowing the end would come quickly. She just had to hold on. She kept his right hand jammed so tight against her breast that it wasn't any help, and her strong legs locked down on his left hand like a vise. She kept his feet off the floor and his head scissored in the crotch of her arm until the gushing stream of blood slowed to a trickle and he whimpered his way to death.

Brewer's blood was already turning sticky by the time she dug the handcuff key out of his pants pocket and un-locked herself. She grabbed his gun as she threw up his blood, then stepped toward the kitchen to wash up. She had just moved out of the living room when the front door shattered and a pistol whipped into the apartment.

She raised Brewer's pistol to fire at the hand that held the pistol, at whoever was on the other side of the door. But she didn't. There was something wrong here, something weird. Somehow, she didn't feel threatened. Then the Big Man moved into the room and aimed his pistol past her, took in the bloody scene behind her without ever aiming in her direction.

"Are you all right?"

She kept her aim pinned on him and followed his movements precisely. "Yes."

"Anyone else in here with Brewer?"

"No."

The Big Man closed what remained of the door and walked past her pistol without even glancing at it. He checked Brewer, then holstered his own pistol and walked straight into her aim.

"You need to get out of here, go someplace safe. I can help you if you want. Actually, I might be able to help you find Jamison."

She stared at him and recognized him, but didn't know him. He was acting too different from the way he'd been in her cell. She lowered her pistol, just a little.

"Who are you?"

"My name is Kane. Jack Kane."

"Whose side are you on?"

His mouth went a little crooked. "My own, I guess. I'd like to help you, though, if you think you can trust me."

Brewer's big handgun was getting heavy. She lowered it a little, wondering what this guy's story was. Wasn't he the enemy? Sure he was. But then, he'd protected her from Jitters back at the Detention Center, so maybe not. And besides, what were her choices? Who else might know where Peter was, assuming he was even alive? Who else knew where the next act of this play might be performed?

"Okay, Mr. Kane. We'll try it awhile and see how it goes. But I keep my gun."

Kane picked up the phone and dialed, turned his back to her.

"Do you know how to use it?"

"Yes. Absolutely."

"Good. I may need the help."

18

It was raining and cold and dark as a nightmare. Jamison was angry and callused, hard and desperate. The scent from Melissa's dress was still in his nostrils, driving him toward trouble, blocking the pain of his wounds, keeping his body's warning signals from reaching his brain.

The cold could not bother him in this condition, and didn't deserve more than a passing observation. It was freezing, so what? He was killing again, had lined himself up at the gates of hell and killed three men in twelve hours. Three more people added to his personal body count. There would be more, he was sure of it, and there was no way to forget any of them. Especially the one who got away. The one who had raped Melissa.

He watched for the crazy man as he marched through the scary forest of rage, never wanting to give in to wholesale slaughter again. His fight with Butler had intimidated the crazy man, but Jamison stayed on guard, determined to fight him like he'd always done and kill only when absolutely necessary, let logic and clear thinking pick his targets. He'd killed Butler, and two men at Casey's house, without the crazy man. He'd hated doing it, but liked the strange feeling of doing it alone, a justifiable approach to killing.

But he wasn't kidding himself. He knew the truth, even as he denied it. He was playing the crazy man's game, a game of unspeakable violence where he would do barbaric things to other human beings, heinous acts he normally wouldn't be able to think about without shuddering. There wasn't an option if he wanted to survive and get Melissa back. It had become a very simple business.

Smithson Lane was a quiet street lined with beautiful houses of distinguished character. Each home was unique, yet true to the Tudor theme of the area. Large porches, steep rooflines and exposed beams. A very upscale neighborhood. Jamison logged in several places to hide as he trod along the sidewalk, just in case he'd brought his troubles with him—killers who might have followed him to Senator Drummond's house, who might hurt Drummond if he got in their way. He hoped it would only take a minute to pick up the information and be gone, leaving the old man to his rest.

He turned into Drummond's driveway, keeping close to a hedge that ran toward the garage in the rear, checking behind him often, keeping a careful vigil against being followed. He passed some windows and peered in, saw Drummond and another man through the sheer drapes. Drummond sat at a table strewn with papers, as though he had just cleaned out his office. He looked very relaxed, sipping from a brandy glass as he picked through the clutter.

The other man was strong-looking and clean-cut, a bodyguard of some kind. Maybe Secret Service, assigned to protect Senator Drummond as he went after those corrupt bastards at Dillon. The bodyguard was pacing the floor. There was a holster on his belt with a large-frame, stainless steel revolver stuck in it.

What the hell? In the bodyguard's right hand was the paper coaster Jamison had given Melissa at the Chamber Restaurant, the one with Blevins's phone number on it.

Jamison looked closer at the papers on the table. There were some Coalition letters there, along with files and disks and the picture of him and Melissa that she'd kept on her desk, the two of them standing knee deep in snow at Sugarloaf. All the items appeared to be from Melissa's office. Drummond had her things spread out on his dining room table, picking through them like garbage. It took five or six seconds for it all to make sense.

His stomach was grinding and his arms were twitching as he whipped his Beretta from his belt, rechecked for a round in the chamber, then ran toward the rear porch. He was going fast, almost running, his side straining his patch job, Melissa's stocking slipping down off it. He covered the last three steps in a single leap then smashed the door with his foot. The glass shattered and the jamb splintered. Somewhere nearby, but not in the house, a dog barked.

He rushed into the kitchen, his pistol cocked and ready at eye level. He was halfway through the kitchen when Drummond's bodyguard jumped into the doorway that separated the dining room. The guard drew his revolver and raised it to fire. Jamison aimed straight at his head and rushed him. He paid no attention to the guard's weapon, concentrated on his own aim as his trigger began to travel, his legs still hurtling his body toward the man.

Three blasts were separated by the smallest margin of time. Jamison felt the second recoil of his Beretta a split whisper before the impact of the other man's bullet. It burned its way into the meaty biceps of Jamison's left arm, just for a tiny slice of time, then punched a hole out the back and exited. He shut off the searing pain like a faucet.

His two shots found their mark and smacked the bodyguard in the face, one below and one just above his right eye, flattened out on impact and ripped the flesh away from his face before they tore the top of his head off. The bodyguard crumpled to the floor and didn't move.

Jamison shifted his aim to Drummond, who was still sitting at the table, looking nice and relaxed with his brandy glass still in his hand. Jamison was short on time; there was no chance those blasts had gone unnoticed by the neighbors.

He dropped his pistol on the table and charged at Drummond, his good right arm leading the way. In the two seconds it took to cross the room, Jamison's anger went to the very edge of sanity. Without a thought he crashed the back of his right hand across Drummond's face, cracking some bones somewhere and opening an ugly gash across the senator's aging hide. But the old man reset himself and remained still, unflinching.

Jamison lunged deep into the old man's face, his spit spraying Drummond's wrinkled skin.

"You son of a bitch! Where's Melissa?"

Drummond dabbed at the bloody gash with his fingers, then held them out and examined them curiously. His face twisted into a toothy smile.

"Who?"

Jamison smashed Drummond's face a second time, not realizing what he was doing until he witnessed it.

"Where is she?"

Drummond tried to stand as a show of authority, or fearlessness. But Jamison wouldn't have it. He spread his right hand into a V and drove it hard across Drummond's neck, lifted Drummond out of his chair and slammed him against the wall. A picture fell and the china cupboard rocked. Jamison bore down hard, compressed the wrinkled neck until all of his fingertips were touching the wall.

"Where's Melissa?"

Drummond stayed calm as he dangled there. His throat strained against Jamison's hand, squeaking in casual gasps as though this whole discussion bored him. Jamison loosened his grip a little, watched how far the old man sank before his feet touched the floor.

Drummond swallowed through the pinch in his throat. "The hell with you, Jamison. And the hell with Melissa Corley."

Jamison crushed the neck again, cracked it around until the skull flopped back and forth.

"Tell me where she is. I'm willing to trade lives here. Yours for Melissa's. That's the deal and it's on the table. But the clock's running. Decide."

He threw Drummond on the floor, watched him huddle by a chair.

"Don't hesitate on my behalf, Jamison. You want to kill me? Go ahead. But keep in mind that if you destroy me, you destroy my work."

"Good."

"Oh? You think so? You think we should go back to the way things used to be?"

"I hate what you're doing!"

"Then who will protect America? If not me, who? The American People? Ha! Do you really think those people who don't read, don't vote, and don't care can adequately decide how this country should handle itself in domestic and foreign policy? Listen to me, Jamison, they're not interested, and wouldn't know what to do if they were."

Jamison went to the windows and looked outside, checked for cops without looking away from Drummond for more than two seconds.

"So you do their thinking for them?"

"Someone has to. They deserve to have *somebody* protecting them and their possessions. Someone who doesn't give a shit about the hows and the whys. You know, Mr. Jamison, Americans only pretend to care if something is legal or illegal, Constitutional or not. In truth, all they really want to know is that they'll be safe, along with their families and their fortunes."

"I think you're wrong. I don't think they want your vision of this country. You're a criminal, and they don't want criminals running their government."

"I'm a revolutionary, Mr. Jamison. All revolutionaries start out as criminals. It's part of the definition. Look at our history, look at Washington, Jefferson, Adams. Weren't they, in most ways, criminals, too? Certainly the British thought so."

Jamison reached down and snatched Drummond off the floor. His side ripped open and spilled more blood down his leg.

"I'm not going to argue history with you. Let's go, you're coming with me."

"Listen, Jamison. You're a smart man. Aren't you tired of seeing every policy and law of this nation bickered over and used as political leverage by two houses and a president?"

Jamison pushed him toward the kitchen but Drummond's feet stuck to the floor, didn't move.

"Well? Answer the question. Aren't you tired of that kind of gridlock? Of course you are. And why? Because Americans are people of action. They hate that their government has become moribund because of idiotic political posturing."

Jamison pushed him again, a hard shove in the back. Drummond moved this time. Jamison picked his gym bag off the kitchen floor, took out the roll of duct tape, and strapped Drummond's hands.

"We've done all right so far, old man. You're not the savior you think you've become."

"You don't think so now. But just wait until the strait jackets that Congress and the president have put on each other prevent America from acting decisively in a national emergency. And it will happen. Hell, it already *has* happened. Everyone's afraid, and unable to act in a crisis. We, as a country, are very, very vulnerable. It's terrifying. If I and my organization hadn't been there to act in America's best interest, our enemies would have destabilized our nation already. There's not anyone else to stop them."

Jamison finished taping Drummond's hands, watching for lights outside, knowing he'd taken too long.

"Let's go for a ride, old man."

"Huh?"

Jamison picked a ring of keys off the counter, pushed Drummond out of the house and over to the garage. He opened the trunk of Drummond's Lincoln, forced him in, taped his legs together while he listened to the sirens in the near distance.

Jamison ripped off one last piece of tape, about eight inches long. "This is for your mouth. You'll have to breathe through your nose, you old goat."

Drummond looked panicked, the first time since Jamison had crashed through the door.

"I can't do that, Jamison. I'll die."

"I hope so."

It was almost midnight when they got to the underground garage. It was completely quiet as Jamison pulled in and stopped at the vacant spot for Unit 213. The other parking place for that condo had a new white BMW parked in it.

He backed Drummond's car into the extra space, leaving plenty of room behind it. He got out and opened the trunk, pulled Drummond's shoulders erect.

"Recognize this place, old man?"

The bumpy trip had taken some of the swagger out of Drummond. He had a dazed look as he shook his head from side to side.

Jamison was too tired to go easy on him. His mind hurt and his body ached too much to ignore the pain any longer. He'd tied one of his socks over the hole Drummond's bodyguard had shot through his arm, and it had stopped leaking. But he was more lightheaded than ever. Coupled with his lack of sleep, too much worrying about Melissa, and too much time in the line of fire, and he could already believe he was a dead man. Being dead was actually beginning to sound like a good thing, an inviting change of pace.

He wrestled Drummond higher out of the trunk, twisted him around, and gave him a better view.

"Oh? Really? Maybe you didn't get a good look. Let's try again."

Drummond actually managed to look dangerous as Jamison bent him around. Right up until the second he spotted the white BMW. At that instant his eyes bulged open and he looked back at Jamison with something else, something new, on his face. It was hope, maybe. Or desperation.

"You know where you're at now, don't you? You recognize your daughter's car?"

Drummond nodded slowly, as if his neck was in a brace.

"Can we leave now or do I have to go through with it? I'm really hoping you don't make me, 'cause it's not something I want to do. But it's your call, she's just upstairs. If I have to torture your daughter to get Melissa back from you, I'll damn sure do it. Won't like it one bit and will hate myself forever. But I'll do it just the same. After you watch her suffer for a while, I'm sure you'll help me. Any father would. So what's it going to be? Tell me now 'cause I'm tired and fussy and short on time."

*   *   *   *   *

Drummond had already decided to tell him. The hard ride had done a good job of convincing him. He was too old to be rolling around in the trunk of a car. And hadn't Jamison gone out of his way to find all the damned bumps in the road?

Why shouldn't he release the Corley woman? She meant nothing to him anymore. He'd had Kane's men pick her up to quiet her, and to flush out Jamison. But her silence hadn't saved his organization, and Jamison wasn't exactly a hard man to find, at least not anymore. Why not give her up? He'd just been waiting for a decent reason, his lifetime in politics telling him that you should only trade when you want something. This seemed to fit the bill.

Besides, he could use this. He'd become a senator by exploiting tough situations like this, by turning them to his own personal advantage. He could do it now by giving her to Jamison. Get Jack Kane to bring Melissa out, nice and easy. Trade her for his own freedom, then let Kane kill both of them. Kane could do that. Sure, it would be easy for a man like him. He and Kane could use this as an opportunity to end their problems with Peter Jamison.

The evidence, well, the evidence would be another story. But he'd already been told of the plan to get that back from the F.B.I. He was confident it would work. The organization that Richard Corley had built would survive this attack, even as it had survived so many others.

He thought about Richard, about how they used to meet at his home when Drummond was a freshman congressman and Melissa was a little girl on her father's lap, sitting there until the meetings turned serious and her father scooted her out of his library. Richard was a brilliant man, a patriot who'd seen the uncertainty in his country's future and decided to protect America from itself. Drummond wondered what Richard would think if he knew his precious daughter had to die in order to protect his organization.

Drummond dragged his stare away from his daughter's car and took Jamison's look straight on. He nodded his head yes, and sincerely meant it.

Jamison pulled him out and let him drop to the ground, cut the tape from his feet and hands, then pulled it away from his mouth. Jamison helped him stand.

"There's a pay phone over there. If you make any kind of sound I don't like, anything at all, we're upstairs. You'll get to watch. Understand?"

Drummond nodded again as he picked sticky residue from his wrists. Jamison prodded him in the back, aimed him toward the phone, poked him several more times as they crossed the garage.

"Local or long distance?"

"Just local, Mr. Jamison."

Jamison dropped some change into the slot and Drummond dialed. He didn't even try to conceal the number, even as he saw Jamison writing it down. Jamison got in close, put his ear next to Drummond's, his hand up against Drummond's throat, making it a little hard for Drummond to speak."

The phone was picked up after four rings.

"Yes?"

Jamison recognized Kane's voice, it was obvious by the way his hand tightened around Drummond's throat and his body twitched with fearful energy. Drummond choked, said nothing more until Jamison worked some of the rigor mortis from his hand. Then he bent out a few kinks and went back to his phone call.

"Do you know where the Corley woman is?"

"Yes."

"Good. I need you to bring her to me."

"All right, sir. I can do that. Where and when?"

Drummond turned so he could see Jamison. He covered the phone and tried to look like he wanted to do a real good job. He asked the question with his eyes.

"Harborplace, in Baltimore. The northwest building. First thing in the morning. Seven o'clock. Make sure that's enough time, 'cause I don't want to wait. No one else comes or you die there, Drummond, and I'll come back for your daughter."

Drummond spoke carefully. "I think Baltimore might be a very nice spot. How about Harborplace? Say, seven sharp? Northwest building?"

"Fine."

"Just you and Miss Corley, please. I think there are going to be some trade negotiations. If you bring more of your staff, they would only complicate things. Understand?"

"I understand, sir. I assume our missing engineer will be negotiating for the other side?"

"Yes. He's a skillful negotiator, too. You would be wise to come alert and prepared."

Drummond was suddenly thrown away from the phone and down onto the concrete. He didn't move, stayed down and watched Jamison race for the phone as it dangled by the cord. He held it for a few seconds and listened, then hung up without speaking, looked tempted to kick at Drummond's head.

19

Blevins stood in the middle of Kane's living room, watching his agents tear the place apart and staring at his walkie-talkie. He'd found little evidence at Kane's house, and none of it was worth a flip. Now the dispatcher was playing some stupid game with him, providing another perfect little annoyance to an aggravating day.

"Say again, dispatcher."

"I have a message for you, 705, and the caller insisted that I shouldn't put it over the airwaves, either radio or cell phone. Call me on a land-line right away. 10-4?"

"Yeah, yeah. Roger that. I'll call right now."

He moved away from Sackett and picked up the phone in the study, an elaborately furnished room in Kane's Northern Virginia mansion. The phone was a complex piece of equipment that Blevins had never seen before. After looking it over for a minute he understood that the high-tech contraption monitored Kane's phone line for traces, pen registers, recorders, and line splices. A small, separate control unit was plugged into the status monitor, which operated a signal scrambling device, an integrated recorder, and an incoming/outgoing call register. Blevins almost didn't want to use the damn thing, afraid of accidentally destroying some evidence. But he wanted the dispatcher's message and, truthfully, wanted to play with the phone a little. So he took the risk.

"This is Blevins."

The telephone's status monitor flashed on and off, the alpha-numeric display signaled that the call was being taped by the F.B.I. office. The damned thing worked.

"Yes, sir, Mr. Blevins. Sorry to bother you in the middle of a search, but I just received a weird call. Since you're Jamison's case agent, I thought you'd want to know about it."

"Go."

"It was a man who called here a few minutes ago. He didn't identify himself, but told me where we could find Special Agent Brewer. He said he'd just left him, and that Brewer was dead. He also warned that he'd assigned several other killers to get Peter Jamison and that we should find him soon and get him under wraps."

"I wish I could."

"I know. Anyway, this guy said he'd come in tomorrow morning and tell us more."

"That's weird all right."

"Sure is. Gets weirder, too. This guy seemed to know every one of our procedures, and was emphatic that we not broadcast any part of his message over the airways. He even said that I shouldn't use our burst transmitter. It was almost like talking to an agent, but I don't think he was one."

"What's the phone number, and did you run it?"

"Just did. It's local, 455-0090. Assigned to a business with no phone book listing, no records in indices, no phone calls— and I mean zero—originating from the number during the last six months. At least not until tonight."

"Doesn't sound like much of a business. Anything else?"

"Just this. The billing address is a mail drop. It's picked up and brought here twice a month."

Blevins snapped to attention, looked around the room, and lowered his voice. "Shit, so this guy called from one of our safehouses."

"It looks that way, yes."

"Okay, good job. Thanks a lot." Blevins hung up, surprised that the status monitor did another light show, displayed a message stating that someone at the F.B.I. office had attempted to trace the call, but that the device had successfully blocked it.

Sackett walked into the study, came over with his head low and his hands in his pants pockets.

"Trouble?"

Blevins took a deep breath and exhaled noisily.

"I hope not. It was just someone worried about Peter Jamison. Said Brewer's dead, killed in one of our safehouses."

"Then the caller must have been Jack Kane. If he killed Brewer, then he might have taken Melissa from him."

"Would he kill her, too?"

"Don't know. He's cold enough, that's for sure. But he's also very smart. There's no way to predict, but I'm guessing he wants the evidence back, the stuff Jamison gave you, the stuff that provided some of the probable cause for this search. I know Kane, so I suspect he'll get it, would never bet against him. He probably plans to barter with Corley."

"Well, even if he does get his hands on our data, Drummond still has a set of copies."

Sackett looked away, seemed very interested in what the agents were doing in the living room.

"I don't know, Blevins. Wouldn't count on it."

"You want to tell me what that means?"

"No. Just that I wouldn't count on Drummond's material doing you any good."

Blevins looked around for something he could kick to the moon, a sacrificial target for some of his evil spirit. A trash can

285

would work just fine. Or a wall, in a pinch. The ass-end of an agent bending over Kane's desk tempted him, but also made him realize he couldn't do a damn thing, forced him to give up on the idea.

"Then I'd better buy some insurance, because Jamison's evidence provided the probable cause for the three searches at Quantico, too. Without it, everything we've seen will be subject to suppression. It will all be fruit from a poisonous tree."

Sackett came back around, looking strange. He wasn't smiling, but he didn't look sad either.

"You're right. Everyone you've accused, including me, will be able to walk. You won't even be able to talk about this without risking a slander suit."

Now, even more than a minute ago, Blevins wanted to grab Sackett by the front of his shirt, twist the fabric in his grip, and lift until his boss was standing on tippy-toes. But he didn't. His men wouldn't understand. Or worse, they would understand, and that would mean they knew about Sackett, making them the enemy.

"Is that what you want, Sackett? To walk? I thought you chose a side earlier."

"I did, Blevins. That's why I'm telling you to be careful. If Kane is after the evidence, you'd better be a step ahead of him."

Blevins picked Kane's phone up again, redialed WFO, asked for the evidence clerk.

"Yes, sir. This is Cunningham, Evidence Tech."

"Listen, Cunningham. I need some clerks and agents to start making copies. Make sure they have plenty of paper because I've got thousands of documents that need to be copied."

"Yes, sir."

"I want you to copy the entire contents of a white file box in the evidence locker. I checked it in on Monday."

The line was silent.

"What, Cunningham? What is it?"

"Sir, that box isn't here. I did an evidence check when my shift began two hours ago, and it was gone then. I've filed an affidavit for the SAC, according to the manual."

"Are you sure, maybe it's—"

"Agent Blevins, I'm telling you it's not here. I know my job, sir. Someone took it."

Blevins let the trash can have it, sent it flying across the room. "Shit!"

* * * * *

Jamison needed to rest before Kane and Melissa showed up at Harborplace, the final meeting where he would get Melissa back, then kill Kane for what he'd done to both of them. His body was desperate for sleep. It didn't have enough energy to keep going and keep healing. His head and eye still ached from his fight with John Butler, he'd hurt his neck rolling into the young gunman at Casey's house, half of his stitching had ripped out of the makeshift patch on his side, and infection was spreading through his left arm, radiating out from the bullet hole he'd gotten at Drummond's but had never disinfected.

But the pain wasn't a problem. He could ignore it easily, would not let it distract him until he was finished. The fear of death didn't bother him either, even as he wondered which of several things would cause it: loss of blood, infection, Jack Kane, the F.B.I., or some other adversary he hadn't yet identified.

But exhaustion was a different kind of enemy. A dangerous one. He worried about it more than everything else combined, and wanted this to end before his body quit completely and collapsed.

He parked Drummond's car in an automated lot ten blocks from Harborplace. It was nearly empty this early in the morning, and he hoped the five dollar cost would cut down on the number of cars and police that entered. He knew he wouldn't get any sleep there, but at least he could give his body a little rest. He wouldn't even be able to do that if cars were cruising around.

Drummond was completely quiet in the trunk, maybe dead. Jamison thought about what that would mean, how it might create a problem for him and Melissa. But it wouldn't stop him. He would just trade Drummond's keys for Melissa, then tell Kane where the car was parked. Kane would have no choice but to make the deal. If there was a problem, he would kill Kane, then take Melissa. It was a simple decision, one he was glad to make now so that he would know what to do if Kane acted dissatisfied with the arrangement.

But worry would not let him relax, and kept reminding him of all the things that could go wrong, the things he hadn't thought of, dozens of little setbacks, some of them bound to happen and cause problems. Kane might not have Melissa with him, might be planning a similar trick on him. Or he might not show up at all. There might be other people there, forcing Jamison to take on more than he could handle. Or the F.B.I. might be onto him, might secure the whole area around Harborplace once he entered their trap. The worst possibility was that Melissa might already be dead.

But deep down, he knew exactly what would happen. In less than two hours he would get Melissa back or he would die trying.

He pulled out of the lot at six A.M., wanting to drive by the exchange point and survey the area before anyone else arrived. It took only a few minutes to get to Harborplace, dimly lit in the early morning hour.

All of the bordering streets were empty as he drove by at five miles over the speed limit. Soon the cars of the early arrivals—the delivery men, bakers, and first-shift workers—

would start filling the streets, and he would be able to drive more slowly without looking too suspicious.

He searched for a good place to park, a spot that was not very open, somewhere he wouldn't be accosted by delivery drivers or shop owners. A place where he could drag a taped-up old man out of his trunk without being noticed.

It couldn't be far away, either. When the time came he would have to control Drummond on a public street in the bright light of morning while he hobbled along in bloodstained clothes. He didn't want to do that any longer than necessary. It could be trouble if the old man started screaming, or if someone recognized him as a U.S. Senator, or if he tried to twist away and forced Jamison to manhandle him, or someone noticed the mixture of wet and dry blood on his pants.

He cruised the city's waterfront a second time, noting the side streets and the high ground and the places of good cover, seeing all of it with a sort of bored concentration. The first employees were beginning to arrive, parking their cars, adding sparks of life to the waking street scene. It was getting safer for him to stop, only twenty minutes to go, not much chance of being harassed by the cops or employees now. He drove around the corner and backed the car in-between two delivery vans with frost on their windshields, got out, and opened the trunk. He looked all around for witnesses but saw none, strained his wounds as he lifted Drummond out of the trunk and shoved him up against the wall of the building, his hands and feet still taped together.

Jamison snatched the tape from Drummond's mouth, the old man's skin stretching long and loose, following the tape a little before letting go.

"You have a nice ride?"

The old man had suffered back there. Hours stuffed in the trunk like a bag of laundry had completely effaced his mask of power.

"No, Jamison. Damn you, it was hard on me."

289

"Good." Jamison untaped Drummond's ankles, and then his hands, ready to hurt the old boy if he so much as twitched.

"We need to talk, old man."

"Is it time to meet Jack Kane?"

Jamison looked around, thought he heard someone walking around the trucks. "Yeah. Almost."

"So then our business is nearly finished. What could we possibly have to talk about?"

Jamison leaned toward him, caught the foul stench of Drummond's body odor. "Just this. I have no choice but to take you out into public, out where you could cause trouble for me. I want you to understand what I'll do if that happens."

Drummond massaged his wrists where they'd been bound.

"You will kill me, Mr. Jamison, then get the Corley woman if you can. If you don't succeed you'll use my daughter as leverage to get Melissa, assuming you can find someone besides me that values her enough to trade. Do I understand you correctly?"

"You do."

Drummond shivered a little in the cold morning air, crossed his chest with his bony hands and hooked them over his shoulders.

"I won't give you any trouble."

Jamison looked at him and almost felt sorry for him. It was over for Drummond, no matter how the pie was sliced up. He would be going down, shamed and humbled, if Jamison lived long enough to tell what he knew. But Drummond was still responsible. Jamison would not forget that Drummond was one of the men who had caused his problems. He deserved whatever happened to him.

Jamison turned away, listened to Drummond's erratic breathing, wondered how close Melissa was to him now. Could he feel her presence? Maybe catch a glimpse of her? Only twelve minutes to go.

He waited, checking his watch a hundred times to make sure it hadn't stopped. He wished he could have gotten here earlier, hours ago, and had the chance to set up someplace safe and watch all the approaches, make sure everything went down nice and clean. But he was stuck dragging Drummond around and didn't want to have him out in the open for too long. So he had no choice but to walk into an unknown area held by the enemy.

At three minutes before seven he headed toward Harborplace, knowing that being on time was the same thing as being late if things were screwed up. He kept Drummond a little in front as they moved down the street. He could watch him there, and use him as a shield if the balloon went up.

* * * * *

Dan Corderman liked to believe he was Kane's friend, or at least the closest thing Kane had to one. They'd worked together at Dillon Security for more than a decade. Kane had never showed him any favoritism, but Corderman was pretty sure Kane liked him. He didn't think anyone else would have gotten away with the stupid crack he made the other night on surveillance, telling Kane how any man would miss his wife while watching Martin tape Jamison and Corley in her apartment. Kane must have liked him to let that go.

Corderman had just returned to Dillon when he'd gotten Casey's call. Casey had badly fumbled security procedures, but was very explicit in what he wanted. Kane was changing sides, he'd said, and was just leaving his office. Corderman had to stop him. His career, and his own life, depended on it. The price was two million dollars, split however Corderman decided. Plus seven-fifty for Jamison, if he happened to get them both. Casey seemed to think it might happen that way.

So he'd followed Kane as he left Dillon's lot, was lucky enough to get to the safehouse without Kane spotting him. He'd called for help along the way, but they didn't get there before Kane left with the Corley woman. Corderman hadn't been stupid enough to take Kane on alone.

Now Corderman was crouched down in a thicket of holly bushes, shivering in the morning air that drifted off the harbor, knowing that his chances of success sucked. Hell, squaring off with Jack Kane was the last thing on earth he'd ever want to do. Even with the three professionals he'd brought with him, he was worried. Kane could come alone and still have a good chance of killing them. Corderman should have brought more men. A dozen more. Twenty, just to be sure.

He was a lot less comfortable now that the sun had come up. He was close to the entrance of Harborside, and ran the risk of being spotted. He glanced along the hedge, gave his second man a thumbs up. The man grinned, as if he'd forgotten who they were about to tangle with, and returned it. Then he shifted around and passed it on to the third man, another fifty feet away, who signaled it to the end assassin. They were ready. Kane was standing on the corner with the Corley woman. Jamison was walking toward them with Senator Drummond. They had a clear field of fire from here. Corderman was trembling.

* * * * *

Jamison and Drummond moved slowly down the sidewalk, which was still pretty empty on this chilly morning. A few people approached them, then passed. None of them paid much attention.

Then he saw Kane and Melissa standing near the corner on the opposite side of the street. But Kane wasn't watching him, hadn't seemed to see him yet. Why? He had to be better than that. If not, Jamison had really overestimated him, and that gave him a lot of worry because every plan he'd made was based on his assumption that Kane was a professional. He had no idea how an amateur might act, but wanted to change his game plan if that were the case. He kept watching Kane, trying to decide which was correct. Kane was glancing up at the high ground, looking plenty edgy as he moved his eyes along the building, not paying any attention to him or Drummond.

A trap? Maybe. Jamison stopped, pushed Drummond down beside two parked cars and scanned the area carefully. This was looking way too easy. Something had to be wrong. He reached behind him, wiggled the Beretta out of his belt with his right hand, felt the bullet wound burning his left arm as he touched the two magazines in his pocket.

"Let's go, Drummond. Stand up and cross the street. It's pretty open from here on in, so if there's going to be a problem this is where it'll happen. If I die, you die. Move."

They crossed without a shot being fired, even though they were easy targets on the empty street. Kane was watching them now, eyeing their approach warily. Melissa was watching, too. Fifty feet away, Jamison reached forward with his bloody left hand, grabbed Drummond's shoulder and slowed him down.

Melissa started to shout to him, but Kane hushed her with a quiet word and a gentle touch to her shoulder. Jamison wanted to yell at him to keep his hands off her, but didn't. He would go slow. Walk easy. Quietly. Getting closer all the time. He would wait for his turn. A few more seconds now.

Kane spoke as they came within easy range. His hands were empty but his jacket was open. Jamison saw the butt of an automatic pistol hanging under his coat in a long shoulder holster.

Kane nodded, then glanced up toward the high ground near the building and made it plenty obvious to everyone.

"Good morning, Mr. Jamison. Mr. Drummond. Everyone okay here?"

Drummond started talking, the politician's ways coming right back to him.

"Hello, Jack. Nice of you to come this morning."

Jamison would not look at Melissa, not even a glance. Oh, God, he wanted to look her over and check for injuries, then appreciate her beauty. But he knew Kane would be watching for it, waiting for the second he looked over to check on her, maybe say something to her. Kane would use that lapse of concentration to kill him.

He glued his eyes to Kane and settled for her blurry image at the edge of his focus, her dark features offset by a tan overcoat, which was probably Kane's. Then he spoke quietly, watching Kane's eyes, knowing they would give him the first warning that the fight was about to start.

"There's not much for us to talk about, Kane," he said. "Drummond for Melissa. I'm prepared to trade and walk away. Are you?"

Kane stepped from behind Melissa, left her alone as he walked over to Jamison and stood still, right in front of him, his arms loose and hanging all the way down. Kane had no protection at all, but didn't act as if it bothered him. It was a damn gutsy move.

"I can understand your hurry, Mr. Jamison. So let's call it a deal. Good luck to you both." He backed away, one step toward the street as if it was all over now. He nodded for Melissa to go to Jamison.

Slowly, she shifted sides, taking her time, carefully avoiding Jamison's line of fire. He was proud of her for thinking like that, and a little surprised. She stepped beside him and turned around.

Drummond moved next, took his first step toward Kane. It was an awkward swap of prisoners, agonizingly slow, pregnant with the seeds of treachery. And this was just the exchange.

Jamison still had to get out of here with Melissa, alive. He looked up toward the high ground, the same place Kane kept glancing, checked for shooters but didn't see any.

Kane held up his big left hand, the palm facing Drummond.

"Don't bother coming to me, Senator. I'm afraid you're on your own. I want nothing to do with you anymore."

Drummond stopped halfway between the two men and looked confused, started to ask something. Jamison looked at him, then at Kane, suddenly very worried and growing more so by the second. If Kane didn't want Drummond, why the trade? What was going on here? Was this just a ploy to get them here so Kane could kill them?

He decided he wouldn't wait for the answer, whipped his pistol up and aimed it at Kane, started to shoot him in the face, suddenly feeling terribly alone. Pulling back on the trigger, hoping that something made sense before he started popping caps.

Kane just stood there, staring back, gazing into the bore of Jamison's Beretta as the trigger traveled and drew the hammer back. Melissa screamed while Jamison watched for the crazy man, wanting to make sure the decision to kill Kane was his own. But the crazy man seemed to be gone, maybe for good. It was just Jamison now, aiming down his sights at the middle of Kane's big face, trying to decide, knowing it was time. Kill or be killed.

If he died here, Melissa would be on her own, alone and unprotected, vulnerable to being victimized once again. It didn't take much in that way of thinking before he squeezed the trigger harder and increased the speed of its travel. Kane watched him with an interested curiosity in his eyes.

The muscles in Kane's face suddenly jumped, made Jamison flinch and almost finish his draw of the trigger. Kane bellowed as he reached over and pushed Melissa toward the protection of the concrete wall. He was still an easy target for Jamison, and not much of a threat.

"Get down!" Kane yelled. "Get down!"

Kane drew his pistol while Jamison fell over Melissa, protecting her with his body. He kept his Beretta pointed at Kane but waited to see where the big man would aim, still ready to kill him if the barrel of his weapon swung anywhere near their direction.

Kane jumped up and beaded his weapon on something Jamison could not see. He fired two shots. The pistol's noise suppresser made the shots nearly silent, but pedestrians in the area saw what he was doing and panicked. Chaos took over and people screamed. It sounded like hundreds of people. Where had they all come from?

Then the background noises faded and Jamison began to hear selectively. A splattering thud up near the building. Kane's weapon seating another round. His own Beretta scraping against the concrete as he hugged the wall. Kane's feet scurrying away, giving the shooters two different target areas.

Jamison popped up and took a quick glance over the wall, saw Kane's target rise a hundred feet away, screaming, his bloody hands covering his face. He fell into the bushes, then all hell broke loose.

Drummond started running, tottering away from the wall and into the street with a wobbly, old-man's gait. He was killed by automatic weapons fire that sputtered down from the high ground and stitched a neat line up his back, from his waist to his skull.

Jamison took his aim off Kane, uncomfortable doing it but having to decide. He peered over the wall and looked for a target, hoping for the chance to start blasting. Gunfire rained down as soon as he did, kept him pinned against the short wall, crouched low over Melissa. He saw Kane catch a burst of rounds high in his right arm and spin around, then muscle his way back against the wall.

One of the gunmen stopped shooting, and Jamison used the opportunity to pop up and fire. As soon as he did Melissa started crawling along the wall toward Kane, distracting Jamison's aim and making him drop back down again. What was she doing? Hell, what was Kane doing? Were they all on the same side now? Was Jamison safe working from that assumption? Were there really any options? He leaped to his feet and fired six quick rounds for effect, just enough to keep the shooters' heads down until Melissa covered the forty feet of kill zone.

Jamison shouted to Kane, feeling strange in their new alliance but trusting Melissa completely. It was her life he was here to save, so if she wanted to team up with Kane, he would too.

"I'm thinking there's three of them left! They're firing alternately, Kane, so we're going to have to rise into their guns no matter how long we wait! Can you still shoot?"

Much of the muscle of Kane's right arm had been blasted away, bloody pieces of meat dotting the sidewalk. His hand and forearm dangled from the denuded bone like a weight on a string. Every time it swung around him, Kane's eyes pinched tight, even as he dropped his pistol and used his left hand to stuff the lifeless right into his waistband. His face was contorted but he didn't make a sound. He picked up his pistol with his left hand and shouted back.

"Yes."

"Okay, let's watch the spray at the next shift of gunfire. Whoever is getting it, the other pop up and unload! Got it?"

Kane nodded, just as Jamison came under heavy fire. Kane jumped up, fired three times with his left hand. Jamison heard one of the shooters cry out as Kane stood there, wide open for a long, long time, maybe two seconds, as if nothing could hurt him, his pistol ready for the next target. But the high ground fell briefly silent, so Kane crouched back down beside Melissa.

As soon as he did, Melissa yelled at Kane, who seemed to argue with her. Shouting at her. The gunfire erupted again and Jamison couldn't hear over it, had no idea what was going on until Melissa jumped up and started running in the direction of Drummond's body. Jamison heard sirens coming and thought maybe she was running to them. But they were still far away, and coming from the opposite direction.

"Damn it, Melissa, get down! Get down!"

She looked back at Jamison with a sad smile, as if this were the last time she would see him, then turned and kept running.

Jamison scrambled off the sidewalk, jumped up and blasted away at the bushes, emptied his weapon, shattered the store windows and set off the alarms. He stood his ground, dumped his spent magazine and slammed a fresh one home, started blasting again, five rounds, ten, twelve, fifteen rounds, as fast as he could sight-in and shoot.

Kane was up, too, blasting with him. Then Jamison saw him get hit, then hit again. He was out in the open, took three or four more hits in the chest before he got back against the wall and collapsed in the middle of a huge red puddle.

Melissa was gone. Thank God, she'd made it out alive. Jamison dropped back below the wall and slammed his last magazine home, hunkered down as the rain of firepower splattered him with shards of chipped and broken concrete. The police were close now. This would all be over soon. He started thinking about ways to get away without having to kill cops. He was proud of Melissa for escaping. Deep-down happy that she was free.

As he sat there, listening to the gunfire that couldn't quite hit him, he looked up and saw a gray Chrysler weaving down the street, going fifty or sixty miles an hour. It slid ninety degrees when it got to Jamison, bounced over the curb and onto the sidewalk, slammed into the wall right beside him. He whipped his pistol around to shoot the driver but stopped when he saw it was Melissa.

"Come on, Peter, get in!"

Jamison ran to the passenger door and started in, catching fire the whole way. But he stopped partway into the car and shot twice, looked down the sidewalk at Kane. He was pinned down and hurt bad, maybe dead, fifty feet away. It might as well have been a mile.

Jamison fired two more shots at the bushes, shouting over the gunfire.

"You alive, Kane? Can you make it?"

Kane was lying on his side. Blood was pumping from his chest like a natural spring bubbling up out of the ground. He wiggled a little, proved he was still alive by stretching his hand up over the planter wall and firing with his eyes closed.

"No. Get out of here."

Automatic weapons fire shattered the car's windshield and sprayed across the roof. Jamison fired again as he checked on Melissa. She was under the dash and pretty safe, all things considered.

"He's not going to make it, Peter," she shouted, her eyes big and desperate and locked onto his. "Come on, get in. Leave him!"

Jamison looked at her face, then looked back at Kane and fired five shots up the steps. What the hell should he do, hot-foot it through this shit after that guy? It would be suicide, and who was Kane to deserve that kind of sacrifice? He should throw himself into the car and let Melissa haul his ass out of there.

But something made him want to get Kane. He found himself lost in time, staring at another victim who lay on the ground, hurt and scared. It was Kane, all right, no question about it. But all Jamison could see was a memory of Melissa, raped and beaten and left to suffer on a Delaware beach. The memory made him feel dirty and helpless.

But this time he didn't have to live with the feeling. This time he could stop it. This time he would not fail.

And it wasn't the crazy man telling him to do it, either. It was something as powerful as the crazy man, except completely different. Something that gave Jamison the choice. Go, or don't go. Entirely his decision.

Peace washed away the dirt and shame and poured energy and confidence into him. And then he was running. By God, running like nature's finest athlete. He felt happy and good and honest, running through the firefight, making each and every decision himself. When to shoot, who to shoot, when to slow. No crazy man dragging him along, no sir. This was all his own doing. Going back to save someone who needed him, someone who had just helped him save Melissa. Absolutely determined not to fail again.

He got to Kane and knelt down, saw a sniper working his way down through the bushes, fired once and got him.

"Let's go, Kane! Help me get you out of here."

Kane's bloody hand was stretched wide open, trying to cover three holes in his chest. The blood was pumping through his fingers, gushing out in a thick, frothy foam. He tried to struggle to his knees but couldn't.

"I can't do it. Thanks anyway. Now go."

Jamison jumped into the open and waited, knowing there were still two shooters left. Then he saw one of them. Just a little of his head, checking Kane's Chrysler. Jamison took careful aim and fired. The shooter rocked back, his body lifted up by the impact, his entire torso a target. Jamison fired again, and now there was only one left, dug in deep at the far end, near the entrance to Harborside.

"We're going together, Kane. Let's move."

Jamison had all the strength now. Much more strength than normal. Crazy man strength, but without the crazy man. He sat Kane up and shoved his left hand under his armpit, the pain of his infected bullet wound blistering its way through his mind and forcing him to scream in Kane's ear.

He dragged Kane sideways so that he could keep shooting with his gun hand, firing at the last sniper once every three seconds, just enough to keep his head down. He helped Kane struggle his way into the car, then dove in on top of him while Melissa climbed up behind the wheel, put it in reverse and stomped on the gas. The tires spun and the smoke rose and for an instant they just sat there as hundreds of horses failed to produce an inch of movement. When the tires finally stuck, the Chrysler shot out into the street, screeching and leaning wildly as Melissa whipped the wheel around and dropped it into drive.

And then they were gone.

20

The emergency room doctors treated Jamison's wounds in a little less than two hours. He would heal fairly well, they said, after a few days of observation and several weeks of recovery. Jamison had wandered away while they filled out the admitting forms, and was now leaning against the wall outside of Kane's hospital room, wondering what was wrong with Melissa.

He understood why they hadn't talked on the way to the hospital. Her top priority had been his wounds, Kane's life, and their own survival. But they were safe now. Melissa had smuggled his pistol in under her coat, and he'd checked every room of the entire floor, pissed off all the nurses in the preop area, and watched the elevators and stairwells with the concealed Beretta ready and reloaded with some loose shells he'd found in Kane's glove compartment.

She sat on the bench near him but didn't move, kept her head down and supported it with her hands. Maybe the stress of the shoot-out had been too much for her. Or maybe it was the relief of being free, that overwhelming feeling of deliverance. In either case, Jamison knew she wanted time alone, and though he wasn't sure of her reasons, he understood the need. Understood it completely, and would give her as much she wanted. He would suppress his desire to hold her, kiss her, and tell her how much he really loved her—loved her enough to be honest with himself and deal with the damage his guilt had caused them, the reasons he'd destroyed their relationship in the first place. Those things were all behind him now. It was over. He was anxious for her to feel better so he could sit down beside her, stroke her fingers, look into her brown eyes, and tell her it had all been his fault. He understood that clearly now, and was so glad to have a second chance.

The elevator dinged. Jamison reached under the jacket which hung off his right shoulder and wrapped his fingers around his pistol, prepared to yank it out and start blasting. Maybe it wasn't over yet after all. Maybe there was more dying left to come.

The elevator doors popped open. Blevins burst out and ran toward Jamison, his men crashing down the bright white corridor in dark uniforms like an invading army. Blevins led the pack, staring at the sling on Jamison's arm and the bandages wrapped around his middle. As he got close the other agents dropped out of the herd, one by one, and stationed themselves along the hall. Most of the nurses stopped what they were doing and watched, while a head nurse made a mad grab for each passing soldier and demanded to know what was going on.

Blevins ran all the way, then screeched to a stop in front of Jamison and set down a briefcase he'd been swinging along the hall.

"What the hell happened, Peter? I just got your message that you were here. Damn, are you all right?"

He poked a finger at Jamison's arm, hit the bullet hole hard, made Jamison jerk away. Melissa rose from the bench and stepped up beside Jamison. A bewildered look crossed Blevins's face, stayed there as he leaned over and gave her a hug. He backed away, looked at the huge bloodstains all over her blue dress, then snuggled up and hugged her again, his bulky armament making the maneuver awkward and comical.

"You, Melissa, are a sight for sore eyes."

She smiled, looked shyly at Blevins. "So are you, Rich. It's been a long time."

"Yeah, you're not kidding. Too long. You okay?" He lifted her hands and spread them apart, leaned left and right, looked her up and down.

She rose up on her toes and kissed his cheek. "I'm fine, Rich. Thanks for worrying about me."

"Sure."

He turned back to Jamison and pointed at Melissa, still looking confused, but quite a bit calmer. "That was you at Harborplace, then. I heard about the shoot-out, and Drummond getting killed. The dispatcher said two men and a woman got away. I figured the woman to be Melissa. Hoped one of the men was you, that you'd stayed alive long enough to cause that kind of trouble. Who was the other man?"

Jamison lifted his right thumb like a hitchhiker, aimed it back at Kane's room. "Jack Kane."

"Really? The security man from Dillon?"

"The very same. He brought Melissa to me."

"No shit? I was searching his house earlier. Man, I should've picked up a program when this show started, so I'd know who all the players were. It would have made everything a whole lot easier."

"No doubt about it."

"No doubt. He really brought her to you? Got shot up during the exchange, I guess?"

"Yes."

Blevins couldn't keep his hands away from Jamison's arm, prodding around, seeing how badly it really hurt, making Jamison flinch and eye him suspiciously.

"Well, good for him. Was he badly wounded? Or was that just a lot of noise about nothing, like this little thing?" He stopped prodding and his grin grew bigger. "Through and through?"

Jamison swiveled his shoulders, moved his bad arm out of Blevins's reach. "Yes. The bullet went right on through, no problem. Drummond's security man did it last night. Enough? Will you leave it alone now?"

"Sure. But what's with the mummy wrap around your stomach?"

"Do you really care, or are you just morbidly curious?"

Blevins laughed and banged his fist into Jamison's good shoulder.

"Just curious."

Jamison groaned, feeling all of his pain now, but also feeling some of the relief that was making Blevins so giddy.

"Hey, give me a break, huh? I ache in places I didn't even know I had."

"I bet. How bad was Kane wounded?"

Jamison kept watching Blevins, trying to guard himself against the next assault on his body.

"He took several hits, was barely alive when we got here."

"Will he live?"

"Don't know. The doctors said he was in bad shape, but were amazed he was alive at all."

Blevins lowered his eyes. "Shame."

"Yeah. But he's a strong man. I think he might make it."

"And Drummond is definitely dead?"

Jamison tried to lift an eyebrow, but even it hurt. Hurt so bad he thought about laughing, glad to be noticing pain again. It amazed him that he'd been able to shut it off and keep going. He thought about how he'd sewn himself together last night and could not imagine how he'd done it. Remembering the feel of the thread drawn through his skin made his knees weak.

"Drummond looked dead to me, Rich, but I didn't hang around long enough to check." He massaged the itchy bullet hole of his swollen arm. "He has to be dead, though. Took way too many rounds to survive."

"Well, the hell with him, anyway. Did he tell you what he'd been doing, the crimes he'd been pulling?"

"Some. Do you think you can stop the others who went along with him?"

"We sure hope to."

"Do you still have my data?"

Blevins shifted to his other leg, looked at Melissa again and smiled big. "Man, she sure looks great."

"Yes, she sure does. Do you have my research data?"

Blevins looked at the floor and dug at it a little with his boot. "Well, that's a problem. I'm afraid your stuff is gone. Missing."

Jamison pushed off the wall, banged his swollen arm in the process.

"Ouch! Damn! How? What happened?"

"It was stolen from our safe. I tried to get copies made earlier, as a precaution against something like this, but it was already gone."

"Then it must have been an agent."

"No other way. A clerk, maybe. But definitely F.B.I."

Melissa nudged in between them. "Rich, will the F.B.I. still be able to prosecute those politicians and corporations who worked with Drummond?"

"Well . . . sure. Yeah, I can still build a case against them, at least the guys at the top, the ones who controlled everyone else. There'll be a lot of low level guys we'll never get, but I can put the head men in jail and leave their organization without any leadership. It should crumble pretty quickly after that."

"Good," Melissa said, then slumped a little and sighed. "It would be nice to get the soldiers, too."

"I think we're screwed on that score. Warden's diary identified a lot of them, but we can't use it because your data was part of the probable cause for that search. And that, my friends, is the law."

"There has to be something you can do, Rich, some way to arrest everyone involved with this corruption."

"Sorry, buddy. Works out that way sometimes. It's American justice, Peter. You can't fight the system."

Jamison pushed hair off his forehead. "Drummond did."

"You want to be like Drummond?"

"No. Of course not."

"Well, neither do I. And if that means letting some small potatoes get away, then that's the price I'll pay. I have faith in the system. Although the wheels of justice grind slowly, they do grind. Very finely. Sometimes it just takes those big ol' wheels awhile to be effective." He turned to Melissa.

"Don't worry though, even if we can't arrest the army that followed Drummond, and even if someone takes Drummond's place and keeps the corruption going, eventually we'll stop it. It's our job. We take that kind of thing pretty seriously."

Melissa stepped into Blevins's face. "What do you mean, if someone takes Drummond's place? You think someone else will take over?"

"Don't know, really." He looked at Jamison and locked up with him. "You didn't tell her?"

Jamison leaned back and grimaced as he shook his head, then looked away. "Haven't had a chance."

Blevins frowned.

"Well, for several years now a rumor's been going around that someone was building a power base, planning to topple the current leadership of that criminal enterprise. Now, it may be true or not, but my guess is that if the rumor is circulating, the chances are good that someone is planning to make a move. It will just depend on how well connected they are. With Drummond dead there will be a huge power vacuum, so I expect someone to try and fill it. You know the old saying, nature abhors a vacuum? Well it's not much different in criminal organizations. The good news is that the person angling for the top spot is probably near the top already, and will go down with the rest of the leaders we arrest."

Melissa tossed her hair back. It moved as a clump, Brewer's dried blood still matting it together. "It's unbelievable that you can't be sure you'll destroy them."

"Yes, ma'am. Good point." Then he turned to Jamison. "How about your friend in there? Kane? Think he might have a lead on your data? Like I said, it would be nice evidence to have."

Jamison didn't answer until he'd caught Melissa's eye, saw how she'd taken Blevins's news. "I don't know. Let's try to ask him. Melissa, you coming?"

Melissa picked at her hair, tried to separate the strands from the blood, still looking angry at Jamison. "In a minute. I just want to get this awful stuff off me first."

Jamison watched her walk toward the bathroom, then told Blevins a little more about Kane, speaking with respect and admiration, almost as if Kane were already dead.

Jamison hadn't been in the room for a while, and he didn't know whether they would still find him alive. Even though the nurses were monitoring him at their stations, he knew they already figured him for dead. It was obvious by the way they treated him. Special. Gentle. As if they were giving him some kind of Hippocratic last rites.

Kane had buzzed for a nurse about an hour ago, needing her help in making a short phone call, wanting to call his family and say good-bye. After Jamison helped the nurse prop the phone against Kane's ear and dial the number, he walked out with her. She was sniffling as she left, already giving up. Her tears had touched him, and made him appreciate that she still had a sensitive nature after years of watching people suffer and die.

Kane's eyes were open when Jamison entered with Blevins, but they didn't reveal whether he was awake or dead. He didn't seem to be breathing. There were tubes and bandages all over his chest and arms, and monitors beeping around his head. But Kane blinked, waved them in with his left hand by making little circles in the air.

"How are you feeling, Jack?"

Kane coughed, whispered. "Better. Pretty good, actually."

Jamison looked along Kane's body, saw the destruction of countless bullet wounds, and knew Kane had to be lying. "Good," he said. "I'm glad."

Kane tried to smile. Somehow he actually managed to do it.

"Listen, Kane, I'm really sorry to bother you, but we need to find a white box of evidence, the stuff I discovered at Dillon?"

Kane coughed again, deep down in his chest and sticky wet. "Yes. I know about it."

Jamison leaned closer. "Do you know who stole it? Where it is?"

Kane coughed some more. This time his body went into convulsions and his monitors went off, buzzing steady tones. Two nurses rushed in and shoved Jamison aside, started fidgeting with the machine and examining Kane. But Kane amazed them by getting himself under control, lying there with a feeble grin on his face, staying perfectly still while the nurses asked each other questions. After a few minutes they backed out of the room, looking at Kane as if they couldn't image how he'd done it.

"Yes," he whispered. "I know who has it."

Jamison moved in very close, tried not to sound excited. "Who?"

Kane shifted in the bed, squeezed his eyes shut and kept them that way for ten or twelve seconds, his face screwed up in a painful grimace. After he settled down he opened his eyes and looked right at Blevins, who was just coming over from setting his briefcase on a nearby tray table.

"I recognize you," Kane said. "You're the F.B.I. agent, Blevins."

"Guilty."

Kane smiled with clenched teeth. "There's an agent in your office named Strick." Kane coughed some more. A big bubble of thick blood formed on his lips, popped, rolled off his mouth and onto the pillow. Neither Jamison nor Blevins wiped it away.

"Strick was instructed to take the evidence from the vault, then hold on to it until he heard from me. I'm sure he still has it."

Blevins's face tightened into stone. "Strick! That bastard. I'm going to crush his balls." He marched to the door and opened it. Jamison could see chaos in the hall. Someone was screaming off in the distance and Jamison panicked for the second it took to be sure the voice wasn't Melissa's. Agents were running to new positions, pushing people out of their way as they crashed down the hall toward the screaming woman. Jamison watched the turmoil as the nurse gave Blevins directions to a phone, kept watching for several more seconds. Blevins made a quick glance back into the room from the doorway to let Jamison know he'd just been appointed to guard Kane.

Kane was smiling and seemed to like the threat Blevins had made toward Strick, was still chuckling about it when his chest went into a spasm. More blood rolled out of his mouth. He grabbed Jamison's sleeve, held on to his arm with a gorilla's strength until he finished coughing. Then he composed himself again, acting like a man who had some unfinished business he needed to wrap up before leaving. Jamison looked at the blood oozing from a half-dozen bullet wounds, then looked at the smile on Kane's face, couldn't begin to understand the reservoir from which Kane drew that much strength and control.

"Jamison, several men were assigned to kill you. Some are from Dillon, some are freelancers. Some are the F.B.I.'s. It will be hard for you to get away, maybe impossible. But it's your only chance. You need to get out of the States, lie low for a long, long time."

"What if I don't? What if I stay and make a stand?" Jamison was hovering closer now, trying to hear every word. Blevins muttered his way back into the room, bitching and moaning about whatever had happened outside, then joining Jamison beside Kane's bed.

"Then you'll die over this," Kane said, glancing at Blevins as he said it. "You've done very well so far, but they'll find you, and kill you. My bet is you'll die right here in this room, along with me. I'm sure they know I'm here, and they can't allow me to live, not after this morning. They will be here soon, could be any minute now, and you'll be killed in the bargain."

Blevins raised his walkie-talkie and held it in front of his mouth, but hesitated before he keyed the mike. "They may be here already, guys. Someone just killed the nurse in charge of the medication cart, stole a syringe and some succinylcholine, or however the hell you say it. Some kind of a paralyzing drug used in anesthesia."

Melissa rushed in and spun around, pushed the door shut then held it closed, braced herself against it as if holding back an army. Jamison watched her, his hand on his pistol, waiting to hear if someone pounded on the door. Twenty seconds later she relaxed and straightened up, looked a little embarrassed as she walked to him, grabbed his good arm, and squeezed it hard. He looked her over and noticed that she hadn't gotten much of the blood out of her hair. He also saw that she was angry. Or was it worry? She threw another panicked glance toward the door as if she wanted to warn him about what was going on outside. He closed his eyes and nodded that he already knew about the dead nurse.

"I'm not running," Jamison said. "I've got a job to finish."

Kane's body convulsed again. He closed his eyes, squeezed them very hard for about a minute before he opened them again. A tear rolled from the corner of his left eye and tracked into his ear.

"That's too bad."

Blevins motioned for Jamison to step away with him. The two of them left Kane, with Melissa beside his bed, and met near the windows. Blevins put his hand on Jamison's shoulder.

"Don't be an idiot, Peter. You're not staying around here, and that's all there is to it."

Jamison whispered, tried to keep Melissa from hearing. "What do you mean, Rich? You know Melissa won't let this go after coming this far. You heard her, she wants all of those people prosecuted. If she's staying, I'm staying. There's no choice here for me."

"I need you alive, buddy. Hell, I need Melissa alive, too. You guys are my witnesses. You have to be able to validate the evidence when I get it back. I just can't let you hang around here and get yourselves killed. Too many people have died already."

Melissa walked over as Blevins finished, probably had heard most of what he'd said. "He's right, Peter. I hate it, but he is. We've done what we can for now. If the F.B.I. can make a case, they'll need us alive to help them. If they can't make a case, well, we wouldn't be able to make one either. We'd just get killed for nothing."

Blevins kept watching the door. Jamison noticed that his hand was wrapped around the grip of the MP5, which hung on a strap from his shoulder, his finger resting on the trigger, his aim following his eyes. It was clear that Blevins was expecting trouble, any minute now. Jamison touched the butt of his own pistol, just for the assurance.

"We'll make the case," Blevins said. "It's just a question of how deep we'll be able to penetrate. But we'll shave off the top few layers, with or without your data. The organization will be destroyed, I promise. It's pointless for you to die now, no matter how you look at it."

Jamison looked at Kane lying in the bed across the room, thinking about how he'd been ready to kill him just a few hours ago. Then he thought about the men who had already died on both sides. The good ones, and the bad ones. Poor, weak Ted Bronovich. Two agents at the Coalition. That ugly animal Butler. The two killers at Casey's house. Three men at Harborplace. Drummond, and his bodyguard. Kane, maybe. And how many had Blevins killed since Monday?

Then he thought about how many more would die. This was shaping up into a war, surely. And war meant casualties. If he were going to do any more to help his side win, he and Melissa could not be among those killed in action.

"Okay, Rich. Let's talk about what you have in mind."

"It's real simple. The Justice Department wants to take away your old lives and give you new ones. They've got a million bucks to carry you two through to old age, assuming you'll testify. So all I want is for you to take the money and get your ass . . . Melissa's, too, to Costa Rica. Hide out there under our protection for six months. A year maybe. Live like sheiks, have a great time. By then everything will be cool and you can come back. If I need you, I'll know where to find you. We have a legal attaché there who will be your contact. I know the guy pretty well, which is why I picked Costa Rica. You can trust him."

Melissa stuck her hands underneath Blevins's bulletproof vest and grabbed his shoulders, gave him a hard squeeze. "Rich, you swear you'll get the leaders of this group, the top levels of corruption. I don't care about the followers because, as you just said, they'll fade away without leadership. But you have to promise me you'll get the leaders, get them all, leave no one capable of running that organization."

Blevins had to think about this. It was obvious by the way he raised his hand to his mouth and held it there. Jamison knew from that simple action that whatever he said next would be sacred.

"I promise, Melissa. I've got enough evidence, even without the data you guys collected. Sackett, the SAC of my office, was in on the corruption, and he's already made a sworn statement to U.S. Attorney Riley, and has agreed to testify. He said the organization was highly fragmented, but that he knows a few people at the top. Almost none below him, though. At least his testimony will help me pry the door open, and from there I can keep moving up the list. If your buddy Kane makes it, I'm sure he can feed me a lot of information that will allow me to work in both directions, pick off most of the soldiers who did Drummond's work. But even if he doesn't make it, yeah, I'll get the top layer. I'm sure. I promise."

Jamison put his hand on Melissa's shoulder, gave it a gentle squeeze. "Rich, what's going to happen to Sackett?"

"He's out. After he testifies in closed court, he'll be out of the F.B.I. I'm not going to prosecute him, though. In fact, I'm going to let him keep his secret, even from his family. As far as anyone at the office knows, he's still the SAC and will be until this all shakes out."

"That's good for our side, I guess. Doesn't seem right, though. Kane's dying, and Sackett gets to walk?"

"I need his testimony. It's as simple as that. But don't think he's not being punished. Sackett has worked for the Bureau since he was twenty. Started as a clerk, then went to college and retreaded through as an agent. Now he'll be out. No pension, no respect, no money. I'd say that's pretty severe punishment."

"Yeah. I see your point."

Melissa picked up Jamison's hand, caressed it without looking at him. "Okay, Rich, I'm willing to hide out. Peter, is that what you think is best?"

Jamison shrugged, couldn't think much farther than his fingers being stroked by Melissa's hand. "Sure. I guess."

Blevins sighed as if he'd expected this to be much harder. "Good, let's go. There's already a dead surgical nurse down the hall. If her death is related to Kane, I don't want you guys here any longer than necessary."

Jamison stepped over to Kane's bed, but stood there for a few seconds, waited until Kane opened his eyes.

"I've got to go, Kane. Thanks for bringing Melissa back to me. I owe you." He touched him on the shoulder.

Kane looked up and grinned with his teeth locked together. "We're even. That was really something, seeing you trot down the sidewalk through that rain of gunfire to help me." He closed his eyes and his body tightened all over. Then he slumped down, deflated, went back to grinning. "It was really a dumb thing, but amazing. Thanks."

Jamison smiled with him, shook his head. Felt good about himself. Then he turned to Blevins.

"Ready?"

"Yeah," he said, then spoke to Kane. "Don't worry, big guy, we'll keep you safe. I have some men stationed right outside your door. They won't let any strangers in here."

He headed to the door and Jamison followed, walking with Melissa. When Blevins opened the door Melissa stopped and turned, gave Kane a sad look then squeezed Jamison's arm.

"Peter, give me a few minutes alone with him. Please. I want to thank him for helping me, and for bringing us back together. It won't take long."

Jamison understood, even though he didn't know the story between her and Kane, and couldn't guess what Kane might have done for her. For all he knew, she might owe him her life. He walked out into the hall with Blevins, closed the door and waited, watched the body of the dead nurse being moved to another room.

21

Melissa walked the few steps to Kane's bed, stood over him, and stroked his forehead. She looked into his eyes and loved the way they looked back at her with complete understanding. They were nice eyes, gentle and peaceful, with absolutely no doubt in them. No fear. No wonder. He seemed to know everything about her, even her deepest secrets. He had acted like that since the first time she'd met the great Jack Kane, face-to-face in an eight-by-nine prison cell.

He struggled to lift his hand, held it in the air about four inches from the bed. He was so sweet, waiting for her to hold it. She picked it up, took the strain of its weight and caressed his fingers. She stroked them, marveling at the strong muscles in his thick fingers, feeling an odd, wonderful kinship with this big man.

Kane gave her a loving look, the same, favorite-uncle's kind of look he'd given her in prison after he'd pushed Jitters out of her cell. He licked his lips, cleared his throat, and squeezed her hand very gently.

"You're going to kill me now, aren't you?"

She stroked his forehead again, gently pushed the hair at the front of his head into a neat line.

"Shhh, it will be all right. You won't feel anything."

"I don't feel much of anything now."

She smiled. "I'm glad. You're not in too much pain?"

"No. I feel numb. The drugs, you know."

"They've given you a lot?"

He glanced away for a second without moving his head, then came back to meet her eyes.

"Melissa, do you really think you can run that organization?"

She looked around the room, then came back to him with quiet confidence. "Of course. Who better than me? After all, I am Richard Corley's daughter. I've spent my life learning how the organization works. I know all the players now. After the F.B.I. eliminates the current leaders, I'll be the only one who knows everything, the only person who knows how to keep the machinery running. It will be easy for me to take over. No one will know it's me, at least not for awhile. I'll do a good job, Kane. I promise. I'll make my father proud."

Kane frothed out some blood and Melissa dabbed at his mouth until she got it all.

"I don't think so, Melissa. In the end, your father regretted what he'd done. He would be impressed by the way you orchestrated this whole thing, though, getting the F.B.I. to eliminate your competition."

Kane's body trembled. But he gritted his teeth, let none of the pain show in his eyes.

She pinched his cheek. "My, my, aren't you the clever one? How long have you known?"

"Oh, I've been suspicious for years, ever since you went to work for the Coalition and started digging around. Every time I heard the rumor that someone else was trying to take over, I thought of you. But you hid your plan well, and I didn't really become convinced until I saw you meet Jamison at Jonah's Bar last week. I knew—" Kane closed his eyes and stiffened his body for ten seconds, but kept talking through the pain. "I knew you didn't love him, knew you were just going to use him. The same way you used Senator Armstrong, then killed him after he gave you the names he knew. Do I have that about right?"

She adjusted his pillow, trying to make him comfortable as she spoke.

"It's funny, you know. I tried to kill Peter once, too, had some men attack us on a Delaware Beach. But he really surprised me by killing one of the men I'd hired, and scaring the other one so badly he ran away. It was so funny." She giggled and glanced away for a second, then shook her head as if not believing her own memory.

"I tried to stop the man from running, but couldn't. So I stripped down and acted like I'd been raped. You should have seen me, tearing at my clothes on the sandy beach, trying to get my tight jeans off before he came over the dune. I tell you, it was a surprise to hear him coming to help me."

"He's a good man. I'm not surprised by him anymore. I once was, but not now."

She felt some pain in her heart and stopped talking long enough to figure out why. She hoped it wasn't for Peter. At least, not just for him alone. Maybe it was for all the people like him. People who left themselves wide open to being hurt, used and abused, over and over again, for love.

"Jack, you know I don't really want to kill you, don't you. But you crossed the line and went back to the other side. Haven't you? Are you really serious about helping Blevins and the F.B.I."

"Yes."

"Then I'm truly sorry to do this. But it does me no good to take over the power, then allow you and Blevins to destroy my army. I've spent too long figuring this out, learning how to eliminate the leaders without hurting the forces they control. There's no way I can let you live."

"I know."

She pulled the syringe out of her pocket, picked up the IV tube and gave Kane a silly grin.

"There's a dead nurse down the hall who didn't need this anymore."

Kane watched her, almost looked amused. "Melissa, what about Jamison? Are you going to kill him, too?"

She stopped with the syringe inserted into the Y-site injection port, her thumb resting on the plunger but not pushing it.

"Now, that's a good question. Truth is, I've grown a bit fond of him, of the way he treats me. I guess, if he'll go along with what I'm doing, I won't. I'm not an animal, you know. I don't kill because I like it. Besides, I need love, too, and Peter's a very nice man. He wouldn't be a bad person to grow old with."

"You're not talking about the Jamison I've seen the last couple of days. He won't go along with you. You know that as well as I do."

She flipped her hair away from her face. "He might. He loves me."

She pushed the plunger of the syringe and the muscle relaxant swept into the IV, then into Kane's arm. She watched the fluid enter his body, then put the syringe back in her pocket.

"Good-bye," he said as his hand fell to his stomach.

She ran her fingers through his hair once more and fixed it neatly. "Give my love to daddy when you see him."

Kane's eyes rolled back and the alarms went off. She raced to the door and threw it open, then shrieked as loudly as she could. "Help! Get a doctor in here, quick! He's dying, he's dying!"

She stood in the doorway and watched to see what would happen. The corridor was plenty chaotic already. Frightened-looking nurses watched their backs while F.B.I. agents milled around with their weapons ready. Several nurses and two doctors raced toward Kane's room and pushed past Melissa, took less than a minute to pronounce Kane dead.

She went back into Kane's room with them, stood there crying, waiting for Blevins and Jamison to shoulder their way into the crowd, hoping Jamison would put his arm around her, pull her into his chest and say something comforting, tell her it would be all right, that Kane was going to die anyway.

But Jamison didn't come into the room. Blevins didn't either. She watched the door, looking out into the hall each time someone opened it, until curiosity moved her feet in that direction.

* * * * *

Jamison kept staring at the four inch screen in Blevins's palm, even after Melissa walked out of frame and headed toward the door. He knew he would be able to see her in a second, if he would just look up and over the heads of a dozen agents. She would be standing at the other end of the long hall, right at Kane's door, looking for him. He did not want to see her.

Blevins pulled the headphones off his head, reached over and pulled the other pair off Jamison's ears, let them drop around his neck.

"You okay? Peter, man, I'm sorry. Real sorry."

Jamison couldn't take his eyes off the screen, kept them glued onto Kane's body, hoping and praying that Kane wasn't really dead. That Melissa hadn't really killed him. If Kane would just move a little, maybe Jamison would wake up from this nightmare and everything would be okay again.

Blevins let him stare for another minute before he snapped the lid over the small screen, wound up the wire that connected it to the receiver of the video recorder. He was cussing, quietly.

Jamison was still staring at the spot where Blevins had held the video screen, scared to death that if he looked up he would see Melissa walking down the hallway toward him. His heart was already breaking, aching so deeply that he couldn't feel any of the other parts of his body, even the shot-up parts. He was absolutely sure it would kill him to look into her eyes.

He turned in Blevins's direction but didn't look at him. "You need me anymore? Or can I go?"

Blevins put his hand on Jamison's back and rubbed it like a father might.

"You want to say anything to Melissa before I arrest her?"

Jamison kept his eyes down, still hadn't looked at anyone since he'd watch her kill Kane.

"No. I don't know what I'd say, Rich." He sighed, and his lip quivered. He bit it so hard that blood squirted into his mouth.

"I understand. If you're ready to take off, I'll assign some agents to go with you. I want you out of here."

Jamison raised his eyes, but lifted them right past everyone around him and looked at the ceiling, fluttered his eyelids a few times.

"Yes. I guess I'm ready. I'd like to know how you knew she would do that, though. How did you know she was the one trying to take over that organization?"

"I didn't. I didn't even suspect her until Kane called me."

"Kane called you? When?"

"About an hour ago. A nurse helped him place it. I was almost here when I got the call, shoot, just a couple blocks away. He called the office and had them patch his call to me. Told me all about the men he'd hired to kill you, then told me that Melissa was probably going to kill him, that she was the only one who could take over the fund, and that he suspected her of orchestrating this whole thing. He knew he was going to die, Peter. But he promised to convince her he wasn't, make it necessary for her to do something about him. That's why it took me so long to get here. I had to go back to the office and get the briefcase camera and recorder."

"Damn you, Rich! You let a man die just so you could put Melissa in prison?"

Blevins didn't look away, took everything Jamison's look was saying. "Yes. It was hard to do, too. Man, you know I love Melissa, almost as much as you do. To stand here and watch her kill a man, knowing I could run down the hall and stop it, keep him alive and her out of jail, well, it was about the hardest thing I've ever done. But Kane wanted it this way. He wanted to end his life doing the right thing. And I wanted to stop the corruption." He paused for a few seconds. "So did you. Remember?"

Jamison turned away, made a little lap in the corridor, rubbed his forehead.

"I bet that tape you just made won't be admissible. And even if it is, her attorney will make you look like an animal for standing by and allowing her to do it. What you've done is despicable."

"You're right. Her attorney will have a field day with it. But it will be admissible, Peter, and it will lead to a conviction. I'm sorry, but that's the way it'll go. I had no choice. I hope you'll understand one day."

Jamison snapped onto him, thought about hitting him with his good right arm. "Rich, you realize you're talking about the woman I love?"

"Hey, don't forget that she tried to have you killed on that beach in Delaware."

"So what? I never said she loved me. Hell, for all I know she still might want to kill me. I can't help that, any more than I can help the way I feel about her. Damn you, Rich, people overlook the sins of people they love. You're a parent, you know that. Could your sons ever do anything bad enough to make you stop loving them?"

Blevins sucked his top lip down and bit it. "No."

"Then don't hold your breath hoping that someday I'll understand. I hate you for what you've done, Rich. I'll always hate you for it." Jamison spun on his heels and headed toward the elevator.

"Wait a minute, Peter. Where are you going? You need some protection, someone to keep you safe so you can testify. My men found Strick and recovered your evidence, but without you it's worthless. You're my key witness. Where will I find you?"

Jamison jammed his finger into the elevator button, turned to Blevins as he waited for the doors to open.

"Go to hell, Rich. You just go to hell."

The doors opened and Jamison stepped in, turned around and watched Blevins staring back. As the doors began to close Blevins turned an angry face to some other agents, pointed at Melissa and yelled, "Put that woman under arrest for murder. Do it!"

22

Jamison rode the elevator down but almost forgot to get off. He just stood there replaying the last few minutes while the rest of the people stepped out and walked away, made room for more people to get on. The closing doors brought him back, signaled him to move, made him lunge through the crowd, hit the safety bar, and jump out. He had no desire to go back up to the floor where Kane lay dead and Melissa stood under arrest.

He felt the stares as he walked through the main lobby of the hospital, his jacket still hanging off his shoulder, concealing his Beretta. His shirt had been cut off by the emergency room nurses, so the rest of his chest was bare except for the gauze and dressing wrapped around his middle, and the sling that supported his left arm. He went through the automatic doors and kept going, out into the cold winter air, tugging his jacket onto his good arm and over his sling, zipping it as best he could. He had nowhere to go, and no plan for when he got there.

He kept thinking about all that had happened since Blevins had arrived at the hospital, blaming him for each and every disastrous turn of events. Everything had been fine until he'd shown up. Melissa was back with him, she was safe, and he was going to live. Kane was dying, but what the hell. That didn't bother Jamison now. Kane had sold out Melissa, had allowed her to kill him in order to provide Blevins with the evidence he needed to charge her. He didn't care about Kane anymore, and regretted that he'd saved him from the sidewalk slaughter, hated him just as much as he hated Blevins.

After a few minutes of walking he caught a cab, had the driver drop him at the front door of Melissa's building, the one place where he could still smell her perfume. Touch things that had touched her, clothes that had been close to her body. See the things she'd valued enough to bring home and make a part of her life.

He wandered through her rooms for several minutes, picking her clothes off the floor and standing the shattered bookcase back up, his good arm and bandaged side straining against its weight. He went to the bathroom and stared at the spot where she'd stood wrapped in a towel and, he realized now, toying with him as he stepped out of the shower and stood naked in front of her. Winding him up with desire. Fueling his devotion. Now he understood what she was really capable of, and his mind despised what she'd done to him, wanted to get her out of it, exorcise her and walk away from this whole mess. Forget he had ever loved her.

But his heart belonged to Melissa Corley and there wasn't a damn thing he could do about it, even if she never loved him back. He felt like a kid in school, loving the Homecoming Queen who would never give him two looks in the same month. But loving her anyway. Getting sweaty palms and a thumping chest when she passed in the hall.

He set a chair up on its legs, pushed some of the debris away, and sat down to think of what to do next. It wasn't easy. Right now, it was incredibly difficult for him to even imagine a future, much less make plans to get him there. He wanted, almost desperately, to live in the past. Just a few hours past, when Melissa was beside him and his arm was around her and they were getting their lives back together. Closer than he'd ever thought possible.

And now, suddenly, she was completely out of his reach, separated from him by Rich Blevins, the F.B.I., a murder charge, and ultimately, a set of prison bars. They had come so close, just two hours earlier this morning.

He tried to stop thinking about it, kept refocusing his mind on his task, kept brainstorming ideas, trying to think of who to call, what to do, and how he could help her. Eventually he came up with a terrible idea. It was full of holes and what-ifs, a ridiculously simple scheme. But it was a plan, something he could put into action right now, before Blevins moved Melissa too far away from him. The fact that the plan could be easily implemented made him grasp on to it with a fanatic's determination, and ignore that the probability of failure was overwhelming.

He called Sackett first, said exactly what he needed to say, didn't care if it offended the man or not. Blevins had said Sackett was on his way out. He was going to testify, then walk away. Blevins, in a magnanimous gesture to which Melissa hadn't been entitled, was going to keep Sackett's secret and let him live out his life as a mystery to those who had worked for him. Let him slip away and disappear. Poof, just like that.

Then Jamison dialed the squad room and demanded that the squad secretary go into the interrogation room and pull Blevins out.

"Damn, Peter, I'm glad you called. Sorry about earlier. Where are you?"

"Melissa's apartment."

"That's not smart. We've located most of Kane's assassins, but there are still a few out there. Melissa's apartment would be a pretty logical place for them to look for you."

"I don't care."

"Okay, fair enough. You don't care. But she's playing you for a fool, Peter, and your pathetic little broken heart is going to get you killed. As your friend, I'm telling you she's not worth it. She's a criminal, plain and simple. You've got to see that, Peter. See her for what she is."

Jamison felt his heart break all over again, for probably the twentieth time today. He knew Blevins was right, knew it was foolish even to think about saving her.

"I know she's a criminal, Rich. I saw what she did to Kane."

"Then get with the program! Get bladed, cover your ass. I'm telling you there are some pretty nasty suckers out there who want to kill you, men who don't know Kane canceled the contract on you."

Jamison looked around Melissa's apartment, amazed to have survived this nightmare, aware that he owed Blevins some gratitude for helping.

"You're right, Rich. As usual. I know I've got to pull myself out of this."

"Now you're talking."

"Yeah. One last thing about Melissa. Okay?"

"Sure, buddy. But make it quick."

"I was wondering if you might cut a deal with her? You could use her testimony to convict a lot of others, let her guide you through your investigation."

"Good thought, Peter. Actually, I already considered it because I like her so much. But murdering Kane was a step too far. I can't plead out a murderer, no matter how much I'd like to try."

Jamison nodded his head, understood and expected the answer. "Just a last-ditch idea."

"Not a bad one, either. Just impossible."

"Last question, then. Is the money still available to me. The money you mentioned in the hospital?"

"Yeah. Sure. Like I said, a million bucks. It's all for you, always has been, locked up in the armory, and it takes two people to open the door. I didn't use the evidence vault because things tend to get lost there."

"It's all mine? I thought half was for me, and half was for Melissa."

"Naw. I said it was for the two of you just to keep Melissa off her guard."

The sound of her name broke his heart again.

"Why's the government being so generous, anyway? Why so much money?"

"Aw, hell, Peter, it's not really that much money. The U.S. attorney figured you'd have extraordinary expenses for a few years, so he added something to cover those expenses to ten years' worth of your current salary. Rounded that number off at a mill."

"You're right, you know. When you put it that way, it's not much money."

"Still better than dying. All you have to do for it is stay alive, and be ready to testify about your data."

"Fair enough. So when can I get the money and haul ass out of here? You mentioned Costa Rica, and that's fine with me. The sooner the better."

"I can meet you with it later. I just need to finish interviewing Melissa, then stop by the bank to get the money converted into whatever instruments you want besides cash."

"Cash will be fine, Rich. Let's just do it, okay? And soon. I'm starting to get nervous hanging around here."

"Man, that's a lot of cash. How about some bearer—"

"Cash is fine. I don't want to die here, Rich, don't want to sit on my thumbs while you do some half-assed banking. Get me out of here, Rich. Now! Get me out before somebody kills me."

"Just hang on, buddy. Hang on, I'll come and get you. You're at Melissa's apartment? I'm on my way."

"No. The airport, Rich. Have some new identification made for me and meet me at Delta ticketing with the money and a ticket to any foreign airport that has flights to Costa Rica. One hour. Okay?"

"Sure, yeah. Okay. One hour. See you then."

Jamison hung up and took one last look around Melissa's apartment. This was the life he was leaving behind. Trading a life of engineering and cherry blossom festivals and weekends in Georgetown for some low-country life in the lesser latitudes. Losing his name and his past and his connections to everyone he loved, or who had ever loved him. Going alone to start over in some foreign country. Blevins had said it would be only a few years before he could come back, but Jamison knew better. He knew he couldn't mark time for that long, would have to start building a new life right away or go insane. He was sure the new life he built would become important to him, and he wouldn't be willing to give it up. It was impossible to imagine any of that now, with his heart aching and loneliness settling around him like fallout. But it would happen, he was sure of it.

There was nothing in the apartment he wanted. He thought about some pictures of him with Melissa, but passed. He walked out the door and down the stairs to the street, caught a cab to his bank, made a quick stop to close his account before leaving forever.

As Jamison had hoped, Blevins beat him to the rendezvous, was standing against a small piece of wall at Delta ticketing, watching Jamison walk up to him. Blevins had changed back to working clothes, jacket and tie with a heavy winter overcoat. He looked like he'd spent the better part of his life standing right there near the ticket counter, as if he were a fixture. Jamison wondered how long he had been there, how long it took to start looking inanimate.

A brown briefcase dangled from Blevins's hands, centered in front of him, a plastic shopping bag behind it. His eyes darted to Jamison, then searched the area, then came back, then searched again. Eyes that expected trouble. Maybe lots of it.

"Come with me, Peter," he said as Jamison got close. "Over here. There's not much time."

He led the way to a recess, a little niche in the wall. Blevins handed him the briefcase.

"One million dollars cash, buddy. The other bag is some new clothes. Be careful, because it's your money now. Tough shit if you lose it. Sign this receipt." He pulled a voucher out of his jacket pocket, grew impatient while Jamison read it before signing.

"Here's a ticket to Mexico City." He handed Jamison a fat envelope. "It's a direct flight, booked under your new alias. I had a new passport and matching identification made up for you. It's all in the ticket envelope. When you land, look for a man holding a sign for Calinda El Torridor Hotel. He'll be one of our agents. He'll make sure you lose anyone who might have followed you. Questions?"

Jamison took the packet. "No, no questions. When will you contact me?"

Blevins held his hand out until Jamison shook it. Blevins smiled when their hands touched, and it made the scab over his eye wrinkle. Had it been only last Friday that they'd boxed? Not even a week ago? It didn't seem possible.

"I'll call you soon, give you a little time to get settled in first. Do whatever your contact agent tells you, all right? He's there to help you. That's just about his only job now. I've told him how important you are to me."

"Thanks, Rich. Will do."

"You'd better go. It isn't smart for us to be standing here. Your plane is loading now. Get on it. Will you be all right, or do you want me to come with you?"

Jamison smiled, felt funny to have Blevins worrying about him now. It was all over. Nothing much left to worry about.

"I'll be all right. Just a short walk and a sit-down, Rich. I think I can handle it. Here, take my pistol before I have to throw it in a trash can."

Blevins took a step back and looked Jamison over, then slid the Beretta out of Jamison's waistband and stuck it under his coat. "You know you look like shit, don't you?"

"Haven't had a shower since you and Sackett came to my hotel room."

"You look even worse than that." He chuckled a little, preened himself like a gorgeous bird.

"I'll make a point of cleaning up when I get to where I'm going. Some clean clothes will help a lot, too."

"Yeah. I bet."

Blevins had started to leave twice already. Made his moves, but hadn't gone. But now he looked ready.

"I'll be seeing you, Peter."

"Can't wait. Take care, my friend."

Blevins waved his hand over his shoulder as he walked away. Jamison watched him leave the terminal, saw a car slow down and stop long enough for Blevins to jump in.

Jamison stood there a moment longer, checked the departure time of the flight and stared at the destination. He pulled the new identification and passport out. He felt bad when he walked over to the trash can and threw the ticket away.

23

Jamison hurried to the Crown Room, hoping it would be empty as usual. Under normal circumstances it would be a good place to meet. Only Delta members had access, and few ever stayed long. It was a nice place to kill time between flights, with free phones and beverages. But not nice enough to hang around longer than you needed. Of course, nothing was normal about Jamison's circumstances, so he walked up to the door expecting anything to happen.

He used his card and opened the door, stepped inside and looked around. He'd been figuring all along that this might be another trap, that he might take a few steps inside the door and get killed. But it was something he had to do, something absolutely necessary, like a victim's family needing to meet the person who'd killed a loved one. Closure, that's what it was. Putting it all behind him, then going forward with whatever portion of his old life survived.

The room was empty except for two people sitting on a sofa at the far end, watching him come through the door. Sackett was one of the people. Melissa was the other. Jamison stopped as soon as he saw them, would not go any farther until he knew what they were thinking. Would Sackett be holding a gun on Melissa, down low where Jamison couldn't see it? Would Melissa think that Jamison had helped Blevins set her up, look at him with hate fulminating in her eyes? He would wait for these answers before moving closer.

Melissa stood up, looked surprised to see him. Sackett allowed her to move, which was a good sign. He sat there with one leg crossed over the other, watching Jamison's eyes go soft as if that were part of his reward for bringing her.

She walked over to Jamison, stopped in front of him and looked like a sad little girl.

"Hi," she said quietly, as her head went down.

Jamison didn't know what to do or say, didn't want to start babbling, wanted to concentrate on what he had to do. Leave all of the unknowns for later. He lifted her chin gently and smiled a little. Then he stepped around her and walked over to Sackett.

"Did you have any trouble?"

Sackett turned his head and looked out the wall of windows, concentrated on an MD-88 rolling by.

"No. There'll be hell to pay when Blevins gets back, though."

"Nobody questioned why you left with her?"

Sackett smirked, chuckled sadly at some joke in his head. "I'm the SAC, Jamison. The Boss. Why would anyone question me?"

Jamison didn't answer. He was destroying Sackett, and hating himself for shredding the last bit of the man's self-respect. Exploiting his sad situation and his love for his family and his needs for the future. He had bought Sackett with blood money, and was ashamed of himself for doing it.

"Where did Melissa get the clothes?"

"Just some things of my wife's. I called her from work, had her meet me on our way here. I didn't want Ms. Corley walking around in that bloody dress of hers."

Jamison set the briefcase of cash on the floor in front of the couch. Sackett didn't even glance at it, just kept staring at the jet outside the windows.

"Thank you," Jamison said.

Sackett nodded while a tear crystallized on his eyelashes, broke free and made a speedy run down his handsome face.

"Sure. I hope it works out for you."

"Yeah. You, too, Sackett. I hope you buy a good life with this money. I swear I'll never tell anyone where you got it. A million dollars should last a pretty long time if you're careful with it."

Sackett reached for the briefcase handle, flipped it back and forth a few times before he closed his fingers around it. He stood up, took a deep breath and gave Jamison a loser's smile.

"It doesn't matter, because I'll know. I'll always know what I've done here."

Jamison bit his lip, cut off the temptation to say something more. He held out his hand and Sackett shook it.

"I've already given Ms. Corley a new passport and I.D. A few thousand dollars, too. So I'd make tracks if I were you. Once Blevins finds out she's gone, he's going to shut this airport down. You know that, don't you?"

Jamison kept biting his lip, feeling even more ashamed of himself than he had a moment ago, and wondering if he could possibly sink any lower. Sackett was probably a decent guy, an honorable man who'd made a couple of mistakes. Jamison was the real criminal here. He was capitalizing on Sackett's errors, using them like some pimp might use a woman's drug habit to get her selling her body. It was a terrible thing he'd done.

Jamison followed Sackett to the door, said nothing else, closed the door after he'd gone. Then he turned to Melissa. God, she was beautiful. To him, she was the exact definition of the word. He tried to look at her differently now, tried to see her with the world's eyes. Why couldn't he convince himself that he didn't really love her, then get the hell out of here? She was free, he had done what he'd set out to do. He should end it here, right now, and he knew it.

But it wasn't going to happen, so he gave up and walked over to her. The room felt like it was a hundred miles across, giving him time for a thousand thoughts which evoked a million good reasons why he should turn and run away.

She had dropped her head when he'd let go of her chin, and was still looking down at the floor when he came back to her. He took a deep breath, rubbed his hands together, crossed them over his chest, looked around the room. She still didn't look up.

"Quite a week, huh?"

He waited, but she didn't move. He could almost hear the hands of his watch sweeping the time away from them.

"What do you plan to do now, Melissa?"

No answer. He couldn't take it anymore, standing so close and not hugging her, not putting his arms around her and pulling her close, feeling the press of their bodies against each other, her hair tormenting his face like it always did.

He walked to the kitchen area, where her gravitational pull wasn't quite so strong, and began to change into the clothes Blevins had given him. She didn't look at him the entire time, not once while he struggled to dress with one hand. He was actually hoping she would look, maybe bring back some of what they'd shared in her bathroom last week.

After he changed, he stuffed his old clothes into the bag then rinsed his face in the sink. When he raised his head and opened his eyes she was standing right there, just across the counter from him.

"You gave Sackett a million dollars to get me free. I want to know why."

He listened to the question carefully, didn't even reach for a towel, stood there with water on his face and her question in his ears.

"Just something I wanted to do. Nothing more to it."

She had her attorney voice going now, nothing too nice, but not quite confrontational, either.

"Rich told me you heard everything I said in Kane's room. Is that right?"

"Yes."

"Then why, Peter? Why would you pay a fortune to save me?"

He picked a towel off the counter, dabbed at his face with his good hand, careful of the scabs on his face. He didn't have an answer she would understand. If she loved him at all, she would have realized already how overwhelming that emotion was, how it forced a person to do things that made absolutely no sense. On the other hand, if she'd never felt it, there was no way to make her understand.

He raked his fingers through his hair and gathered up the few things he had, got ready to go.

"Do you need money, Melissa? I got a little over thirty thousand dollars when I closed my bank account. If you need some traveling money, it's yours."

She shook her head hard, as if she'd just seen Elvis and couldn't believe it.

"Why are you being so nice? I tried to kill you."

"Yeah, I know. I'm a fool. Do you need the money or not?" He walked around the counter and headed toward the door.

"No," she said, still shaking her head. "My daddy left me a lot of money. I've never wanted to use it, though. But I've got cash stashed all over the place. Would you at least let me repay the money you gave Sackett?"

He shot to her eyes and checked to see if she had offended him on purpose, then decided she hadn't. She looked confused and bewildered, but there wasn't a hint of haughtiness anywhere on her face.

"No, but thanks."

It was time for him to go. Blevins would be hitting the ceiling soon, and Jamison had to be on a flight before then.

Melissa should be, too, but he wasn't about to tell her what to do. He put his good hand on her right arm.

"One question, Melissa. Did you ever love me, even a little? Or was it all a pretense?"

She didn't know the answer, he could tell by the way her head tilted and her eyes looked at him.

"I . . . I think I may have loved you, Peter. Might love you still. I'm just not sure. Honestly, I've never been sure what love is. But if I've ever been in love, it was with you. But I really can't say for sure. Don't want to mislead you anymore."

It felt great to hear her confess that maybe, just maybe, she might have shared some part of the feeling he had for her. It made him happy as he turned to leave.

"Well, I love you, Melissa. Don't really want to anymore, but I can't help it."

"Then I should tell you I love you back. After all, you just paid a million dollars for me. I kind of feel like an indentured servant."

He had already turned away, had managed to start walking out on her. Leaving her behind. His brain ignoring his heart's demands to beg her to come with him. He wasn't going to turn back now, regardless of what she said.

"Good-bye, Melissa." He stared at the door knob twenty feet away. "Hope you get to be in love some day. It's a wonderful feeling."

Then he struggled against every power of nature, fought his way to the door as if walking against a beating wind. It took all of his strength to turn the knob, but once done, he pulled back on the door and stepped through it. Shuffled away, trying to remember how to find the ticketing area.

"May I help you, sir?"

Jamison looked up. The line in front of him had vanished, and the perky woman in the blue uniform was waiting with a smile of forced patience on her face. He slid his paper bag forward with his right foot, then stepped up to the counter.

"I understand there's a flight to Zurich that leaves in fifteen minutes. Are there still seats available?" He'd never been to Zurich before, and had never wanted to go there. But it was the next international departure.

She tapped her keyboard. "Let me see . . . yes, sir, through JFK. There's a seat in first class." She rose up on her toes and looked Jamison over, raised her eyebrows as if the words *first class* might cause him to faint. "One-way or round trip?"

"One-way," Jamison said.

The direction for the rest of his life. Never coming back. Never seeing Melissa again. One-way.

"Your ticket will be three thousand six hundred forty-two dollars, sir. Would you like me to book that?"

"Yes."

"Are you traveling alone?"

Melissa's voice suddenly snapped him out of his trance. "No," she said. "Make it two."

Jamison jumped a little as she put her elbows on the counter. The ticket agent looked at Jamison. He closed his eyes.

He could actually see it happening, could imagine them rushing for their gate with Jamison carrying nothing but a plastic bag of dirty clothes and all his cash. Not exactly the typical first-class-to-Zurich passengers.

But Melissa would be beside him. He wouldn't even have to look to prove it. He would hear her feet slapping the tile floor, and her voice giggling as if they were getting away with a silly prank. All the while his heart would be thumping away with the pleasure of knowing that the next several hours would be spent sitting beside her.

Of course, tomorrow might be different. Anything could happen. Blevins might be enraged enough to come after them. Melissa might go out for coffee and never come back. She could kill him whenever they slept together. It was even possible that she would discover she loved him.

But tomorrow could wait. Right now was all that mattered. And right now, Melissa was willing to come with him, her legs ready to move along with his, their lives, at least for the next several hours, moving in the same direction. The woman he loved would be going to Zurich with him. He would take nothing else for granted. Had never taken her for granted. The essence of love.

"Sir? Will that be two tickets?"

He opened his eyes and looked at Melissa. He loved her so much it hurt, still noticed each and every breath she took, still tried to inhale the air that left her lungs. But she was different now. She wasn't crying on a beach, and she wasn't in any danger. She did not need him anymore and didn't care about him. She had given him a chance to love, and he would always be grateful. But he had to leave her, had to go somewhere new and start over. There might even be another woman out there for him, someone who would reflect back some of the love he had given her. It seemed unlikely, but possible.

"Sir?"

He took Melissa's new passport out of her hand and gave it to the ticket agent. Started counting out the money. "No. Just one."

Melissa put her hand on his arm. "You're not coming? You don't want to be with me now?"

Jamison watched the woman recount the money, waited as she processed the ticket and handed it to Melissa. He did not look in Melissa's direction.

"Gate 23. It's boarding now."

"Peter?"

He turned and walked away.

Advance preview of

HEAT SYNCH

A POLITICAL THRILLER

BY

WES DEMOTT

NOTE TO THE READER

ADMIRAL HOUSE PUBLISHING, Box 8176, Naples, FL 34101
AdmHouse@aol.com

The Library of Congress has catalogued this hardcover edition as:

DeMott, Wes
Heat Sync / Wes DeMott.— 1st edition

p. cm.
ISBN 0-9659602-8-5 (hardcover)

ADMIRAL HOUSE first hardcover printing Spring 2000

10 9 8 7 6 5 4 3 2 1

Printed in the U.S.A.

1

It's just a theory I have, and I wonder if women would agree. But don't men say a lot about themselves when a short-skirted woman slides out of a car or chair?

Some make a show of looking away, as if they're above such indiscretion. These men are saints, or, more likely, they're too polite, dishonest, or scared to follow the natural instincts that keeps our species alive. So I don't trust them.

Others look away, then steal a glance, then look away again. Cowards.

A few sneak a sheepish peek then act like they're sorry, exploiting the woman's natural tendency to forgive anyone who apologizes, even if insincerely.

Creeps ogle lasciviously. Enough said about them.

And then there are the few who take a steady look, which is what every damn one of them wants to do. This guy, in my opinion, has courage. He does what nature tells him to do without apology or shame or intimidation.

As for me, I am twenty-eight, healthy, hetero, and one of the guys who looks away, steals a glance, then looks away again.

I also might be a liar.

Unfortunately, women in short skirts never seem to be sliding out of cars or chairs when you need to find out what kind of man you're dealing with. That's the problem I'm having now. Not a lot of short-skirted women at Basic Underwater Demolition School. I would know and tell you if there were. Honest. They'd stand out.

So I brace myself at rigid attention, staring at my executive officer's I-love-me wall of plaques and photos while he stands up and comes around his desk toward me. He has a scary walk. Even the sound is scary. Don't ask me what that means, because I can't explain it. If you ever have someone walk up to you like that, you'll understand. Trust me.

"Thompson . . ."

That's my name around here. Not Henry or Hank or H.T., like my friends back in Lafayette, Indiana, call me. Thompson, Lieutenant J.G., junior grade.

None of us has a first name anymore. Makes sense, too. An instructor would have a tough time sounding vicious if he shouted, "We're training you to be SEALS, the deadliest small-force threat in the world. Killers! Survivors! Do you have any idea what that means, Hen-*ry*?"

There are two Thompsons in my class, which means we snap to attention twice as often as the others. Everyone thinks it's funny. Obviously, a good sense of humor isn't essential to being a SEAL. Glad I left mine at home.

"Sir," I bark back.

"Thompson, this is Colonel Maddigan, from the Pentagon. He has new orders for you. They're voluntary, just like here."

"Sir, new orders? I haven't graduated yet, sir."

This was it, what I knew had been coming. Fifteen percent of SEAL applicants get accepted; seventy-five percent leave before they graduate. Cold is the biggest reason, the enemy. Cold water, cold weather, cold, cold, cold. You sit around and shiver for hours, then they demand your best.

I would never quit, but I wasn't going to graduate, either. The cold would win. The handful who could endure it had spent hours trying to teach me some way to stop shaking. Maybe I just didn't have enough body fat, which made me wonder if this was a problem that could be solved with potato chips and ice cream.

"You've tried like hell, Thompson. We've all seen it. But you won't graduate. It's nothing to be ashamed of; it's just physiology. Few men make it. You've gone further than most, and have led your class in many aspects of the training, especially in stealth skills. Which is one of the reasons the colonel is here."

I wasn't really hearing his consolation speech. I was staring at the SEAL's trident—the Budweiser—on his uniform, accepting for the first time that I'd never wear it. I decided that it was too big anyway.

My X.O., Lieutenant Commander Nance—Thumper to his peers, of which there can't be many—stood about eight feet away, allowing Colonel Maddigan room to start making slow laps around me. He, too, was scary, which surprised me. I've always thought of the Pentagon as the military's corporate headquarters, and the people who work there as being soft. And after all, how many tough guys do you think there are at IBM's home office? Maddigan makes me believe there might be a few.

"Lt. Thompson," Maddigan says while he's still behind me.

I'd like to about-face quickly, but figure I'd bump noses with him if I did. So I stare straight at the wall of awards. Maddigan circles around in front, then backs three feet away. He's about forty-five, maybe a few years older, so I figure he needs the distance to bring me into good focus.

"Sir?"

"Have you ever heard of the Joint Services Personal Warfare School?"

I searched for an acronym that might ring a bell. Everything in the service has one, and the trick is to figure it out before the time's up. JSPWS. JeSPWaS? JoSPeWS?

"Well, have you?"

Time's up.

"Sir, no sir!"

Maddigan smiles, and it bends the scar that dribbles down his neck. He looks scarier smiling than he does frowning. IBM headquarters might be a kick-ass place after all. How would I know?

Maddigan wanders off to a corner of the room and leans into it. Commander Nance picks up the story. "It's another elite force, Thompson. Much like here. The best from all the services and some of the intelligence communities, trained to work independently." He grinned. "And not much of the work involves bathing in freezing water. That's been your only set-back here."

"Yes, sir."

"It's a secret project, Thompson. After graduation, you will work for a variety of government services, from the CIA to DEA, and lots of folks in-between. Your life's going to change if you take this assignment."

"Yes, sir."

"If you want my opinion, I think you'd do well at JASPERS."

Jaspers? Not fair. They hadn't used all the letters. And they'd thrown in some that didn't belong. "Thank you, sir."

"You'll be promoted to full lieutenant upon graduation."

"Your confidence is appreciated, sir."

"Questions?"

"Sir, a hundred, sir." I love this place. The most commonly used word is *sir*. Usually the first and last word out of your mouth.

"Any that won't wait?"

"Sir, no sir."

"Yes or no? On the school."

"Sir, yes sir."

He looks over at the colonel as if they might be old friends. I can't tell exactly, as I'm still staring straight at the wall and can't see Maddigan. But my X.O.'s face has victory on it, like he's proud to offer me up to Maddigan. It makes me proud, too, and makes me look forward to being a Jasper, if that's what they call themselves. More likely something like operator, which was a *real* SEAL, something I would never be.

But operator, Jasper, meat eater, what the hell? Maddigan looks like someone I'd be proud to fight beside—even though I

4

already sensed that the fighting he did wasn't the kind that got reported in the papers. Still, it mattered a lot that Maddigan made me feel proud by association. I couldn't imagine him sneaking a look up a woman's skirt. Sir, no sir.

"Well done, son," said Maddigan as he came back into view. Then he hands me some papers, which I guess would be my orders, and shakes my hand, which I guess might break my fingers. "Report to Camp LeJuene for initial training as soon as you clear from Coronado. If you do as well there as you've done here, we've got some work waiting for you upon graduation."

Camp? Camp was like fort to a navy man, like saying barbecue to a Hindu or anchor rode to a pilot. It didn't have much meaning. The navy has bases, air stations and vessels. Camp is for Boy Scouts. And Jaspers, apparently.

"Aye-aye, sir." I suddenly had a need to sound maritime.

Maddigan had looked away, but snapped back onto me. He smiles a little, his scar bending out of line. I smile a little, too, wishing I'd had a tougher problem with acne as a kid so that I, too, could have that "this face means business" look. I was fairly sure that all my face said to Maddigan was, "pretty nice guy, doesn't like cold water." Nothing else came, even though I kept straining. It looked like Maddigan was going to burst out laughing, so he said good-bye to my X.O. and walked out.

Commander Nance also shook my hand like hell. Around here, you should really think about it before you stick your paw out there for someone to mangle. I winced and he smiled.

"Congratulations, Thompson. You'll do fine there. It's been a pleasure having you under my command. I'm sure our paths will cross again."

"I hope so, sir."

"Dismissed."

So much for social pleasantries. I left.

In matters of the heart, wallet, and military, I am usually pretty slow-moving, and tumble major decisions around until all the dangerous edges are smoothed off. I've been that way since . . . well, I guess I've always been that way. All of my relatives were farmers, except for my dad. And even he recently surprised everyone by leaving the U.S. Marshals to return to the ground. Anyway, farmers are tedious decision makers because the wrong crop or weather guess can put them out of business.

All of which made me a little surprised at myself for accepting these orders so suddenly, and wonder if it wasn't just a reaction to washing out of BUDS. So I did what I've done for the last two years, something I could never have considered if I hadn't met Rachel Sullivan.

We met during my first job after O.C.S., while I was part of the navy's White House detail. She was, and still is, President Robinson's press secretary. Which kind of puts me a heartbeat from the presidency. Neat, huh?

I feel pretty cool as I call her, just going through the White House switchboard, thinking about what's going on up there at the seat of power.

"Henry, hello."

She calls me Henry in a way that's fine with me. It's beautiful when she says it, and she never makes it sound like I'm the candy bar. I've been a million laughs to people I meet who must think they're the first one to put an *Oh* in front of my name, as in, "Oh. Henry. Hello. Ha-Ha." Maybe ten million laughs. Which is why I prefer H.T.

"Guess what, Rachel?"

"You've been promoted to general."

"The navy doesn't have generals."

"I know. It was a joke. Admiral?"

"That's right, good guess. I was standing by the Coke machine and a guy came up and pinned a star on my collar. My lucky day."

"I'll say."

"Try again."

"I'm pretty busy."

"I've been transferred back to the East Coast."

"Really? That's great. Katie will be so excited."

Katie is Rachel's nine-year-old daughter, conceived while Rachel dated the guy who ran up the tab I'm now paying. That's the way I see it, anyway. As Rachel tells it, the marriage ended before they finished their first football season together, leaving

6

Katie with a disinterested father and Rachel convinced that no man is trustworthy. A tough act to follow.

Katie, however, lets me play the role of dad, which I cherish. I call her Kitten, although she says she hates it. I don't believe her. She looks too happy when she protests.

"Yeah. I'm glad she'll be excited. Was kind of wondering what you thought."

"Fine with me. You know you're welcome home."

Home is a word I have trouble with. Goes back to my dad and my own family. But it sounds nice when Rachel says it.

"I've washed out of the SEALS."

"I kind of assumed that. Sorry. I know it was important for you to do well. What happened?"

"I got cold."

"A cold?"

"Nope. Just cold."

"Oh." Then, "You're kidding, right?"

"Nope. Kind of a long story."

"I can imagine."

"So, no one else has taken my place in your life? No threats out on the horizon that would keep me from coming back?"

"They're everywhere, Henry."

She's kidding. I was the first man she dated after her marriage, and it was a *long* time after. I couldn't believe my luck. Smart, fun, beautiful, successful, and not dating anyone. But I play along with her warning because I love her and she needs to do this.

"I know they're everywhere," I say. "I worry constantly."

"I've always been honest with you about how I feel, Henry. But relax for now. No one has come out of the shadows while you've been gone, if that's what you're asking. Your clothes aren't out on my front porch yet."

"If you ever do that, please put the valentine underwear on the bottom of the pile."

"Will do."

"Along with the—"

"Henry, I'm pretty busy here."

"Right. Well, I just wanted to know your thoughts."

7

"Does it sound interesting and challenging?"

"Yes."

"Then do it. Just make sure you're not going as a reaction to your . . .what did you call it—washing out? Of BUDS?"

"I've thought about that. But it does sound like a good opportunity."

"Then take it."

"It's should be exciting, too. It's a secret school."

"That's nice."

"Don't you want to know what it is?"

"No."

Rachel has little interest in the military. She was born and raised in Covington, Kentucky, across the Ohio River and one decent tee-shot from Riverfront Stadium in Cincinnati. No military there, so no reason to get interested in it.

"I can't tell you about it, of course, but it'd be fun to hear you beg."

"Uh-uh."

"Just a little?"

"Henry!"

"Okay, okay. Thanks for the advice. My orders give me ten days to report. Can you take some time off? Maybe take Kitten out of school and go to Williamsburg for a few days?"

"Probably. Can't really commit until I talk with the boss. But Congress is out of session and President Robinson hasn't had a decent death threat in days." She laughs. What an exciting sound. "So there's little for me to meet the press about. Unless somebody starts lobbing political hand grenades, it should be pretty quiet around here."

The death threats always worry me. It seems that threatening President Robinson has become some sort of national pastime. I don't care much about Robinson because, truth be known, he seemed to leap from Religious Right to Rabid Right as soon as he hit office, upsetting lots of the people on both sides of the aisle, conservatives and liberals alike. The joke was that he'd traveled so far to the right that someday he was bound to bump into Teddy Kennedy, who'd be coming around from the other direction. Even the Coalition of Conservative Christians—the powerful organization he'd built and used to win the presidency—was gaining its senses and distancing itself from Robinson, being as careful as possible not to piss off the guy who still controlled their television network and college.

But the threats make me worry about Rachel. It's terribly easy to be an incidental victim—collateral damage. No training required. If someone bombs the Oval Office, I'll probably lose her. It makes me sad just thinking about it.

"This will be fun, then," I say to Rachel as I try to push away my concern. "I'll pack today and leave tonight. Be home tomorrow."

"Katie and I will bake a cake."

"I hope not. Maybe Kitten can do it alone, while you're at work."

"That's funny."

"Really?"

"No."

"A cake sounds nice then."

"Too late."

"Pie?"

"Henry, I'm pretty busy."

"Me, too."

Not really. I've got a locker's worth of clothes to dump into a seabag, then a wait at the terminal for an eastbound transport plane.

"Then I'll see you tomorrow. Want to come by work? President Robinson says you're always welcome, if he has time in his schedule."

"I'd rather surprise Kitten. Pick her up at school."

"She'd love that, I'm sure you know."

"Yeah. She's a good kid."

"She's lucky to have you for a playmate."

"Ouch."

"Because you two operate on the same—"

"Rachel?"

"Yes?"

"I'm pretty busy here."

She laughs again. Man, I love that sound.

9

"Fair enough, Henry. See you tomorrow after work."

"Can't wait."

She hangs up and I hang up. Then I call the base operator at North Island Naval Air Station and ask her to connect me to the terminal. There's a flight to Norfolk that leaves in three hours, and I intend to be on it. A few days with the two women I love, then on to become a Jasper.

I still think operator sounds better.

2

During the flight to Norfolk I met an army captain named Bill something-or-other who works at Fort Eustis. Fort, I'm guessing, is the army's name for camp. Anyway, he dropped me off at the Amtrak station in Newport News for the three-hour ride to D.C., which arrived at Union Station early. Imagine.

It's been a lucky trip, except for the fact that the club car—which I understand used to be a glorious aspect of train travel, but which now amounts to nothing more than a counter on one side of an aisle—ran low on everything but candy an hour out of the station. But I'm home, bathed, and ready to go pick Kitten up at school. Things could be better, but it would take Rachel to make that happen.

Kitten's school is one of those inner-city places where the teachers know all the students and suspiciously eye any interloper they don't know well. Lots of people who work on Capital Hill send their kids here. It's private, expensive, and—

I'm guessing here—subsidized by some little line item in a bill about fighting forest fires, or immigration, or who knows what.

Of course, that's fine with me because a little girl I love gets the benefit of a safe, excellent learning environment. I think everyone should be so lucky, but don't get me started on that. I'm tolerated, but not liked, by Rachel's politician friends because I keep reminding them that every parent would love to have their children go there.

Anyway, the last bell rings and, like elementary schools everywhere, there's an explosion of noise. I love that sound. Innocent kids laughing and shouting and having fun. Again, I think all of us should be that lucky.

I hide behind a drink machine and watch Kitten coming down the hall, talking to another girl, then giggling. As she passes I jump out and grab her. She jumps and shrieks so loudly she scares me. Really. So I jump, too, trying like hell not to shriek with her. Then she recognizes me and jumps way up into my arms—but not before a stern-looking educator makes a few hasty steps toward me. She stops as Kitten kisses and hugs me, then turns away without smiling. I think she's mad she didn't get to fight with me, maybe wrestle me to the ground and beat me with her erasers. Obviously, it's still my lucky day.

"Hi, H.T.," Katie says with so much enthusiasm that I want to hear it again. I notice her little girlfriend is looking like she's sizing me up, maybe gauging me for a boyfriend or something. I'm flattered, but taken.

"Kitten, how are you? I've missed you so much."

"Really? How much?"

This is a tough question for anyone. Your arms aren't quite big enough, and the universe is too big for a little kid to grasp the analogy.

"If love was a ship, I'd be the *Titanic*."

"That's all?"

"And the *Carpathia*."

"The what?"

12

"Another ship." I couldn't help throwing out the arm that wasn't supporting her. "A big one."

This seemed to satisfy her, and she squeezed my neck again, still strapping her skinny little legs around my middle.

"How long will you be here?"

"A few days."

"Does Mommy know?"

"Of course not. I just came to town so that I could see you. You know that."

"Did not. You came to see Mommy."

"And you."

Are girls born with that look? The one that says, "Sure, I'll buy that. As long as you know that I know what we both know." Kitten gave it to me, but held it too long. She still needs a little practice.

"Okay. Got me. Yes, your mommy knows."

"Told you so. You guys going to get married this time?"

"What's that?"

"What's what?"

"Marriage?"

She pulls my ear. She loves to play with the little hangy-down part. "You know what marriage is, silly. You and Mom put rings on, then walk around all the time holding hands so they don't slip off."

"Where did you hear that?"

"It's a joke. Kind of. Just made it up."

"Funny."

"Really?"

"No."

Now she pinches my ear, hard. It doesn't hurt, but I grimace anyway and tilt my head her way. "Ouch."

"Take me home. I need an after-school snack."

"Me, too."

So we head home, on foot, which gives us lots of time to jump over fire hydrants and climb on fences. I vault parking meters for her, which she thinks qualifies me for a spot on the Olympic gymnastics team. Got to love kids.

"H.T?"

"Yup?" I look her in the eyes, because I know this voice is serious.

"Are you and Mom *ever* going to get married?"

I was the oldest of three and, until I lost contact with my family, was always the one my brother and sister cornered with their tough questions. I know better than to be dishonest, or evasive. Even at nine, kids know who they can trust for the truth. So I give her my best shot. "I hope so. Do you?"

"You know I do. But why's it taking so long?"

I exhale big, which makes a lot of kids roll their eyes. But Kitten doesn't. She just keeps watching me.

"Marriage is a big step, honey. Your mom married your dad, and it didn't work out. She wants to be sure next time. I don't blame her for that. I hope you don't, either."

"My birth-dad was a loser. You're not. Big difference."

Birth-dad? I've never heard her say this before, but I like it. It sounds like she's pushing him out to make room for me. "You probably shouldn't say that. It's tough being an adult. You and I don't know what happened with your dad." These words stick hard in my throat. I still want to high-five her for the loser comment.

"Well, whatever happened to him, my mom's crazy for not grabbing you right now. All of my girlfriends think you're really cute."

I blush, and marvel again at the magic of little girls.

"Thank you. Any of them I should meet?"

"Amie thinks your gorgeous."

"Do you think she'd marry me?"

"She wants to marry someone, that's for sure. That's all she talks about."

"So I've got a shot?"

This time I get a slap on my arm. "You're marrying my mom."

"I hope so."

We go back to playing, which is fun because it so rarely happens in my adult life. Playing in the navy, the types of jobs I've done lately, meant live-fire and multiple targets, escape and evasion tactics, training to administer death and destruction in a world of unseen enemies. No wonder hopping over fire hydrants with Kitten is such a gas.

She and I are so close it scares me a little. I love Rachel more than I would have ever imagined possible. But I love Kitten just as much. Maybe more. Something about her fresh innocence draws me to her. Somehow, I always feel worthwhile when we're together, like she draws something good out of me that would have shriveled up and died if not given an outlet. I guess, said simply, she makes me happy with myself.

So, being close like that, I have to fight the urge to sit her down on the curb and ask why she thinks her mother's holding out on me. What am I doing wrong? What could I do better? I'm fairly intelligent, decent-looking, honest, and faithful. And, I love them both. What's missing?

But I don't do that. I love Kitten too much to put that kind of pressure on her, to use her as a source of information, to risk turning her against her own mother—a woman I love without limits. So, I relish in the magic of adolescent play. Soon enough, I'll be at Jasper school, and I've got the sneaking suspicion that the innocence of today will be beaten, brutalized, and murdered if I don't hide it securely in one of the safe little eddies of my heart.

As we walk along on this beautiful fall day, Kitten tells me her plans for Halloween, that she's going as a nun, or sister, or whatever they're called these days, complete with black habit and wooden ruler. She wants to know why grown-ups stop wearing costumes, and I remind her that Rachel and I went as Raggedy Ann and Andy to one of those intimate Washington parties for a few hundred people last year. I, a lowly lieutenant, ended up sitting next to a four-star admiral who actually *came* as an admiral—Lord Nelson. I felt pretty stupid with my red yarn hair and patched, ill-fitting clothes, sitting next to this dashing figure from another century. I kept mumbling my name so that he couldn't look up my service jacket and sink my career. Kitten laughs at my story and remembers thinking that I was adorable. I bet.

We race for the front door of Rachel's town house, which is in a comfortable little neighborhood just up the hill from Georgetown, walking distance from the shops. Nothing fancy. Well patrolled and outrageously priced. You could buy a decent farm in Indiana for what this place cost.

I know that Rachel's dad helped her with the down payment when she was suddenly promoted into her current position. President Robinson had fired her boss for using a cuss word during a press conference, and Rachel got his job, office, media exposure, and need for privacy. Her language has been fit for the angels every since. Mine, too, although I've never cussed much. Have never seen an angel, either, but wouldn't be surprised if they were around. How would I know?

Kitten has her key out before me and opens the door, then runs to the refrigerator. I check the answering machine. There are two messages. The first is from Rachel. "Hi, Katie, it's Mom. I hope Henry is there with you. If not, go next door and stay with Gretchen until I get home. Henry, please don't let her eat a lot of junk."

I pause the machine to give Katie the word. "Your mom called," I shout toward the kitchen.

"What did she say?" I hear these words spoken through a mouthful of something that sounds like cookies. Or chips.

"Uh, nothing much. But go easy on the junk food."

"These are fat-free chips."

"Sure. And nutrition free, too. One more handful, then eat an apple. Or drink a glass of milk."

16

"Chocolate milk?"

"Eat the apple."

The phone rings, and I answer it.

"Hi, it's me."

"Hello. Same here."

"Same what here?"

"Me."

"What? Oh, never mind. Did you get Katie from school?"

Kitten walks in, polishing an apple on her sleeve.

"Who?"

"My daughter. A nice little girl, nine years old, thinks you're pretty special—for some unknown reason."

"You'll have to be more specific. That could be a lot of people."

"Let me talk to her, please."

"Who?"

"Henry, I'm pretty busy here."

She says that a lot. She has an important job, I guess.

"Sure. Hang on."

I hand the phone to Kitten, who bites off a big chunk of apple just before she says hello.

"Apple," she says almost immediately, in answer to some typically mom type of question.

"H.T. gave me chips, but I knew you wouldn't want me to eat them." She winks at me. I smile and tug on her hair.

"We'll be fine. No, don't worry. I'll do my homework before we do anything fun. Here's H.T." Then she covers the phone and whispers, "You're in trouble."

"Thanks. You're a stinker." This seems to makes her happy. I pretend to tremble as I take the phone. "I didn't do it."

"What? The chips? Forget it. Listen, Henry, something's come up. It's going to be extremely busy around here. I won't be home until late, and definitely won't be able to take any vacation. I'm very sorry."

This does not surprise me. Rachel was thrown into her job a little too green, if you ask me, and it takes her lots of time to do it as well as she desires. I'm glad she demands a lot from herself, but it sure gets costly on this end.

"Hey, I understand. It's not a problem. I'll take Kitten out to dinner, then something fun. I'll have her in bed by . . . what's her bedtime now? Nine?"

"Around then, yes. If you need to go out later, call Gretchen, the lady next door. She's almost always home, and loves to come over and take care of Katie. She stays with her when I'm out of town, and is very good."

"I know. We've met."

"That's right. I'd forgotten."

"Anyway, I don't have any plans. I'll see you when you get home."

"It'll be late."

"Can you tell me what's up?"

"Sorry. Watch for me on CNN."

"Will you be telling the truth this time?"

"Gotta go. See ya. Thanks."

"Take care, Rachel. I . . . I'll hold down this end."

I want to say that I love her, but can't. Protocol. I mean, I *do* love her, and can't wait to tell her. But she knows how I feel, I'm sure, and if she wanted to exchange the words, she'd start it. If *I* do it, it might make her uncomfortable. Wouldn't want that. So I walk around with a heart full of I-love-you's that I'm saving for the day I can use them. Of course, I get to use a slew of them on Kitten, who is now plopping down in front of the television.

"Uh-uh. Homework first."

"Can I just watch one show? It's educational. The science guy."

"Nope. Homework. Then we'll go get something to eat."

"You're mean."

I give her my nastiest snarl and most vicious look, which doesn't scare her a bit. I'm glad. "Homework. Arrgh!" And then I chase her up the stairs.

I'd forgotten about the other message, which Rachel might have wanted. But now I'm thinking it might be a good excuse to call her back later and see if she could slip away for dinner somewhere near the White House. I listen to her voice say she's not home, then get startled by the deep voice that comes on next.

"This message is for Lieutenant Thompson. Colonel Maddigan here. I got this number off his travel itinerary. Please have him call me at 703-695-5805. Right away. Thank you, ma'am."

I look up and see Kitten on the stairs, looking worried, or curious. "Who was that, H.T.?"

"I guess, sort of, he's my new boss."

"I don't like him. He's scary."

"You should see him walk."

"Walk? He walks scary?" She sticks her arms out like Frankenstein and wobbles toward me. "Like this?"

I crouch down like a wrestler about to attack. "No. Like this!" I lunge at her and she scoots back up the stairs. I go back to the phone and dial.

"JCS Director of Operations, Deputy for Special Operations, Staff Sergeant Armentrout speaking. This is an unsecured line. May I help you, sir?"

"Colonel Maddigan, please."

"Yes, sir." There's a click, then another.

"Maddigan."

Maddigan answers his own phone and doesn't mention his rank. I'm not one bit surprised.

"Sir, Lt. Thompson. You left a message to call you, sir."

"That's right, Thompson. I need you to get to work. Ready?"

"Sir?"

"I need you at Camp LeJuene right away to start training. Sorry about canceling your leave."

I look at the staircase, and imagine Kitten hurrying through her homework so that we can play.

"I understand, sir."

"Good. I'm sending a car for you; a plane's ready at Andrews. I'll see you at LeJuene in a few days."

"Aye-aye, sir."

"And Thompson?"

"Sir."

"Dig deep on your way down there. You'll need to be hard as a diamond."

"I can do that, sir."

"I know you can. Sorry about your leave. That is all."

He hangs up, and I'm worried. Not about being hard at Camp LeJuene. I can do that. It's not my favorite side of myself, but I can, when necessary—and assuming there's not a freezing ocean involved—be cold and hard and heartless against the threat of an enemy. What worries me now is whether or not I'm tough enough to go tell an adorable nine-year-old that I'm leaving her. Some things in life are incredibly difficult.